'A gripping story of love, loss and murder' **Jane Casey**

'I couldn't stop reading' **Gytha Lodge**

'Brings a real fresh feel to the police
procedural genre' **Robert Rutherford**

'I raced through it!' **Russ Thomas**

'An astonishing debut' **Tina Baker**

'DC Eve Starling is feisty, fearless and
so relatable' **Louise Jensen**

'An enthralling mystery' **Rob Parker**

'An incredible book' **Jen Faulkner**

'An essential read for crime fiction fans' **Adam Hamdy**

'Twisty, heart-breaking and compelling' **Claire Allan**

'Well plotted, perfectly paced and full
of surprises' **Susi Holliday**

'I loved it' **Amanda Jennings**

'A powerful story that kept me up late' **Christie J. Newport**

'Absolutely sizzles with suspense' **T. Orr Munro**

'Everything you'd want from a debut and
then some' **Alison Belsham**

Readers are giving *The Deadly Spark* five stars!

'An amazing debut novel'

'Fantastic storyline with a brilliant twist'

'I loved this'

'Absolutely riveting'

'Brilliant'

'Everything you want in a psychological thriller'

'An assured debut, complete with compelling characters and a layered mystery'

'I actually gasped out loud'

'Really hooked me'

'Kept me on the edge of my seat'

Roxie Key is an author and copywriter with a degree in creative writing. She lives in Northampton with her wife and daughter. *The Deadly Spark* is her debut novel. Find out more at www.roxiekey.com

THE
DEADLY
SPARK

ROXIE KEY

ONE PLACE. MANY STORIES

This novel is entirely a work of fiction. The names, characters and incidents portrayed in it are the work of the author's imagination. Any resemblance to actual persons, living or dead, events or localities is entirely coincidental.

HQ
An imprint of HarperCollins*Publishers* Ltd
1 London Bridge Street
London SE1 9GF

www.harpercollins.co.uk

HarperCollins*Publishers*
Macken House, 39/40 Mayor Street Upper,
Dublin 1, D01 C9W8, Ireland
This edition 2024

1
First published in Great Britain by
HQ, an imprint of HarperCollins*Publishers* Ltd 2024

Copyright © Roxie Key

Roxie Key asserts the moral right to be identified as the author of this work.
A catalogue record for this book is available from the British Library.

ISBN: 9780008500474
Trade paperback ISBN: 9780008500443

MIX
Paper | Supporting
responsible forestry
FSC™ C007454

This book contains FSC™ certified paper and other controlled sources to ensure responsible forest management.

For more information visit: www.harpercollins.co.uk/green

This book is set in 10.7/15.5 pt. Meridien by Type-it AS, Norway

Printed and Bound in the UK using 100% Renewable Electricity at CPI Group (UK) Ltd, Croydon, CR0 4YY

All rights reserved. No part of this publication may be reproduced, stored in a retrieval system, or transmitted, in any form or by any means, electronic, mechanical, photocopying, recording or otherwise, without the prior permission of the publishers.

This book is sold subject to the condition that it shall not, by way of trade or otherwise, be lent, re-sold, hired out or otherwise circulated without the publisher's prior consent in any form of binding or cover other than that in which it is published and without a similar condition including this condition being imposed on the subsequent purchaser.

For Laura and Hallie – my very own bunch of Keys.

Prologue

I stop as close to the cliff's edge as I dare. I allow myself a few deep breaths before grabbing the phone from my pocket.

Hot tears prick at my eyes, threatening to trickle down my face, but I can't lose my nerve. Limbs trembling and palms clammy, I inhale the cool summer evening air as I take in the view. The grass illuminated by the sunrise, blades ruffling with every breath of wind. The sea glittering for miles, the horizon unbroken. The thundering noise of the waves crashing over the rocks below sounds closer than it actually is . . . almost three hundred feet to the bottom.

Such a long drop.

The sensation of the phone vibrating in my hand makes me start. Without looking at the glowing screen, I hurl it into the ocean with as much force as I can muster, watching it sail through the air before being swallowed by the dark depths below. A spike of adrenaline burns through my body as I envisage myself stepping over, imagining the sensation of my body slicing through the cold air, plummeting into the darkness of nothing.

I take a step closer. Just a few metres away now. Any minute.

The sound of a dog barking in the distance makes me jump,

and I turn on the spot, squinting in the weak light. Then, I see him. And he sees me. I don't have much time.

I turn back to face the edge of the cliff, break into a run up the grassy slope.

And leap.

Chapter 1

Eve – Now

The Fitbit on my wrist performs a celebratory buzz as I hit my daily step count target. *It's not even 6 a.m.*, I think to myself smugly, slowing to a fast walk so I can chuck some water down my throat. I live for this time of year. The sun rises before five and I'm usually out the door shortly after, trainers on, the coastal wind whipping my face as my feet pummel the pavement that leads to the beach.

'Take that, Bells,' I say out loud as my avatar slides into first place. DC Bella Cortez and I have been competing for as long as we've known each other. On my first day in the CID as a detective constable five years ago, she'd added me to the team's step count competition. Within a couple of weeks, everyone else had dropped out, but Bella and I never stopped taunting each other. We soon progressed to lunch dates, post-shift drinks, and wild ideas of running the Brighton Marathon together to raise money for the Sussex Police Charitable Trust. It hasn't happened yet, but our friendship has grown stronger and stronger.

I pause to lean against the rusting promenade railings, pastel turquoise paint tarnished beneath my fingers, and watch the sea lapping against the pebbled shore. It's my morning ritual, enjoying the peace before the usual onslaught of selfie-snapping tourists and ever-ravenous seagulls. Just me, and anyone else mad enough to be up at this time.

My phone vibrates in my arm strap, shattering the peace of the summer morning. I slide it out of its pocket and see a text from Bella. Smirking, I prepare myself for a ribbing about overtaking her again, but I flinch when I see her message.

You heard about the fire?

If there's been another arson attack, this would make it the fourth in the area this year. Our team isn't the one investigating the serial arsonist who keeps breaking into people's homes and destroying their lives, but we haven't missed it on the news. As Brighton residents, we're all too aware of the destruction fire can cause. I can't help but let my gaze drift to the sorry remains of the West Pier, burnt to a smoking carcass in 2003. I remember standing on the pebble beach with my jaw hanging open, gripping my mum's hand as we watched it go up in flames.

But another memory, far more recent, is the one that sends a shiver snaking down my spine, and I send a silent prayer of thanks that I, Detective Constable Eve Starling, am not on this case.

***

4

Stale air pumps into the incident room, the sound of the ancient air-conditioning unit buzzing in my ears. DCI Gillian Harbrook rushes through the door in an emerald-green suit tailored to her tall, athletic frame, clutching files to her chest in one hand, a coffee in the other, and her phone wedged between her ear and shoulder. Not for the first time, I wonder if I should make more of an effort with my appearance. Gillian burns bright in outlandish colours I've got zero hope of pulling off. I smooth out my plain white tee, worn with my usual dark blue jeans and a black leather jacket slung over the top, my feet shoved into Converse trainers. A black mane spirals from my head, refusing to be tamed.

Judging by her tone, the conversation isn't going well, and I feel grateful not to be on the receiving end. She has the unique ability to be utterly terrifying and likeable in equal measures, a combination I find both puzzling and fascinating. She knows how to switch her warm, Geordie accent into something far frostier. I live in fear of disappointing her.

Gillian ends the call abruptly and sets everything down on the table. 'Absolute arsehole,' she mutters, reaching for the remote control for the projector screen. She turns to me, honey-coloured hair falling in a neat crop around her tanned face, which she arranges into a calm smile. 'Eve. You're early.'

I pull out a chair. 'Just needed five minutes. The others are on their way.'

'Everything okay?' Her expression tells me it's a loaded question. I know she's remembered the anniversary is tomorrow.

'Probably best I'm keeping busy.' I offer up a half-smile.

'Good.' She approaches me and rests a hand on my shoulder. 'If you need anything, you know where I am, pet.'

I smile, but I feel awkward, wanting to project a strong, capable image. 'I'll be fine.'

She considers me for a moment. 'I know you will.' Her hand drops. 'How's the new recruit getting on?'

'Tiana?' I search my brain, having barely paid any attention to DC Tiana Banks, a slight, dark-skinned woman who wears her afro hair tied back from her pixie-like face. 'Er, fine. I think. I haven't had much of a chance to talk to her yet.' The reality is I'm harbouring bitter feelings towards her for swanning into the CID on a fast-track scheme, bright-eyed and bushy-tailed, a detective at the age of . . . well, I haven't thought to ask.

I know how petty it sounds, but I've done my time in uniform, years on the beat, exam after exam, earned my detective constable status. I took my sergeants' exam months ago, hungry for the next stage, refreshing the internal jobs board so often you'd think I was trying to get hold of Taylor Swift tickets. Desperate to prove I got my dream job on my own merit, and not through my connections. In Tiana's first week, I asked her to sift through some phone records, and she missed a crucial piece of information I later discovered when double-checking her work. I don't think I'd have got away with that.

Gillian reads my mind. 'Give her a break.' Her voice softens. 'She's young. And she's got potential, just like you did when you started.'

My cheeks flame, and I think back to when she hired me. She's the younger sister of my old next-door neighbour, Charlie. But Charlie was more than just a neighbour to me. Still is, actually. More like an uncle, making Gillian like an aunt. Maybe even a big sister. I'd grown up calling her Gilly, looking up to her in the way that teenagers often do with young adults who seem to have everything together.

After my life fell to pieces, Gilly and Charlie were the only ones who looked out for me. I clung to them because there was no one else. When I graduated with first-class honours in Criminology, she was the one who encouraged me to apply to be a police officer and work my way up through the ranks, just like she had. I've always been unashamedly in awe of her, and secretly pleased that I have a stronger bond with her than anyone else in the team does. When she was promoted to detective chief inspector, calling her ma'am took a lot of getting used to.

'Yes, ma'am. Sorry.'

'Don't apologise, just do me a favour,' she says. 'I was going to ask you this later, but seeing as you're here . . . she needs a coach. She's great at problem solving but I want her to work on her people skills, and her eye for detail. That's where you come in.'

My eyebrows rise in surprise. 'You want me to mentor Tiana?' It's not what I expected, but the truth is, I'd dance off a cliff with a smile on my face if Gillian asked me to.

'Exactly. You possess the skills she needs to thrive. She's young. You can mould her. A mini-Eve, if you will.'

I grimace. 'No one wants that, ma'am.'

Gillian laughs. 'Just don't pass on your hot-headedness and we'll all be fine.'

I'm still processing Gillian's request when a commotion in the corridor signals the arrival of the others. DS Jason Hooper strides into the room like he owns it, followed by Tiana, eager to get a good seat at the table. Bella breezes in, always the coolest person in the room, the rest of the team trailing in her wake. The sound of chairs scraping is followed by the usual hushed silence that Gillian's presence solicits.

She stands beside the projector screen, her arms folded and her expression serious. I love seeing her in action. 'In the early hours of Monday morning, a fire was set at 11 Buchanan Drive, deliberately. The fire service was called in at 3.22 a.m. You'll have seen it on the local news, no doubt. Or bloody Facebook.'

I dig my nails into my thighs as she continues. *Why the hell has this case landed in our laps?*

'What is this now, the fourth fire like this in the area?' Jason's gaze is intense.

'Yes. Except this one's different. There were fatalities.' She presses a button and two photographs flash up on the screen. 'The 999 call came in from a neighbour, but it was too late. Lisette Dupont and her daughter Sylvie died. Sylvie,' she says, tapping the photo of the smiling child with eyes like chocolate buttons, 'was just five years old. I attended the post-mortems yesterday afternoon and the pathologist confirmed there was soot in their lungs, making smoke inhalation the cause of death. To give you an idea of the state of the bodies, their identities could only be confirmed via dental records.'

A flicker of a memory seeps into the edges of my consciousness, but I bat it away. *Not now.*

Gillian continues. 'The photos I'm about to show you are particularly gruesome. You may look away.'

But I don't. As much as I struggle, I force myself to look as two more photographs appear on the screen. Two bodies, one unmistakably a child, charred to the point of being unrecognisable. Any clothes they were wearing had completely burned away, and both their postures were curled over with flexed knees and elbows and clenched fists, like a boxer defending against a blow. I lean back instinctively, nausea swirling through my body until I'm finally forced to avert my eyes, focusing on a crumb on the carpet.

'Pugilistic stance,' says Gillian, staring at the pictures thoughtfully. 'Not shielding themselves from the fire as you might think. Caused by the shrinkage and stiffening of the muscles due to extreme dehydration.'

I suppress a shudder. I glance over at Tiana and notice how her facial expression is neutral, as if she's not affected by the gruesome images on the screen in front of her. How does she do it?

Gillian clicks onto the next slide, showing a photograph of the house, cordoned off with scene tape. 'The fire was set from *inside* the house, but there was no sign of forced entry. No broken windows, no smashed locks. We can assume the perpetrator was either known to the victims, or gained entry some other way. A key under a plant pot, a window

9

left open, a back door unlocked, et cetera. There was a set of keys dropped in the hall, but these could have already been in the house. Either way, the M.O. doesn't match the other three fires.'

'But it could've been the same person,' says Jason. 'They might have switched up their strategy.'

'Possibly. Not ruling it out, Jason. But it's unlikely.'

'Hold on. Do we know who those keys belong to?' I ask. 'The ones found dropped in the hall. Does someone else live there with them?'

Gillian clicks and brings up a photo of a set of keys attached to an assortment of key rings: a tiny dream catcher I recognise from one of the seafront market stalls, and a metal heart bearing the slogan 'World's Best Stepmum' in purple enamel. 'These were the keys found in the hall. We know Lisette has a partner called Anya Fernsby, who is obviously a suspect, given the nature of the fire and the presence of the keyring.'

I jot down the name.

'There's no chance it could've been accidental?' asks Bella.

'Absolutely not,' Gillian replies. 'Too many suspicious factors. This is officially a murder inquiry.'

'Where was the seat of the fire?' Jason asks, pen poised to write his careful notes, neat as an English teacher's on the first day of term.

'The fire investigation officer confirmed it was a wicker washing basket, placed just outside Lisette's bedroom door on the second-floor landing and set alight,' says Gillian. 'The damage is mostly confined to the second-floor landing and stairwell. The basket and its contents are in the lab, but the crime scene manager's report states there was an accelerant splashed inside the basket, along the landing and down the stairs. It's some form of hydrocarbon: petrol, white spirit, something like that. They'll confirm what type ASAP.'

I force myself out of my frozen state, knowing I need to engage. 'Was there anything outside Sylvie's room?'

'No. Just the one fire, directly outside Lisette's bedroom door.'

I frown, my detective brain kicking into gear, overshadowing the side of my brain that wants to run and hide. 'The deliberate positioning of the fire makes it sound like Lisette was a clear target. What about Sylvie? Do we think it's possible that the perpetrator didn't know there was a child in the house?' *Or didn't care*, I think to myself.

Gillian clicks her manicured fingers at me. 'Good thinking.'

'Any chance of DNA?' I ask, hoping there would be a scrap of something to lead us to the killer. A single hair, a spot of blood or a speck of saliva. Sometimes that's all it takes.

Gillian purses her lips. 'The CSIs didn't recover much. The fire saw to that. But here's hoping.'

'What about the smoke alarm?' asks Bella.

'Batteries vanished.'

Bella sits back in her chair, deep in thought. I wonder what she's piecing together with her brilliant brain.

'Why didn't she just jump out the window?' asks Tiana.

11

'Because her five-year-old daughter was trapped in the room next door,' I snap, my face growing hot as a memory tugs at my sleeve. 'Would you jump?'

Tiana bites her lip but doesn't retaliate, and I feel Bella's hand squeezing my knee as a gentle warning. *Calm down.*

Gillian chooses to ignore my outburst. 'Yes, it's likely she wouldn't have attempted to escape without her daughter. Okay.' She clears her throat, moving on. 'Evidence. The CSIs found something of interest at the scene.' She gestures towards another image on the case board. 'An empty bottle of white spirit recovered from a nearby shrub. The lab's checking to see if the fluid in the bottle matches the chemical splashed over the washing basket. Plus, we have the keys found on the carpet.' Gillian fixes her impenetrable gaze back to us. 'Tiana, you'll be exhibits officer on this one. Eve, can you rally the troops and get house-to-house inquiries sorted, pronto? Jason and . . .' She pauses, and her eyes land on Bella. 'Jason and Bella. The CSIs are finished up now. We've got confirmation that the house is safe to enter. I want you two to go and check it out today and tell me what you both think. See if you spot anything else.'

'Sorry, ma'am.' Bella sits up straighter in her seat, face flushed. 'I've got an interview with a witness from the Stacey Jericho case in an hour. Can we go first thing tomorrow?'

'Ideally needs to be today,' says Gillian. 'The fire investigation officer will be there at one.' Her eyes slide to me with uncertainty.

My stomach lurches, but I can't let my past hinder my career. 'I can go,' I say with more confidence than I feel.

Gillian's eyes linger on me, a flicker of understanding passing between us. She nods and stands up straighter, her eyes sweeping the room. 'Excellent. We need to get this fucker. Do *not* let me down. And, guys? Tread carefully. You know as well as I do that when a child is killed, the local community watches us *very* closely indeed.'

That's something I'm all too aware of.

Chapter 2

I can still smell the reek of smoke on the coastal breeze as I pull up behind a parked patrol car just outside the three-storey terraced townhouse. Either that, or I'm imagining it. I spot Jason climbing out of his car on the other side of the narrow road, lined with the type of vehicles that signify that whilst this is one of the more affluent parts of town, it's by no means a wealthy area. Despite the shimmering afternoon heat, his tall, sturdy frame is enveloped in his trademark grey jacket, and he plunges his hands in his pockets as he strolls over to me.

'Hey.' He reaches out and gives my shoulder a quick squeeze. 'You okay?' His deep voice is gruff and gravelly.

I press my lips together as a small group of teenagers wander past the house with curious looks on their faces at the crime scene tape, the blackened windows. 'Just about.' One of the teenagers raises a phone to take a picture and I hold up a hand, shooting her a look that makes her lower the phone immediately.

He surveys me as if worried I'm going to break down. 'Remember what I said about—'

'I know,' I say, not wanting another conversation about counselling. It's not happening. 'I'll be *fine*.'

But my stomach jolts as I turn my attention to the house, painted duck-egg blue, faded with time, with white-framed bay windows adorning the front, paint flaking at the edges. The windows on the top floor are blackened. The outer cordon has been removed now, the CSIs confident they've collected all the evidence, but the inner cordon still remains. A young police officer stands just outside it, his face anxious, eyes wide and darting. A rabbit in the headlights. I don't recognise him, but from his nervy demeanour I'd put money on him being new to the force. I remember that panicky feeling all too well.

'DS Hooper.' Jason gestures at me with one hand. 'DC Starling.'

After he logs us into the crime scene, we pull on white forensic suits over our clothes and stretch on protective gloves, masks and overshoes before stooping underneath the blue-and-white scene tape that separates horror from normality; a threshold into hell. POLICE LINE DO NOT CROSS. Five short words that say so much. An acrid, smoky stench fills my nostrils, making my eyes water, and buried memories resurface, circling above me like a vulture.

Waiting.

'Afternoon, detectives.' A stocky man with salt-and-pepper hair greets us in the hallway. 'Martin Grove, fire investigation officer.' He reaches out a thickset hand to shake each of ours in turn, and we introduce ourselves.

'We okay to take a look around?' I ask.

Martin nods. 'I've got half an hour. Ask me any questions you need.'

I note the lack of destruction as I glance around the ground-floor hall, but there's noticeable smoke damage on the first-floor landing. By the time we reach the second floor, we're surrounded by charred carpets and wallpaper curling away from the walls. I can see from the concentration of charring where the blazing washing basket had been strategically placed.

'So we know the fire started here.' I point at the carpet outside Lisette's room. 'Do you know how the fire spread throughout the rest of the house? And how fast?'

'Pretty fast. We believe the arsonist splashed more of the accelerant across the landing and down the first set of stairs, judging by the burn patterns.' Martin gestures at certain areas of the carpet where the charring is more concentrated.

'Right,' I say. 'So it's likely that the fire started in the washing basket, and then ignited the accelerant on the landing?'

'That's a working theory,' Martin replies, 'but I'll know more when the tests have been confirmed.'

A thought strikes me. 'Is it likely that the perpetrator would have traces of the accelerant on their clothes?'

'It's possible. It would depend upon how they did it, how fast, and their state of mind.'

We're silent for a few seconds as we take in the state of

the place. My eyes drift to Sylvie's bedroom door and I try to ignore the growing pressure on my chest. 'And how did Sylvie's room get so damaged so quickly?'

Martin strides over to the charred remains of Sylvie's bedroom door. 'These older houses don't tend to have fire doors. Current building regulations state that all new builds with three or more storeys require FD30 type doors – fire safe for thirty minutes. If these had been installed, it may have been a very different outcome.'

I'm usually numb to death and suffering. After five years on the job, I've seen my fair share of the worst of humanity. But when I find myself standing in the doorway to Sylvie's bedroom, with its collapsed bookcase now devoid of books, and the remnants of unrecognisable objects that I assume are toys scattered across the blackened carpet, a fissure appears in my carefully constructed shell. I gaze upwards, remembering the plastic glow-in-the-dark stars I used to have on my ceiling as a child, and wondering if Sylvie had lain in bed last night, gazing up at a ghostly green constellation before she fell asleep for the last time.

I'm overwhelmed by the sudden urge to get out of the house. 'I'm done,' I tell Jason, my voice muffled through the disposable mask, and he gives me a knowing nod before I make my way downstairs. As I walk over the stepping plates to the front door, my eyes lock onto a photo of Lisette and Sylvie smiling into the camera, in a frame decorated with painted pasta shapes. Two pairs of deep brown eyes, the same crinkle at the corners, stare out of the photo at me as if imploring me to bring them justice, and I can almost imagine the little girl trapped in her room, not knowing what to do. I hope, more than anything, that she slept through and had no idea what was happening. Without warning, a series of images unfold in my head with vivid clarity, one after the other.

Flames.

Smoke.

Hospital.

Casket.

I shake my head violently and the memories dissipate, retreating to the corners of my mind.

***

After removing and bagging our protective gear, we cross the path to Jason's car. I stop and turn back, taking in the scene in sombre silence.

Jason leans against his car and follows my gaze towards the house, the afternoon sun soaking everything in a golden glow, making it more beautiful than it should ever be. He pulls a packet of cigarettes from his pocket. Is he serious? I glare at him. 'Don't you think that's a bit insensitive? Sarge,' I add, as I remember his rank.

'Ah.' He glances at me apologetically before sliding them back into his pocket. After a moment he speaks again. 'Initial thoughts?'

'Someone wanted Lisette dead and was ruthless enough to not give a shit about killing her daughter. We need to find the bastard who did this.' I grit my teeth. It's clear someone had planned to murder this woman; we've already got enough evidence for that. Finding out who is a different matter.

'Eve.' His voice carries a subtle warning note and he looks at me sharply. 'Keep your anger in check.'

I take a deep breath and nod. 'Sorry, Sarge.' He shoots me a smile. Jason knows me inside out and I appreciate his advice. And if I'm going to find out what happened here, he's right: I need to keep control of my anger.

***

I'm exhausted when I traipse through the door to my flat. Probably more emotionally than physically, but I can't summon the will to even go for a walk, let alone another run like I normally would. Seeing that house, that fire damage . . . The stench of smoke clings to the insides of my nostrils and I know I won't be able to relax until I can get rid of it.

Millie appears and snakes her warm feline body around my legs, leaving a layer of tortoiseshell fur attached to my jeans.

'Hey, girl.' I reach down and stroke her soft head. She purrs and presses her face into my hand, lapping up the attention. I bend down to fuss her a bit more, but she darts across the flat in the direction of the kitchen, pausing at the door and looking back at me expectantly with her tail curled at the tip like a question mark.

'It's just cupboard love with you, isn't it?' I sigh, following her into the kitchen to sort out her dinner. She's an ideal pet.

I'd actually wanted a dog to go running with, but changed my mind after looking after Dave, Jason's dog. They're really needy and I'd never have the time to give enough affection to one, not with my job taking up everything I have. Plus, having a cat is a bit like having a link to my past. I remember Ajax with fondness; I never saw him again after that night.

Once Millie is fed, I run the hottest shower I can stand. I scrub my skin until it's raw and wash my hair three times to get rid of the stench of smoke that has settled over me like a suffocating blanket. I pull together a dinner for one, consisting of chicken flavour instant noodles with a side of stir-fried vegetables. I haven't been eating enough green stuff lately. After inhaling my dinner whilst scrolling through a news article about the fire, complete with incorrect assumptions, I complete my usual ritual of triple-checking the gas hob's off before collapsing onto my sofa and pulling my origami book off the sofa.

I've never told anyone about this hobby of folding col-oured paper into weird and wonderful designs. Well, except for Charlie. He knows why I do it. I'm embarrassed that my only social life consists of a handful of work friends . . . my family non-existent, my old friends long dropped off the radar. I wonder if they ever think about me. Just as I settle on a complex dragon design that I'm sure will take my mind off things for a couple of hours, my phone buzzes. It's Bella.

Tony's being a wanker. Fancy some company?

Sure! BYOB, I text back immediately, knowing I've got no alcohol in the kitchen: I never do. I text again: I'm picking the music this time. Her fondness of heavy metal for ambience is at odds with my preference for chilled acoustic and I'm too tired to put my ears through that so soon after last time.

Feeling bad for her, but happy to have a distraction, I heave myself off the sofa and attempt to make the flat look presentable, shoving the origami book deep under the sofa. Tony's such an arse about Bella's job, having a go at her whenever she's working late on a case. He just doesn't *get* it. I decided a long time ago it's easier being single. I have to answer to no one and I can do what the hell I like.

Chapter 3

Eve – Then

I'm kneeling on the carpet, staring at Mum's round tummy and running my hand over the smooth skin with its funny little red stripes. It's getting so big. 'Hello, little brother or sister,' I whisper into her belly button.

'You're going to be such a good big sister.' She smiles down at me.

'I'm already a big sister.'

Mum laughs. 'Ajax isn't your brother.'

I scoop up the ginger kitten that's playfully batting at my socks, trying to get him to sit still on my lap. 'He is. Aren't you, Ajax?'

Ajax ignores me, taking a flying leap off my legs, no longer interested in me or my socks. I pretend not to be disappointed.

'Hey, do you want your favourite tonight? It *is* Friday . . .'

I open my eyes wide, distracted. 'Pizza?' She never lets me have pizza. Except on special occasions.

Mum nods. 'I read your school report, my little smart cookie.'

I grin. 'Can we do the cinema thing? Can we watch *The Parent Trap*? Please.' I love it when we put a video on, turn off the lights and eat hot, buttery, salty popcorn from the big brown mixing bowl.

She reaches out and strokes my cheek. 'Of course we can. Your dad'll be home soon. Go and check if the video needs rewinding and I'll pop the oven on.'

I watch her rock backwards and forwards to try and get out of the armchair, and wrinkle my nose. Being pregnant looks like a lot of hard work, and I decide I'm not going to ever be pregnant.

She waddles to the kitchen with her hand pressed to her back. I hope the baby comes soon. I'm a bit bored of waiting. I wiggle myself across the living room, seeing if I can get all the way to the TV without standing up. I can. I turn everything on and pick out the video. We only bought it a few weeks ago but I've watched it seven times. I snap open the plastic case and pick out the tape, before pushing it into the video player and watching it gobble it up like a slice of toast.

I hope Mum's all right.

***

We're snuggled up on the sofa when it happens. I finish my last slice of pizza and wipe my hands on the blanket when no one's looking.

'Ow.' Mum's hands go to her tummy and she screws up her face.

Dad's face goes white. 'Another contraction?'

I pause the video so no one misses anything. Mum nods. 'They're getting closer together.'

I don't know what a contraction is but I don't want it to happen to me. It looks like it hurts.

'Is it time?' he asks. *Time for what?* I look from one to the other, confused.

'Might be.' Mum winces and wiggles around a bit.

'But we haven't finished the film yet.'

Dad puts his hand under my chin. 'Sweetie, your mum might be having the baby very soon. I need to take her to the hospital.'

My mouth opens wide. 'Oh!' I pause to think. I guess we can finish the film when we're back from the hospital. Maybe the baby would like it. 'Can I bring my book?'

'No, darling,' says Dad. 'We're going to take you over to Grandma's.'

'I don't want to go to Grandma's! She treats me like I'm six or seven when I'm actually eight. She doesn't have anything fun to do and her food is rubbish.'

'Sorry, Evie. But we can't take you to the hospital with us.' Mum's talking to me but she looks like she's in pain. I bite my lip. I think I need to do what they say.

I stomp up the stairs and dive under the bed to try and find my rucksack. I shove in my pyjamas, toothbrush, a dress, socks and knickers for tomorrow and my favourite book: *Five on a Treasure Island*. I reach for my teddy, and then stop. If I'm going to be a big sister, I need to grow up. I don't need a teddy. I zip up the bag and go back downstairs. We rush into the car, and Mum wails in pain.

I suddenly wish I'd picked up my teddy after all.

Chapter 4

Twenty minutes have passed since Jason and I arrived at Monique Dupont's house. Lisette's older sister can barely keep her hands still, her nails digging deep into the dark skin of her forearms in a futile attempt to stem the tears that flow steadily down her cheeks. Her black hair is styled into hundreds of tiny plaits that create a pattern on her head. Monique's parents, Clarisse and Frederic, huddle together, hands fiercely gripping each other, the mugs of tea I'd made for them going cold on the coffee table. I remember the last time I saw my parents holding each other like that; just after Frankie was born. I feel a pang of sadness at what once was.

I glance at Jason, who gives me an encouraging nod. 'I'm so sorry for your devastating loss. But I promise you all, we're going to do everything in our power to find the person who did this, and bring justice and closure to your family.'

A sound like a wounded animal tears through Monique's throat. 'It is so painful. Who in their right mind would do something like this? And to a child?' Her stricken eyes fix on to mine as if searching for an answer. One I can't yet give.

'That's what we're trying to find out. What we need to do is build up a picture of Lisette. The more we know about her lifestyle and movements, her friends and her enemies, the better we know her.' I speak in the most soothing voice I can manage, reaching out to touch her gently on the forearm. Monique needs delicate handling if I'm going to get any information out of her. We don't have time to waste.

Jason nods in agreement. 'The better we know your sister, the more likely we are to find out what happened that night.'

Monique dabs at her dark eyes with a crumpled-up tissue. '*Je suis désolée.*' Her shallow breathing slows as she warms to me. 'It is all just so . . . so *raw*. And we've had journalists knocking at our door already, strangers messaging us on Facebook.'

'We know,' I say softly. 'And we promise we'll do what we can.' There's rarely a good time to speak to the victim's family. It's never easy for them, even when months have passed. I know too well the agonising, lingering pain of loss. I understand the desire to bury the memories, deep into the ground where they can't resurface.

'Tell us about her.' I direct my question to Lisette's parents. 'What was she like?'

Despite her deep sadness, a smile plays upon Clarisse's lips and her eyes shine at the memory of her daughter. 'Oh, she is – *was* – wonderful.' The switch to past tense sends a ripple of empathy through me. 'I know everyone says that about their loved ones when they pass away, but she truly was the kindest person you could ever meet. She was a head teacher, you know. She adored her work.'

I smile in encouragement. 'What kinds of things did she like to do? Where did she go?'

'She was a family girl at heart. She spent most of her time with our little family . . .' Monique gestures at her parents. 'She . . . she was such a good mother to Sylvie.' She breaks down again at the mention of her niece and takes a few moments to gather herself once more. 'We have dinner together every Friday evening. Sylvie would tell us stories about aliens and draw pictures of planets and spaceships. She dreamed of becoming an astronaut, you see. Such huge ambition for such a tiny girl. And Lisette would tell her she could do anything if she put her mind to it. She just told her she would need to work hard, and she would get there. She even bought her a little astronaut helmet of her own.'

I smile. 'Sylvie must've been so lucky to have had Lisette for a mother.'

'What about Sylvie's father?' Jason interjects. 'Is he on the scene?'

Frederic frowns. 'He's not in any trouble, is he? I really do not think he had anything to do with this. He is a good man. He adores his daughter.'

'We have to explore all avenues, Mr Dupont,' says Jason. 'There are routine practices we've got to follow.'

Clarisse nods and squeezes her husband's hand. 'We understand. His name is Mark Maynard.'

'Thank you.' I note it down. 'How long had they been separated?'

27

Frederic rubs at his eyes. 'A few years now. I don't remember exactly.'

'What sort of relationship did they have in recent months?'

'As far as I know, it was a good one. They were friends.'

I make a note to speak to him anyway. 'And do you know if she'd been in a relationship with anyone recently?'

Monique nods. 'She has – *had* – a girlfriend. Anya Fernsby.'

I cast my mind back to the set of keys found attached to the 'World's Best Stepmum' keyring. 'How long had they been together?'

'Five or six months, I think. She will be devastated. They were crazy about each other.'

I gaze at the three pairs of dark eyes trained on my own. 'Have any of you heard from Mark or Anya today?'

Frederic nods. 'Mark has been round. He is beside himself.'

Jason straightens in his seat. 'You've not heard from Anya at all?'

All three heads shake in response. Definitely something to follow up.

'Did Lisette and Anya have any relationship problems that you knew of?' I tap my pen against my notebook.

'No.' Clarisse shakes her head firmly. 'They were so good together.'

'Okay.' Jason pauses. 'How about you? Could you tell us where you all were in the early hours of Monday morning?'

Frederic's eyebrows shoot up, his hands resting on his thighs to steady himself. 'Us? Why do you need to know that?'

28

Jason holds up a hand. 'Just a necessary step in the investigation. To rule you all out.'

Clarisse and Monique stare at each other with wide eyes, and then back at us. 'I was at home with my husband and my son,' says Monique. 'They can both tell you the same.'

'And we were both asleep,' says Clarisse. 'Here. In this house.'

'We have a security camera on our front door. You are welcome to check,' adds Frederic. 'We have not left the house since Sunday afternoon.'

'And what time was that?' asks Jason.

'Around 7 p.m.,' Frederic replies. 'I went to the shop on the corner for a few things. We watched a film, and then went to sleep.'

'Which film did you watch?' I ask, putting him on the spot. Usually the best way to tell if someone's lying.

'The one about the old people living in India,' he replies without a pause. 'The sunflower hotel or something like that.'

'*The Best Exotic Marigold Hotel*,' supplies Clarisse.

'And what did you buy from the shop?' asks Jason.

Frederic's eyebrows draw together but he answers immediately. 'A bag of popcorn and some fresh bread for the morning.'

'What about her close friends?' I ask, satisfied for now that the Duponts are unlikely to be key suspects. 'Can you name any?'

'Orla Fernsby is the friend she mentioned most,' says Monique. 'Anya's sister. That's how she met Anya.'

I note down the name, planning to hunt her down on Facebook and see if she could help to shed any light. 'Did she have any enemies? Anyone who had an issue with her?'

All three members of the family shake their heads, and Monique's voice cracks. 'I can't think of a single person who would want to hurt my sister, or our poor, beautiful Sylvie.'

At the sound of her granddaughter's name, Clarisse breaks down. 'If only she had been staying with us as planned. If only she had not been sick.'

My head snaps up from my notebook, halfway through a word. 'Sylvie was meant to be with you last night?'

Clarisse nods, running her hand over her face. 'She would still be alive. *She would still be alive.*' She rocks back and forth, her hands gripping opposite forearms as a wave of grief drags her under.

Jason and I stare at each other, his eyes wide at the prospect of a potential suspect who knew where Sylvie was meant to be that night, but who didn't know those plans had changed. This changes everything.

***

Jason gives me the side eye as we shuffle forward in the queue, and I pretend to devote my attention to the selection of cakes and pastries on offer. Casey's Coffee is the café second closest to the station, but by far the best.

'You all right?'

'Uh-huh.' My eyes shift to the coffee menu, as if I don't know it off by heart.

'You sure?' he presses.

'Yes. An Americano and a cappuccino please,' I say when the barista turns her attention to me. 'It's just . . . the arsonist only trapped *Lisette* in her bedroom, not Sylvie. On the night she was supposed to be staying with her grandparents. It's almost as if they'd deliberately targeted Lisette, with the intention of sparing her daughter. Who would do that?'

Jason shrugs. 'Someone who loves Sylvie?' He slides a fiver across the counter to me. I slide it back. 'I've got this.'

He tries to hand it back to me, and I bat it away. 'Bugger off.'

I tap my card against the card reader before he has a chance to try and pay again.

'You've got no respect.'

My face flushes. I'm worried I've overstepped the mark, but he's smirking.

'You git.' I nudge him with my elbow, before taking both coffees. We step out onto the street, narrowly avoiding a swooping seagull. Clouds hang low in the sky, thick and oppressive, carrying the imminent threat of a summer downpour. It already smells like rain, before a single drop has hit the pavement. I quicken my pace, fumbling at the receipt in my pocket, wondering what I could turn it into.

He's quiet for a moment before he tries to probe me again. 'You seem a bit . . . off.'

'Thanks so much,' I retort, voice laden with sarcasm.

'No, I just . . .' He sighs. 'I know I was a bit harsh yesterday. Sorry.'

'I'm just—'

31

'I know.'

I pause. 'You're right. I do need to keep my anger under control. In other news, Bella and I are speaking to Mark Maynard this afternoon,' I add.

'Good. After what we just heard . . .' He looks sideways at me. 'You know, if you need to talk about—'

'I know,' I interject. 'I'm fine, though.'

He opens his mouth as if to say something, but glances skyward as the heavens burst open. 'Oh, fuck.'

Chapter 5

Anya – Then

I glance at the clock again; it's five past five. I'd pointedly let the customer know I was closing up at five when he'd walked through the door at ten to, and he'd assured me he was just having a quick browse. Typical. I'd had barely any customers all day, except for the usual midday rush, packed with people making the most of their lunch hour by browsing musical instruments, vinyl records and music-related gifts. All I have to show for it is a mucky floor, and a few sales of guitar straps and plectrums with 'Brighton' emblazoned on them. I'm grateful to the customer who purchased a vintage Fender Stratocaster guitar for over a grand this morning, but tomorrow and Sunday are the big-money days.

I turn off the Fleetwood Mac record, cutting Stevie Nicks off mid-sentence, and the customer's eyes snap up from the record he was gazing at. *Nevermind* by Nirvana. *Good taste*, I think, giving him an approving nod.

'I'm sorry, it's gone five isn't it?' His dark eyes, exaggerated by thick-framed glasses, lock onto mine. The faint hint of fine lines around them places him in his thirties. A sense of familiarity dances at the edge of my memory. *Do I know him?*

'It's okay,' I lie. 'But I'll have to kick you out in a bit.'

He smiles as he approaches the cash register. 'Big Friday night plans?' he asks, as I ring up the record and hand him the card machine. It beeps as he taps his card against it.

I nod, my head filled with grand ideas of a quiet night in. 'Raving and misbehaving. Would you like a bag?'

'Go on then.'

I slip the record into a paper bag and hand it to him.

'Thanks.' He pauses, holding my gaze. 'Do we know each other from somewhere?'

'I was *just* thinking that.'

'Actually, you sound far too posh to know me.'

'I am not posh,' I say, although I often get teased for being well spoken.

'You didn't go to uni round here, did you?' he asks.

'Yes.' *That can't be it*, I think. He's years older than me. 'Graduated two years ago,' I hint.

He lets out a laugh. 'Ten for me. Where d'you drink?'

'You assume I drink?' I raise an eyebrow.

'You're, what, twenty-three? Of course you do.'

'Presumptuous of you,' I say. 'But correct. Mainly The Beachcomber. The little one in the arches with the tiki parasols out front.'

'Could be it.' He turns to leave. 'You look like someone I'd remember,' he adds, over his shoulder.

My face flushes as I lock the door behind him. Was that flirting?

Chapter 6

Eve – Now

If I felt emotionally drained after my conversation with the Duponts this morning, it was nothing compared to how I feel right now, perched on a bar stool beside Bella in Mark Maynard's kitchen, watching him pace the cramped room like a caged lion. His black hair is coiled tightly, and he wears a pair of jogging bottoms and a T-shirt bearing the logo of a band I've never heard of. Grief flows out of him in waves which I can almost feel myself absorbing.

'Mark, I know you don't feel like talking to me today, but the first few days are crucial.' I keep my voice gentle. 'Can you think of anyone who'd want to hurt your ex-girlfriend or daughter?'

He stops at the breakfast bar and fixes us with a stare. His eyes are red-rimmed and raw, two deep pools of pain and desperation. 'Why aren't you out there, looking for the person who did this?'

'We have a team on the case,' I assure him, in my calmest voice, despite the pressure I'm feeling to solve this case fast.

'Officers are undertaking door-to-door inquiries as we speak. We're getting hold of phone records. We're scouring local CCTV footage. Mark, we know it's tough, but we need you to answer our questions.'

'You know it's tough, do you? Like fuck you do.' The words are angry, but all I see is fear and sadness. 'The bloody press won't leave me alone, you know.'

'I'm sorry.' I soften my voice further. 'Please. Can you think of anyone?'

He shakes his head and drops onto the stool opposite me. 'No.' His eyes are fixed on a small purple hair elastic sitting on the breakfast bar, a couple of black hairs still wound around it. He picks it up and fiddles with it. 'Our relationship didn't work out, but I don't have a bad word to say about Lisette. My girlfriend doesn't get how I can be friends with my ex.'

'Is your girlfriend close to Sylvie?' asks Bella.

He nods, stretching the hair band over his fingers and twisting it. 'They're . . . they were best pals.'

'What's her name?' she probes.

He looks back up at Bella, eyes wide. 'What?'

'Your girlfriend. What's her name?' she repeats.

His brows crease. 'What's this got to do with anything?'

She tenses beside me. I know she struggles with reluctant interviewees. 'Please answer the question.'

'No.' He shakes his head. 'No. I'm not under caution. I don't want her involved in this.'

'We need to know who knew Lisette,' I explain gently.

He bristles. 'Well, she didn't *know* Lisette. They'd never

met. She doesn't know their address. So leave her out of this. Please.'

I decide to back off for now. We'll find out anyway. 'So there were no problems in your relationship with Lisette? None at all?'

He shifts in his chair and his eyes drop back to the hair band. 'No. There weren't.'

I raise an eyebrow. 'Are you sure?'

He shrugs, then sighs. 'Well . . . we had a disagreement about child maintenance payments recently. Nothing major.'

I straighten my spine, my attention snagged. 'What brought it on?'

He raises his hands in a helpless gesture, then lets them fall into his lap. 'Work's not going great so I'm short on cash. My girlfriend's pregnant. I asked Lisette if I could delay the payments a bit. Just 'til I'm back on my feet. She wasn't happy.'

I lean back on my stool. 'What's going on with work?'

He frowns. 'What's this got to do with anything?'

'Please. Answer.' I can sense Bella getting frustrated by the shortness of her tone, and I will her to take it easy on him.

He slumps against the back of the stool. 'I've got a burger van. I pitch up at events, festivals, that kind of thing. Was doing great but lately there's been a load of new kids on the block. People don't want burgers no more; they want Yorkshire pudding wraps and Mexican street food.' He shrugs. 'I can't compete.'

'So this disagreement . . . when did it happen?' I ask.

He drags his hand across his face. 'Few weeks back, maybe?'

'Did you have just the one argument about it?'

He pauses, followed by an incredulous shake of the head. 'Wait a minute. I know what you're doing here. This had *nothing* to do with me. Even if you think I'm capable of killing my ex, you think I'd kill my own daughter—'

'We're not saying that at all, Mark,' I interject. 'I know you're hurting. But ruling people out is a crucial part of narrowing down the suspects.'

His head drops and the fight evaporates from him as quickly as it appeared. 'I want to help. But you have to know, we had nothing to do with this. *Nothing.*'

'I've just got one more question,' I say, and he glances back up at me. 'Where was Sylvie supposed to be on Sunday night?'

'What d'you mean?'

'Where were you expecting your daughter to be on Sunday night? On the night of the fire?'

He stares at me for a few seconds, trying to figure out if I have some kind of ulterior motive. 'At home,' he says, his voice firm.

I nod. 'Thank you. Would you be willing to give us a DNA sample and fingerprints down at the station, and have a quick chat? For the purposes of ruling you out?' I brace myself.

He freezes, a look of utter panic on his face. 'You'll find my fingerprints in Lisette's house. I've been there loads of times.'

'It doesn't mean you're a suspect.'

But the panic in his eyes tells me otherwise.

Bella and I exchange glances once we're back in her car, the dash coated in a fine layer of dust. I write 'clean me' with my finger and Bella flicks me on the arm.

'I think he's lying.' She starts up the car and swings it around a corner. Her thick, dark hair is pulled back into a ponytail that swooshes with the movement of the car, revealing the scattering of stars tattooed across the back of her neck. I know she has many more, most of which I haven't seen. The late afternoon sun appears between a gap in the buildings, casting a golden glow over the car, her olive skin like something out of a skincare advert.

'He really had to think about his answer. He *knew* she was supposed to be at her grandparents' house last night. He knew *exactly* what you were getting at.'

I purse my lips, fiddling with the radio and settling on a station where Florence and the Machine were singing about the dog days being over. 'I'm not sure, Bells. He's a grieving father. He's probably not thinking straight right now.'

'God, you're so hard on Tiana yet you're nice as fucking pie when it comes to your suspects.'

If anyone else had said that, I'd have flipped out, but potty-mouthed Bella can get away with saying anything to me. 'I always get them to talk though, don't I?' I shrug. 'I'd like to hear him out. And I'm *not* hard on Tiana.'

The traffic thickens as we approach the main coastal road. 'Assume the worst; anything else is a bonus,' says Bella, as if imparting some piece of ancient wisdom on me. 'And yes, you *are* hard on her. You're supposed to be her mentor now, right?'

'Yes. I guess I'm just a bitter old hag.' I grip the dashboard as Bella swings out of a junction onto the main promenade, bustling with the late crowd ready to catch some late afternoon rays with a post-work pint in the sunshine.

'You're twenty-bloody-eight,' she snorts. 'And what does that make me at thirty-one?' I feel her finger prodding my thigh, accusingly. 'She's only a few years younger than you. Remember how nice I was to you when you started? Now look at us.'

'What, you think the three of us are going to be all *Sex and the City* now? Who's going to be the fourth? Jason?'

She winks, and I roll my eyes. 'Oh, stop it.'

'Oh come on. You're telling me you wouldn't go there, given half the chance?'

'You're practically married. And no.' I stare out of my window, avoiding her gaze.

'Tony's a knob,' she retorts, as she turns the car into the station car park. 'Jason's . . . y'know?'

I change the subject. 'Anyway, are we going for a drink after work?'

'Yes, and we're taking young Tiana with us.'

'Uh-huh,' I say, opening up Facebook to see the latest comments on the case. 'Oh, for fuck's sake.'

'What?' Bella parks up and turns to look at me.

'The story is trending. There's a bloody hashtag: #BrightonFireStarter.'

40

***

When we get back to the office, every corner is filled with the aroma of someone's microwaved leftover curry, lingering from a late afternoon lunch break. My stomach complains embarrassingly, and I rummage around in my desk drawer for something to eat, uncovering nothing but old Polos and a squashed, out-of-date cereal bar. I slam the drawer shut, wrinkling my nose. I don't have time to pick something else up. 'Has anyone got hold of Anya Fernsby yet?'

A non-committal murmur Mexican-waves around the office.

'Can't get hold of her.' Tiana pipes up, her back poker-straight, her head popping up over her monitor like a meer-kat. 'Phone's been switched off all day. Uniform have been round but no one's answering. We've tried her sister Orla twice but she's not picked up.'

I frown and drop into my seat, firing up my computer.

'I'll keep trying,' she says, her voice bright.

'Thanks . . .' I tap my foot impatiently as the damn thing whirs to life, resisting the urge to smack it.

'Is there anything else I can do?' Tiana asks, hands poised on her keyboard.

I glance at her. I know I need to spend some one-on-one time with her, but right now I just don't have the headspace. 'No, it's okay. Thanks though.'

Jason stops at my desk. 'How you getting on?'

'We had a chat with Mark Maynard this afternoon.' I raise an eyebrow. 'Sylvie's dad.'

41

'Oh yeah?'

'Yep. He's playing happy families but let slip about a row about child maintenance payments.'

'Interesting.'

'Gonna get him in for DNA and prints. He doesn't seem chuffed about the idea. He's also refusing to tell me his girlfriend's name. Tiana called Lisette's sister and found out anyway, but still . . .' I shrug. 'Why hide it?'

'Funny that.' He stretches his arms above his head, his joints cracking, and I grimace. 'What about Lisette's girlfriend? Anya, is it? Found her yet?'

I shake my head. 'Gone AWOL. No one home, phone off. I'm going to try her sister, see if she can help locate her.'

'Good plan.'

'Have you seen the tweets?' I ask. '#BrightonFireStarter. They think it's the same person who started the other fires from the looks of it.'

He grimaces. 'I'm not surprised. I'm going for a smoke; update me after.'

I give his back a disapproving look before calling Orla Fernsby, who answers after what feels like an eternity.

'Hello?' she says, voice shaking.

'Am I speaking to Orla Fernsby?'

'Yes.' Her voice is thick like treacle as she suppresses a sob.

'I'm Detective Constable Eve Starling. Orla, is now a good time to talk?'

There's a pause as she sniffs and composes herself. 'Sure. Is . . . is this about Lisette?'

'I'm trying to trace your sister. Have you heard from Anya in the past twenty-four hours?'

'No,' Orla snivels. 'I really need her right now. And I'm sure she needs me after what happened, but she's not home, she's not at the shop, her phone's off. I've been running around all over the place trying to find her—'

'Slow down, slow down,' I say. 'When was the last time you spoke to her?'

'Sunday evening,' she sobs. 'It's just not like her to disappear like this.'

Chapter 7

Anya – Then

I let myself into my older sister Orla's house. The cottage, just outside of Brighton on the outskirts of the woods, is so beautiful. I love being here. Orla is sprawled across the sofa with a glass of rosé in one hand, her silky hair cascading in waves around her shoulders. I'm reminded that my hair hasn't been cut in so long that it's becoming acquainted with my waist. She beams at me. 'Hey, sis. How was the shop?' We inherited Melody Laine from our parents, each sharing responsibility for running it. It's a lovely way to keep their memories alive.

'All good.' I shrug off my jacket. 'Sold the Strat.'

She stretches over to give me a high five. 'Nice work.'

'Where's Ruben?' I glance around the room for my cousin. 'Didn't he say he was joining us tonight?'

'Running late.' Orla rolls her eyes.

'Aunt Andrea again?' I guess, knowing Ruben has been clashing with his mother quite a bit lately.

'Probably.' She stretches and climbs off the sofa. 'You okay to wait in for Ruben while I pick up a Porta Pizza?' She's never one to wait in for a takeaway. Too impatient.

'Sure.' I'm more than happy for an excuse not to go back out into the cold. I *always* feel the cold. 'I need a drink anyway.'

In the kitchen, which is as familiar to me as my own, I start the ritual of making the perfect gin and tonic. Three cubes of ice. Two tantalising slices of grapefruit. A shot of Tanqueray. A can of Fever-Tree.

'Back in a bit,' I hear Orla calling from the front room, followed by the sound of the front door slamming, key rattling in the lock. I raise the glass to my lips, feeling the sensation of the ice-cold drink sliding down my throat.

It's not long until the door goes again, and I open it up to see Ruben standing there, holding a bag of what looks like beer cans. He grins, holding the bag aloft, and closes the door behind him. I look at him properly, noticing the shadows under his eyes. The smile that's anything but authentic.

I can't help but frown. 'Are you okay?'

The fake smile slips and he shrugs. 'All good.'

'What is it, Ruben?' I step closer.

'It's nothing. I'm all right.' His eyes drop to the carpet as he kicks off his shoes.

'No, tell me. Something's wrong.'

'I . . . don't want to talk about it.' His eyes are still on the floor, and he fiddles with the toggle on his hoodie.

'You sure?'

He nods wearily.

'Is there anything I can do?'

His eyes meet mine, and he looks as if he's about to ask me a question, but he doesn't.

'Ruben.' I reach out and touch him on the forearm. 'It's me. You can ask me. You know that.'

'I need money,' he blurts out.

'What's going on? Are you in trouble?' My mind races through every possibility: credit card debt? Unemployment? Gambling?

He's silent.

I pause. 'How much do you need?'

'I wouldn't ask if I wasn't desperate.'

'How much?'

'Five hundred.' His face flushes.

'That's fine,' I say. I can spare a bit of my savings. 'Cash or transfer?'

'Cash please.' Relief floods his face. 'Are you sure?'

'Of course,' I say. 'What's family for?'

'You're the best.' He smiles. 'I'll pay you back ASAP. Promise.'

'You'd better.' I wink.

'Please don't tell Orla,' he says. 'She's so . . . *together*.'

'And I'm not?' I joke, but it falls flat.

'It's just a bit . . . embarrassing. You know she's the sensible one out of us three.'

'Of course I won't tell her. Come on, let's choose a film before Orla gets back and picks something rubbish.' I'm still wondering why Ruben needs the money, why he doesn't feel like he can tell me right now. But I decide I trust him enough not to press him further on this. After all, I'd do anything for him . . . he's family. And I don't have much of that left.

We're flicking through Netflix when Ruben hovers on a film called *A Long Way Down*. 'How about this?'

I read the blurb and my pulse quickens. 'Ruben, it's about suicide. No. Find something else. Please.'

He's silent for a few seconds, before he mentions the thing we've not spoken about since it happened. 'Do you ever think about her?'

He doesn't have to say her name for me to know who he's talking about. 'Of course I do,' I say, although my voice wobbles as my mind catapults me back to that night. Images and sounds flash in my mind. Fireworks. The reflection of the moon on the sea. The crashing of the waves against the rocks.

A scream.

Chapter 8

Eve – Now

When I arrive at work the next morning, Gillian is at an appointment, so the noise level is naturally higher. A pile of cupcakes complete with star-shaped sprinkles sit on a tray on the communal snack table and everyone crowds around it.

'Morning, Eve. D'you want one?' Tiana smiles at me as I pass. We'd had a laugh last night with Bella, but the way she's sucking up to everyone still sends a flash of irritation through me.

My stomach growls. I've forgotten to eat breakfast again. 'I'm all right, thanks.' I drop into my desk chair and fire up my emails. 'Too early for sugar,' I offer by way of explanation.

But five minutes later, a cake drops onto the desk beside me. I glance up at Bella, wearing a disapproving frown reminiscent of my old head teacher.

'Stop being funny with her,' she says. 'Eat the damn cake. She's all right, you know.'

'I'm not.' I glance back at my screen and she sighs before stalking back to her desk. The cake sits uneaten as I dial the number for the Forensic Management Team.

'Eve, how are you?' Tim's jovial Yorkshire accent rings out, a note of genuine pleasure in his voice that never fails to make me smile.

'Hey, Grim Tim.' I use my favourite nickname for him. 'I'm fine,' I lie. 'How's things?'

'Ah, you know . . . muddling through. What can I do for you? You'd better not be chasing me up on anything.' I can tell from his voice he's kidding but I feel bad all the same.

'Of course I am,' I say. 'Why else do I call you? It's that house fire on Buchanan Drive. The wicker washing basket and an empty bottle of white spirit?' I rattle off the exhibit reference number and Tim taps away at his computer. I hear music in the background: The Arctic Monkeys singing about something happening when the sun goes down. Tim always works to loud music. I tap my fingernail in time to the beat.

'Buchanan Drive? The team were looking at this this morning actually.' I hear the click of the mouse followed by a silent pause.

My heartbeat quickens. 'Yes?'

'We've checked it. Eve . . . it's not the answer you're after.' I hear the note of regret in his voice at letting me down. 'No trace of, well, *anything*. Either the DNA completely burned away in the fire, or your arsonist is *seriously* good at this.'

'And the bottle?' I try keep the hope out of my voice.

'Now, there *is* something I can tell you about that. The traces of fluid inside the bottle match the chemicals on the laundry basket contents. *And* we recovered prints from it.'

'Please tell me you got a match.' I cross my fingers under the desk.

'Nope. Nothing on the database.'

'Shit. Okay.' I suppress a frustrated sigh as the pressure inside builds further. 'Thanks, mate. Appreciate your help, as always.'

'No worries. Speak soon.'

Tim hangs up, and I rub my forehead in frustration. It's something, but not what I'm hoping for. This is going to make things bloody difficult for us. I wish we had more time.

Jason appears at the side of my desk clutching a sharing bag of Doritos, crunching loudly. I wrinkle my nose at him. 'It's not even 10 a.m.'

He shoots me a grin and pops another one into his mouth. 'Never stopped you scoffing Maltesers for breakfast.'

'That's different. That's necessary.'

He leans against my desk and brushes the orange crumbs off his fingers and into the bin. 'How's it going?'

'All right.' I look up at him. 'Just been on the phone to Grim Tim. Only thing he can tell me is the white spirit definitely started the fire, and that there are prints on the bottle – no matches though.'

He frowns. 'Has everyone in the street been spoken to? Someone must've seen something.'

I shake my head. 'All but one. Number ten, directly opposite. Uniforms have been round three times but no answer.'

'Can you get round there and try?'

'I can give it a go, Sarge.'

'Great stuff. You eating this cake?'

I shake my head, and he swipes it.

***

50

I find myself standing in front of Lisette's house with my hands in my pockets and my heart in my throat. The collection of flowers, cards and teddies that have been placed outside the house by mourners is growing by the day. I can't bear to look at it, yet at the same time I struggle to tear my eyes away, thinking about the two people who once lived happily there. People who had lives. Who had hopes and dreams. But just one spark of a match and a splash of white spirit tore everything apart in moments. My nails dig into my palms as I vow once again to get to the bottom of this. A chill settles into my bones, despite the warm, gentle breeze, and I suppress the urge to run. To get as far away from this street, this case, this *fear*, as possible.

'Come on.' Bella gently tugs my arm as an elderly woman approaches with a pink stuffed rabbit, gently placing it by the front gate and gazing sadly at the house. 'You've stared at it long enough, mate.'

Snapping out of my reverie, we cross the road to stand under the porch roof of number ten and I rap my knuckles loudly on the door. The sound of booming bass reverberates through the house; someone's definitely in. After my second bout of hammering on the door, followed by a rattle of the letterbox, the music finally ceases and the door creaks open. A single blue eye appears in the crack and stares at us.

We hold up our warrant cards. 'DC Eve Starling and DC Bella Cortez,' I inform him. 'Do you have a moment, sir?'

One blond eyebrow shoots up and the gap narrows even more. 'Don't wanna talk to no pigs.' He has a lazy, drawling voice.

I slide my boot into the gap between the door and the frame to stop him slamming it in our faces. 'There was a fire here in the early hours of Monday morning.' I gesture towards the house opposite. 'Did you see anything?'

He stares at me for a moment as if weighing up his options. I see his tall, gangling frame slump dejectedly as he opens the door wider. He doesn't invite us in, but from what I can see of the inside of the house, I'm not interested in setting one foot inside.

'What's your name?' The man looks like he's barely reached adulthood. His eyes are unfocused and framed by dark shadows that stand out against his pallid complexion. His blond hair is closely shaved. My eyes drop to the track marks on his arm and he yanks his sleeve down to cover them up.

'Zachary.' He scowls at me and shoves his hands in the pockets of his grubby hoodie.

I pretend I haven't seen anything. 'Zachary what?'

He pauses. 'Zachary Samson.'

'You live here?' I ask.

He slumps against the doorframe. 'Yeah.'

'Anyone else live with you?' asks Bella.

'Few mates.'

'Can you tell me their names?' she prompts.

He scowls. 'They didn't see nothing.'

I step forward. 'But *you* did?'

He stares down at me, running his eyes over my body in a way that makes a knot of discomfort unfurl in the pit of my stomach. 'Yeah. Yeah, I saw something, *Detective*.'

I fix him with a stern gaze that would make Gillian proud, waiting for an answer. 'Well?'

'Saw a fire.'

'Was it you who called 999?' asks Bella.

He looks sheepish. 'Couldn't find my phone.'

'Do you know who did?'

He shrugs, but says nothing.

'Did you see how it started?' I ask.

He shakes his head. 'Just came outside 'cause . . .' He pauses, glances to the left then back at me. ''Cause I heard a noise. House was burning.'

'What noise?' *Why is he acting shifty?*

Another pause. 'Don't remember.'

'What exactly did you see?' I urge him.

He rolls his eyes. 'Nothing. Just fire in the windows.'

I try to stem my frustration. 'Was there anyone else around?'

He glances skyward for what feels like a full minute, then back to me. 'Saw a girl pegging it from the house.'

My pulse races as I scribble everything down in my notebook. 'What time?'

He shrugs. 'Late – 3 a.m. maybe? Four? I dunno.'

'What did she look like?' asks Bella.

His drags a hand down his face. 'Umm . . . brown hair. She had a rainbow jumper thing on. With buttons down it.'

'A cardigan?' offers Bella.

'Yeah. Whatever.'

'Thank you. Is there anything else you can tell us? Anything else you noticed?'

'Nah.' He shakes his head, reaching up to scratch the side

of his face. It's bristly with patchy stubble and peppered with acne scars. He grabs his phone from his jeans pocket and his eyes widen at the screen. 'Look, I've got to go . . .' He slips the phone back into his pocket.

'We just need to take a formal witness statement from you,' I say. 'It won't take long.'

His eyes slide down to where his phone is. 'My brother needs me. Family emergency.'

'It won't take long,' I repeat, stifling a flutter of annoyance.

He shakes his head. 'Like I said, my brother needs me.'

'What happened?' asks Bella.

'I don't know yet. I just know he needs me, all right?' He slides his feet into a pair of trainers that look like they've seen better days.

I cave. 'Would you be willing to come down to the station and give a formal witness statement?'

He looks me up and down again, and I fight the urge to punch his lights out. 'Yeah, man. When?'

'Today please. Once you've sorted out things with your brother. I'm sure you can understand the urgency.'

'Sure.'

I note down his number. 'Thanks for your time, Zachary.' I resist the urge to shudder as we walk back to the car, feeling his eyes on our backs the whole time.

'What an absolute *gent*.' Bella's lip curls. 'What d'you think?'

'Not sure.' I turn back to Lisette's house. 'He was acting weird, like he was covering something up. But maybe he *did* see someone. Lisette's girlfriend Anya has brown hair. Not many people wear rainbow cardigans at three in the morning; what if she owns one?'

'Maybe he was off his face,' says Bella. 'He seems the type.'

'Or . . . maybe he was the one who did it, and is lying to us.' I stare at the door as it closes.

***

On the way home, I decide I don't want a solitary night at home, folding paper shapes. Instead, I head towards the street where I grew up and pull up outside my old home. Or at least, a new version of it. All traces of my family are completely wiped of course, and a new family is living there, blissfully unaware of the tragedy that happened all those years ago. Yet, like every time I come here, I avoid looking at it for too long. An estate car is pulled up on the drive, and a toddler's scooter leans against the wall in the front garden. It looks like it's in a much better state than when my family resided here. Images flash before my eyes, that I mentally bat away. I shudder, before turning off the engine, stepping out of the car and knocking on the front door of the adjoining house. After a few seconds, Charlie appears, eyes squinting against the evening sun. Charlie, the man who stepped in when my own parents failed miserably at their most basic of responsibilities.

His face splits into a wide smile. 'Evie.' He opens his arms and pulls me into a comforting hug. 'Come on in, pet, come on in. Can I fetch you a brew?' I nod, knowing that by 'brew' he means hot chocolate and not the tea I can't stand.

We sit side by side on his sofa, with me clutching the same black-and-white-striped Newcastle United Football Club mug that Charlie used to give me when I was little. I use a teaspoon to scrape off the foamy top and slurp it from the spoon. It's familiar and soothing.

He sips his tea, as strong as a builder's brew. 'How're things?'

'They're okay.' I stir the spoon in my mug, letting the powder that had settled at the bottom swirl around in the hot milk, before bringing it to my lips.

'My sister keeping you on your toes?' He shoots me a grin.

'Always.' I suddenly remember what I have in my bag for him. 'Here.' I pass him the origami seahorse I'd made last night when my mind was spiralling.

'I remember when Frankie mastered this one.' He takes it gently in his thick fingers, turning it over and examining the sharp edges and angular folds. 'You're good at this.' His eyes lift back up to me, realisation dawning on his face. 'You only do it when you're struggling. Talk to me.'

I pause. 'We're investigating an arson case. Gilly might've told you?'

'Oh.' He gently places the paper seahorse on the coffee table. 'She doesn't talk to me much about work. Likes to separate – you know how she is.'

'I do.' I wish I could learn to separate.

'I saw it on the news. How's it going?'

'It's difficult,' I admit. 'A young girl died in the fire.'

'Oh, pet. Gilly's not making you . . .?'

I hold up my hand. 'If I want to be taken seriously as

56

a detective, which I do, then I can't let my personal issues get in the way of my work. I was actually doing okay before we started this investigation. I was getting somewhere. But I've just got to push it to the back of my mind and get on with it, you know?'

'Aye, I understand. And are you talking to anyone about it? Getting things off your chest?' He gazes at me with concern. 'Are you still having counselling?'

'Not for a while. Like I said, I thought I'd come to terms with it all, but standing inside that house just brought it all flooding back to me and now I don't know how to get rid of it.' I stare directly at the wall ahead of me for fear of bursting into tears. The thought of spending another second in a therapist's office makes me want to hide under a duvet. I was *fine*. And I can *be* fine again.

He slides a comforting arm around my shoulders. 'Once you've solved it, you'll have found justice for that little girl. And you will solve it – I know you will. You're a proper smart cookie, Evie.'

And in that moment, it's like being hurled back in time. To getting my school report, to my mum calling me a smart cookie, to Dad wrapping his arm around my shoulders. Before everything went so horribly wrong. A conflicting feeling bubbles to the surface. I miss them. *I miss them.*

Chapter 9

The baby's crying again.

'Mum?' I shout over the banister, painted glossy and white with chips on some of the corners. I pick at a blob of dried paint while I wait for her to answer.

There's no reply. I go back into the nursery and stand on my tiptoes to peek over the side of the cot. She's just lying there, her arms and legs kicking all over the place, her little face dark pink and screwed up like a wet flannel. I pull a face back at her, and she stops crying to stare at me. I stick out my tongue, and her eyes go all big and round at me. The crying's finally stopped. That's all it took.

Frankie's been alive for a whole two months, but all she really does is cry and sleep and dribble. I can't wait until she gets a bit older, and we can have secret conversations and play cops and robbers together. I crouch down and push my arm through the bars of the cot, holding it near her hand and hoping she'll grab onto it with her tiny little fingers. She does.

58

'What d'you want, Evie?' Mum stands in the doorway, rubbing at her forehead in the way she does when Dad's annoyed her. When he's stayed out all night. 'You all right?'

'Uh-huh.' I nod. 'Frankie's stopped crying now.'

'Thank f— goodness for that.'

Mum looks different now. Her face is pale like she's sick, and she doesn't put her make-up on anymore. And she's got these weird dark patches under her eyes, like when she used to wear eyeshadow, only now it's underneath instead of above.

***

It all changed a few months ago. I remember being in bed, making a tent out of my duvet, shining a torch so I could read my book when I was meant to be asleep. It was my favourite Enid Blyton that's full of stories about elves, pixies and goblins. The cover was smooth and shiny, and I kept it by my bed every night. I heard a weird noise coming from downstairs, so I snuck out of my room and sat on the top step in my pyjamas, listening.

I heard Dad's voice first. 'We're being avicted.' I didn't know what *avicted* meant, but then Mum started crying so I knew it must be bad.

'What are we going to do? They can't chuck us out on the streets. Can they?'

Mum's words scared me. I imagined what it might be like, all of us snuggled into sleeping bags by the side of the road, begging people for money, like the poor men in the city. I always want to give them my pocket money but Mum says no.

'I've got us on the waiting list for a cancel house.' *A cancel house?* I hated it when they used words I didn't understand.

No one said anything for a minute. Then Mum spoke again. 'How long do we have?'

'A month. The cancel know we've got a newborn. We'll be top of their list.'

'Can't you just find a job?' she said, her voice high and panicky. '*Any* job? It doesn't matter what it is.'

'You don't think I'm trying?' he says, his voice louder now.

I wanted to run downstairs and give her a cuddle, but something told me I shouldn't. I'd heard enough. I ran back into my bedroom and hid under the covers.

***

And now we're living in the cancel house. It's a lot smaller than our old house, and we had to sell a lot of our stuff so we could fit inside. I learned that our house was part of a cancel estate, which means it's full of lots of people like us, who don't have much money either. People who don't have jobs anymore, like Dad. Maybe that's why it's called a cancel estate. Everything's cancelled.

Dad's different too, now. He doesn't read me bedtime stories anymore. He smells a bit different, too. Especially when he's been drinking. That happens a lot now. And they always argue when it happens.

'Mum, is it Friday?'

She looks at me with a frown. 'Yes.'

I hug my knees to my chest, digging my toes into the carpet. 'Can we have a cinema night?'

Mum does one of her really big sighs and turns away. 'Not tonight, Evie.'

I turn to look at Frankie, who's still holding on to my finger.

I sing my favourite song from the radio to her, 'You & Me Song' by the Wannadies, about how it's always me and her forever, and she makes a funny little gurgling sound in response.

I think we're going to be okay.

Chapter 10

Anya – Then

I clutch two cocktails close to my chest as I turn around, colliding with the person standing directly behind me.

'Oh God—'

'Shit, I'm so sorry!' The man in front of me holds out his hands to steady me, but it's too late. My top is saturated with ice-cold alcohol, and I shudder. 'Was that my fault?' he asks.

'Well, you were standing pretty close,' I snap, slamming the two almost empty glasses onto the bar and shaking excess liquid from my bare arms. We've only been at The Beachcomber for an hour and I'm not ready to go home yet.

'Let me buy you another round,' he offers. 'It's the least I could do.'

'*Two* rounds, and I'll let you off.'

'Fine.' A smirk. 'Four lemonades, is it?'

'Mojitos,' I correct him, wanting more than anything to ask him to take them to Orla while I stand under the hand dryer, but knowing full well not to take my eyes off him. You never know what someone might put in your drink.

We lock eyes and I see a flash of recognition on his face. 'It's you.'

'Me?' I look at him properly, taking in his glasses, remembering him from Melody Laine. 'Oh, of course. Nirvana man.'

'Nirvana man?' He laughs. 'I've got a name, you know.'

'You never told me,' I retort.

'It's Matthew.' He smiles at me. 'Or just Matt. You?'

'Anya,' I reply. 'Who would *really* appreciate it if you'd get those cocktails so she can go and dry off.'

'Noted.' He turns back to the bar and I bite my lip. He's all right, really. I lean onto the bar next to him, trying to ignore the liquid seeping into my skin, and watch as he buys four mojitos before carrying them over to our table.

Orla's eyes widen as I approach. 'What happened to you? And, erm, who's *this*?'

'This is the man who spilled our first round of drinks over me.' I shoot him a grin. 'I'm just going to go and dry my top.'

She laughs. 'Thanks for saving us fifteen pounds.'

'Never mind my wet clothes.' I roll my eyes and head in the direction of the toilets. 'Back in a minute.'

'Hey, wait.'

I spin around and see Matthew behind me.

'I hope you don't mind me asking, but d'you fancy a drink or dinner sometime?'

I wasn't expecting this at all. A mixture of intrigue and trepidation swirls around my head. Should I? He's quite a bit older than me. Orla would freak out; she's so overprotective. He's not my type, but then again, I've never dated my type. But there's definitely *something* there . . .

'Sure, go on then.'

'Don't make me twist your arm!' He smirks.

My smile widens. 'You'd better give me your number.'

Chapter 11

Eve – Now

'The last time Anya was seen by anyone was by her sister on Sunday evening.' I stir two sugars into my second coffee of the morning, pinpointing on Google Maps the music shop that Anya co-owns with her sister. 'She was meant to open up on Tuesday at nine, but never showed up.' It's already Friday; she's been missing for four days. How has it already been four days?

'Her shop?' asks Tiana.

'Yeah.' I load up the Melody Laine website on my phone and show it to her. It's a simple design, clearly made by an amateur, but it does the job. 'It's a music shop in the North Laines. Sells second-hand guitars, music books, that kind of stuff. Uniform have been round there every day this week but there's been no sign of her.'

'I've never played an instrument in my life.' Bella takes my phone and scrolls through the website. 'But I wanted to be in a metal band. *Obviously.* I was so jealous of my brother when he started one with his friends. They wouldn't even let me play the drums. Can't be that hard, can it? Just bash them to a beat.' She tosses the phone back to me, and I feel a little pang in my stomach, at the memory of Frankie, face pressed up against a shop window, lusting after a piano we couldn't afford, her little fingers desperate to create something. Mum dragging her away, laden with more shopping bags and impatience than she could comfortably carry.

'Anyway, just had the ANPR data through.' Bella pulls up her emails, her eyebrows almost disappearing into her hairline as she reads. It doesn't take long for her to home in on the exact information she needs. After a few minutes, she speaks again. 'You'll never guess where her car was last seen.'

Tiana and I crane our necks to look at her screen as she swivels it towards us. 'South Hill Barn Car Park?' Tiana frowns. 'Where's that?'

'It's the car park by Seaford Head.'

I raise my eyebrows. 'Seaford Head? As in, the cliffs?'

Bella nods.

Tiana stiffens. 'And it hasn't been seen since?'

'Nope,' I say, knowing exactly what she's thinking.

'If it's still there . . .' I shake my head. But a quick call to the car park security company confirms that Anya's car is still parked up where it was left in the early hours of Tuesday morning.

'Shit. You don't think she's thrown herself off the cliff, do you?' Bella's eyes widen.

'Only one way to find out.'

***

It doesn't take long to discover that a young woman matching Anya's description was spotted jumping to her death on the early hours of Monday morning. Despite searches, no body has been found, but the car is confirmed to be Anya's and still hasn't been collected. The report, filed by the Seaford division of Sussex Police, had flagged on our system once we started digging, leading us to our witness. We're standing in view of where it had happened, where he'd seen it; I can't tear my eyes away from the cliff's edge, imagining her stepping over.

'I was walking my dog,' says Dennis, the witness who'd seen the whole thing unfold and contacted the emergency services. 'I always have a look, just in case. It's no Beachy Head, but people, still, y'know . . .' He reaches down to his black Labrador and strokes its head protectively, as if protecting his pet from the same fate. 'It's just so sad, what with that poor girl and her mother dying, and now this . . . what's happening to the world?'

'What time was this?' asks Bella, scrawling in her notebook. That unintelligible scribble no one else can decipher except for her.

'About 5 a.m. I'm an early riser,' he adds when he catches the grimace on Bella's face. She'd get up at half eight and roll into work if she could get away with it.

'Can you tell us *exactly* what you saw?' I hug my arms around myself. It might be summer, but the wind is fierce up here today.

'Well, I was walking over there, by that gate.' Dennis points a stumpy finger in the direction of the main path, then turns to face the sea. 'And I saw this woman, just standing over there, by that hillock.'

Close enough to have seen it was Anya, I mentally note down. No trees or shrubs in his line of sight, either. 'Was it a clear morning?' I probe. 'Any fog? Rain?'

'As crystal,' he says. 'Sun was starting to rise, no clouds.'

'Had you ever seen her here before?' asks Bella.

'No. Didn't recognise her. Not from where I was standing, anyway.'

'And how long was she stood there for?' asks Bella.

'Not long. I saw her turn back to look at me, maybe ten, twenty seconds after I'd spotted her? Then she just . . . *jumped*. I shouted out but I was too late. I rang 999 straight away.' As he remembers the incident, his face turns ghostly white underneath his grey stubble.

'Was she alone?' I ask. 'Or was anyone with her?'

Dennis shakes his head sadly. 'Completely alone.'

Bella glances up from her notebook. 'And she didn't say anything to you?'

'Not that I could hear from where I was standing.' He hugs his jacket closer to him. 'All she left behind was a stripy cardigan.'

'A stripy cardigan?' I ask sharply, remembering Zachary's words. *She had a rainbow jumper thing on. With buttons down it*. 'What colour?'

He shrugs. 'All kinds.'

'Bright colours?' Bella supplies, her ponytail whipping in the wind.

The Labrador whines and Dennis pulls a treat from his

pocket to satiate his dog. 'Yes. Like a rainbow,' he says, after what feels like an age.

What does this mean? 'Thank you so much, Dennis. We really appreciate your time.'

***

We burst into the office and my eyes sweep the room, looking for Jason.

Tiana is sitting at her desk, absorbed in paperwork. I really need to take her out with me sometime soon.

I stop in front of her desk. 'Tiana. Where's Jason?'

She lifts her head. 'In the kitchen.'

Bella is hot on my heels as I dash out of the room and shove the kitchen door open. Jason's leaning against the fridge holding a pint of milk in his hand. When he sees us, his face stretches into a warm smile. 'Coffee?'

'No, thank you.' I hover anxiously as he unscrews the cap, sniffs the milk, shrugs and splashes it into a mug.

Jason glances back at us. 'You two all right?'

'It's Anya Fernsby. She's killed herself,' I say.

'Anya Fernsby? Lisette Dupont's girlfriend?' His eyebrows shoot up.

Bella nods.

He frowns as he pulls a butter knife out of the drawer and begins stirring his coffee with it, ever resourceful.

'Shit. When?'

'Early hours of Monday morning. The day of the fire,' I say.

'Right.' He pauses, a concerned look on his face. 'We've got briefing in ten. Update the boss there.'

Bella pauses as if she wants to say something, but thinks better of it and leaves. I turn to follow her, but Jason calls me back.

'How're things?' he asks.

'Fine,' I say instinctively.

'Sure?'

I hesitate. 'I had a wobble yesterday, but I'm fine now.'

'I told you to speak to me if that happens.' His face is full of concern.

'I know, but . . .' My face crumples. 'I don't want to be a burden.'

'Eve.' He drags me into a hug. 'You're not on shift this weekend are you?'

I shake my head.

'Good. Just take some time out. And remember, I'm here for you, okay? I've been there before. Always will be.'

'Thank you,' I whisper into his chest. I'm grateful, I truly am. But how can he understand what it feels like to have had no one for so long, and then to suddenly have people care so deeply about you?

***

I break the news in the incident room.

'So he just didn't bother showing up?' Jason crosses his arms over his broad chest and his face folds into a frown.

'No, Sarge.' I sit a little straighter. Zachary Samson hadn't shown up yesterday evening as promised, and I'm kicking myself for not taking his witness statement there and then. 'He said he'd swing by yesterday to give his statement. I've tried calling, but no answer.'

Gillian stares at the case board, littered with photographs and hand-scrawled notes. 'Lying little sod.'

'I can pop by tomorrow, see if he's in?' Tiana offers.

'Thanks, Tiana.' Gillian casts her sharp eyes over the incident room. 'What about Mark Maynard?'

'He's in on Tuesday to give us his prints,' says Bella.

'Alibi?' Gillian asks.

'None yet,' supplies Jason.

'Get him in. Question the shit out of him. What else?'

'Zachary's not the only one who's vanished,' I say. 'We're looking into the disappearance of Anya Fernsby, Lisette's other half. According to her sister, she's missing, and—'

'You think this Anya woman has something to do with the fire?' Gillian asks.

'Possibly. Zachary Samson said he saw a woman with brown hair and a rainbow-striped cardigan fleeing the scene. He—'

'Is probably off his face?' interrupts Gillian, one eyebrow raised. 'Eve, he might well see rainbows wherever he goes. Unicorns, fairies, the bloody works.'

'Yes, but a witness saw a woman in a rainbow-striped cardigan jumping from Seaford Head on Monday morning. And Anya's car has been in the car park since then,' says Bella. 'We're waiting for access to her phone records.'

71

Gillian's face remains neutral. 'Worth looking into. Good work.'

Jason smiles at us across the table and I try not to look too pleased with myself. 'That's not all,' says Tiana. 'She's in the will.'

I turn to look at her. 'Anya is in Lisette's will? When did you find this out?'

'The family sent through a copy today. I've been chasing it for days. And get this . . . none of them seemed to know Anya is named in the will.'

'Did they seem surprised?' asks Jason.

'A bit,' she says. 'They'd not even been together six months. Seems pretty fast to me. Especially when you've got a kid.'

'What was she planning to leave to Anya?' I ask.

'Half of everything. Any equity in the house, six and a half thousand in Premium Bonds, and her pension of course. The other half to Sylvie. Either they were insanely serious about each other, or she was coerced.'

'Get in touch with the solicitor she used. I want their opinion.' Gillian continues. 'And what about the other suspects' phone records? Mark? Zachary?'

'I've scoured them but I can't see anything useful,' says Bella. If there was anything useful, Bella would've spotted it instantly.

Gillian glances at her watch. 'Right. It's late. Get the hell out of here.'

We don't need telling twice. I snap my notebook shut and shove my notes into my folder. Jason sidles up next to me, Tiana and Bella. 'Pub?'

I smile. 'I'll pass. I'm working late.'

Jason winks. 'Sucks to be you.' But I don't mind. I don't have much else going on and I can't stop thinking about this case. When the office is quiet after hours, it's the perfect time to get my head down and do some digging on Anya's past. I'm so eager to get going that I don't even care that I'm missing out on after-work drinks. And it doesn't take me long to see it. Something that makes me pick up the phone and call Gillian immediately.

Chapter 12

Anya – Then

The restaurant I meet Matthew at has a roaring fireplace, candles and squishy armchairs that almost swallow you whole. It's all very romantic, and perfect for a chilly autumn evening. Matthew orders a bottle of red wine, despite my protests. I'm not a red wine drinker, but I've left it too late to actually say that and now I'm stuck with it. My eyes scan the menu for something that I can't spill down my top, which I realise, all too late, is dry clean only. My favourite one as well, a vintage clothes shop find, made from intricate white lace. I settle on spaghetti carbonara (white sauce: perfect) and take tiny sips of the wine, trying not to make a face at the bitter taste. I've always had this idea that I'll grow into liking things like red wine, olives and hummus once I'm a proper adult, but at twenty-three I'm yet to enjoy any of these things. I'm suddenly very aware of how sophisticated and mature Matthew is compared to me.

'So you know what I do for a job,' I say. 'What about you? How do you pay the extortionate cost of living in Brighton?'

'I work for the fire service,' Matthew replies. 'Preston Circus.'

'Admirable.' I eye the muscular build of his arms. I'd trust him to pull me out of a fire. 'What's that like?'

He shrugs. 'Highs and lows. Could do without drunken students setting off fireworks.'

'I bet.' My face reddens at the memory of doing drunken dares as a student. Not setting off fireworks, but I definitely ended up doing a couple of stupid things with my friends after one too many shots. 'Makes owning a shop seem boring.'

He interlocks his fingers under his chin. 'Not at all. How long have you had it?'

'Two years. My sister and I took over running it a few years ago.' I find myself twirling a lock of hair around my finger, and silently berate myself. *Stop being so stereotypical.*

'Pretty impressive for a grad to have a shop in such a prime location,' he says. 'Rent must be through the roof.'

'It used to belong to my parents.' I force another sip of wine to stop my voice cracking. It's still hard to talk about them. 'It's been in the family for generations.'

'Oh.' He gazes at me, dark eyes full of understanding. 'Was it always music?'

'No. It was a clothes shop once. But there are so many of those already, we decided to switch to instruments. My sister and I source the stock from all over the country. Get vintage guitars and stuff restored, sell it for a profit.'

'Very savvy.' He raises his eyebrows. 'You like music then?'

'Only as much as life.' I welcome the distraction from talking about my parents. 'Guitar's my thing.' I mime playing one.

A waiter interrupts by placing our dinners in front of us, and my stomach rumbles in response. 'This looks amazing.' I twist a fork into the pasta and spiral it onto the prongs.

Matt reaches for his cutlery. 'So have you always lived in Brighton?'

'I grew up in Seaford.'

He swallows a mouthful of steak and cocks his head to one side. 'Seaford? Why'd you move?'

'It's more fun here.' I don't let slip the real reason I convinced my sister to up sticks and move from our hometown.

'True,' he agrees, returning his focus to his dinner. 'Whereabouts are you based?'

'I've got a little flat over in Whitehawk. You?'

'Ahh. I'm looking for a place at the moment. The landlord had to sell up so I'm just crashing in my mate's spare room.' His face reddens in embarrassment.

'Places come up all the time. Anyway, it must be fun living with your friend.'

'It's fun for a week, until you realise your mate snores like a trooper and leaves his boxers on the bathroom floor. I might live on my boat,' he jokes.

I laugh. 'It's pretty lonely living alone. Make the most of him.' I pause. 'Wait a minute, did you say boat? You have a *boat*?'

His face reddens even more. 'It's just an old thing. In the marina.'

'Wow. That's pretty cool though.' I wonder what kind of boat it is. How big it is. I'm about to ask a question when Matthew speaks.

'Anyway. Enough about that. You said you're lonely.' He locks eyes with me. 'I could always come and keep you company. Or you could come and stay on the boat.'

I feel a little jolt of something in my stomach. 'What did you say?'

He bites his lip, and it's really quite attractive. 'I don't mean . . . just like, as a mate. Sorry, that was a bit forward of me.' He lets out a nervous laugh.

'It's okay.' I smile in encouragement. 'That would be lovely.'

Maybe it would be nice to hang out with someone who didn't know me when everything happened.

***

Once I get home, I check my phone and frown. Two missed calls and three messages from Ruben.

I need your help.

An, please answer.

Are you there???

I ring him back as I shrug off my coat and he picks up immediately. 'Mum's kicked me out.' He doesn't even say 'hi'.

'What?' I splutter, dropping onto the sofa. 'Why?'

He mumbles something about not seeing eye to eye, and him having to stand on his own two feet.

'Where are you living?'

'I'm staying on my friend's sofa for a bit. But he said I can only stay a couple of weeks. I need to get some money together for a deposit for a flat.'

I pause, hearing nothing but his breathing at the end of the phone. 'And that's why you're ringing me? For more money?'

'I'm sorry.' His voice quietens. 'You know I wouldn't ask unless I was desperate. I trust you. We always look out for each other . . . don't we?'

I sigh, remembering how Ruben had convinced Aunt Andrea to take me and Orla in when our parents drowned, and stopped us being put into foster care. How Ruben had shared everything with us, including his bedroom, until we went to university.

How he had kept my darkest secret.

The way I see it, I have two options: offer up my sofa, or give him the money. 'How much do you need?'

'Just a grand. That'll get me into the flat in Moulsecoomb. Then I'll pay you back. The whole lot within three months. Promise.'

I close my eyes. 'Okay. But no more, all right? Please.'

He promises this will be the last time. I believe him.

Chapter 13

Eve – Now

'How was the weekend shift?' asks Bella.

'Made a little discovery,' I say, bleary Monday-morning eyes fixed on my computer screen. I'd skirted on the edge of sleep all night, listening to rainforest sounds that did little to help. Despite my minor breakthrough on Friday night, the growing pressure of this case is taking its toll on me.

'About what?' asks Bella, hurling a balled-up crisp packet into the bin, standing up and stretching. 'God, I need to run. I'm seizing up like an old woman,' she mutters.

I fold my own crisp packet into a perfect triangle and drop it neatly into the bin. 'Anya. *Look*.' I tap the screen with my fingernail.

She peers over my shoulder and her eyes widen at the report on my screen, filed by DC Janet Kane. *Anya Fernsby, aged 15, interviewed in connection with the suspicious death of classmate, Poppy Fallon, at Seaford Head.*

'As in, DI Janet Kane? Short but scary?' I say, remembering the petite, pinched-faced woman with an expression that

79

had made me permanently anxious in her presence. And my God, did she have a presence. She'd worked in our division for two years and then upped and left to join the Met last year after getting promoted again.

'Yep,' says Bella. 'Avoided her like the plague.'

We slide our eyes back to the report. From what I'd read of the case, Poppy's death was ruled as suicide. But the location . . .

'Seaford Head,' Bella whispers, echoing my thoughts. 'And that's where Anya killed herself too? Same spot?'

'Looks like it.'

'D'you think there's anything in it?' asks Tiana, who's been listening in from her desk.

I shake my head slowly. 'Honestly? I've got no idea. If she was traumatised about the deaths of Lisette and Sylvie, which anyone in their right mind would be, she *might've* been driven to suicide. Most people go to Beachy Head if they want to die, but she went to exactly the same place her friend killed herself. It could've given her the idea.'

'I wouldn't go to Beachy Head if I wanted to top myself,' says Bella. 'There's always someone around to talk you out of doing it, isn't there? The chaplaincy team. Those absolute angels,' she adds.

I nod. 'You're right. I think we should speak to some of her school friends and see if they can tell us anything about Anya's involvement in Poppy's death. She might've confided in them, things she never told the police.'

'An admission of guilt?' Tiana suggests.

'Maybe.' I sit back in my chair. 'If she was responsible

for Poppy's death, even if it was accidental, then she's got away with it once. Who's to say she wasn't responsible for the Duponts' deaths too?'

'But she killed herself . . .' says Tiana.

'The guilt could've got to her,' says Bella. 'It's just a theory. We've still got Mark and Zachary to figure out.'

'I'll speak to Orla, get her scheduled in for an interview. See if there's anyone else she can think of who might have some info for us.'

***

I hate delivering bad news. But when the news is ambiguous, it's somehow worse. *Your sister* might *be dead, but we can't be one hundred per cent sure.*

Sometime after Orla has digested everything we've told her, she blinks back at me with red-rimmed eyes. 'When will you know for sure?' Her hands grip the mug of strong, sweet tea I'd made her earlier, slowly going cold.

'If she's found alive, or if her body is discovered.' I rest a hand gently on her forearm. 'She hasn't been found yet, but from what the witness has said, I'm afraid it does look like she took her own life.'

A shudder tears through her body, and she puts down the tea. 'Why?' she croaks, bringing her feet up onto the sofa and hugging her knees.

'We're hoping you can help us with that,' I say. 'Have you had any worries about the state of her mental health?'

She takes a moment to think, staring at a photo of her

81

sister on the mantelpiece. 'When we were teenagers, she had a bit of anxiety and depression. But it passed.'

'Do you know what triggered it?' asks Jason.

'Maybe losing our parents and almost going into foster care?' she snaps, glaring at him as if willing him to challenge her further.

'I'm sorry.' I keep my voice soft. 'We have to ask these things.'

Orla lets out a deep breath and drops her forehead onto her knees. 'Sorry, I just . . . I want to help. It's hard. So much has happened. I'm surprised she turned out as well as she did.' Orla pauses, and looks back up at us as if she's remembered something important. 'There was something else that really affected her though.'

'Go on,' I say.

'She was really shaken up after a girl at our school died. We all were, obviously, but she was more affected than the rest of us. She saw it happen.'

I nod in sympathy. 'That's understandable. Can I ask who the friend was?'

'Her name was Poppy.' Orla twists the fabric of her sleeve around her finger. 'Poppy Fallon.'

'And what happened to Poppy?' Jason presses, his knee bouncing up and down, the way it always does with he's focused, making my chair shake. I nudge him with my shoe and he stops.

Orla's voice shudders. 'Poppy killed herself at Seaford Head. She was up there with Anya on the night of the fireworks display. Anya followed her up there and tried

82

to convince her to step away from the edge, but Poppy didn't listen.'

'Thank you,' I say. 'Can you think of anyone else we should speak to about Poppy's death? Close friends of Anya's at the time, perhaps?'

Orla exhales. 'God. It's been a few years, I don't know if I can remember their names.' She glances out of the window for a few moments, then back to us. 'I'll try and have a think.'

I nod. 'I know it must be tough to talk about, especially with everything going on. We have a few more questions for you.'

Orla grips a tissue as if it's a life raft and nods for us to continue.

'How was Anya and Lisette's relationship?' I ask. 'Was it a happy one? Or did they have any problems?'

'They seemed so . . . so *content*. Anya and Lisette, they . . .' She sniffs into her tissue. 'They were so happy.'

'No issues at all?' asks Jason.

She shakes her head. 'Nothing either of them told me about.'

Jason continues. 'What about her relationship with Sylvie?'

'They adored each other. It was so sweet.'

'Okay.' I look up from my notebook. 'Is there anything else about her you think we should know?'

Orla eyes me suspiciously. 'Why are you focusing on her so much? Her grief drove her to suicide. What more could you need to know? She's not a suspect, is she?' A shadow of worry crosses her face when I don't answer immediately. 'She wouldn't. She *couldn't*.'

Jason leans back in his chair, eyeing her closely. 'You don't think she's capable?'

'No,' she splutters. 'Never in a million years. Look, what does this have to do with the fire? What are you not telling me?'

'We're not assuming anything at this point.' Jason drums his fingers on his leg. That man is always fidgeting. 'We've still got a lot of avenues to explore. And a lot of questions to answer.'

Orla stares at him, waiting for the next question.

'How would you describe your relationship with your sister?' he asks.

'Really good,' says Orla. 'Mostly anyway. There were a few months last year where she was a bit distant, but I don't think it has anything to do with this. It can't.'

'Can you tell us a bit more about that?' I ask gently.

'There's nothing much to say.' Orla glances down at the carpet. 'She was seeing someone. A guy, I think. I got the feeling it was a bit intense, maybe. It didn't last long.'

'You didn't know who it was?' I ask.

She shakes her head tightly. 'She said she was seeing someone but wouldn't tell me who. Said she wanted to keep it under wraps for a bit. I got the impression I wouldn't have approved.'

'Was it Lisette? Had she met her by this point?' His knee is bouncing again.

'No. She didn't meet Lisette for a while after that. Anyway, she'd been seeing this other person for a few months and then early this year when it all ended, she was back to her normal self. I actually think it was around the time she met Lisette that she got better.' She pauses to reflect, her face wistful. 'And now they're both gone. I've lost both parents. My sister. My friend.' She gazes back at us with a vacant expression, as if struggling to comprehend the avalanche of terrible luck that she had become buried under. Jason gives me a small nod, and we take it as our cue to leave.

'Thank you so much for your help. We'll leave you in peace. It'll take a while to sink in.' I leave a leaflet for a local bereavement charity on the coffee table. Just as I'm shrugging my jacket back on, Orla looks up at us as if only just seeing us for the first time.

'If this is a straightforward suicide, why are *you* looking into it?' Her eyes widen, eyebrows knitted together. 'Aren't you detectives?'

Jason and I glance at each other.

'We're investigating the deaths of Lisette and Sylvie Dupont,' says Jason. 'If there's a possibility the two deaths are linked, we need to know about it.'

'Linked?' Orla whispers. 'You think it might not have been a suicide? My sister could've been murdered by the same person who killed Lisette and Sylvie?'

I pause, almost relieved she hasn't made the connection, that she doesn't realise her own sister is a suspect. 'We don't know anything for sure yet.'

***

We're sifting through local police reports after lunch, Bella and Tiana with much more enthusiasm than me, when we find it: seven logged complaints from Lisette Dupont against Zachary Samson in the past twelve months. *Seven.* I squint as we scroll through the list. Most of them are noise complaints, where he'd been playing loud music until the early hours. I remember the racket coming from his house when we called round, and I wouldn't have put it past him to not give one single shit about his neighbours. The one that concerns me sticks out horribly: *racist and homophobic slurs.*

'Absolute bastard.' Tiana shakes her head slowly. I've never heard her swear before.

I nod in agreement, and click on the report. It was the same night England got knocked out of the World Cup, and Lisette was putting her bins out, when Zachary shouted at her in the street. Rage simmers away inside me and I draw in slow, steady breaths.

'Maybe you're onto something,' says Bella, and I know she's remembering my words . . . *maybe he was the one who did it, and is lying to us.*

I sit back in my chair, thinking about what I'd thought, what I'd said. Had he known about Lisette's girlfriend, and deliberately put her in the frame to save his own skin? Had he found her spare key and set the fire himself? I think about the fact that Tiana had gone round every day since he was meant to come in and give his witness statement, and he hadn't answered the door once.

'Jason.' I wave him over.

He rolls his chair over to me and pinches one of the crisps

from the packet on my desk. I slap his hand away, and he feigns a hurt expression.

'Listen,' says Bella. 'You know Zachary, the one we can't pin down?'

'You found him?'

'No,' I say, 'but look at this.' I tap Bella's screen and show him the complaints.

He lets out a long, low whistle. 'Seems like a right arsehole.'

'I know,' I say. 'D'you think there's something in it?'

He rubs his stubbled chin. 'I think it's worth looking into. Not sure he has the intelligence to go through with a plan like that though.'

'Fair point, but I still want to check it out after my interview with Mark tomorrow. Want to come with? See if you can terrify him into an admission?'

Jason grins. 'Always.'

Chapter 14

Anya – Then

Matthew's dog Bowie rests his soft brown head on my lap and I scratch him behind his silky ears.

'You're officially accepted, then.' Matthew walks out of my kitchen, clutching two mugs of coffee.

'Looks like I've got a new pal.' Bowie leans into my legs as if to remind me he's there, and that I should resume the ear-scratching immediately, which I do.

'He doesn't do that for everyone, you know. You should feel honoured.'

Matthew passes me a mug. I inhale the rich aroma and close my eyes. Coffee. It's one of my favourite things, along with bubble baths, the feel of a guitar in my hands, and takeaways from Porta Pizza. It's the little things.

'Really?' I ask.

'Nah. He's a massive softie. But I do think he likes you a lot.' He pauses. '*I* like you a lot, too.'

He sinks into the sofa beside me, shoving a sequinned

cushion out of the way and almost knocking over my potted palm tree. I make a mental note to declutter my flat.

'Matt, you're not going to ask me out, are you?' I grin, but I'm nervous. We've been on several dates and things are going well, despite me deflecting questions about my teenage years. I've had a feeling this conversation has been coming for a while, and I've been looking forward to it and dreading it in equal measure. I like him. There's *definitely* a spark. But then there's the age gap, and Orla's inevitable disapproval.

His face flushes. 'Well, I wasn't going to say, "will you go out with me" exactly.' He throws his head back to stare at the ceiling, where I have draped fairy lights from corner to corner. 'How do you do this? I'm rubbish at these conversations.'

I grab his hand and pull it into my lap, and he turns his head back to me.

'So am I. "Awkward" is my middle name.' I pause, unsure if I want to put a label on it. 'How about we say we plan to spend a lot of time together, just you and me?'

'That sounds very good to me.' He runs a forefinger over the musical note tattoo on my inner wrist.

'Good.' I lean over and kiss him deeply before drawing back and gazing at him. 'Matt . . .'

His brows knit together in concern. 'What? What is it?'

'Nothing, it's just . . . are you okay if we don't tell people about us for a bit? I'd kind of like to stay in our own little bubble.' I leave out the bit about my sister. I can deal with that another time.

'That sounds perfect.'

Chapter 15

Eve – Now

When Mark arrives at the station, exactly one week after our investigation kicked off, his demeanour has changed for the worse. Last week, he'd been upset and defensive, but this morning, his shoulders are slumped in defeat.

I reach out to shake his hand. 'Mark. Thank you for coming in.'

Up close, I can see Mark's eyes are red-rimmed and bloodshot. 'Can we get this over and done with? Please. I've got a funeral to arrange.'

I nod. 'Of course. Please come with us.'

We head into a side room where I take his prints, swab the inside of his cheek, place it into an evidence bag and seal it shut. He's docile and compliant throughout the whole process. I offer him a drink, which he refuses.

'Mark, we'd like to ask you some questions.'

He gazes at me. 'Am I under arrest?'

'No,' I say. 'We need to clarify a few things after our conversation on Wednesday. Would that be okay?'

He shrugs. 'Sure.'

'I'd like to ask you again about your relationship with Lisette. You say you got on well after the divorce, and just had this one disagreement. Now, I don't know about you, but I don't know any couple who have split, and not had at least a handful of arguments. Especially when a child is involved.' I fix him with a stare. 'Is there anything you're not telling us?'

He glances down at the table, then back at us. 'Look . . . of course we argued sometimes. It was never anything serious; that's why I didn't mention it. I don't want you reading into anything.'

Jason leans forward. 'What did you argue about?'

He throws his head back and stares at the ceiling, so we can only see the underside of his chin. 'Maintenance payments. Custody. Whether I could take Sylvie on holiday or not. When I was allowed to introduce her to my girlfriend. Just usual broken-family stuff, you know?'

'Mark, can you look at us please?' I say.

He returns his gaze to us and frowns.

'Where were you expecting Sylvie to be on the night of the fire?' asks Jason.

He pauses, glances at Jason, then his eyes slide to me, wary and suspicious. 'You asked me this before.'

I nod.

'She was at home. Where else would she be?' His voice cracks, and he covers his mouth with his hand, muffling his words. 'If only she'd been with me.'

'So you didn't know she was supposed to be with her grandparents?' Jason asks. 'With Lisette's parents?'

He drops his hand from his face. 'No. No, I didn't know that.'

'Are you sure about that?' I press, remembering his slow reaction to the same question earlier this week.

'I'm sure. Why are you asking me? What does all this mean?' He rubs one hand over his upper arm repeatedly.

'We think the attack on Lisette was targeted.' I pause. 'Someone who didn't know Sylvie was in the house.'

It takes a few seconds to sink in. 'No,' he whispers. 'Lisette and me . . . we had our disagreements, but I never wanted to *hurt* her. I swear.' His eyes plead with us. 'You have to know I didn't do this. Have you investigated that girlfriend of hers?'

'Anya Fernsby is dead,' I supply.

Mark says nothing.

'Can you tell me where you were on the night of the fire?' Jason's eyes burn darkly.

'I was at my girlfriend's place.'

'And can she confirm that?' he presses.

He nods.

'Can you prove you were there?' I ask. 'Did you see anyone else?'

'I mean, it was just the two of us.' He raises his palms to the ceiling and lets his hands drop back into his lap. 'How can I prove it other than her word?'

Good question, I think to myself. 'We'll speak to her. And on the subject of your girlfriend . . . why did you refuse to tell us her name? We found out anyway. We know her name is Georgie Peters.'

His eyes drop to the table. 'I don't want her getting involved.'

Irritation bubbles away inside me. 'Mark. Eyes up please.' Our gazes lock.

'What are you hiding from us?' Jason asks. 'We'll find out either way.'

His shoulders slump. After a pause, he speaks again. 'Lisette wanted to meet Georgie. To know who was looking after Sylvie. Georgie refused, didn't want anything to do with my ex. I told Lisette it wasn't going to happen, and she flipped out; said she was going to stop me seeing Sylvie. But it doesn't mean anything.' He jabs his finger onto the table to emphasise his last three words.

'We're going to need Georgie to come down and give a DNA sample and fingerprints,' says Jason.

Mark looks like he wants to cry.

***

I knock on Zachary's door later in the afternoon, but this time it's silent inside. I shake my head at Jason, then knock again, louder.

He crosses his arms, his face folded into a frown. 'You tried ringing?'

I feel a swell of irritation and resist the urge to roll my eyes as I crouch down to peer through the letterbox. 'Every day since he gave me his number, Sarge.'

And it isn't just me; no one's managed to get hold of him on the number he gave, and he hasn't answered the door to anyone since I was last here. I listen at the letterbox and can hear the faint sound of coughing coming from the back of the house. When I lean around the wall, I see a side gate. 'Let's try round the back.' He follows me to the gate, and I rattle the latch. 'Locked.' I eye the gate. It doesn't look too high.

He reads my mind. 'You can't climb that. You're too short. Let me.'

'Less of the short.' I glare at him. 'And give me a leg up, Sarge.' Remembering my manners, I flash him a smile. 'Please.'

He glances skyward. 'Fine.' He interlinks his fingers, creating a platform for me to stand on, and I scrabble against the gate until my head and shoulders are above it. I cast my eyes over the garden, littered with junk: empty cans and beer bottles, a discarded disposable barbecue, a single white plastic garden chair that has gone mottled green. There's no one there. He gives me another shove, and I fold myself over the gate, hinging painfully at the hips until I can reach the rusty old bolt on the other side. With fumbling fingers, I yank it across and the gate swings open with a creak, and with me still dangling over it. I drop to the concrete before my head goes crashing into the wall.

'Graceful.'

'Pipe down.' I dust myself off and we make our way around to the back of the house. The sound of coughing floats through an open window, and we stride up to the back door. I rap on the glass panel. My eyes adjust to the shadowy darkness of the inside of the house and I see a man slumped at a table, face illuminated by the beaming blue glow of a phone screen.

I knock again. 'Police. Open up.'

His head snaps up and he gazes at me in confusion, before stumbling to the door and pulling it open. He squints in the sun, his eyes darting from me to Jason. I don't know who he is, but he's not Zachary.

'What you want?'

We hold up our warrant cards. 'We're looking for Zachary Samson,' says Jason.

His eyes dart between the two I.D.s 'Who?'

'Zachary Samson?' I prompt him. 'He lives here. I spoke to him last week.'

The man scratches his ear. 'I don't know no Zachary.'

Jason and I exchange looks. 'How long have you lived here, mate?' asks Jason.

'Few days.' His body sways on the spot.

'What about the person who lived here before you?' I ask.

The man stares at me. 'I don't fucking know, do I? I just turned up.'

I realise we're going to get nothing out of him. 'Mind if we come in and take a look around?'

The colour drains from his face. 'Nah. No way, man.' The door slams shut before we have a chance to react, and he slinks back into the darkness. I don't think either of us were expecting someone so out of it to react with such speed.

Jason's face is thunderous after further attempts to get

the man's attention prove fruitless. 'We'll come back with a warrant. I need some lunch. And a bloody smoke.'

'You can do that when we get back to the office,' I retort as I storm after him, and he gives me a playful eyeroll.

***

I leave Jason to have his much-needed smoke while I head inside the office, wondering about Mark and Zachary, but also Anya. Each one has behaved suspiciously. Each one could have accessed the house; Anya's keys were found in the hall, Mark could have easily still had keys, and Zachary could've seen where Lisette kept her spares. Anya has killed herself; Zachary's done a runner. Mark's the only one hanging around and cooperating with us, but even then, I'm not convinced he's telling us the truth and his alibi is weak.

I grab a mug of coffee and a cereal bar before I begin the laborious task of checking Anya's phone records, which have finally been released.

'That's not going to keep you going.' Jason stops at the side of my desk, motioning towards the cereal bar that's hovering halfway between the desk and my mouth.

I lower my snack. 'Are you monitoring my diet now, Sarge?'

He grins. 'If you flake out on us, it looks bad on me. Want anything from Casey's? My treat.'

I consider it, my head cocked to one side. 'Go on then. A bacon sarnie wouldn't go amiss.' I smile at his retreating back. Sometimes I feel like Jason is the big brother I never

96

had, the way he looks out for me. He's certainly as bloody annoying as one.

I hear Bella put her phone receiver down and shortly after, her head pops up over her computer monitor directly opposite mine. 'No luck with any of Anya's school friends. None of them had anything helpful to say about Poppy's death,' says Bella.

'Not ideal,' I say.

'Nope.' She pauses. 'You all right? You look grumpy.'

'Anya's phone records,' I mumble, not even bothering to rearrange my face.

'Ah,' she says.

I grimace.

'That looks fun,' she adds. The irony is that she isn't being sarcastic.

'You'd love it,' I reply, not taking my eyes off the list of numbers.

I mark off the ones I recognise. Lisette. Orla. The local doctor's surgery. A number that I manage to link to her cousin Ruben; I'll get Tiana to track him down later – he could be useful. Plenty of unanswered cold callers. Not much in the text messages; everyone uses WhatsApp now, and that's encrypted. There's one number that showed up a lot in the months before Anya and Lisette got together, and then a couple of times the day before Lisette and Sylvie's deaths. But when I look it up, it tells me there's no subscriber information held.

A burner phone?

Chapter 16

Eve – Then

'Are we having a party for Frankie's first birthday?' I dangle the fluffy rabbit toy by its foot and my sister reaches out to grab the floppy ears with her little fingers. Each time she comes close to catching it, I swing it out of the way.

'No. Please stop winding your sister up.' Mum's lying back on the sofa with a glass of wine in her hand, staring at something boring on the TV.

'Why not?' I know I'm whining but I can't help it. I plonk the rabbit on Frankie's lap and she gurgles happily as she jams the tail in her mouth.

'Please don't whinge.' Mum looks like she wants to cry. After a moment, I jump to my feet and flop onto the sofa next to her, leaning into her warm body, hoping she'll reach an arm around me and pull me in for a cuddle. But she doesn't move, and I feel a weird little pain in my stomach, like a snake's wriggling around in there. I don't like it at all.

A huge wail comes out of Frankie's tiny little mouth and Ajax shoots out of the room like a bomb's gone off. I look up at Mum, but she's still sitting there, stuck in the same position as if she's run out of batteries. I slide off the sofa and shuffle across the living room on my knees. I try pulling a face at my sister, but her wailing has turned into screaming, with her eyes shut so tight that she can't even see me. I look back at Mum, but she's crying too now, and I don't know what to do. I'm shaking a bit but I pick Frankie up and put her over my shoulder. She's a lot heavier now, and it's not easy to carry her. But as I rub her back, her loud cries turn into quiet whimpers.

I sing my favourite song to her, and she stops crying completely. I'm so proud of myself, I try to catch Mum's eye but hers are squeezed shut. I feel the snake in my stomach slithering about again. Things are weird now. And I hate it.

'Where's Dad?'

Her eyes open, and I notice that they're a bit red. She drinks a mouthful of wine. 'Spending all our money down the bloody pub, no doubt.'

'Oh,' I say, remembering how my school shoes make my feet sore, and how Mum keeps saying we can't afford new ones yet. Is it because Dad's spending all our money down the pub? How will we afford to buy clothes and toys for the baby then?

***

I miss my old dad. Even when he's here, it's him but it's *not* him. Because he's not the same dad anymore. This one's full of anger and stinks like an old cigarette.

When I wake suddenly in the middle of the night, everything's pitch-black, except for the My Little Pony night-light that glows soft blue in the corner of my room. My mouth is really dry, and I reach for my cup of water but knock it to the floor, soaking the carpet. I wiggle my legs out from underneath the sleeping cat, climb out of bed and tiptoe to the door, across the hall and down the stairs. It doesn't matter what Mum says, I don't like getting water from the bathroom tap; it's too close to the toilet. I know my way around the new house now so I don't bother turning on the light. My eyes have got used to the darkness, but I wrinkle my nose at the disgusting smell coming from downstairs.

'Aurgh!' The liquid on the floor is cold against my bare foot and squelches horribly between my toes. I jump back onto the bottom step and my fingers fumble around for the light switch. I blink a few times against the bright light and then I realise my dad's fallen on the floor in the hallway, lying in a pool of sick. He looks dead. I scream so loudly I'm sure the whole street can hear me. 'Dad!' I rush to his side, shaking him hard, and his head wobbles strangely from side to side, his tongue hanging out of his mouth. I might've found it funny if I wasn't so frightened.

'What are you making that racket for?' I hear Mum's footsteps thumping across the landing. 'What are you doing out of—' She stops dead when she sees what's happened.

'Dad won't wake up.' I feel hot tears stinging my eyes and running down my cheeks. 'He's been sick and he's fallen over and he won't wake up and I think he's dead.' The words rush out of my mouth like water streaming out of the bath taps.

Mum races down the stairs and stares at Dad, shaking her head. 'You stupid, bloody idiot,' she whispers.

Why is she calling Dad an idiot? My heart is jumping up and down on a trampoline inside my chest. 'We need to call an ambulance.'

'No we don't. He's drunk.' Then she says a swear word, the one I'm definitely not allowed to repeat. She steps past me, avoiding the puddle of sick, and turns Dad onto his side, shaking him so hard I think he's going to knock his head on the floor.

Dad groans and I hug my knees to my chest, relieved that he's alive but so scared of what's happening in front of me.

'Get back to bed, Evie.'

But I'm frozen to the spot.

'Please.' She turns around and says it again, slowly and quietly. First, I think she's angry with me but she looks scared, like she's pleading with me to go. I don't think I've ever run up the stairs as fast, and I don't dare look back. I dive into my bed and bury my face in my pillow, my head full of things that frighten me.

Chapter 17

Anya – Then

I'm organising a display of sheet music books when the bell tinkles to let me know a customer has entered the shop.

'Morning.' I turn around to greet them, and I falter when I see who it is, and the state of him. 'Ruben? What happened to your face?'

Ruben is pale. A bruise blooms across one cheek, a rainbow of crimson, violet and navy. His bottom lip bleeds. 'I'm in a bit of trouble.'

'No kidding.' I lead him to the sofa at the back of Melody Laine and he collapses into it. 'What's going on?'

'I owe some people some money.' He stares at his trainers, the laces on his right foot loose.

I try to catch his eye but he keeps his gaze down. 'You owe me fifteen hundred.' I didn't ask any questions when he asked me for a thousand more, but it's time for him to start talking. 'Who do you owe money to? And for what?' I probe.

He glances up at me then back down at his feet.

'If you won't tell me, then I can't help you.' I cross my arms over my chest.

'It was just a few pills,' he says to the floor. 'I was meant to sell them, but I took them, and now I owe the supplier money. The interest goes up every day. They turned up at my house.' He suddenly stands up and grabs my arms, his eyes wild, the words tumbling out of him faster than I can keep up. 'You've got to help me. Please. I'm *family*.'

I jerk my arms out of his grip. 'You haven't paid me back the money I've already lent you.'

'You've got tonnes of money, right?'

I'm furious. 'This ends now.'

He drops to the floor, sobbing. 'I'm desperate. Please, An. I don't know what else to do, except . . .' He looks up at me, eyes pleading. 'Except end it all.'

Something inside me physically aches for him. I've been so close to how he's feeling now. I reach my hand out for him to grab, and drag him to his feet and into my arms. 'Don't you *dare* do anything stupid.' My voice is muffled, my mouth pressed against his T-shirt, his collarbone protruding. 'Are you eating?'

'Sometimes.' He snivels into my hair.

I stand back, holding on to both of his shoulders with my hands. 'How much more do you need?'

He bites his bloodied lip, and then winces. 'Two grand will pay them off. Another grand will cover this month's rent and bills.'

It's my turn to grimace.

Seeing my expression, he grabs my hands, eyes pleading.

'Listen. I've got a job at the chippy. I get paid at the end of the week. And I *promise* I won't go near the drugs again.'

I soften. 'You mean it?'

He nods in earnest. 'I don't want this.' He gestures at his face, and then at me. 'I don't want to do this to you.'

I exhale deeply, knowing I'm going to give in. 'You'd better be telling the truth.'

Chapter 18

Eve – Now

When I arrive at my desk the next day, my phone's ringing.

'Hello?' I put my coffee on my coaster off centre, and spill half of it over my desk. 'Shitting hell.'

'Language, DC Starling.'

I catch the spilled coffee with a tissue. 'Grim Tim! Sorry. You okay?'

He laughs. 'I'm good. I've got a bit of news for you.'

My ears prick up, desperate for good news. 'Oh?'

'So we've run Mark's prints through the system. Got a match for the ones found on the smoke alarm.'

'The smoke alarm that had its batteries removed?'

'Uh-huh.'

'This is big,' I say, gripping the phone. '*Really* big.'

***

I bump into Gillian in the kitchen at lunchtime. 'Not seen you in a couple of days. Good weekend?'

She leans against the counter with her arms folded, shooting a dirty look at the teabag someone has left in the sink. 'Oh, lovely. Romantic picnic in the park with Eddie celebrating our anniversary.'

I sense a subtle tone of sarcasm in her voice. 'How was it?' I probe, fishing the teabag out of the sink and flinging it into the bin.

'The twat forgot to pack a bottle opener and tried to open a beer by tapping the lid against a brick wall. Ended up glassing his own hand and we spend a beautiful five hours in the delight that is Brighton A&E.'

'Oh, shit. He okay?'

Gillian rolls her eyes. 'He had surgery. Went through an artery, would you believe it? That man.' She shakes her head fondly and grabs a mug from the cupboard. I slide the coffee canister across the counter to her and she scrapes around the bottom of it with a teaspoon. 'How about you?'

'Nothing new.' I shrug. 'Can't stop thinking about this case. Even when I'm not doing a weekend shift, I spend the whole time thinking about it anyway.'

She looks sharply at me. 'Don't let this take over your life.'

I wave her off. 'I won't. It's just so . . .'

'Close to home?' she offers lightly.

I nod. 'Seeing all those flowers, those teddies—'

'This is a completely different situation,' she says, her

voice gentle. 'I *know* it's difficult, but try not to link the two events in your head.'

I smile weakly. 'I'm trying.'

Gillian reaches for my shoulder and gives it a squeeze. 'We've got you, okay?'

'I know.'

She stirs her coffee. Black, no sugar. Straightforward, to the point. 'What's the latest?'

I lean against the counter. 'Still haven't got hold of Zachary.'

'Suspicious?'

'Absolutely,' I say.

She nods. 'And what about Mark? How'd the interview go?'

'He's definitely a suspect. They've had a fair few rows about Sylvie and child support payments. The night the fire was set, Sylvie was meant to be at her grandparents' house, but the plans had been cancelled last minute – I'm not convinced he knew this. I wonder if he'd meant to kill Lisette, but accidentally killed Sylvie too? His girlfriend provided an alibi but there's no other evidence he was at her house.'

'It's a theory.' Gillian raises an eyebrow.

'There's one more thing though,' I say.

Her eyes dart to me. 'I'm listening.'

'Mark's prints were found on the smoke alarm . . . Remember the batteries were missing?'

'Jesus.' Gillian looks at me sharply. 'Haul his arse back

in here as soon as you can. Preferably yesterday. And you're still looking at Anya as a suspect?'

'Yes. And we've got something else on her. I've looked through her records and she was investigated in connection with the death of her friend when she was a teenager. Her friend died in the same spot she did. And she's been in contact with someone using what I suspect is a burner phone the day before the fire.'

Gillian smiles. 'Nice work. Keep me updated. And remember what I said about Frankie.'

'Will do, ma'am.' I open up the coffee canister. 'Oh, for crying out loud.'

'What?'

'You nabbed the last of my caffeine supply. You do realise it's my lifeline?'

'The boss's prerogative.' She laughs. 'There's a stash in my office. Bottom drawer on the left of my desk. Help yourself, but don't tell anyone what you saw in there.'

She winks, squeezes my upper arm affectionately and swoops out of the kitchen.

***

I make my way to her office, clutching a mug of hot water and a spoon, and set it down on her desk. Reaching for the bottom drawer and sliding it open, I discover a canister of Nescafé nestled amongst several packets of fizzy sweets. I laugh to myself, wondering if the protein shakes and detox teas are all for show. As I reach over to scoop up the coffee, my eyes fall on Gillian's open handbag, and the little bundle of orange-capped needles tucked in next to her purse. I had no idea she was on medication and I wonder if she's okay.

***

Later in the afternoon, I watch Mark through the window into the interview room. Unlike most occupants who tend to slump in the seat, stare blankly at the wall or pick at their fingernails, he paces relentlessly, tiger-like. It reminds me of how he behaved in his kitchen last week while I waited for him to answer my questions.

'He's so tense,' says Tiana, moving her gaze from the window to me. 'Do you think he's guilty?'

'It's a theory.' I echo Gillian's words from earlier. 'While I remember, did you manage to speak to Ruben? Anya's cousin?'

'Eventually,' she replies. 'He was about as useful as an inflatable dartboard.'

'They spoke a lot,' I say, not moving my eyes from Mark.

'They were close,' she agrees. 'He's devastated, but has absolutely no idea why Anya jumped.'

Tiana switches her gaze back to Mark. After a pause, she turns back to me, squaring her shoulders as if preparing herself for a difficult task. 'Eve, I'd like to sit in on an interview soon. I've watched you a lot, and I think I'm ready.'

I glance at her, a determined, confident look on her face

masking the insecurities I know lie beneath the surface. I nod. 'I'll speak to Gillian.'

***

Mark stops on the spot when I enter the room with Jason by my side. 'Why am I here? *Again?* I was only bloody here yesterday.'

I gesture to the chair. 'Please, sit down.'

He glares at me but does as I say. 'Am I under arrest this time?'

We lower ourselves into the seats opposite him. 'No,' says Jason. 'We've got a few more questions for you.'

'Fine.' Mark opens his hands to the sides. 'Be my guest.'

'Mark, could you please tell us the last time you were in Lisette's house?' asks Jason.

He freezes. His eyes dart between Jason and me. 'Um, I dropped Sylvie off, like, the week before—' The words get stuck in his throat. I don't push him to complete the sentence.

I flick through the calendar at the front of my notebook and remind him of the date. He nods, his eyes squeezed shut.

'Okay. And did you go *inside* the house?'

He opens his eyes. 'Just in the hallway. I was waiting for Sylvie to go to the loo. Me and Lisette chatted for a bit, then I took Sylvie to the cinema to see that film with the singing bloody koala.' He pauses, hands clasped together in a silent prayer, eyes squeezed shut as if holding in the

110

tears. Gripping tightly on to the memory, as if it might leak out of the cracks and be forgotten forever.

'Were you left alone at any point?' asks Jason.

Mark opens his eyes and frowns. 'What is this, exactly?'

Jason repeats his question.

'No,' says Mark. 'I wasn't *left alone*. Can you please tell me what you're getting at?'

'The smoke alarm at Lisette's house didn't sound when the fire started.' I watch him for a hint of a reaction, but there's nothing other than confusion.

'Well . . . why wouldn't it go off?'

'There were no batteries in it,' I reply. Still no flicker of guilt. 'What would you say about that?'

'Shit.' His eyes widen. 'She forget to replace them?'

Jason leans forward. 'Or . . . they were removed.'

Mark jumps back in his chair as if a firework has gone off in front of him. 'No. No way. I know where this is going. You can't pin this on me.'

'Your fingerprints were found on the casing of the smoke alarm,' I challenge him.

'Of course they were! I used to live there. I changed the batteries tonnes of times. I was probably the last person to change them. *Shit*. I'm not talking to you again without a solicitor.' He stands up and stalks towards the door, staring at us until we let him out.

'We'll be in touch with you and your solicitor then,' says Jason to Mark, who storms out of the station without so much as a second glance over his shoulder.

Jason and I look at each other.

'He's got a point.' I think of the half-hearted attempts I put into cleaning my flat. 'When was the last time you wiped down your smoke alarm?'

'I'll ask my cleaner,' he retorts, and I roll my eyes.

I watch Mark from the window as he speeds out of the car park, his tyres screeching on the tarmac. I can't help but think he's hiding something that might just help everything slot into place.

Chapter 19

Anya – Then

Ovingdean Beach has more sand and fewer pebbles than Brighton seafront, and is perfect for Bowie to burn off some pent-up energy. It's quiet; this time of year brings with it fewer tourists. As soon as Matthew lets him off the lead he bounds across the sand and straight into the freezing cold sea, emerging almost immediately, dripping wet and full of joy. We watch Bowie dig a huge hole, kicking up a shower of sand behind him, before getting distracted by a golden retriever and chasing after it in the unabashed, joyful way that dogs do.

I try not to look up at the cliffs towering behind us. They're so beautiful, but how can I look at them without being reminded of what happened? But I find myself staring up at them anyway, squinting in the sun.

'You okay, An?' Matthew's voice cuts through my reverie. 'What's up there?'

'Nothing.' I shake my head. 'They're just so . . . *big*.'

He follows my gaze, and for a second, I think I see a dark

expression cross his face, but it's gone before I really register it. Maybe he's got a bad memory of these cliffs too. 'That's one word for them. Bowie!' he shouts suddenly. 'That dog.'

Bowie has raced off, too far into the sea for Matthew's liking. 'Bowie!' he shouts again.

I can see the dog's happy face as he paddles in the gentle waves. 'He looks okay, Matt.'

Matthew shakes his head. 'I don't like it when he goes in the sea. Bowie!'

The dog doesn't register Matthew's shouts. I laugh. 'Are you sure that's his name?'

'Of course it's his name,' says Matthew. I sense he's not in the mood to joke around. Eventually Bowie comes back to the shore, a slimy piece of seaweed dangling from his tail.

'Stupid dog,' says Matthew, but ruffles him on top of his soaking-wet head with fondness. 'You've got to stop scaring me like that.'

Bowie pants, his pink tongue lolling like a piece of ham, and we both laugh.

Matthew wraps an arm around me. 'Fancy hanging out at the boat for a bit?'

The excitement must have shown on my face because he laughs. 'I'll take that as a yes.' He attaches Bowie's lead and we make our way towards the marina. Orla and I have spent countless evenings after a couple of drinks wandering around the marina, picking our favourite boats. If she gets drunk, she likes to tell the story about how she once snuck onto an unoccupied boat to have al fresco sex with her ex-boyfriend, at which point I slam my hands over my ears. My heart races at the thought of what Matthew might have in mind.

Bowie's claws tap on the boardwalk behind me as Matthew leads us towards the boat. It's bigger than I expected, painted white and navy, with a sun-bleached deck. Some of the paint is peeling but it looks pretty in a rustic kind of way. Two comfortable-looking deck chairs sit side by side, and I imagine lounging there together, wrapped in a cosy blanket, watching the sun go down. I can't wait to see inside.

'This is amazing!' I squeal, as we climb onto the deck. I slip off my shoes and the wood is cool under my soles. 'I've always wanted to go inside one of these.'

Matthew unlocks the door and lets me inside. It's so tidy and minimalist, the total opposite of my place, but I love it. There's a little table and chairs next to a tiny kitchen area, a sofa for two opposite a TV that's probably a bit too big for the space it's in, and a double bed in a cosy corner, dressed in hotel-style white waffle bedding. The door at the opposite end leads to a miniature bathroom. My eyes land on the empty glass, plate and cutlery on the draining board, the paperback propped open on the pillow, the dog bowl on the floor, and the half-full washing basket. 'Matt . . .' I turn to him. 'Are you *living* here? I thought you were joking when you said that.'

He shrugs. 'For a bit. Turns out living with my mate was more annoying than I thought. I prefer it here.'

'Is Bowie all right here?' I ask, concerned.

'He's fine.' Matthew strokes one of the dog's ears. 'He loves it. He thinks he owns the marina.'

I laugh. 'Fair enough. It must be an adventure for him.'

Maybe it could be an adventure for me, too. Matthew kisses me on the cheek and gently eases me towards the bed. I melt into him, feeling safe, feeling comforted. This could work out, couldn't it?

Chapter 20

I'm sitting in front of Mark for the fourth time and he looks different. Uncomfortable and squirmy. Bella takes her place next to me, opposite Mark's solicitor, and starts the recording tape, running through the usual spiel before getting to the nitty-gritty.

'Mark, when we spoke yesterday, we told you that your fingerprints were found on the casing of the smoke alarm at Lisette's house,' I say. 'The same alarm that had its batteries removed at some point prior to the fire. Do you remember?'

He nods, but doesn't say anything.

'We'd like to ask you a bit more about that,' I continue, clasping my hands on the table between us.

Mark's solicitor speaks. 'DC Starling, DC Cortez . . . if you're insinuating my client set this fire—'

I smile tightly at him. 'We're just clarifying the facts.' I turn back to Mark.

'I understand you're getting a lot of pressure from the public to solve this case, but before you go any further with your claims, my client can prove he was not at the scene of the fire.' A confident, smug look settles on the solicitor's face and we lock eyes.

'Go ahead.' I glance at Mark, who appears to be sinking lower into his seat, his face slick with sweat. He looks embarrassed. *Why?*

The solicitor holds his hand out and Mark hesitates before dropping a phone into his open palm. Bella and I watch intently as Mark's solicitor unlocks it and navigates to the photo and video gallery.

'As you know, Mark's girlfriend Georgie gave him an alibi for the night of the fire. The video I'm about to show you proves she was telling the truth.'

'Why was this not shared before?' Bella asks.

The solicitor wordlessly hands me the phone and my breath catches in my throat at the sight of a woman on the screen, slowly removing her clothes. I can clearly hear Mark's voice from behind the camera, egging her on. I turn down the volume.

'Right,' I say, fast-forwarding the video, which moves quickly on to what I can only describe as homemade pornography. There are more videos, all of them geo-tagged and timestamped, starting at around midnight and ending at four in the morning. It must have been quite a session; I'm exhausted just thinking about it.

Mark's eyes remain on the table throughout the whole conversation. Humiliation radiates from him and it's all I can do not to release a nervous, highly inappropriate laugh.

'We'll take this and get it checked by Digital Forensics,'

says Bella, dropping the phone into an evidence bag and sealing it up. There's no hint of embarrassment on her face. 'Thank you for bringing it in. We'll have it back with you once the video has been extracted.'

Mark's solicitor smiles. 'I think that brings our conversation to a close, unless you have any further questions for my client?'

I smile. 'Nothing more from me. We'll be in touch.'

***

'Fucking *hell*,' says Bella as we make our way upstairs. 'That was pretty hardcore.'

'Each to their own.' I try to rid myself of the mental image of Mark and Georgie going at it like amateur porn stars.

'There's no way I'd film myself having sex,' she says loudly, attracting several pairs of raised eyebrows as we enter the office. 'With anyone,' she clarifies. 'I can't think of anything worse than watching that back. Me and Tony tried mirrors once. It was *vile*.'

'I'd watch it,' offers Jason with a smirk.

Bella shoots him a dark look as she passes. 'Zip it, pervert.' But her tone is playful. She turns back to me. 'Danny's going to have a right old time checking this footage.'

I snort. 'He's seen worse.'

Gillian catches my eye through the glass partition to her office and beckons me over.

I slip through the door. 'Morning, ma'am.'

She stops typing and glances up at me. 'How'd the interview go? I couldn't watch. Had an appointment.'

I drop into the seat opposite. 'His alibi definitely checks out.'

'How so? Sorry,' she says, covering her mouth to yawn. She looks exhausted, and I wonder if she's okay.

'We were just shown a video with a timestamp that proves he was . . .' I pause '. . . otherwise engaged.'

'Was it a sex video, Eve? Don't beat around the bush.'

'How do you *do* that?'

'There aren't many things people film on their phones at that time of morning. Obviously, I'm *not* speaking from experience.'

A laugh escapes my lips. 'Fair enough.'

'Where does this leave you?' Her expression turns serious.

'The video is with Digital Forensics to check it's legit, but my best guess is that it is. If you were going to make up an alibi, I think you'd go for one that doesn't involve a team of detectives seeing you stark-bollock naked in the throes of passion. We've got a warrant to search Zachary Samson's place, so Jason and I are heading there after lunch. And the team are still searching for Anya Fernsby's remains, but nothing has been found yet.'

'What's that gut of yours telling you?'

I pause. 'Honestly? I was convinced it was Mark. But with Zachary's disappearance and the revelation that he had issues with Lisette, I'm zoning in on him.'

'And, Anya?'

'I can't see enough of a motive there, not to do something

like this. Yes, there's the will. But is that *really* enough to drive someone to brutally murder the woman she loves, and her five-year-old stepdaughter? Someone who's known for being kind and loving?'

Gillian raises an eyebrow at me. 'Assume nothing, believe no one, challenge everything,' she says, rattling off the team's ABC mantra.

'Oh, don't worry,' I say. 'She's not off my radar yet.'

Chapter 21

Anya – Then

I'm torn from the safety of sleep by a banging on the front door. My eyes, gritty and bleary, register the time: 2 a.m. I decide to ignore it, and shove my head under my pillow.

Bang bang.

Whoever it is, they're not letting up. I haul myself out of bed and yank open the curtains. An orange glow from the streetlight floods the room and I squint into the front garden.

It's Ruben, crouching down, his face pressed up against the letterbox.

I throw open the window, letting in the autumn chill. 'Ruben, what the *hell* are you doing?'

He staggers back from the door and stares up at me.

'Let me in,' he slurs.

'You *promised* you'd lay off the drugs. You're off your face.'

'I'm not.' His words blend into one, magnifying the blatant lie.

'I'll call you a taxi and you'll go home.' I grip the handle, ready to slam the window shut.

'You can't just get rid of me,' he mumbles. 'I'm not . . . I'm not *her*.'

'Shut up,' I hiss, blood rushing in my ears. 'I'm coming down.'

I grab my dressing gown off the back of the bedroom door and hug it around me, shoving my feet into slippers and racing down the stairs. I pull the front door open, and he's standing there, looking worryingly ill. He stumbles into the hallway and I push the door shut behind us.

'What the *hell's* going on?' I guide him into the living room and he slumps into the armchair, dropping his head into his hands. I notice his fingernails are bitten and filthy. He looks even more scrawny than last time I saw him, and the bruises have faded, although I can see a fresh one blooming across his jawline.

He raises his head from his hands, his eyes wild. 'You've got to help me.'

'I *have* helped you,' I say. 'Four thousand, five hundred pounds. And you've not paid a penny back.'

'Can't put a price on family,' he mumbles.

'Oh, you can,' I retort, deciding he needs tough love right now. 'I love you, and I appreciate everything you and your mum did for us, but this *has* to stop.'

His eyes flash dangerously. 'I don't know how much longer I can keep covering for you.'

I freeze. 'You don't mean that. You don't know what you're talking about. *I* don't know what you're talking about. You're off your face.'

'You'd have ended up in foster care if it wasn't for us.' He leans back into the armchair, closing his eyes. 'You'd have ended up in *prison* if it wasn't for me.'

I swear my heart stops beating for a few seconds. 'Please don't do this,' I whisper. 'It was an accident. You *know* it was an accident.' I thought he was sure about what he saw that night. I was convinced.

He responds with silence.

'Ruben?'

A snore.

I close my eyes, pressing the heels of my hands into the sockets. There's a good chance he'll forget this conversation in the morning. I turn to go back upstairs, but a twinge of guilt makes me drag the throw off the back of the sofa and lay it over him. Love is so complicated, especially when it comes to family.

Chapter 22

Eve – Now

This afternoon's search of Zachary's place reveals nothing. Nothing related to the case, anyway. When we'd turned up and the same lad answered the door, the colour drained from his face quicker than Jason can down a pint. We haven't yet found out his name, but he's already been taken to the station. Now I'm standing in the middle of the living room, my gloved hands on my hips, eyes sweeping the room for any clue as to where the hell Zachary has got to. But it's a mess of drug paraphernalia, bits of foil, teaspoons, lighters, empty crisp packets, pizza boxes and, weirdly, a teddy bear. The sight of it conjures an image in my mind of the teddy bear I'd left behind that day, eight years old and frightened of what was about to happen, clueless about what it meant for our family. How things would end up.

'Probably rammed with drugs,' says Jason, snapping me out of my trance. A CSI bags the bear up as evidence, and it looks strange next to all the needles. There's enough here to send these guys down for a good seven years. Longer, if we find evidence of intent to supply.

I gingerly open a door, immediately wishing I hadn't. I try not to retch at the sight and stench of the shit-streaked toilet. 'Where the bloody hell has he gone?' I shut the door as quickly as possible.

He shrugs. 'He never planned to come down to the station. You should've taken the statement here, to be fair. I would've.'

I round on him. 'I didn't know he was gonna do a bloody runner, Sarge. He was cooperative at the time.'

He holds his hands up in mock surrender. 'All right, tetchy. Just saying.'

The two CSIs descend the stairs, laden with evidence bags, nodding at us to let us know they're done. 'Got a shit ton of prints,' says the taller one. 'Will take a while to get through them all, mind.'

'We don't have the luxury of time,' I snap, thinking of the flurry of comments on our Facebook page, the pressure from Gillian's bosses. 'Make it a priority. Please.'

She frowns. 'We'll do what we can.'

I thank her, wondering if any of the prints found in this wretched place would link back to the prints discovered on the white spirit bottle. Whether Zachary was involved somehow. He disappeared into thin air, like he never even existed . . . Was this purely because of the fear of getting caught selling drugs, or something much more sinister?

***

'You ready to go?' Bella raps her knuckles against my desk.

'One sec,' I say, shutting down my computer. 'Just need the loo.'

She glances at the time. 'You've literally got three minutes before we're past the cut-off point for guaranteeing a good table.'

'All right, all right, I'll be quick.' I leap from my chair.

'I'll go without you,' she calls after me, as I rush to the bathroom, nearly crashing into Gillian as I push open the toilet door. 'Oh, sorry—'

'It's okay.' She bustles past, her eyes red-rimmed and bloodshot.

I reach out to touch her on the shoulder. 'Are you okay?'

Her face splits into a smile. 'Of course I am,' she says, brushing off whatever has bothered her. 'Never better.'

I know the smile is fake. I know there's something wrong. But before I can coax her into telling me, she turns on her heel and leaves me standing there.

With a deep sigh, I make my way into the toilet and shut myself into a cubicle. Gillian's always so strong. What could've happened to make her crumble like that? Work pressure? But she's so together, so composed. I never thought I'd see the day Gillian Harbrook cried at work.

I peel the wrapper off a tampon and try to lift the flap to the sanitary bin, but it's stuck. Something has wedged itself in there. 'For fuck's sake,' I mutter to myself, resisting the urge to shove it until it snaps. And that's when I see it. A pregnancy test announcing that whoever had just been in here was definitely not pregnant.

'Two Kopparberg strawberry and limes, please. One alcohol-free, one regular,' I ask the barman when I've finally got his attention. It's busy today, the beautiful weather bringing everyone out in droves. I peer over my shoulder and see Bella has snapped up a table in the sun. 'Get the one with the parasol,' I mime to her, pointing at a group of lads leaving a table in the shade. She rolls her eyes, but sidles over to it and drops her bag on the seat. She might enjoy sitting in blistering-hot sunshine, but my pale complexion could do without burning today.

I pay for the ciders and pick them up, the condensation cooling against my clammy skin. I weave my way through a group of women on a hen party, complete with several inflatable penises, and drop into a seat at the table.

'Bella, this is shit.' I pass her a bottle.

'I got the table you wanted.' She pulls a face at the parasol.

'Not the table. The case. It's been nearly two weeks. Anya's body still hasn't been found. Zachary's still on the run. Mark—'

Bella snorts.

'Stop remembering the sex video.' I flick her on the forearm. 'I'm trying so hard to remove it from my brain. As I was *saying*, Mark's no longer a suspect—'

'But *you* think he still is.' She peels the corner of the label on her bottle, eyeing me across the table.

'I think he could've been involved, but I can't prove it. Was Anya involved? Maybe. But *why*? And until I pin down

Zachary and figure out his part in all this, I won't be able to prove anything. Gillian's probably going to hand this over as a cold case and it'll be my fault—'

'Hey,' she says, her eyes burning into me. 'You're *not* the SIO on this case. You've done everything you can. If we fail, *we* fail. Not *you*.'

'I know, it's just that ever since I passed my sergeants' exam I've been waiting for a big case like this to prove myself. I'm so bloody ready for the next step.'

'I *know*.' She smiles. 'I have faith in you, Eve. You're destined to run this department.'

'What about you?' I ask. 'You could do your sergeants' exam—'

'No,' she says, cutting me off. Her phone buzzes and she grabs it, peers at the screen, then places it face down, cheeks flushing. She carries on speaking as if it hadn't happened. 'I've told you I'm not ready. Not yet.'

'Bella.' I pretend I haven't seen anything. 'You're more than good enough. You're always uncovering stuff the rest of us don't notice. You have the patience of a saint with all your data and numbers and spreadsheets . . .'

'An eye for detail isn't enough.' She takes a swig of cider. 'I can't interview like you do. You have a way with people. You just need to get your angry outbursts in check.'

I smack her playfully on the arm. 'You'll get there. Maybe one day you'll be as narky as me.'

'Maybe.' She shrugs. 'I *am* happy, you know. It's not all about promotions for me. I'd like to keep hold of what remains of my work-life balance for a little longer, thank you very much.' Her eyes momentarily shift to her phone, then back to me.

'Just make sure Tiana doesn't overtake you,' I mutter.

She rolls her eyes. 'Shut up and drink up.'

I bring the bottle to my lips and drink deeply. It's sweet and cold, and it's exactly what I need right now. I flinch as someone behind me sparks up a cigarette.

'Want to swap?' she asks.

I pause. 'No. It's okay.' My eyes close and I rest my forehead on the table. 'Why is this case so hard?' I groan.

'We'll get the fucker, I promise you,' says Bella. 'You won't believe how many people are looking for Zachary Samson and Anya's body right now.'

I really hope she's right.

Chapter 23

Eve – Then

I stare at the thick white envelope in my surprisingly still hands. Chaos breaks out around me as one by one, envelopes are torn open with varying degrees of enthusiasm, and in some cases, extreme trepidation. A wave of nervous excitement seems to pulsate through the busy school hall, but still, I don't open that envelope. My eyes are transfixed on it, yet all I can think is how much it really doesn't matter what's inside. Because it doesn't change a thing whether I get straight As, or fail all three subjects spectacularly.

Eventually, my fingers find the corner of the envelope where the flap isn't quite stuck down, and rip it open. I slide the results from the safety of the envelope and out into the world, where I have to acknowledge their existence.

I don't know what the fuck to do.

***

'Evie.'

I glance up from the front gate to see where the voice is coming from. My next-door neighbour, Charlie, is standing in his perfectly preened front garden that puts our oblong patch of dry, weedy grass to shame.

'Hey, Charlie.' I drop my hand from the gate and turn towards the guy I wish was my actual dad. I've known him since we moved into this house, almost ten years ago. I remember how he looked after me when I came off my bike and got grit painfully embedded in my knee, and when I broke my arm falling out of a tree in the park. Charlie and his younger sister Gillian stepped in when my own parents repeatedly failed me.

I frown. 'Are you all right?'

'Aye, I'm canny. How about you? Results day, eh?' I love his warm Geordie accent.

'Uh-huh.' I pin a stone to the pavement with my Converse, and scrape it along the ground, making a rough white line on the tarmac.

'So . . . ?' He brushes his gloved hands together and bits of dry soil shower into the flowerbed.

I shrug. 'I did all right. How's Gilly?' I look back up at him, imploring him to understand my desire for a change of conversation.

'Oh, she's all right. But don't change the subject, pet. Come on, now. What did you get?' He holds his arms out wide in an open, friendly gesture.

'I got an A, B and C.' I shrug. 'Easy enough to remember, I guess.'

His face splits into a wide smile. 'Well done! Come here, smart cookie.'

He opens the gate to his front garden and I allow myself to be enveloped into a hug. I have to admit, it feels comforting. And it's easier to talk when I can't see his face. 'I'm withdrawing my application to East London,' I mumble into his T-shirt.

Charlie plants his big hands firmly on my shoulders and gently pushes me back so he can see my face. 'What? Why would you do that, Evie?'

My face crumples. 'How can I leave her? With *them*?'

His own face softens. 'Are things that bad?'

I fix my eyes on his muddy gardening boots, a leaf stuck to the toe of the left one. 'They're just . . . useless,' I mutter. 'And they're both still drinking. Can't get them to stop.' I laugh awkwardly. Things have got worse over the years. It started with Dad drinking his problems away after he lost his job and Mum dealing with the fallout, until it took its toll on her, too. It was so slow, I didn't really notice how bad things were. How distant, how zombie-like, how *sad* she'd become. The over-reliance on alcohol that they both seem to have succumbed to.

Charlie hooks a finger under my chin and tips my face upwards. 'Listen to me, pet. You're not to go messing up your own future, d'you hear me? Me and Gilly will keep an eye on your sister. Remember, I can hear everything through those walls. Paper-thin. And she's a smart kid, you've taught her plenty.'

I smile weakly at him. He's right, Frankie's only nine but

she's developed skills no normal kid should possess. I'd tried to teach her well, keeping her clued up in all the things she might need should I take the plunge and go to university. She knows how to cook most basic things, but what I've managed to teach her relies purely on the dregs in our kitchen cupboards, which leaves little to our culinary imaginations. I've taught her how to use the washing machine, and how to hang and fold the clothes so we can get away without ironing them. The iron had broken years ago, and never been replaced. She can operate the old hoover, even though most of the attachments have been lost over the years.

She knows what to do in any emergency situation I can think of. Books are a luxury neither of us have access to in the house, but I've signed her up for a library card. She knows precisely how much vodka to pour down the sink and replace with water before they'll notice. I've blurred the line between sister and parent, but who knows what a parent is supposed to be, anyway?

I puff my cheeks out, letting a sharp burst of breath blow past my lips. 'I'll think about it. Me and Frankie . . . we haven't discussed it yet.'

He gives me a squeeze on the shoulder. 'I'm here if you need me. You remember that, Evie Starling.'

I smile, and turn back to the house, where I see Frankie's angular little face peering from her open bedroom window at me. I wave, and she leans out. 'Code red,' she whispers, just loud enough for me to hear.

For fuck's sake.

I rush through the gate, shove my key in the lock and

swing the door open, immediately hearing raised voices. Ajax darts from the kitchen, making a little chirruping sound as he winds his sleek body around my legs in greeting. His pointed ears are flicked back in a way that tells me he's anxious. I reach down and run my hand over his silky back, and he purrs.

'. . . well if you hadn't turned into such a miserable bitch, maybe I wouldn't have shagged her!'

Something thuds against the closed living-room door. Ajax and I both jump. My eyes slide to the top of the stairs where a skinny pair of legs stands frozen on the top step.

'Frankie?'

At the sound of my voice, the legs descend with caution, and my sister appears. Her freckled face is pinched in worry, one hand gripping the banister.

'You okay, sis?'

Her eyes dart in the direction of the living room as another unknown object is flung against a wall. 'Yes,' she murmurs. 'My homework's in there, though.'

'Don't worry, we'll get it later. When's it due?'

She bites her bottom lip. 'Tomorrow.'

'Tomorrow? Not like you to leave it to the last minute.'

'I needed help. It's English.'

The one subject my smart little sister can't stand. I'd gone round my friend's last night and stayed later than planned. Guilt floods through me.

'Shit. Sorry.' I glance at the door. 'I'll get it.'

'No!' She reaches out a hand to stop me, but I'm already storming towards the door. I fling it open. Mum stares at me with forlorn eyes, and Dad whips around on the spot, anger emanating from him like sparks of electricity.

'Don't mind me. You carry on.' My eyes scan the room, and I spot Frankie's school bag resting against the side of the sofa.

'Your mother's a twat.' Dad's voice is slurred.

I glare at him as I grab the bag. 'Yeah? Takes one to know one, doesn't it?' I stalk towards the door and slam it behind me, knowing they'll be too drunk to remember what I said. I hold the bag triumphantly in front of me, but a twinge of worry flickers through me. Dad's been cheating on Mum. She must be going through hell. Are things going to get even worse?

I smile. 'Come on, let's get out of here.'

We link arms and head off down the street, singing the 'You & Me Song'. It always seems to make the hard times a bit easier.

Chapter 24

Anya – Then

'What's your favourite memory?' asks Matthew. We've been sitting on the boat all afternoon, painting it with a fresh coat of bright white, passing the time by asking each other the most random questions we can think of as we make the most of the dry weather.

'Easy.' I barely have to mull it over. 'When our parents took us to Disneyland Paris. It was the last holiday we had together before they died.'

'That's a lovely thing to remember.' Matthew shoots me a warm smile.

'Okay.' I feel myself welling up. 'Most embarrassing memory?'

He laughs, shaking his head. 'Texting my dad instead of my ex, Dana.'

'Oh, God.' I stifle a laugh. 'Please tell me it wasn't—'

'Oh, it was.' He reads my mind. 'Never lived it down.'

I let out a howl of laughter. 'Ever send a sex text again?'

'Absolutely not.' He pauses to dip his paintbrush into the

can, pondering his next question. 'I've got one. What's the worst thing you ever did?'

Matthew's question catches me off guard.

'The worst thing I've ever done?' I repeat, my mind racing.

'Yeah.' He absent-mindedly scrapes the excess paint off his brush.

'I don't know,' I say, buying myself some time as my heart pounds. 'What's the worst thing *you've* ever done?'

He glances thoughtfully at me, as if weighing up whether or not to tell me. 'I got a girl pregnant. A stupid, drunken thing. We were . . . far too young. It really affected her. But I've spent most of my adult life feeling guilty about it.'

'Oh.' I sit back on my heels, numb with shock. 'You've got a child?'

'No.' He turns back to his paintbrush, offering no explanation.

I pause. 'Did she have an—'

'No.' He looks back at me sharply. 'The baby died.'

'Oh, God. I'm so sorry. How old were you both?'

'Young enough.'

This conversation has got pretty dark, pretty quick.

'Tell me yours,' he says.

'What?'

'The worst thing you ever did.'

I swallow, desperate for a drink. For a distraction. 'I don't really know,' I lie.

'Am I dating Miss Perfect?' He raises an eyebrow at me.

'Of course not! I just . . . don't feel ready to talk about it.'

'You can tell me anything,' he probes.

'I . . . hit someone's dog with my car,' I lie, standing up and stretching, wiping paint off my hands with a cloth soaked in white spirit.

He looks at me, face blank. 'That's it? The thing you don't feel ready to talk about?'

I nod. 'You know how much I love animals. The dog . . . it belonged to a child. I've always felt guilty.' I feel my face flush from the lie. 'Want a drink?' I keep my voice bright and breezy.

He frowns at me, opens his mouth as if wanting to ask another question, then decides to drop it. 'Can you grab me a beer, please?'

I shoot him a smile and slip through the door before he has a chance to probe me further. I pull my phone out of my back pocket and I glance at it for the first time in hours. Three missed calls and four messages. *Orla.* My stomach plummets as I remember. We were meant to have lunch today. I check the time: 3 p.m. I'm *hours* late. When I return to the deck without the drinks, Matthew notices my worried expression. 'What's happened?'

'I was meant to have lunch with Orla today. She was waiting for me at the café.' I ring her three times but she doesn't pick up.

He puts his paintbrush down and leans over to scratch Bowie under the chin. 'What are you going to tell her?'

'I guess I'll have to tell her the truth. I forgot. What else can I say?'

He straightens up. 'But what will you say you were doing instead? You said you wanted to keep us a secret.'

I raise my palms to the sky, unjustifiably irritated at him, when it was really my fault and not his. 'I don't know. I can just say I felt ill or something and forgot to let her know. It doesn't matter, I need to go and see her.'

***

I knock on Orla's door and she eventually answers.

'Hey, sis.'

She looks at me, stony-faced. 'All right?'

'I'm sorry.' I wring my hands together.

'For what?' She turns away from me and walks back into her flat.

'Forgetting our lunch.' Worry twists in my gut as I follow her inside.

She shrugs.

'Orla.'

Her head snaps back to me and she explodes. 'It's fine, An. You've been a crap sister lately, so this is just another thing to add to the list. Don't worry about it. It's just lunch. Who cares?'

The accusation stings and is followed by a strained silence. I recall with a jolt that I cancelled on her last week and I've been rubbish at texting her back because I've been so distracted by my shiny new relationship. I've completely abandoned her. My fiery, overprotective sister, who cares about me more than anyone else.

It must show on my face because she softens. 'Sorry. I didn't mean that. I never see you anymore. I miss my little sis.'

I take a tentative step further into the room and we sink into sofas opposite each other.

'So where have you been disappearing off to lately?' She says it in an offhand way as she fiddles with her sleeve, like she isn't actually that bothered where I've been, but I sense the question has been burning inside her for a while now. I want to tell her – I really do. She's my sister, my best friend – I normally tell her everything. Well. *Almost* everything. And I'm bursting to tell her about Matthew. To chat into the early hours over a gin and tonic. But what if she flips out? I swallow, my throat dry and sticky. I feel a sharp pain in my finger and realise I've been picking at the skin around my nails as I've been talking, leaving them a sore, unsightly mess.

'Well . . .' I make a snap decision. 'I've been seeing someone.'

'Who?' Her eyes widen, forgetting about her annoyance with me at the promise of potential gossip.

I instantly regret telling her, and shrink back into myself. 'We're keeping it a secret for now.'

She wrinkles her nose. 'Why? Is he a weirdo?'

'No!' I snap. 'We're just, you know, enjoying being in our little bubble for now, without letting anyone else in.'

'Well don't go getting yourself pregnant or anything,' she warns me in that big-sister way of hers.

'I'm twenty-three, not sixteen,' I remind her.

She waves a hand dismissively. 'Someone's got to look after you. And I don't know this guy, so I don't know if *he* will, do I?'

'He will,' I assure her. 'You can meet him soon. Promise.'

She sighs. 'You're being weird lately. But, look, I'm happy if you're happy.'

'I *am* happy.'

Orla nods, and gets up to make a cup of tea. I relax into the sofa, relieved that we've not fallen out over my incompetence as a sister.

'Have you heard from Ruben lately?' she asks, over the sound of the kettle boiling.

I hesitate, unsure whether to say anything. I remember his words when he first asked me about the money . . . *please don't tell Orla. She's so . . . together.* What would he do if I told her? Would he tell her *my* secret?

'We've texted a bit. He seems really busy though. Not seen him since we all got together last,' I lie.

'We'll have to sort something soon.' She sets a cup of tea down on the coffee table.

'Yeah,' I say, even though I've seen more than enough of him lately. 'We should. I'll speak to him.'

Chapter 25

Eve – Now

I creep as close to the cliff's edge as I dare to tread, bracing myself against the strong summer wind, staring down into the crashing ocean waves below. It's been eleven days. Is Anya still down there? I wonder how bad things must get for someone to give up on life, like so many people who've tragically been driven to this very spot, and other similar ones along the coast. Even with everything that has happened to me, I feel lucky those dark, disturbing thoughts have never crossed my own troubled mind.

Jason's voice cuts into my trance. 'This place gives me the creeps.' He shudders, flicking his cigarette. 'Every time I look at someone I wonder if they're here to top themselves. Shall we get a move on?'

I'd made Jason come to Seaford Head with me, in the hope that I might be struck by a bit of inspiration up here. So far, it's lacking. I can't shake off the worry I feel about this investigation. Zachary's still missing, Mark's been crossed off the suspect list and Anya's dead.

I turn my face away from the cloud of stinking smoke Jason has emitted. I *wish* he'd stop smoking around me. 'Fine. Let's go get some lunch.'

We traipse back in the direction of the car park, Jason debating the merits of fish and chips versus a crab sandwich, but I'm lost in thought. Just before we reach the main path, I turn and stare out to sea one last time. I'm standing in the same spot where our witness Dennis saw Anya jump. The seed of an idea plants itself in my brain.

'Keep up,' barks Jason over his shoulder.

I hold up a hand. 'Wait. You see that little hillock, over there?' I point where Dennis gestured a couple of days ago.

'What the fuck's a hillock?' He follows my gaze. 'Oh, that. What of it?'

'Wait here.' I stride in the direction of the small hill, no more than a metre in height, and then I stand on top of it, glancing back at Jason, who's looking at me like I've gone mad. Maybe I have. I turn back in the direction of the sea. There are a few metres between me and the edge of the cliff. The idea has fully taken form now, sprouting stems and leaves. But I need Jason's eye. I look back at him; he's not moved, but is still staring quizzically at me. Once more, I turn back to the sea, and I step off the edge of the hillock, landing a couple of feet short of the cliff's edge and crouching down. I'm safe enough, but that doesn't stop my heart pounding itself into a frenzy at the thought of losing my footing and toppling over the edge.

Jason's frantic voice booms behind me. 'Eve! *Eve!*'

Heavy footsteps pound on the grass behind me. I stand

up and turn to face him, brushing myself off. To my shock, his face is pale and tear-streaked.

'Jesus *fucking* Christ, what did you just do?' He quickly wipes a hand over his face. 'Are you trying to give me a bloody heart attack?'

'No.' I reach for his arm, touched by his concern, but he shrugs it away from me.

He steps back. 'Don't pull a stunt like that again, d'you hear me? I'm already bloody worried about you as it is.'

'I'm sorry, but don't you see what this could mean?'

He stops dead, and stares at me. 'No.' His voice is a degree or two colder.

'Jason, Anya jumped *here*. Look how easy it could've been for her to fake it.'

He stares at the edge of the cliff. 'Sure. If the witness was standing in exactly the right spot . . . I don't know.'

'If I fooled *you*, think how easy it would've been for her to fool a stranger? Think about it,' I continue. 'It was so early in the morning. No one was about. So why did she wait until someone was walking their dog near enough to see her? What if she did exactly what I just did? And rolled away before Dennis rushed over? Let's at least consider the idea.'

I can tell he's mulling over what I'm saying, but still furious with me. His gaze drifts to the sea. 'Maybe.'

'Will you forgive me if I buy you lunch?'

He sighs, his anger seeping away. 'You really scared me.'

'I didn't know you cared so much, Sarge.' I smirk.

He turns back to face me, his dark eyes burning into mine. 'I need you and Bella to get hold of as much CCTV and road

145

traffic camera footage from Monday morning as you can. If your crazy theory is true, then you need to prove it by finding Anya. And yes, fish and chips would contribute towards you being forgiven. Fish and chips every day this week.'

I suppress a smile as we trudge back to the car, unable to help feeling a little proud of myself for this potential breakthrough. This could mean everything . . . to the case, and to my career.

Chapter 26

Kate – Now

I stretch out on the lounger, resting my paperback open on my stomach, closing my eyes to block out the sun. The warmth comforts me, and I feel myself melting against the towel beneath me. After everything that's happened, I decide I'm never leaving this place. I smile, and stretch my legs, pointing my toes and placing my interlocked hands underneath the back of my head.

A great thundering crack causes my eyes to snap open and I realise I'm not lying in the sun on holiday; I'm lying on my back in the long grass, staring up at a sky darker than ink. I expect to see lightning. Am I not in the middle of a storm? But no lights flash in the sky, and not even a sliver of moon softens the bleak darkness. A scream forces me into a sitting position and that's when I see them. They're standing there, right on the edge of the cliff. Dangerously close. I climb to my feet and it's like I'm moving in slow motion, as if invisible ropes are tied around my wrists and ankles, pulling me back down to the ground.

Another ear-splitting crack rips through the night, and a fissure opens up in the ground ahead, zig-zagging towards me with menace.

The ground ahead crumbles away, revealing not an ocean, but a raging fire. I try to reach them, to shout at them to run to safety, but my legs still won't move and no sound escapes my lips. One by one, they descend into the flames. The words swim around my head, over and over again: it's all my fault. It's all my fault. It's all—

***

I jerk awake, my eyes darting around the room. There's no fire. There's no crumbling cliff edge. I'm safe. *I'm safe.* I allow my eyes to close and wait for my heart rate to return to normal, before kicking the covers off and hauling my exhausted body out of bed. I push the nightmare to the back of my mind and whip back the curtains, squinting as sunlight streams in, bright and hot. The initial anxiety of my arrival in Plockton is ebbing away, although I'm well aware I haven't come close to dealing with what happened. A life without fear shimmers on the horizon, but it's at night when my guilt hits me where it hurts, and I'm plagued with all the thoughts and worries I manage to bat away during the day. I sleep, but it's poor quality, peppered with nightmares, which over-the-counter sleeping tablets do little to reduce.

My unrecognisable new reflection stares accusingly at me from the window pane and I shiver. Kate Smith the nobody. Kate Smith the invisible. Kate Smith, who will never again love another human being until the day she dies, because everything Kate Smith touches falls to pieces.

***

I pad into the living room where Peggy sits in the big armchair, gazing out of the window at the summer scene beyond its frame. I feel a swell of fondness for the old woman, with her silver plait and her kind eyes. When I turned up at her house two weeks ago, clutching a job advert for a live-in housekeeper, I was expecting to be turned away. No I.D., no references, no fixed address, no documents. But Peggy Colton took a chance on me, despite her initial suspicions. With a stab of guilt, I remember what I'd said to her . . . *I'm running from someone. My ex . . . he's after me. He's . . . heavy-handed.* She'd taken me in immediately.

Even though it was only a half-lie, guilt simmers away inside. But since then, I'd transformed her home from dusty and cluttered to sparkling clean. Her crippling multiple sclerosis means she struggles to do it herself, and her distant family mean she'd been painfully lonely before I came along just a few weeks ago. We'd soon settled into a comfortable familiarity with each other.

'Morning.'

She turns to me and smiles. 'Morning, lassie. How'd you sleep?'

'Really well,' I lie.

'Are you sure? Only I thought I heard you shouting and crying. I thought you might be having a nightmare, but I didn't want to frighten you by coming in.' Her eyes shine with concern.

'I might've had a nightmare, but I'm okay. Sorry if I woke you.'

She waves a hand at me as if to say, 'Don't be so silly.'

'You've had a few since you moved in. What do you dream about?'

I press my hands between my legs and drop my gaze. 'I don't really remember.' *Lies, lies, lies.*

'Okay, pet.' She reaches out and pats my knee. 'Well, if you ever want to talk . . .' She tails off, as if worried she's overstepped the mark.

'Thank you.' I look up and smile. 'It means a lot.'

Chapter 27

Anya – Then

I toss and turn all night, and not just because of the guilt I'm feeling over letting Orla down earlier today. No. Tonight, there's a constant stream of sounds playing over and over inside my mind so I struggle to drift off for a long time. The roaring of the bonfire. The chatter of the crowds. The fizzing of the children's sparklers. The booming and crackling of the fireworks, so loud in my head it makes my body jolt. I can almost feel the October chill dancing on my skin as if I'm really back there, my hands as cold as a cadaver's. The peals of laughter from the crowds morph into one terrifying scream, and then I see it: Ruben's face, white with shock, looming in the darkness, inching closer and closer and closer . . .

Bang.

My eyes fly open. For a few unbearable seconds I think I'm back there, lying on my back in the long grass, a stone digging into my shoulder blade, my sweaty hands covering my face. Trembling. The realisation that I'm safe in my bed settles over me like a soft, thick blanket. The bedsheets are damp and twisted underneath me, so I haul myself out of bed and throw open the window, letting some of the muggy summer heat out. A cool breeze snakes its way in. Then I see the figure, lurching down the alley, my gate swinging on its hinge.

Bang. That was the sound that snatched me from my nightmare. Not the memory of the fireworks.

With a creeping sense of dread, I ease open the bedroom door. I don't know why I'm scared; I clearly saw the person running *away* from my flat, not towards it. But I'm terrified all the same. Why would anyone be in my back garden? The living room is cloaked in darkness, moonlight slicing through a gap in the curtains. A sweeping glance across the room tells me no one has been inside. Every plant, candle and cushion is exactly where I left it. I pad barefoot across the carpeted floor towards the kitchen, where a nearby lamppost casts a chink of eerie yellow light through the glass pane in the back door.

And that's when I see it. Something is attached to the door handle, silhouetted against the textured glass. I don't want to open the door, but at the same time it's all I *can* do. I slowly turn the key in the lock and open the door with a soft click, before cracking it open a couple of centimetres. Cold air curls itself around my bare ankles. After assuring myself no one's there, I open it a little more, and my eyes fall to the awful thing tied to the handle. With shaking hands I untie the ugly bunch of flowers. No blooming flower heads with sweet aromas, no lush foliage and glossy leaves, no thick green stems full of life. No, the stems of these flowers are gnarled, brown and dried, with nothing but round seed heads topped with spiky crowns.

Poppies. *Dead* ones. Tied together with a black velvet ribbon. I drop them to the ground and slam the door shut as my heart seizes with paralysing fear.

Chapter 28

Eve – Now

'Knock, knock.'

It's the Monday morning after my revelation on the cliff top and I'm still feeling the rush of a potential breakthrough. I glance up from my desk and Bella is standing in front of me, holding two takeaway coffees. 'I'm all yours.'

'Lifesaver.'

She hands me one of the drinks and I wrap my hands around the corrugated card cup. I scoot over and she grabs an empty chair, wheeling it over and squeezing it under the desk beside me.

'I've done a bit of digging.' She opens up her laptop and turns to face me. I can hear her phone vibrating on the desk beside her, but she ignores it. 'None of the local taxi companies have a record of anyone booking a cab from Seaford Head that night. So, if your theory's correct, there's no way Anya left via taxi. And we know she abandoned her car. So, she must've left on foot, if she left at all.'

'She could've got a lift from someone,' I point out.

'Yes,' says Bella slowly, 'but I got in touch with a few bars and restaurants along the route she'd have been most likely to take if she were, say, heading to the train station. And . . .'

She spins the laptop to face me. A grainy, greyscale CCTV image shows someone walking with their head down, along a dark high street. A person with a bag slung over one shoulder, wearing jeans and a long-sleeved top, arms wrapped around their torso as if they're cold. As if they'd left their cardigan behind? I can't make out their hairstyle, as whoever it is has tugged a beanie hat tightly over their head.

Bella runs a hand through her hair as her phone buzzes again. 'It's black and white, but could it be her?'

I play the footage again and frown. 'Could be. Did you get any footage of them from the front?'

'Just one – quality's shite though. I've sent it to Danny to see if he can sharpen it up, but he's stacked at the moment.'

'Show me anyway.'

Bella flicks to another window and hits play. I watch the person walking towards the camera this time, but she's right. I can barely make out a thing. 'I see what you mean. Are you going to answer that?' I ask, as her phone rings for the third time.

'No.' She abruptly switches it off but doesn't elaborate, carrying on as if nothing had interrupted us. 'That's not all I've found.'

'What else?'

'Whoever this person is, let's assume it's a her, was picked up on CCTV at various train stations.' She pulls up a map and taps on each station in turn. 'Brighton. St

Pancras. I actually lost her at St Pancras because it's such a huge station, but I hounded the staff who were working that day and a bloke who was checking tickets remembers her because she was crying and he was concerned. He remembered offering her a tissue, having a conversation with her about where she was heading. That helped me trace her to Edinburgh.'

'Nice work,' I say. 'So you think she's in Edinburgh?'

'Well, I lost her again at Edinburgh and didn't want to assume she'd left the station,' Bella replies. 'It took a bloody age, but I managed to catch her on CCTV getting on a train to Inverness. That's where we lose her again.'

I stare at the map. 'Jesus Christ . . . how much further north can you get?'

'Well, she could have gone to John o'Groats,' reasons Bella. 'But I'm seriously hoping that's not the case.'

'What would I do without you?'

'You'd be well and truly screwed, pal.' She sits back in her chair and sips her drink.

'You're not wrong.' I pluck the lid off my coffee and tip in two sachets of sugar. 'Surely there's a high chance she'd have been seen by a member of the public. She's quite striking to look at . . .' I pull up a photo of Anya, her light brown hair tumbling in beachy waves over her shoulders, tucked behind one heavily pierced ear. Her vivid green eyes gaze warmly back at the person taking the photograph; someone was bound to have noticed her.

'Not as striking as you ladies.'

I roll my eyes as Jason enters the office with a smirk

on his face. He sits on the edge of my desk, peering at the notes scattered across it. 'What's the latest?'

'I was telling Eve how I believe I've traced Anya to Inverness, and then you walked in and interrupted us.' Her words are frosty, but her tone isn't. Like she's pretending to be pissed off with him, but not doing a very good job at it. I smirk, remembering her words in the car the other week . . . *Oh come on. You're telling me you wouldn't go there, given half the chance?*

He whistles. 'Long way.'

'We don't know if she stayed there.' Bella turns her face away from Jason and back to her monitor. 'It's the last suspected sighting of her. But it's a start.'

'Does her sister know?'

'Not yet,' says Bella.

'Are either of you free to come with me and tell her this afternoon?' asks Jason.

I pause before offering, wondering if Bella would be up for making small talk with Jason during a car journey, given her blatant crush on him. It'll be the first time I've had to deliver the news that a loved one was in fact suspected *alive* rather than missing or dead.

***

'We have some news.' I brace myself for the inevitable flurry of emotion. I glance at Jason, who nods once. 'We've reason to believe your sister didn't take her own life.'

Orla's eyes widen, and her fingers grip the arm of the sofa. 'She was murdered?'

'No,' I say hurriedly. 'We don't think she was murdered.'

'Wait. What?' She claps a hand to her mouth, eyes shining with tears. 'Are you trying to tell me she's still alive? Please tell me she's still alive.' She sobs, her body sagging with relief, in anticipation of what she wants to hear.

'We can't confirm that,' says Jason. 'But we believe she faked her own death. Do you have any idea where she might've gone? Or why she ran away?' We're pretty sure Anya is in Scotland, but we want to hear what Orla has to say first.

'Run away?' She squeezes her eyes shut, then opens them again. 'Why would she run away?'

'We were hoping you could help us with that,' I say.

'It doesn't matter.' Orla's face splits into a tearful smile. 'She didn't kill herself. She's *alive*.' She stands up and paces the room.

'Like my colleague said, we can't be a hundred per cent sure; she's not been found.' I clasp my hands together on my lap. 'We'd like to speak to her in relation to the deaths of Lisette and Sylvie Dupont.'

The colour drains from Orla's face, and she stops to turn to us. 'Why would you want to speak to Anya about *that*?'

'Because we have reason to believe she faked her own death not long after Lisette and Sylvie were killed,' says Jason. 'We've reason to believe she headed up north straight afterwards. And we have to be honest with you – she's a suspect in our murder inquiry.'

'No.' Orla shakes her head firmly. 'No. That can't be right. My sister wouldn't do something like that.'

'In order to rule her out, we need to find her first,' I say gently. 'When was the last time you saw her?'

'It was the day before she died – disappeared, I mean. Sorry, I can't . . .' She tails off and wrings her hands, still pacing the room.

I can't imagine what it must feel like to find out your sister has taken her own life, then to find out she's potentially alive and also a murder suspect. 'It's okay.' I smile encouragingly. 'When you last saw her, how did she seem?'

Orla sinks into the sofa. 'She seemed okay. Like I told you before, she was happy. They were in *love*.'

I pause. 'Do you have any idea where she might be?'

Orla opens her mouth to speak, then hesitates. 'I honestly don't know.'

I'm certain she's protecting her sister. 'Are you sure?' I press her.

She shakes her head, then shrugs. 'Maybe London?'

I make a note, but I'm convinced Orla's trying to throw us off the scent. I remember Gillian's words . . . *assume nothing, believe no one, challenge everything*.

'Did she have any savings put aside that you know of?' probes Jason.

'I've no idea,' says Orla. 'I'm sorry. I don't know where she is or how she's getting by.'

'It's okay,' I say. 'We'll do our best to track her down. There's one other thing I need to ask.'

Orla nods once for me to continue.

I choose my words carefully. 'In order to rule Anya out of the investigation, we need to get hold of her fingerprints.

We'd like to send our CSIs round to dust Melody Laine for prints, as we can't gain access to her flat at the moment.' *We'll break in if we need to,* I add silently.

Orla looks aghast. 'Why do you need her prints?'

'Like I said, it'll help rule her out.' *Or in.*

'Okay.' Her voice turns into a strangled sob and she nods. 'Okay. I can give you access.' I thank her, and the room falls silent for a moment.

Jason and I exchange looks. 'I think that's enough for today,' I say, standing up. 'Thank you for your time. We'll be in touch the minute we find anything.'

***

Jason, Bella and I pile into Gillian's office, unable to wait until this afternoon's briefing to update her.

'This better be good.' She taps furiously at her keyboard. 'I've got a meeting with Rani in fifteen. Make it snappy.'

Superintendent Rani Sharna waits for no one. Bella jumps straight to it. 'Anya Fernsby faked her suicide.'

Gillian's hands freeze on the keyboard and she tears her eyes away from the screen. 'I'm interested. Go on.'

Jason explains what we've discovered so far and Gillian shakes her head. 'So where's she hiding?'

'We think somewhere in Scotland,' I say. 'As far up as Inverness. Nothing more specific than that.'

Gillian folds her arms. She still looks tired. 'What else?'

'We've traced her on CCTV to Inverness, but lost her after that. The CSIs are checking Melody Laine for prints this

week, to cross-reference against the crime scene evidence,'
I say. 'Should help rule Anya in or out.'

'Okay.' Gillian glances at her watch. 'Right. Got to go.'
She downs the dregs of her coffee and slings her bag over
her shoulder. She pauses at the door and gives us a smile.
'Good work. Update me later today.'

We stand outside Gillian's office after she's gone.

'I think Anya did it,' I say. 'Why fake your death if you've
got bugger all to hide?'

'Agreed. Why did it have to be Scotland though? How the
hell's anyone going to find her there?' Jason groans.

Bella rolls her eyes. 'I think that's the point, Sarge.'

Chapter 29

Anya – Then

I've been feeling uneasy since I woke up, despite having pushed the dead poppies to the back of my mind. In the bright light of day, getting scared of a bunch of dry flowers seems utterly ridiculous. It was obviously some local idiot doing a dare or playing a stupid game. Probably some kind of social media trend. The poppies had gone straight into the bin . . . but I still can't shake off the unsettling feeling that lingers behind.

Every time a customer enters Melody Laine, my stomach does a little jolt. I feel *horribly* tired. I barely slept last night, plagued with mental images of a hooded figure creeping around my back garden.

The bell tinkles and Matthew walks in, carrying a brown paper bag. 'Hey, you.' He places the bag on the counter in front of me. 'Brought you some lunch.'

I smile weakly. I'd texted to tell him I wasn't feeling great but hadn't expected this. 'What is it?'

'Sustenance,' he supplies. 'A chicken sandwich and

ready-salted crisps. Got it from your favourite café, told them to hold the mayo.'

I take the bag gratefully. 'Thank you. Are you on your way to work?'

He nods. 'I'll be home by eight, if you want to hang out?'

'Yes,' I say, a little too eagerly, desperate to be away from my flat. 'I can get us a takeaway.'

'Sounds perfect.' He leans over the counter and kisses me. I don't want him to go. In the few minutes he's been in the shop, I've almost forgotten what happened last night.

'Do you have to leave?' I immediately regret my obvious neediness.

'The people need me,' he says. 'Hey, are you all right? You're shaking.'

I force myself to stop. 'I'm fine. Honestly.'

His face creases in concern. 'Is something else up?'

'I . . . there were some noises outside my flat last night. Woke me up.' I pause, contemplating telling him what I'd found, then thinking better of it. 'Probably a fox or something. But I didn't sleep well after.'

Matthew steps back and looks at me, his hands grasping mine. 'Stay with me tonight?'

Relief washes over me; I think I'll feel safer sleeping next to someone else. 'Thank you. It'll be nice to get some rest.'

***

'Want a glass of wine?' Matthew calls from the little kitchen.

I shake my head and kick off my shoes, the remnants of

my headache still lingering unpleasantly. 'Just a cup of tea, please.'

As the kettle boils, I sit on the sofa and gaze around the boat, which is in its usual clean and tidy state. White walls, simple furniture. Meticulously neat. It amazes me that anyone can live this way, although I have to admit, I find it quite calming. I like being here. I wonder if he hates my flat, with all the cushions, plants and candles. If I were to move in, would he let me bring some of my clutter with me? Would there even be any room for me? *Don't get ahead of yourself*, I scold myself. *Don't start thinking about moving in together*. My mind tells me to take it slow, but deep down I'm enjoying being in a couple, and all the security it brings.

'You all right?' Matthew's voice makes me jump. He kisses me on the cheek and hands me a steaming mug. 'You're frowning.'

'I'm fine.' I wave him off. 'I just need to get a good night's sleep.'

'You'll be right as rain in the morning,' he assures me, leading me to the sofa. He sinks in beside me, and I lean into him, intertwining our fingers. The boat gently rocks in the wind. This feels good. This feels safe. *Do not mess this up, Anya Fernsby.*

Chapter 30

Kate – Now

After finishing my morning jobs and errands, I head off on a long walk along the beach, taking in the breathtaking beauty of the Scottish coast. I stop to look at the boats bobbing in the distance, the near-empty shore littered with tiny pebbles, and the little rows of white and pastel-coloured buildings neatly lining the coastal road . . . It reminds me of being at home. I've been taking this same route at a similar time for several days, so I don't have to think about where I'm heading. I can simply focus on the sound of the sea and the pebbles crunching underfoot, and count to one hundred over and over again as I trick myself into thinking everything is fine, and that I'm guilty of nothing.

My eyes slide to the couple who have stopped a few feet away. Their little girl is stomping in the waves as they break on the shore. She must be about five. As if someone has pressed a rewind button in my brain, my mind catapults me to the past. Back to Sylvie, wrinkling her nose in disgust at the clothes labelled 'girls' in the supermarket. ('Why do all the girls' clothes have to be so *sparkly*?') The neatness she'd obviously not inherited from Lisette. Everything lined up, parallel or perpendicular. Her love for outer space, and anything to do with it. Those little eyebrows that scrunched up with indignation when things didn't go her way.

I miss her like a limb. It still physically hurts when I think of her. I'd only just got to know her. And now she's gone. I reach up to my head and grab a handful of hair, feeling that familiar, soothing pain as I tug hard at the roots to try and dispel the memory of standing there, watching the fire rage. I reach the end of my route and turn on the spot to come back again.

'Hey.'

I almost crash into the woman who stands in my path, towering over me.

'Sorry.' I steady myself. 'I didn't see you.'

She steps back and reaches into her pocket. 'It's okay. I think you dropped this yesterday.' She holds out my black beanie hat. I hadn't even noticed it'd gone missing.

'Thank you.' I take the hat and stuff it in my pocket.

I start to walk off, but the woman talks again and I stop.

'Mind if I join you?' She has a strong Scottish accent but she sounds different to Peggy. I wonder where she's from.

Of course I mind. This is my alone time. I'm not here to make any friends. 'Of course I don't mind.' My mouth betrays me, and I continue along my path, the other woman falling into step beside me. Her flame-orange hair forms a swishing curtain and half-hides her freckled face from

166

view. I think she looks a bit older than me but I can't be sure.

'Sorry to be so bold,' she says. 'I'm new round here. I don't really know anyone. I'm Hazel, by the way.'

'Same. I'm Kate.'

'You've been doing this walk every day, rain or shine. I remember you because of the hair,' says Hazel, when she sees my frown. 'Don't worry. I've not been following you or anything.'

'Oh.' My new hairstyle is a deep mahogany pixie cut, accompanying the bright blue contact lenses disguising my naturally green eyes and the tattoo cover-up I'd had done before arriving in Plockton. The musical note I'd had etched into the skin of my inner wrist since I was eighteen was now expertly covered by a bright peacock feather tattoo. I'd been so set on making my appearance look different to before that I didn't even consider a style like this might make me stand out in a place with a population of less than four hundred people. It's not exactly incognito. 'So, if you're not from round here, where did you come from?'

'Glasgow. Needed a bit of an escape from the city life. You?'

'London,' I lie. 'Same kind of thing, really.'

'That's a long way to go.'

I have a lot to run from. 'Yeah.' I shrug.

'Think you'll hang around?'

I nod, rubbing my arm where my skin is turning pink. 'I reckon so. You?'

'Aye. My job means I can work anywhere.' She roots

167

around in her bag for something and then tosses me a tube of factor fifty. 'Here you go.'

I catch the bottle, taking it as an invitation to probe. 'What do you do?'

'I'm a writer.'

'Like a journalist?' Panic patters across my skin and a wave of nausea engulfs me.

She smiles. 'Like an author.'

'Oh!' My worry evaporates. 'Anything I might've heard of?'

'Probably not.'

'Try me.' I slather the sun cream over my forearms.

'*No Way Out*?'

'The one about the escape room?' I gasp when she nods, popping the lid back on the bottle. 'You're Hazel Morgan?'

'Guilty.'

I shake my head in disbelief as I hand the sun cream back to her. 'Wow.'

She waves a hand dismissively. 'I hate talking about myself. Tell me about you.'

I feel my shoulders sag in embarrassment. 'I'm a house-keeper. It's just to keep me going until I decide what I really want to do.' I'm suddenly desperate to present a more interesting version of myself, which competes with my deep-rooted desire to remain anonymous. I scramble for something in my brain but come up with nothing.

'What do you think you might want to do?'

I shrug. 'Honestly? I have no idea.'

When we reach the end of the beach, Hazel turns to me. 'Sorry if this sounds a bit forward, but d'you fancy doing this again?'

Do not get close to anyone. Do not let anyone in. Do not take any risks. Focus on what you're here to do. To lie low, and find him.

'Sure.' I smile.

'What's your number?'

I hesitate, before giving her the number for the cheap pay-as-you-go phone I'd picked up in Inverness. We part ways, and I head back home with a spring in my step, despite having broken one of my self-imposed rules. I'm sure everything will be fine. We probably won't even meet up. And if we do, I'll keep her at arm's length; it'll be easy enough.

***

On the way back, I'm overcome with the urge to try and find him again. The man who single-handedly tore my life apart, piece by piece. I stop on a bench about a mile away from the house. Even though I bought it under a fake name, I never use my phone inside the house, in case I'm somehow traced. I switch it on and navigate to Facebook. I've almost exhausted the list of people with his name, but it feels like every time I search, another one has popped up. It's frustratingly difficult to remember which profiles I've looked at, which ones I haven't, and which ones have simply changed their profile picture since last time I checked their pages. Privacy settings don't help either, nor do people who choose profile photos of anything but their face, so I can't tell who they are.

'Where the hell *are* you?' I mumble to myself, my determination refusing to wane. He can't have vanished off the face of the planet.

But then again, *I* did.

Chapter 31

Later that afternoon, my phone trills to life and I grab it from the cradle.

'Eve, hi. It's me.' Tim's voice exudes excited energy. He's found something.

I grip the receiver. 'What is it?'

'Got results on those prints on the bottle. They match to a set found all over the back office of Melody Laine that don't belong to Orla. The number of times these prints appear suggest it's someone who works there. A *lot*.'

There's only one person other than Orla who would've left prints all over the back office. 'Grim Tim, I could kiss you.'

'It's her,' says Jason, after I announce the news about the prints to the rest of the team.

'Slow down,' says Gillian. 'I know we're desperate to solve this but what does this tell us exactly? That a set of prints found at the shop was also found on the bottle? So, someone who had visited Anya's shop had touched this bottle at some point? It's not enough.'

'It's circumstantial, yes,' I admit. 'But the prints were found all over Melody Laine, including the back office. The desk, the laptop, the filing cabinet, the safe, the till buttons. Everywhere. It's not just a visitor. It's someone who's been there a lot.'

Tiana pipes up. 'It could've been planted.'

'By who?' Jason pulls a face in her direction.

She bites her lip, shrinking back into herself. 'It's just a thought,' she says, almost apologetically.

Gillian folds her arms. 'Don't rule it out, Tiana.'

Another thought strikes me. 'The bottle *could* have been taken from Lisette's house. Say, from under her sink. Which could explain Anya's prints.'

'Possible,' says Gillian. 'But that would mean our killer would be pinning their hopes on finding something suitably flammable in Lisette's house before being rumbled. Once you catch up with her, you can at least confirm that the prints are hers, and that she'd come into contact with that bottle at some point. That might be enough to crack her into talking. And don't forget, Zachary Samson's still a suspect.'

A murmur of acknowledgement ripples around the table.

'Are we one hundred per cent sure Mark Maynard wasn't involved?' I ask.

'His alibi checks out,' says Tiana.

'Yes,' I say, quelling a flash of irritation. 'But it's not that simple. Anya's prints were on the bottle, Mark's prints were on the smoke alarm. Anya was in touch with someone using a burner phone the day before the fire. What if it was him? It's almost as if they were working together, don't you think?'

Everyone's eyes fall on me. I can't tell what Gillian is thinking. 'When you find her,' she begins – and I note the use of 'when' and not 'if' – 'you can figure out if she knows him. And if so, how. Any more for any more?'

'Danny's sharpened up the CCTV footage of the woman heading towards Scotland on the train,' says Bella. 'It's clear enough for us to confirm it's Anya.'

The atmosphere in the room is thick with anticipation. We're creeping ever closer.

'Great work.' Gillian gives her a brisk nod.

As everyone files out of the incident room, my eyes shift to the case board, where Anya, Mark and Zachary's faces stare down at me. *Which of you did this?* I demand silently.

Chapter 32

Eve – Then

I step lightly off the train at Brighton station and take a deep breath. It's the type of cool, clean air that you can't find in London, which always feels muggy and a little bit grubby.

I can't wait to see Frankie. It's been a tough year, my criminology course challenging me more than I ever thought it would. And it's not just the academic side of it; I'd taken it as an opportunity to, not reinvent myself exactly, but present an improved version of myself to the world. A version of me who isn't a parent to her sister. Who doesn't have parents who depend on alcohol to get them through the day. A relaxed me. A witty me. A fresh start. But now it's time to give my brain a rest; God knows I've earned it. The stresses of my first year finally melt away as the summer stretches out ahead of me, long and hot.

And yet.

As I round the corner and my house comes into view, I feel myself automatically slow my pace as apprehension floods my body, like a poison seeping through every vein.

I stop at the front gate with its peeling paint, staring up at the house. My eagerness to see my little sister gives way to a crushing dread that prevents me from moving forward. After a few moments, the front door flies open and I jump as Ajax streaks out of the house in a frantic flash of orange and white.

Mum goes to close the door but pauses when she realises I'm standing metres away. For a single, hopeful second, I think her face is going to split into a smile, but her shoulders sag as she waits for me to say something.

'Hey.' I raise my hand in a pathetic wave.

She does smile then, but it's a sad smile. One that doesn't reach her eyes. She flicks the ash from her smouldering cigarette onto the pavement. *When did she start smoking?*

'You're back.'

I reluctantly make my way up the short path. The peeling gate closes behind me with its familiar but unsettling creak, and I wipe flakes of paint off my hand and watch as they fall to the ground like ugly snowflakes. Mum turns her back as I approach her, and I think about the kind of welcome my friends will be receiving from their parents, imagining tight hugs, *I missed you*'s and favourite meals hot from the oven. I can't remember the last time Mum or Dad embraced me, or told me they love me. With a deep breath, I step back into the house where happy memories are trodden into the carpet like discarded cigarettes, replaced with memories that make me want to run away and never come back.

One small step for Evie.

God, it's become so much worse since I was last home. As

it was always me and Frankie doing the cleaning, I never realised how bad it actually was, or how bad it could get if I wasn't around. The acrid stench of cigarette smoke is overwhelming, and I can't ignore the multitude of empty vodka bottles littering the kitchen worktops, no matter how much I want to. Things have got bad around here. What the hell's going on? I need to speak to Frankie. And I *have* to find Charlie.

'Uni going all right?' Mum's voice is monotone. Devoid of emotion.

'Yeah.' I pick up one of the empty bottles and search for the bin. It's overflowing.

Mum watches me, leaning on the doorframe with her arms folded. Just staring.

I drop as many bottles as I can fit into a plastic carrier bag and tie the handles in a knot. I turn to her, the bag dangling from my fingers. 'Are you okay?'

She shrugs. 'Been better.'

I drop the bag by the door and pause, before taking a step forward as if to hug her, but she sparks up another cigarette, instantly creating a barrier between us. Embarrassed, I turn to throw open the window instead. 'Where's Frankie?'

'Her room.'

I pass the front room on my way up and spot Dad passed out on the sofa, wearing nothing but his underwear. He's snoring deeply, the sound of his rhythmic grunts competing with the blaring sound of the TV. I hurry upstairs and gently push open Frankie's bedroom door. My ten-year-old sister sits on her bed hunched over a sheet of paper she's transforming into what looks like a cat. The windowsill behind her is littered with origami creations. Her face lights up and she drops the paper cat when she sees me.

'Evie!' She slides off the bed and crosses the small room, folding herself into my arms.

I pull her bony little frame close. 'Sorry I was gone so long, chicken.'

'I missed you.' Her muffled voice is absorbed by my denim jacket. 'Are you a police lady yet?'

'Not just yet.' I step back to look at her, taking in her appearance. Her T-shirt rides up, exposing a sliver of skinny midriff, and her leggings finish halfway down her calves. Her heels hang off the back of her flip-flops, at least a size too small, if not two. I wonder about her school shoes.

'Those clothes don't fit.' I smooth her hair back from her narrow face and check her over with concern. 'You had a growth spurt?'

She yanks her top down self-consciously. 'Dunno. Maybe.'

'I'm gonna pick you up some new clothes, okay?'

She nods with enthusiasm. 'Thanks, Evie. Maybe then the other kids will stop calling me names.'

Anger surges through my body like an electric current. Has the school not noticed what's going on here? And where the hell's Charlie? And Gilly? They promised they'd look out for her. My head, which a day ago had been filled with the intricacies of criminal law, now bursts with images of my sister being neglected. Ignored. I'm seriously doubting whether I should go back to university now I've seen what a state my parents are letting themselves, the house, and

Frankie get into. Maybe I should try and finish my degree through the Open University, so I can keep an eye on things at home. Perhaps I don't even need to do the degree after all.

I cast my mind back to when I was Frankie's age, having to learn from Charlie how to cook dinners, how to wash clothes and change the bedsheets, and then passing the same skills on to Frankie. I wonder if he ever reported Mum and Dad for their blatant neglect. It's bad, but it's never bad *enough*. There's always someone else worse off, isn't there? But why has he not intervened?

'What have the other kids been saying to you?'

She shrugs, and walks over to the window, leaning the heels of her hands on the sill. The stiffness of her delicate shoulders communicates that she's not ready to discuss it, so I decide not to push it.

I cross the small room and place a hand on her shoulder. 'Has Charlie or Gilly been round much?'

She glances over her shoulder at me and gives me a sad smile. 'They did a few times after you left. Then Dad told them to bugger off and leave us alone, that we didn't need their charity. It's a shame because they always brought nice things with them. You know that lovely crusty bread I like? And marmalade without the bits.'

'I do know.' My heart feels heavy after hearing that. So they did try to help, but my ignorant parents decided to push them away.

'But sometimes I find a little bag at the bottom of the garden, by the hole in the fence. Sometimes it's got boring stuff in it like soap or toothpaste or socks. And sometimes it has chocolate buttons in it.' She grins.

'Fairies?' I open my eyes wide with pretend wonder.

She rolls her eyes. 'It's obviously Charlie or Gilly, you idiot.'

I laugh and ruffle her hair, masking my sadness that she's growing up so fast. Too fast. But at least they're looking out for her in the only way they feel able to.

Chapter 33

Anya – Then

'I've got a surprise for you.' Matthew smiles at me from the breakfast bar, his hands wrapped around a coffee, as I emerge from the bathroom in a cloud of coconut-scented steam and fluffy towels.

'A surprise?' I gaze quizzically at him as I towel-dry my hair.

'I'm taking you on a date.' His eyes crinkle at the corners, and the twinkling lights from our mini Christmas tree reflect in his glasses.

'Tonight? Where?' I sling my hair towel onto the bed and approach him.

'It wouldn't be a surprise if I told you.' He wraps his arms around me.

'You're very sweet.' I lean my damp forehead against his chest and breathe in the woody smell of his aftershave. It had been a long day and I got caught in the rain coming home. Half an hour ago, the thought of stepping back outside would have filled me with horror, but I'm thawed out now, and the Christmas lights are up in town, which always makes me feel warm and cosy.

Within an hour, we bundle into a taxi and get on the road. Matthew still won't tell me where we're going, but I can tell it's away from Brighton. I don't really know of any good places to go, west of Brighton. But I soon recognise where we are, and within half an hour we pull up on a high street I realise with a jolt that I know all too well.

'Matt, why are we in Seaford?' My insides are swimming as I climb out of the taxi. I haven't been back here since Orla and I left for good. I promised myself I'd *never* come back here.

His face splits into a smile. 'I'm taking you back to your hometown. I thought you could show me around a bit. There's a Christmas market on tonight as well.'

He thinks I want this. But why would he know any different? I've not told him *anything*.

I force a smile. 'That's such a lovely idea. Shall we get some food? I'm starving.'

We find our way to the German Christmas market and squeeze onto a small wooden table, steaming mugs of mulled wine and a paper plate of bratwurst sausages in front of us, and I have to admit, I'm having a nice time. We'd never had a Christmas market when I lived here, so there's no association. No triggers. I relax, enjoying the woozy feeling of wine, every inch of me feeling toasty and everything looking a little blurry around the edges.

'Let's go for a walk,' Matthew says, later in the evening.

'I don't want to go out into the cold,' I whine, but I follow him anyway, winding my scarf tighter around my neck. His gloved hand grips mine, and our breath hangs in little clouds in front of our faces before vanishing. But it's not as bad as I thought it would be, being back here. Alcohol certainly helps, and I can't help but smile. It's been a lovely evening so far.

'Where are we going?' My voice slurs.

'Just taking in the sights.' Matthew walks in front of me but backwards, his hands in his pockets, and an impish grin on his face. 'You're drunk.'

'No I'm not,' I lie. 'See?' I point to my feet, which as far as I can tell, are walking in a perfectly straight line.

He turns around and crouches down. 'Come on, jump on my back.'

I clamber onto him and let him take the weight for a bit. It feels like we're walking up a hill, and I'm sure I could sleep for a year.

It feels like forever before he stops and drops me to my feet. We're standing on grass, dampened with sparkling dew, and the bitter wind stings my cheeks. It's really dark and cold, and I'm not sure where we are. I shiver.

'Look,' he whispers, gesturing behind me. I turn on the spot, and gasp. We're staring out over a glittering sea. But that must mean—

'No.' I stumble backwards. *'No.'*

'What is it?' Matthew's face twists in worry. 'Are you okay?'

'I can't be up here.' My mind searches wildly for a reason, any reason, other than the truth, because I can't possibly tell him that. 'I— I—'

'Anya, what is it? I thought you'd love it up here, it's so beautiful—'

'I've got a fear of heights,' I splutter.

'You never told me that.' His face is dark with concern.

'It never came up.' I back away from the edge, my entire body trembling. 'Please, *please* can we go? I want to go home.'

He stares at me for a few seconds, before nodding, reaching out an arm for me to grip onto. I lean into him, before bending over and emptying the contents of my stomach onto the grass.

I can't believe I'm back here. I vowed never to set foot in this place again.

Chapter 34

Kate – Now

The minutes crawl by each night. I do everything I'm supposed to. I sip my chamomile tea and spritz my pillow with the little bottle of lavender spray that Peggy left in my room after a particularly bad night. I take deep breaths . . . in for four, out for six. But all I can think of is her. Her slender fingers with their neat, square nails, never painted. Her coils of black hair, spiralling across the pillow each morning, tickling my face. The way she never quite managed to close a cupboard or door properly. *A walking whirlwind*, I would call her. The slight upturn of her nose. Everything. All those things that made her *her*. All gone. While I stood there and watched it happen.

No matter how much I try to occupy my mind with cleaning things that are already clean or exploring new routes around Plockton, Lisette and Sylvie hover painfully on the periphery of my mind, waiting to be given my full attention. Poppy, too. She's always there. A constant reminder of what happened. And Orla. I've *never* been without my big sister for this long. It's weighing me down. Will I be able to keep up with my own lies and keep a lid on my past? And will I ever be able to find *him*? I'm determined to track him down. And when I do, I'll turn him in. I mentally list all the places we went together. The café, the smoothie place, the Italian restaurant, the bar . . . What if there was CCTV?

I don't know how long I've been standing here, a damp cloth redundant in one hand, the other tugging painfully at a lock of hair, and I don't know how long Peggy's been hovering by the door, observing me with concern.

'Kate, pet . . .'

I jump. 'Peg! Sorry, I was in a daydream.' I spray the window and reach up to wipe it with the cloth.

She crosses the room, leaning on her walking stick and shaking with the sheer effort of the movement. When she reaches me, she stretches out an arm and gently touches the side of my head. 'Why do you pull at your beautiful hair?' I stop cleaning and she tucks a short lock of hair behind my ear, before gazing deeply into my eyes. 'There's a lot going on in that mind of yours, isn't there?'

'I . . . I don't know why I do it. I don't *realise* I'm doing it.' My hands always find their way to my hair at stressful times.

She squeezes my arm. 'Be careful, lassie. You're a kind soul and you don't need to do that to yourself.'

I hastily brush away a tear. My life is one huge lie, and I spend every day with a sick feeling of guilt in the pit of my stomach mixed with a low, rumbling panic like distant thunder, wondering if it would be easier to turn myself in. But I can't think like that.

'I'm going to lie down.' Peggy gently takes the cloth from my hands. 'Why don't you take the afternoon off, go for a long walk or something. Anything, as long as it takes your mind off whatever's troubling you. And talk to me if you need to. I know I'm not your mum, or your gran. But I'm ever so fond of you.' I watch her as she makes her way slowly to the bottom of the stairs, heaving herself up the steps one by one.

Deciding to take her advice, I head straight for the coast. It's early, and the beach is quiet. I find a bench and settle down, before navigating to Instagram using my fake profile. I'd planned to carry on searching for *him*, but it's been a couple of months and I'm painfully homesick. I can't risk getting in touch with anyone from my old life, but there's nothing to stop me checking up on them.

I start with Orla. Immediately I know something has changed. Her posts have been sporadic since that night. Since she lost her sister, and her friend. No photos of nights out and videos of prosecco glasses clinking together, just thoughtful posts and emotional quotes. I hover my mouse over a photo of a patch of wildflowers in the sun. The caption makes me stifle a sob in my throat.

A month has passed, and the flowers are blooming for you.

#AlwaysInOurHearts #MissYou
She's still hurting. The ripple effects of that night have spread so far. I close down Instagram and open up Facebook.

I'm too scared to log in, in case somehow the police are tracing my online activity or one of my friends sees me online. A thought strikes me: I wonder if Poppy's Facebook profile is still active? It's been so long . . . but a couple of taps and there it is. Frozen in time. I stare at her profile photo, her face tilting up at the camera and smiling, until the guilt becomes all-consuming. It's like a form of self-harm.

Curiosity makes me click on my own profile, where I see the comments people have posted. All the people who think I'm dead. I chew on a fingernail as I read through them, all the pain and sadness coming through from the friends and family who loved me.

Next, I navigate to Google, search my name, my *real* name, and click onto the first news article that shows up in the results. It's similar to the one I'd read in the paper yesterday, how I'm wanted in connection with Lisette and Sylvie's murders, but when I scroll down to the comments, I'm nearly sick.

Disgusting, child-killing scum. Why don't we hunt her down and set fire to her while she sleeps? See how she likes it! – Andy K, Norfolk

Hope someone stabs her in the stomach before the police find her. – Matthew T, Sussex

Move over Myra Hindley, we've got a new sicko on the loose! Hope the police catch her and lock her away for good. – Fatima T, Fife

Myra Hindley? Am I really being compared to *Myra Hindley*? I'm not even named as a suspect, I'm just wanted in connection with the case. Surely these commenters are jumping to conclusions? I swallow the lump that sits like a stone in my throat and I scroll back up to read the article again. I stare at the photo of beautiful little Sylvie, with her big round eyes like a doll's, and her head of tightly coiled hair, laughing and waving a toy rocket at the camera. She really was the sweetest child I've ever met. No wonder everyone wants me dead. I'm about to click away from the page when something drags my eyes back to the comments.

Matthew T.

The blood drains from my face, my whole body shivering as if someone has dumped a bucket of ice-cold water over me. It *must* be him. How many Matthew T's can there be in Sussex? I click on his name, hoping it'll take me to some kind of profile, but I find nothing. I take a photo of the comment on my phone before viciously scrolling back to the top of the web page so I can focus on something other than his vile comment glaring at me from the screen, but it continues to swim in front of my eyes, refusing to budge.

Hope someone stabs her in the stomach before the police find her.

Chapter 35

Eve – Now

'Late night?'

I'm caught mid-yawn by Jason, passing my desk on his way to Gillian's office. I stifle it. 'Sorry, Sarge. It's still early.'

He laughs. 'I'm kidding. We're going out for a drink after work for my birthday. You up for it?'

I'm so tired. But what's the point in going home to my lonely little flat with nothing but origami and my own thoughts to occupy me, when everyone is out having fun? 'That would be a big fat yes.'

He laughs. 'See you down The Half Moon tonight then? Weather's looking decent.'

I nod.

Gillian's office door opens and she leans out. Her expression is unreadable and that makes me nervous.

'Eve, Jason, can I see you in my office for a moment? You too, Bella.'

Everyone's eyes slide to us as we make our way across the room and file into Gillian's office.

'Ma'am.' Jason gives her a nod.

'Sit, please.'

We do as we're told, and she drops into her chair. 'Have you been keeping an eye on the news?'

'Of course,' I say.

'So you'll have seen this?' She swivels her computer monitor to face us, and a newspaper article bellows the words **SUSSEX POLICE: ARE THEY UP TO THE JOB?**

My stomach drops. I haven't seen *this*.

'When was this?' asks Bella sharply.

'Today.' Gillian's lips are pursed. 'But the tweets have been going for weeks now. #BrightonFireStarter. Our murderer is gaining celebrity fucking status. Please tell me you have an update so I can give Rani some good news, instead of having to deliver the news that both, I repeat, *both* of our remaining suspects are still on the run, a month after our investigation began.'

'We don't know enough about Anya Fernsby to release her name as a suspect yet,' I say. 'But—'

'No buts.' She rounds on me. 'Why haven't you found her yet?'

'It's all in hand,' says Jason, smoothly. Which is sort of true, but after all the excitement of being the one to discover Anya is still alive, and Bella tracing her to Inverness, things have fizzled out. I've rechecked phone and bank records, and I've rewatched the train station CCTV footage until I can memorise the layouts of every train station that links to Inverness. I've been back and forth with the Inverness division of Police Scotland, and short of driving up there and looking for her myself, I'm stumped. I don't know what to say to Gillian.

'Sort it,' she snaps, standing up, not giving me the chance to speak. Our signal to leave. 'Do you understand how much pressure I'm under to solve this?'

We leave as quickly as we can. My legs are shaky; it's been a while since Gillian last tore a strip off me, and I'd almost forgotten how fiery she is. I'm on my way to the kitchen when Tiana slams down her phone and turns to face us, looking pleased with herself.

'I've tracked him down.'

'Who?' I ask.

'Zachary,' she replies. 'He's been found dead.'

We stop walking. 'What?'

'He's been stabbed to death.'

'Where?' I ask.

'In the chest—'

'No, *where*,' I repeat, 'in the country.'

She flusters. 'Oh, yes, of course, sorry. He was found when a drug den was raided over in Guildford.'

Bella frowns. 'Guildford?'

'He was picked up by a mate the day after you interviewed him and he's been holed up there ever since.'

'*Shit.*' I glance at the ceiling. 'Tiana, can you do some digging into exactly what happened? We need to know if this is connected to our case.'

One suspect missing, another one stabbed to death. Is *anything* on this case going to go right?

'What a shitter of a day.' Jason drops onto the seat between Tiana and me, exhaling deeply.

191

'Cheer up, birthday boy.' I nudge him with my elbow. 'What you having?'

He leans back in his chair with his hands behind his head. 'What are *you* having? I need inspiration.'

I flash him a grin. 'A rather large glass of the good stuff. And by good stuff, I mean Coke.'

'Oh yeah. I sometimes forget you're one of those rare creatures who's teetotal. Go on then, I'll have a pint of Guinness please.' He hands me a pound coin. 'And get some Ziggy Stardust on the old jukey while you're at it.'

I roll my eyes.

'Come on, it's my birthday!'

The rest of the team give me their orders: a cider for Tiana and a large glass of red for Bella. I weave my way through the punters and reach the bar, leaning forward to get the bartender's attention. Jason's right. It *has* been an awful day. Stacey Jericho, who the team have been trying to track down for well over a month, has been found. Well, her body has been found. We didn't get to her quickly enough. Jason was the one to find her remains, following a tip-off from a member of the public who'd found a shoe and bra in the woods nearby. The body had been shoved unceremoniously into the hollow of a tree, all clothing removed. Add that to the newspaper article, another flurry of social media comments, Gillian's simmering rage, and the fact we're a month into our investigation and our progress is questionable, we're all feeling bitterly disappointed and fed up. Tonight will give me a much-needed chance to unwind, but I'm more motivated than ever to solve this case now.

'What can I get you, love?'

Rolling my eyes at the casual use of the word 'love', I rattle off the order and while I wait, I queue up some of Jason's favourite songs on the jukebox.

When I return to the table, laden with drinks, Bella gazes dreamily at me with her arms outstretched. 'Who needs a man when I've got you to bring me alcohol?'

I playfully shove her. 'Stop it, you.' Bella and Tony are going through a rocky patch, but she's not revealed much of it to me. I don't think she really knows what she wants to do about it all. The rare few times I've met him, he was moody and uninterested in striking up a conversation. All I know is that he has an issue with her career, and her long working hours had caused a rift in their relationship that has now become a chasm neither of them seem able to cross. I understand; I've never met anyone who's stuck around long enough for me to fall in love with them. Much easier to stay single. Who else could possibly compete with my job? I realise how sad and pathetic that sounds and stare into my glass.

'Anyone for darts?' Bella announces after downing half her wine. She glances at Jason, who's absorbed in his phone and isn't listening.

Tiana can't jump up quick enough. 'Go on then.'

'Here we go.' Jason glances up from his phone and shields his face from an imaginary dart. 'Watch out, everyone. Take cover.'

I feel a sting of jealousy at the sight of my best mate getting pally with someone else. Add that to the fact that she's not really talking to me about Tony, and I'm wondering if I've done something wrong.

I end up sitting listening to Jason as he sinks pint after pint, his conversational skills slowly going down the drain. I don't blame him, he needs to let off some steam. I just need to figure out how *I* can let off steam. Running helps, but it doesn't block out my spiralling thoughts. I just can't bring myself to drink. Not after that night.

Bella's phone vibrates on the table in front of me and I can't help but slide my eyes to the glowing screen. A message from Tony.

You slut.

Shock ripples through me, and I reach over and turn it face down so no one sees it. Last thing she needs is Jason seeing something like that. But why is Tony calling Bella a slut? What the hell is going on with those two?

''Scuse me,' I say to Jason, standing up.

'Where you going?' he slurs.

'Getting some fresh air.'

Once I'm outside, standing as far away from the smokers as I can, I allow myself a few deep breaths. I thought tonight was going to be a laugh, but with Bella refusing to open up to me, and Jason steadily getting wasted, I realise who I'm missing: Gillian. I really hope she's in a better mood tomorrow.

Just as I decide I've had enough, that I can't possibly enjoy myself tonight while the killer is still on the loose, a voice slurs from behind me. 'All right?' Jason appears from the shadows, the glowing ember of a cigarette illuminating his face.

'Don't smoke near me,' I mutter, sidestepping to the right. He shuffles closer as if he's not heard what I said.

''S'not going to plan, is it?' he says from behind a cloud of smoke.

'What isn't?' I edge further away.

He waves a hand in front of him, as if trying to conjure something. 'This . . . this case. We're not getting justice. For *her.*'

'We will,' I say, with more confidence than I feel.

He flicks his cigarette. 'She didn't jump.'

I frown at him. 'I know. *I* discovered that.'

He looks at me like he's only just noticed I'm standing there. 'What?'

'You've had way too much to drink.' I shake my head.

'Come back inside.' His words roll into one.

'Give me a minute.'

He turns around and knocks a glass out of someone's hand. 'Careful, mate,' he says to the unsuspecting bloke who's just lost a whole pint of lager. 'I'm a copper.'

I cringe, turning away. I can't be around people when they're like this.

Chapter 36

Anya – Then

A shadow of nausea passes over me and my skin erupts in beads of sweat, trickling over me like ants.

Matthew stares at me. 'You okay, An?'

I gape wordlessly at him.

'You're so pale.'

I push myself off the sofa and fumble my way to the bathroom before the inevitable happens. The door ricochets off the wall as I fall through it, dropping to my knees before the toilet bowl. My body shakes uncontrollably.

'An, you poor thing.' I feel his hand resting heavily on my back.

'No.' I wave him away, not wanting to be seen like this. My face burns hot with embarrassment.

He rubs my back, not sensing my need to be alone. 'That mulled wine must've been strong.'

I spit into the toilet and wipe the corner of my mouth on my sleeve. He helps me to my shaking feet and over to the sink, where I rinse away the taste with peppermint mouthwash.

He brushes a strand of hair away from my face. 'Stay here tonight.'

I give a weak laugh and gesture at my limp form. 'Like I have a choice.'

He pauses. 'You can . . . stay as long as you like.'

I gaze up at his face, blurry and concerned behind the dots swimming in my eyes. I squeeze his hand. 'Thank you.'

He hands me a glass of water and I take it with quivering hands.

'Listen, I've got to get to work in a couple of hours.' His hand rests on my forearm. 'Are you gonna be okay here on your own?'

I nod, the slight movement of my head making me wince. 'I'm going to sleep it off.'

He kisses me on the forehead. 'I'll be back soon.'

I'm woken by a hand shaking my shoulder roughly, with a frantic kind of urgency. My eyes blink until the person crouched next to the bed swims into focus.

'Matt?'

He's looking at me with a panicked expression that whips up my anxiety like a snow globe being shaken furiously.

I sit bolt upright, steeling myself. 'What is it?' Fear seizes me with an oppressive fist. 'What's happened? Why is it so cold in here?'

'The door was open when I got home. I think someone's been in the boat. Are you okay?' His eyes dart over me as if checking for signs that something's happened.

'What?' I untangle myself from the duvet and stumble

out of the bed. 'How? It was closed. It was *locked*. I locked it.' My voice shakes as my eyes sweep the room, as if expecting someone to leap out and throttle us.

Matthew touches me lightly on both shoulders. 'They've gone. You've got nothing to worry about.'

'Did they take anything?' I stutter.

'The keys have gone.' He rubs a hand over his face, stress radiating off him in waves I can almost see.

My eyes widen. *I locked the door . . . didn't I?*

'I'll call someone now. Get the locks changed. Just in case.'

A ghost of self-doubt shivers down my back. Do I actually remember locking the door? I'm sure I do. Or do I just remember doing it yesterday? My head is spinning with worry as I pull the door open and step out onto the freezing cold deck, the early evening sun low in the sky and casting a golden haze over everything. It's really quite beautiful.

'What's that?' Matthew points to the bistro table set we keep on the deck. A vase I don't recognise is positioned in the middle of the tiled table, and my knees buckle beneath me when I see what's inside the vessel.

'Anya, what's wrong?' Matthew grabs me before I fall.

I can't tell him that the sight of the gnarled, dead poppies has upset me. I *can't*.

'Nothing, I . . .'

'What is it?'

'It's just the shock.' I pull myself together. 'The break-in. And that.' I wave a hand at the poppies. 'It's *creepy*.'

He holds my gaze for a few seconds before sweeping up the vase and emptying it into the murky green water.

'All gone.'

Once he has gone inside, I remain on deck to get a bit of fresh air. I pull out a chair to steady myself, when I notice a scrap of paper on the seat. With trembling fingers I unfold it and read the words that make me feel so dizzy I grip on to the back of the chair.

I KNOW WHAT YOU DID

I huddle miserably in the corner of the sofa with my feet tucked underneath me, while the locksmith replaces the boat locks. The wind roars outside, and I shiver. This is all my fault. Why had I left that door unlocked? My mind drifts to Ruben. Was he behind this? After we went back inside, we realised my phone and laptop were missing. Is this a warning? He must have followed me. He knows where Matthew lives; he could turn up any time he likes and tell him everything. All because I've stopped giving him money. I force myself to take a couple of deep, calming breaths. I'll call him once I get hold of a new phone, sort this out . . . before he goes to the police.

My mouth stretches open as a yawn forces its way out. I'm exhausted. After the break-in, I'd triple-checked the lock and wedged a dining chair under the handle. But despite these extra precautions, I found myself tossing and turning all night. I was wrenched from sleep several times during the night, so sure I'd heard slow steps on the wet boardwalk outside, but it was only ever the sounds within my own head. More than once my fingers found the handle of the paring knife that I'd tucked between the mattress and the bed frame, in response to the normal creaks and groans of the old boat which, up until last night, I'd been totally accustomed to.

But everything is fine this morning. And we're both okay.

Matthew appears, grasping two mugs of steaming coffee, one of which I take with grateful hands.

'Matt, I've been thinking . . .'

He sinks into the sofa, turning his head towards me, an odd expression on his face.

'Do you . . .' I falter. 'Do you want to meet my sister?'

He exhales deeply.

'What? What is it?'

He runs an exasperated hand across his face. 'Now's not a good time.'

'Why?' I place the mug down and angle myself towards him, ready to state my case. I pause, when I see the annoyance etched into his face. 'What is it?'

The sound of the locksmith's electric screwdriver whirs through the strained silence.

He gestures around the boat. 'This. I know you're stressed, but . . . come on. You left the door open. Let a stranger root through our things.'

'You're mad at me.'

'Yes,' he says, blunt as anything.

A seagull shrieks outside, and I flinch. 'Right.' I fumble around for the right thing to say. 'I just . . .'

'If you can't tell me what's troubling you, how can I trust you? Why take things further if I can't trust you? I'm here for you, An, but . . . I can't help you if you won't tell me what's going on.' He removes his glasses and rubs wearily at his eyes. 'There's *clearly* something playing on your mind.'

My face reddens. I can't tell him about the money I've been dishing out to Ruben, about him refusing to pay me back. There's no way he can find out what Ruben knows. But I don't want it to be over. And if I tell him, it *will* be. 'I promise I'll tell you. When I'm ready.'

Chapter 37

Kate – Now

I fiddle with the hammered silver ring wrapped around my finger, pressing the turquoise glass stones embedded into it, remembering when she'd given it to me.

'It's stunning,' I'd said, after I'd opened the little gift box it was nestled in. 'Thank you.'

She'd smiled then, so beautiful and radiant. I'd slipped the ring onto the fourth finger of my right hand: the perfect fit.

'Do you like it?'

'I love it.' I'd wrapped my arms around her, my face nuzzled into her neck. 'And I love you.'

'Did you see they announced the new *Strictly* judges last week?'

'What?'

I shake my head as Hazel repeats her question, bringing me back to the present. We're walking back from a late lunch from our favourite café, the one that does the warm, crumbling scones where Hazel sits for hours, working on her books, drinking coffee after coffee. 'I'm a walking

202

stereotype!' she'd said, laughing. I glance at her; cheeks flushed pink from the warm sunshine, more freckles emerging by the day. She repeats her question.

'Oh. Yeah.' I peer through the window of the charity shop at all the knick-knacks at the front, cupping my hands around my face to shield the light away from the glass.

Hazel stands beside me, eyes following my gaze. 'I'm nipping in. You coming?'

A bell tinkles as we enter the shop, and a rosy-cheeked woman looks up from her book and smiles at us. I wander through the narrow spaces between the clothing rails, my fingertips brushing against textures of satin, cotton and wool as I pass by. My eyes scan the shelves, which are a jumble of sparkling trinkets and retro vinyl records. And then I see it: a polished guitar sitting propped against the wall. I pick it up gingerly to inspect the shining rosewood surface and notice how all the strings are still intact. It looks almost brand new. I turn the price tag over and gasp in surprise. It's only £20.

'What've you seen?' Hazel wanders over, a navy-blue scarf printed with white birds tossed over one forearm, and a stack of books balancing in her other hand. 'Oh, that's lush. D'you play?'

I cock my head. 'Sort of.' I cast my mind back to my old job. My old life. Melody Laine. I wonder how Orla's coping, looking after the shop by herself, dealing with the death of her friend. Dealing with the death of me. The hot, searing pain of loss hits me in my gut, seeping through my veins like a toxin.

'I taught myself using videos online.' I shrug. 'I'm really

not that good. But it's therapeutic.' Maybe it'll help, picking up a guitar again. Perhaps it's the distraction I've been looking for?

'I wish I could play. You'll have to play me something sometime.' Hazel looks wistfully at the instrument.

'Yeah . . . maybe.' I blink hard, my dry eyes suffering with the discomfort of wearing contact lenses all day, every day.

We pay for our purchases and step out onto the pavement. A soft light washes over everything. Plockton is a beautiful place, and I hope, one day, I'll feel something close to contentment. Of course, the pangs of guilt will always lurk at the edges of my awareness, and the empty feeling inside will always be there. But hopefully, in time, I'll feel normal. Maybe I'll even be able to relax. But no. Not until I find out where Matthew is hiding. Once things die down in Brighton, I could go back and track him down properly, turn him in, make him pay for what he did. Could I?

We cross the street and pause to lean on the stone wall that overlooks the sea. I rest the guitar against it. We don't say anything; it's peaceful and not many people are about. Hazel places her carrier bag on the ground and slips her phone out of her jeans back pocket.

'Selfie?' She leans back against the wall and before I have a chance to protest, she snaps a picture of us. It's quite a flattering photo really; the sun has given our faces a golden glow, and Hazel's hair is as red as fire. My lips are slightly parted, turned up in a half-smile, my eyes open wide, caught unawares. They look unnaturally blue. Even with my coloured contact lenses, my short mahogany hair, I still look a bit like me.

I still look a bit like me. Fear spikes in my chest as I remember the comments about me online. 'Delete it. Please.'

'Why?'

I search for an excuse. 'I look awful. Please get rid of it.'

She frowns at me. 'Okay,' she says slowly. 'Take another?'

'No,' I say quickly. 'I . . . I don't want any photos of me online. I'm funny about things like that.' I let out a nervous laugh. 'Sorry. I'm a bit weird about it actually.'

She shrugs, and deletes the image. 'If you're sure.'

I can't risk it. I'm fairly confident no one would recognise me, but I know there are programs out there, image search functions that comb the internet for photo matches to find missing people, or criminals on the run. I'm not ready to be found. Not until I've found Matthew first.

'Fancy a coffee tomorrow?' She slides her phone back into her pocket.

I pause. I've already seen her twice this week. I can't get too close. I've risked enough. 'I'm a bit busy. Maybe next week? Friday?'

'Deffo. See you, then.' She cheerily waves me off, seemingly not bothered by my odd behaviour. That's what I like about Hazel. We haven't known each other that long, but she seems to take me at face value, and that's exactly what I need right now. It's nice to have a friend, one who doesn't ask too many questions, who's happy to join me for lunch, or a coffee, or a walk, without digging around in my past. We can talk about music, books, politics, what was on TV last night, and I can present my new personality to this person without fear of her finding anything out. And it feels good. It feels safe. As long as I keep her at arm's length.

I stop off at the shop to pick up a bunch of flowers for Peggy. She'd never say as much, but I know she's feeling down about the fact that Ingrid didn't call her on her birthday yesterday. I'd seen her checking for missed calls at least four times, hoping for a call from the granddaughter who hasn't visited her in over three years.

I can't help but scan my eyes over the newspapers for any mention of my name, half-expecting to see my own face staring back, next to the headline **KILLER WOMAN**. I know how it must've looked as I stood in front of that house while it burned. He might not have been the only one who saw me. There are at least forty houses on that street. Who else was peering through their curtains? Who else might have seen me running, desperate and afraid? I envisage a team of detectives sprawling across the country, trying to hunt me down, leaving no stone unturned. A feeling of dread washes over me once more.

I rush home, looking forward to finishing up for the day and trying out my new guitar. Peggy's in good spirits when I return.

'Hello, lassie.' She appears at the end of the hall, beaming. 'Is that a guitar?'

I feel my face flush. 'It is. You don't mind, do you?' I hadn't thought about whether she'd be okay with me playing an instrument in her house.

'My dear, I can barely hear a thing at the best of times.' She hobbles towards me, her body curling over like a comma. 'But no, I don't mind. I used to play the guitar myself, before the arthritis kicked in.' She strokes the dark, glossy wood with the tip of a gnarled finger, gazing wistfully at it. 'I'd love to hear you play.'

'Oh, well I'm not very good. I'll see how it goes.' I blush, thrusting the bunch of blooms into her hand. 'These are for you. I thought you might like something to brighten up your room.'

'Thank you, pet, that's so kind.' She takes the flowers from me and breathes in the sweet scent of rose, freesia and alstroemeria, before turning around to find a vase from the cupboard under the stairs. 'But don't think you've distracted me from that guitar, young lady,' she calls over her shoulder as she walks away. I glance fondly at the guitar and prop it against the wall, before shrugging off my jacket and grabbing the vacuum cleaner from under the stairs.

It might seem like a simple thing, but the guitar is one of the only things connecting me to my past. The old me. The life I'd rebuilt, before everything went wrong again.

Chapter 38

The news about Zachary's murder has soured Gillian's already dire mood. 'If we'd have found him quicker, we'd have a witness with a pulse to interview,' she snaps. 'A breathing suspect to grill. We don't have a formal witness statement from him so we can't use what he said as evidence. We don't have prints from him, so we can't link him to the evidence. This is absolute fuckery.'

'I know,' I say, when all I want to ask is how the hell would we have known he was going to do a runner? 'Our most likely suspect is still Anya. She has the motive; she was in Lisette's will. She definitely had the means and the opportunity. And on top of that, she faked her death. Zachary had a few rows with Lisette over the years but quite frankly, I'd be surprised to find he'd been sober long enough to plan something like this. It's a setback, but we've still got some cards to play.'

'We'd better bloody have.' Gillian folds her arms. I wonder again about the negative pregnancy test, and Gillian's tears.

A world apart from the woman standing here, eating us alive. 'You've probably all seen the headlines today.'

I grimace. I was scrolling through local news this morning and saw another headline roasting us for having not found Lisette and Sylvie's killer yet. The headline **SUSSEX POLICE: ALL PLAY & NO WORK** printed next to a photograph of a uniformed police officer taking a lunch break, leaning against his car in the sun, glancing at his phone. The comments section is brutal. The fact that this officer isn't even *on* this case, and very much deserves to have a lunch break, isn't mentioned in the article.

'Tiana, stay close to the investigation into Zachary's murder,' Gillian continues. 'Surrey Police can keep you in the loop. Find out if there's any link at all to this case. If Anya arranged for the witness to be wiped out.'

'Yes, ma'am.' Tiana scrawls in her notebook.

'Bella, dig into Anya's bank records again. Check her online activity. Has she used her phone since Eve last checked them? If she's on the run, she's bound to have slipped up somewhere. They always bloody do.'

Bella nods. 'Got it.'

Gillian looks sharply at me. 'Eve, I want you to set up a video call with DI Glenn Sloan from Police Scotland. Take him through what you know, find out what he knows. Collaborate.'

'No problem.'

'He's a smarmy sod, but please keep him on side.'

'Will do, ma'am.' I smile at her, but she doesn't return it.

Glenn is late. I've been sitting in this meeting room for fifteen minutes, and by this point, I assume he's been dragged off to something urgent.

My phone buzzes, and I glance down at the screen. It's Bella.

He shown up yet?

I tap out a reply.

Nope.

The phone immediately rings and I press it to my ear.

'Bells?'

'Got something for you,' says the voice at the end of the line. 'Just wanted to tell you before I update the boss.'

'Oh God, *please* let it be something good,' I groan.

'I reckon so,' she says. 'Anyway, we're still looking into Anya's online activity. From what we can see so far, she hasn't slipped up yet. Digital Forensics are combing all the main social media platforms for new profiles created in the past few weeks, listing similar interests or variations of her name. I think they're hoping for a rogue geo-tagged selfie to pop up somewhere but I think she's too calculated for that.'

'I hope this gets better.' I reach for my glass of water and completely miss my mouth, spilling cold liquid down my shirt. I swear loudly.

'I'm sorry,' says Bella. 'No need for the F-bomb.'

'Ugh, not you. Spilled my drink. Carry on.' I dab at my shirt with a tissue.

'Anya's bank statements tell a different story.'

'Now you're talking.' I pause. 'Hold on, didn't we already check those?'

Bella is silent for a few seconds. 'It was missed.'

'By who? Not you, surely. You've got eyes like a bloody hawk.'

Another pause. 'Tiana checked them. Don't start, Eve.'

I bite my lip. 'I didn't say anything. Tell me what you've found.'

'The last time she used her bank card was the day before the fire. She withdrew a grand. But it's part of a pattern. She'd been withdrawing large sums of money regularly for the past few months. All cash. Her bank account is pretty much cleaned out.'

'How much?' I ask.

'Just shy of five grand,' says Bella.

'Holy fuck. Who needs five grand in cash?' I open my mouth to say something else when I realise there's a face on the laptop, watching me with great interest. 'Got to go.'

'You make quite the first impression, DC Starling,' says a deep voice in a thick Glaswegian accent. The man on the other side of the screen has a slim, pale face, with closely cropped black hair, the same length as the salt-and-pepper stubble on his face. His eyes are framed by thick eyebrows, one of them currently raised.

'DI Sloan.' I'm suddenly very much aware of the wetness seeping through my shirt. 'Excellent.' I arrange my face into something resembling an enthusiastic smile.

'Sorry I'm late.' He suppresses a smirk. 'But it seems like you were preoccupied too.'

'Just getting an update on the case while I was waiting for

you.' I place emphasis on the last three words, and immediately regret it when I remember Gillian's words. *Please keep him on side.*

'Ah yes, the case. I've not had a chance to familiarise myself. I've seen the social media campaign against your division though.'

My face flames. The tweets and Facebook comments have been coming in thick and fast since the second newspaper article and it's done nothing to improve Gillian's sour mood. I launch straight into it. 'The person we're looking for is Anya Fernsby. She's a twenty-three-year-old woman from Brighton, who staged her suicide just hours after her girlfriend and stepdaughter were killed in an arson attack. A witness saw her at the scene of the fire; however, that witness is now dead. We're not sure if his death is linked yet. The prints found on the accelerant that was used to start the fire were linked to Anya. She was also a benefactor in the victim's will. We've traced her to Inverness train station but that's where we lose her.'

'Assume you've flagged her on the PNC? Alerted ports, border control and airports?'

I grit my teeth. 'That's the first thing we did.'

'Yet she's evaded you.' He sits back in his chair.

'We have no idea where she is,' I admit. 'We believe she may be in some kind of disguise, living under a different name. Can you get your team to Inverness train station, question the staff? Someone might remember seeing her. We have some CCTV images of what she looks like, and what she was wearing.'

'Aye, we can do that. We'll need to revisit the CCTV as well. If all we know is that she was last seen in Inverness, there are countless places she could have gone on to from there. It'll be like looking for the proverbial needle. If we can find the platform she went to, we'll at least be able to trace which onward train she took.'

'Thank you,' I say. 'I'll email over the CCTV stills shortly.'

'You're welcome. And I hope you have a dry shirt on next time we speak.' He winks and I smile tightly, realising all too late that the water has turned part of my shirt transparent.

I end the call and close the laptop lid, thinking about what Bella had told me. Why had Anya withdrawn so much cash in the lead-up to the fire? The theory that Anya was after the money from Lisette's will doesn't stack up. Not only did she have plenty, she was planning to go on the run with the money she had, so there must be another reason.

Chapter 39

I breathe in the warm, aromatic scent of Spanish cooking, taking in the hum of chatter and the sound of cutlery tapping against crockery. I lose myself for a moment, thinking about the second dead poppy delivery, the intruder on the boat. It must have been a warning from Ruben. But what if it's not? What if someone else knows what happened?

The weight of Orla's hand on my shoulder brings me back to the present, back to Platos Pequeños, our favourite tapas restaurant.

'Are you okay?' she whispers, and I nod. I *have* to be.

'I'm fine.' I subtly try to shake off her hand. 'It's fine. I'll be fine.' *Stop saying fine*, I tell myself.

I've been invited along after getting upset about Matthew's behaviour last night, crashing a dinner and drinks with her friend Lisette. Conscious of the fact that I'm potentially spoiling a lovely evening between friends, I don't do much talking. But despite my sudden shyness, Lisette makes me feel at ease instantly, drawing me in with her warmth,

214

her intense eye contact, the little furtive smiles she keeps directing my way. Is she like this with everyone, or just me? Every time she leans in to speak to me over the noise of the restaurant, I hold my breath, silently begging my cheeks not to flush, my breathing to slow.

I do know that I like her in a way I definitely shouldn't like my sister's friend . . . and it has disaster written all over it.

We're a few hours into the evening and I can't face drinking alcohol, despite the gentle cajoling from the other two. Not after how ill I felt last week. But right now, I'd give anything for that woozy feeling of alcohol-induced confidence. My eyes sweep the dimly lit cocktail bar, looking for Orla, and land on someone else. That mermaid hair. The sharpness of her jaw. Even the leather jacket she's wearing. That's her . . . it's Poppy. I blink, and she's gone. I strain my eyes and squint into the darkness, checking every single person in the room, but she's vanished. I scold myself; of course it wasn't her. *Stop being so stupid.* I catch Lisette's eye again for the fourth time tonight, certain her eyes are lingering a little longer than necessary.

I finally spot Orla and beckon her over to the sticky sofa and pat the empty seat beside me. She shuffles over and giggles as she stumbles. 'You okay?' she shouts in my ear over the thumping sound of Walk the Moon telling everyone to shut up and dance.

'Yeah.' I lean over to put my drink down. 'Listen, what's Lisette's deal?'

'Deal?' asks Orla, confused.

'I feel like she keeps staring at me.' I hide my hands in my sleeves self-consciously. 'Is she . . . is she *gay*?'

Orla bursts out laughing and claps a hand over her mouth to stifle the sound.

'What's so funny?'

She shakes her head, still laughing at some joke I'm clearly missing out on.

'Seriously, *what*?'

'She literally asked me the same question about you. You've been staring at each other all night.' She takes another sip of her prosecco and eyes me meaningfully before continuing. 'I told her you were as straight as a pole of course. Right?'

There's something in the way she says 'right?' Like she's challenging me. But she can't know. No one knows . . . I stay quiet, and look back at Lisette, who's standing at the bar, waiting patiently for her drink.

'She *is* gay, though,' she adds, not noticing my silence. 'And I think she's a bit gutted you're straight.'

I'm pondering this when I see him, snaking his way through the crowd, smiling widely at us both.

'Ruben!' Orla leaps from her seat and pulls our cousin into a hug. 'I didn't think you'd make it.'

He breaks away from her and glances down at me. 'Long time no see, An.' He spreads his arms to invite me in for a hug. I'm so angry with him right now, but painfully conscious of how one more wrong move could tip him over the edge and send him blabbing about what he thought he saw. So I oblige. When Orla leaves to go to the bathroom, I step back instinctively.

'What do you want? I said no more money.' My hands clench into fists, nails embedding into my palms.

He has the decency to look ashamed. 'It's only temporary. Anyway, Orla invited me.'

'I know you broke into our place,' I accuse him. 'I know it's you leaving the poppies.'

He pulls a face. 'Broke in? What place? What poppies? What are you *on* about?'

'The boat,' I snap. 'After I told you no more money, someone left a bunch of dead *poppies* at my flat. Then a few days later, someone broke into the boat and stole my phone and laptop.'

'The boat?' he repeats, a look of pure confusion clouding his face.

I shake my head in disbelief. 'What is it? A warning? A threat?'

'You've lost it.' He stares at me.

'When you ended up on my doorstep last week, pissed as anything and asking for more cash, you said you could only keep my secret for so long.'

His expression darkens. 'Anya, I know I'm a complete waste of space right now, but I'm not a *blackmailer*. I told you, I'm sorting my shit out. I was in a bad way last week, and I'm sorry if I said something to upset you.'

'Upset me?' I round on him. 'You threatened me. I've given you thousands of pounds. You've not paid a penny back and then you *threatened* me. You stole my stuff.'

Something in his expression snaps. 'For fuck's sake, An. Maybe I shouldn't have bothered saving your arse from

217

prison. Maybe I *should* tell them what I really fucking think happened.'

My world tilts and I grab his forearm. 'No. *No.* Please. You know it was an accident.'

He shakes his arm out of my grip. 'I haven't got a reason to keep your secret anymore. You're not doing anything for me.'

'Ruben, please. *Listen* to me. There's no secret. What you know, it's the truth.'

'So why did you convince me to say I was never there? To lie to the police?'

'Because it was easier. I was protecting you,' I insist.

'You put me in a shitty position – you do realise that, don't you?' His eyes dart to Orla coming back from the bathroom, then back to me again. 'Just think about where your loyalties lie, all right?' He throws a look of contempt my way before backing off and then weaving through the crowds.

'Everything all right?' Orla glances at our cousin's retreating back with a frown.

'Yes. All good.' I force my face into a bright smile. 'He's gone to chat to his mate.'

Orla, Lisette and some of Orla's friends she's bumped into have been on the dance floor for a while, but I don't have the energy for it. I glance up and see that Lisette has broken away from the group. I catch her eye, and she smiles as she walks over and sinks into the seat next to me.

'Hey.' I'm suddenly nervous. Why am I nervous? 'We've not talked much yet.' I sip my drink.

'No, because you are the elusive Anya.' She has a sparkle

218

in her eye. 'I cannot believe I am only just meeting you tonight. You are all over Orla's Instagram.' I instantly warm to her, finding myself gazing into her deep brown eyes and listening intently to the velvety French accent passing her lips. Deep red lips. I can't stop staring—

'Orla's told me all about the music shop you both own.' Her voice brings me back down to Earth. 'I must bring my daughter there. She keeps asking me for a recorder.'

'You've got a daughter? What's her name?'

'Sylvie. She is the light of my life.' She shows me a photo on her phone of a pretty little girl, with dark hair styled into hundreds of tiny plaits, her big brown eyes staring into the camera like two buttons as she grips on to a doll that's wearing a space suit in her pudgy hands.

'She's gorgeous, Lisette. How old is she?'

'She's five.' Lisette stares proudly at the photo. 'She is so smart, too. She wants to be an astronaut.'

'So ambitious.' I try to remember what I wanted to do when I was five. A musician, I think. I'm not sure where all my confidence has gone. I look up at Lisette. 'What do you do?'

'I am a head teacher at Sylvie's primary school.' The smile on her face tells me she loves her job.

'Really? That's incredible.'

She laughs. 'Yes. It is very rewarding.'

***

We've been deep in conversation for over an hour before Orla declares herself ready to get a taxi home. Keen to continue talking, we wave her off. Another hour passes, our drinks remaining untouched, when I feel a prickle of unease spread across my skin, as if someone's watching me closely. The bar's still busy, with the buzz of people letting off steam after a long hard week at work, and I sweep the room with my gaze, trying to work out if it's pure paranoia, or if there's a pair of eyes on me. I lock eyes with Ruben, and my body fizzes with nerves. I turn back to Lisette. 'Shall we get out of here? I'm losing my voice from talking over all the noise.'

We walk home together arm in arm, wrapped up against the late winter chill . . . Neither of us suggested getting a taxi. I feel like I'm bonding with Lisette in a way I'd never quite managed to with other friends. I already feel like I know everything there is to know about her, from stories about Sylvie, to her life in France before moving to England. I slow my pace as we get closer to home, unable to bear the thought of the night ending.

'Anya.' She turns to me during a short but comfortable lull in the conversation. 'Would you like to stay at mine? To save you walking the rest of the way home?' Anxiety patters across my chest and my stomach churns.

'Are you sure? I don't want to impose.'

'Of course. I can set up the sofa bed. Or, if you want, you can share with me,' she suggests lightly. My heart is pounding. Why though? I've bunked up with friends before. That's all this is.

'Okay.' I nod. 'If you're sure.'

We lie side by side, chatting long into the early hours, but still never discussing anything to do with either of our sexualities . . . which is why it comes as such a surprise when we kiss, as naturally as if we're in a long-term relationship and kissing each other goodnight. As naturally as if it's simply meant to be. We stare at each other in shock as we register what's happened, before collapsing into each other, our bodies and limbs a tangled mess in the sheets, all thoughts of Matthew a distant memory for one blissful night. *This*, I think, *is how it's meant to be for me.*

Had I known what would happen five months later, I'd have run away and never looked back.

Chapter 40

Kate – Now

No matter the weather, I religiously complete a two-mile walk around Plockton every day. More so since I saw the comments online. I enjoy the rhythmic thump of my boots hitting the ground and being surrounded by miles of lush Scottish landscape. I lose myself daily in the sound of the coastal wind rushing around my ears and the screech of the seagulls . . . These are the things that remind me of the home I might never be able to return to. The sister I might never see again . . . unless I manage to get Matthew locked up where he belongs.

A fresh flood of fury runs through me as I think about what he did. I wonder how long it'll take for this to become a cold case, for the police to move on to something else and give me the chance to fly under the radar and get myself back to Brighton. But what if I'm found first? I need to get my story straight . . .

'How are things going at Peg's place?' Hazel's voice interrupts my thoughts. Sometimes she joins me on my walks, and today is one of those days. We're on the last leg of the walk, the final half a mile.

'Really good. She's sweet.'

'Why did you move here anyway, to the middle of nowhere? I've been meaning to ask.'

I feel a jolt in my stomach at the thought of delving back into my past, and feed her the same old half-lie I told Peggy, about running from an abusive ex-boyfriend. I try to move the conversation on. 'Anyway, how about you? You never told me why *you* came here.'

'My dad died when I was eighteen, and I ended up blaming my mum because she didn't make him go to the doctor. It wasn't her fault, but I needed someone to blame. We were so close, and I screwed it all up. I guess I wanted a fresh start.' She lets out a deep sigh.

'Do you still speak to her?'

'We send Christmas and birthday cards. I've seen her once since I moved out. I know I need to try again with her. I guess you probably think I'm awful, don't you?'

'I don't think you're awful.' I stop and look her straight in the eyes. 'We've all done things we're not proud of. No one's perfect.' She nods solemnly at me and we carry on walking but I stop again when I see it: my own face staring back at me from the front cover of a tabloid newspaper.

A man behind me tuts loudly as he sidesteps around me to avoid a collision, and I start walking again. My head reels as I read the headline over and over again as I pass, hoping I've read it wrong and that the words might morph into something else before my eyes. **WOMAN WANTED**

IN CONNECTION WITH BRIGHTON MURDER. The words shout angrily at me from the page, bold accusations in black and white.

I see my own face taking up half the page. It's a photo taken from my Facebook account, one that I don't really remember being taken. I'm not smiling. It looks like I'm in the background of a picture of someone else, frowning about something. The journalist has picked the worst possible photo they could find, to make me look like I have the potential to kill. My own deep green eyes burn into me from the paper, my long brunette waves looking strange now I'm so used to my pixie crop. My face looks odd without the bright blue eyes I've since become accustomed to. But it's unmistakably me. I feel my face flush deep scarlet and I hope Hazel hasn't noticed. The conversation stops flowing because I can no longer contribute, and I'm trembling.

Hazel's voice brings me crashing back down to Earth. 'Kate, you all right, mate?'

'Yes.' I wrap my arms around myself in fear, as if I can protect myself from the inevitable. It feels like the past is catching up with me, reaching out of the darkness to wrap its tentacles around me, pulling me backwards to face up to what's happened.

Hazel reaches out and grabs my shoulder, squeezing it comfortingly. 'What's wrong?'

'Nothing.' I force a smile.

She frowns. 'Come on, Kate. Something upset you. What's going on? You can tell me.'

'It's nothing,' I say quickly. 'Please don't worry. Listen,

224

I've just remembered I've got to get some bits for Peg.' I nod towards the shop. 'I'll see you tomorrow.'

'D'you fancy a drink later?' Hazel's voice sounds hopeful.

I hesitate, but the thought of a gin and tonic does sound appealing, so I force myself to smile. 'Sure, why not? See you about eight?'

'Great stuff.' Hazel nods, and hesitates before giving me another shoulder squeeze, and making her way home.

I bend over and put my hands on my knees, exhaling deeply as I mentally run through my plan for if I get caught. I'll tell them everything, and do everything in my power to find Matthew. There'll be CCTV, phone records, *something* the police can access to prove my innocence. Until then, I need to keep trying to track him down. It's a solid plan, I'm sure of it.

But something tells me that my world could so easily come crashing down around me for the third time.

Chapter 41

Eve – Now

My phone rings, and DI Glenn Sloan's name flashes on the screen. I wrinkle my nose, remembering his creepy wink last time we spoke.

'DC Starling,' I say, my voice stiff.

'DI Sloan. Got an update for you.' He skips straight past the pleasantries.

'Okay, shoot.' I grab my notebook, trying not to get my hopes up.

'We've spotted her.'

My heartbeat quickens. 'Where?'

'Inverness Station.' There's a note of smugness in his voice, knowing his team looked in the same places as us, and found something we missed. 'Your suspect had removed her beanie hat and hoodie, and concealed herself within a large group of teenagers who were too drunk to notice she was walking with them.'

'Where did she go?'

'She boarded a train on platform six, which was heading towards Kyle of Lochalsh.'

'But you don't know where she got off?'

'I'm not a magician. There's barely any CCTV along the Kyle line. But you can consider your search area significantly narrowed.'

'Right, sorry. Thank you, DI Sloan. Is there anything else you can tell me?'

'Aye. Officers in Dingwall and Kyle of Lochalsh have been briefed to keep their eyes peeled for her. It's a large area, but a sparse population. I'll have someone my end share all possible onward routes from these areas with you.' He pauses and lets out a sigh. 'Not much more I can do, I'm afraid.'

'No, that's really helpful. Thank you.' I grip the receiver tightly.

***

'There are fourteen stops along the route,' I inform the team. A map of the route, from Dingwall to Kyle of Lochalsh, appears on the projector screen of the operations room, next to a satellite view of the area. 'Garve, Loch . . . Loch-something.' Bella snorts as I try and fail to pronounce it. 'Anyway, most of these are small, unstaffed platforms with no CCTV. No one we can ask if they saw Anya.'

'Not ideal.' Gillian folds her arms across her chest.

'I know,' I say. 'Sloan's team have sent over some useful info. Bus, coach and ferry routes from each train station, information on the local areas, local taxi companies, a list of recently stolen vehicles, some helpful contacts in the local forces.' I watch Tiana spreading out the printouts detailing the onward routes and studying them while we talk.

'Question is, did she stay put in one of these fourteen places, or has she gone elsewhere?' Gillian looks sharply at me. 'What would you do if you were on the run?'

'After a twelve-hour train journey, I don't think I'd be going much further, ma'am. Unless I had a particular place in mind. But if I were running on limited resources, with just the cash I had on me, I'd settle in the first safe place I could that wouldn't rouse suspicion. But I'm not Anya.'

'If she did move on to somewhere else,' says Tiana, glancing up from the printouts and maps, 'we could be looking at a huge area. Possibly as far up as Stornoway.'

'Tiana, Bella. Can you pair up to give me a list of all possible, *likely* places she could have moved on to, and work with local transport providers to get some posters up? And get hold of any CCTV you can.'

'Yes, ma'am.' Tiana looks pleased. I don't know why; I wouldn't want that job. Is it because she gets to work closely with her new pal?

'Jason and Eve, can you liaise with Corporate Comms to get Anya's face out there, *up there*?' she says, meaning the Highlands. 'I'm talking targeted social media posts to anyone based along the Kyle line, and north of that. And local newspaper appeals, please. Ideally, front cover. Ideally, tomorrow.'

I feel a buzz of excitement. Despite the obvious uncertainty, it feels like we're getting a bit closer.

***

It's late when I finally shut down my computer. I stand up, stretch my arms over my head, and pick up my bag; my eyes are stinging with tiredness and too much screen time. The sound of someone sneezing makes me jump. I turn on the spot, and see Gillian in her office, dabbing her nose with a tissue.

I hover in the doorway, unsure if she's still angry with me. 'Are you okay?'

'I'm excellent.' She smiles as she drops her tissue in the bin, but no amount of make-up can hide the shadows sitting stubbornly under her eyes. 'Are *you*? You look concerned. Come in.'

I close the door behind me and sink into one of the seats opposite her.

'Why are you here so late?' she asks.

'Tying up a few loose ends. Why are *you* here so late?'

She raises an eyebrow. 'You're all about the questions lately.'

I blush. 'Sorry, I'm just . . .'

'Just what?'

'Worried.'

'About what?'

I pause, unsure if I should even be bringing it up. But she's not just my boss, she's my friend. 'You.' I fix her with my gaze.

She cocks her head. 'Me? I'm fine, Eve. What makes you think I'm not?'

'Well, you were crying when you came out of the loo the other day. I don't mean to pry, but there was a pregnancy test jammed in the bin when I tried to open it. I realise it could have been Tiana, or Bella, but . . . you'd just come out crying.'

Her smile slips. 'Ah.'

'And I didn't know you were ill.'

She frowns at me. 'I'm not ill, Eve.'

'But . . . I saw syringes in your bag. I didn't mean to look; I leaned over to fetch the coffee, and I saw them.'

'Okay.' Gillian closes her eyes. 'Okay. Look, I haven't told anyone this, but—'

'You don't have to tell me anything you don't want to,' I interject.

'It's okay. Those needles *are* diabetic needles, but they're also used in IVF. When you saw me in a bit of a state in the ladies', I'd had a failed cycle.'

My stomach drops. 'Oh, Gilly. I'm so sorry.' It explains all the absences and the appointments. And the tiredness.

She gives me a sad smile. 'Looks like Eddie and I . . . well, we possibly left it a little too late.'

'Will you try again?'

'Yes,' she says firmly. 'One *hundred* per cent yes.'

I smile at Gillian's determination, hoping the tenacity she displays on the job will serve her well in her own personal battles. I hope more than anything they can make it work.

Chapter 42

Anya – Then

'Hey, you.' *I smile at the woman sitting at the café table as I approach. Lisette turns around, her face splitting into a heart-stoppingly beautiful smile, and she stands up to wrap her arms around me.*

I breathe in the scent of her perfume, floral and exotic.

'It is so good to see you again.' *She steps back, drinking me in with her eyes and I bat away the guilt that insists on bubbling its way to the surface. She doesn't know about Matthew; Matthew doesn't know about her. And I simply cannot stop thinking about her.*

She entwines her fingers with mine, and in that moment I realise what I need to do. I need to leave him.

I just have to pick my moment.

***

I'm tugged from my dream at the sound of kitchen cup-boards opening and closing. I roll onto my side and watch with bleary eyes as Matthew cracks some eggs into a bowl, feeling a pang of guilt at what I'm about to do. What I *need* to do. Because I can't keep on lying to myself, to everyone. It's been two days since my illicit night with Lisette, and I feel sick with guilt and sick with longing. The churning in my stomach is too much. I've done this terrible thing behind Matthew's back that'd break his heart if he found out. I know, more than anyone, how much guilt affects you, mentally and physically. God, I've been plagued by it since I was fifteen.

Since that night.

'Morning.' Matthew waves a whisk in my direction. 'Pancakes?'

I nod, swinging my legs out of bed and padding across the small space to lean against the breakfast bar. Can I do it? He's so good to me. But I don't love him. And . . . I already feel like I'm falling for Lisette. As crazy as that sounds.

'What are you deep in thought about?' Matthew slides a pancake onto a plate and passes it to me.

'Nothing,' I mutter, settling myself down on a stool and staring down at the pancake. My stomach flips at the thought of eating it.

He squirts lemon and scatters sugar over his pancake, and cuts off a piece, skewering it on a fork. It's halfway to his mouth when he pauses, staring at me. 'Is something wrong, An?'

I hesitate. I can do this, can't I? I have to. 'Matt . . . I need to talk to you about something.'

He gazes sideways at me, lowering his fork to his plate. 'Something's up. Tell me.'

I push the plate away and lean my elbows on the cold, hard surface in front of me. 'I've . . . met someone else.' The words are out in the open, and I can't take them back now. I take a deep breath.

Matthew twists in his seat to stare at me. 'You *what*?'

I drop my head into my hands. 'I've met someone else. I'm so, *so* sorry.'

'What the fuck, An? Who is he?' He slams a hand on the breakfast bar, catching the side of his plate, sending his fork flying. '*Well?*'

My eyes slide from the table to his face, and it's not just the anger I'm expecting. It's panic. And fear.

'You don't need to know who it is.'

He laughs, but it's a sharp sound. 'I think you'll find I do.'

I shake my head. 'It doesn't change anything.'

'Who is he?' His voice is quivering.

'It's not a he,' I whisper.

His dark eyes burn into me, darker than I've ever seen them. He slams a fist on the bar, and I jump.

'I didn't want to admit it to myself, Matt. I wanted to push it down like it wasn't really a part of me. Last time I tried to come out . . . God. I can't even *begin* to tell you how awful it was. But it *is* a part of me, and I can't force myself to be something I'm not anymore. I've been doing it for so long, and it's *exhausting*.'

He stares at me. 'What happened when you tried to come out last time?'

I can't look him in the eye. 'It's not important.'

'You at least owe me the truth.'

Our eyes finally meet. Mine, red-rimmed and his, dark and intense. I can't tell him the whole story, but maybe I can tell him *something*. 'I had feelings for my friend. I thought she felt the same; she was giving me all the right signals. But . . . I was wrong. We argued, and she said some awful things about me, about my family. It was horrible. We never got a chance to make up.'

'Why?'

I pause. 'She was killed. In an accident.'

He frowns. 'What kind of accident?'

My eyes drop to my knees. 'I don't really want to talk about it, Matt.'

His hand reaches out to grip my forearm and I flinch. '*Tell me*.'

'No. I can't. I'm sorry, Matt.' I shake my arm out of his grip and slide off the stool. 'I need to leave. Let me leave.'

It all happens so quickly, I'm not even sure I have a chance to take it in. His fingers curl into a fist and he draws his elbow backwards as if he's about to punch me in the face. I bring my arm up to protect myself, automatically curling my own hand into a fist in case I need to fight back, but nothing happens. When I lower my arm, he has his hand over his mouth, his face white with shock.

'What the *hell*, Matt?' My heart is hammering, adrenaline shooting around my body, surging me forward. 'Were you about to *hit* me?'

'No.' He shakes his head furiously. 'I'd never do that. I love you. I was just going to whack the worktop. I'm sorry. I didn't mean to scare you.'

I back away, and his mouth is set in a grim line as he watches me toss my possessions in a bag. He doesn't seem sad at all.

Chapter 43

Kate – Now

There's a chill in the air; autumn is definitely on its way. I stand outside the old village pub, staring at it, but I can't go inside. I just can't do it. I can see through the steamed-up windows that the place is full. Everyone in the village must be in there for the open mic night. I can hear a man singing his heart out to Rod Stewart's 'Maggie May', Hazel's at the bar, and I'm still frantically trying to think of an excuse for my behaviour earlier on.

I can't go in there.

I think about what I'd be doing in another life, if I'd made better decisions . . . if I'd never met *him*. I'd be the first one up there, singing without a care. I remember karaoke nights with Orla, and singing in the kitchen with Lisette, and then try not to remember, because it's agonising.

The door opens and Hazel's face appears, bringing with it a waft of that smell all pubs seem to have: beer-soaked carpets and smoke, despite the fact no one's smoked in a pub for years. 'You just gonna stand there and freeze your tits off?'

I step back instinctively, as if the mere presence of me will alert the punters that I'm the woman in the newspaper. 'I can't go in.'

She considers me for a few seconds, then nods once. 'Hold on.' The door closes, and I watch her gathering her coat through the window. She downs a drink and then bustles out of the door.

We fall into step, the lampposts illuminating the darkness, our footsteps echoing in the empty road. I link her arm in mine. Little clouds of condensation bloom with every breath.

'What's up, mate?' she asks once we're out of earshot of anyone who could be lingering outside the pub. We are completely and utterly alone.

My pulse quickens, but I can't bring myself to say anything yet.

After a few moments, she speaks again. 'You're hiding something.' She doesn't sound like she's accusing me of anything, she sounds like a concerned friend.

I summon up the courage to speak. 'Something bad happened.'

Hazel nods. 'Okay.'

I try to speak but the words catch in my throat. 'I . . .' I can't do it. I clam up completely.

She spins me around to face her. 'What is it, Kate? You can talk to me.'

I squeeze my eyes shut against her intense gaze, and then open them again. We lock eyes. There's a connection, the air fizzing between us and suddenly I want to talk. To tell her something. Not everything, but *something*. I'm so tired of keeping this secret, this thing brewing inside me, growing, threatening to burst open. The real me is at risk of leaking out of the cracks and I am *exhausted*.

'My . . . my girlfriend died in a fire. So did my stepdaughter.' A silent sob rises in my throat. I can't bring myself to tell her the rest.

'Oh, Kate.' She wraps her arms around me. 'I'm so, so sorry.'

I don't know why, but I feel safe with her. Something tells me I'm safe. There's a connection between us: I've not felt anything close to it since I first met Lisette, although it's not romantic this time.

'I was blamed,' I mumble into her shoulder. 'But it wasn't me.'

'Kate . . .' She hesitates. 'Are you the woman in the paper?'

My whole body freezes. I pull back, out of her embrace. 'Why . . . why do you think *that*?'

She chews her bottom lip. 'You always seem to be buying hair dye. You're sketchy about your past. You're weird about having photos taken . . .' She pauses. 'And you look a bit like her.'

I feel like I've been punched in the gut. If Hazel has noticed, then who else might? What if someone else has recognised me? What if Peg recognises me?

'I was . . . framed.' The last word comes out as a whisper, a word I'm too scared to say out loud.

Hazel tenses beside me. 'Oh, shit.' She pauses, as if

238

contemplating what to say next. A sense of apprehension creeps through me as she exhales deeply. 'Really?'

I nod.

'Bloody hell, Kate.'

'Please don't tell anyone who I am,' I plead. 'Please. I can't face up to what happened. I lost everything. I can't do it again. I just *can't*.'

She eyes me cautiously, then shakes her head. 'I won't breathe a word. I . . . I know I don't really know you that well but I like to think I am a good judge of character. In fact, I *know* I am. I have a strong feeling that you're telling the truth – I don't think you did it. But . . . who's framing you, Kate? And *why*?'

I shake my head tightly. 'I've already said enough. I . . . I can't tell you.'

I feel my face flush with humiliation. I need to lie low for a while.

* * *

I still can't find him. Despite it becoming a daily obsession since I saw his name in the comments section online, he appears to have vanished off the face of the planet. *Just like you've done*, says a voice in my head. I could go back now. I could go back and tell the police what I know. That he had set me up. Framed me. Make it look like I killed my girlfriend and stepdaughter in cold blood. *They won't believe you*, says the voice again. *They'll know all about Poppy by now.* My past is tarnished, and no number of fresh starts is ever going to make that fact go away. But a huge part of me longs for home. For the hustle and bustle of Brighton. For my big sister. How long should I wait for it to be safe?

'Who's Matthew Taylor?'

I twist around on the bench to see Hazel standing behind me, holding a fat doughnut that looks like it's been glazed in bright pink lip gloss. She takes a sticky bite.

I lock the phone and slide it into my bag with a frown. 'What are you doing here?' I'd come to the beach for some privacy, like I always do when I go searching for Matthew.

She sits on the stone wall behind me and props her trainers up on the back of the bench. 'Sorry, didn't know I wasn't allowed on your beach.'

I blush, but she's laughing. 'I didn't mean it like that.'

'Who is he then?'

'Who?'

'Matthew Taylor.'

'Just someone.'

'Gonna need more than that.' She scrunches up the paper her doughnut was wrapped in and shoves it in her pocket. 'Wait . . .' Her voice turns serious. 'Is this who framed you?'

I nod. 'I'm trying to track him down.'

She climbs over the back of the bench and slides onto the seat beside me. 'I'm an excellent social media stalker. It's a great avoidance tactic when I'm meant to be doing other stuff. So if you need help finding someone, I'm your woman.'

I return my gaze to the waves lapping against the pebbled shore. Imagine if we found him. If I could have some kind of proof he exists before I get in touch with the police. Imagine if I could stop running, stop glancing over my shoulder. Imagine if I could be Anya again, Anya Fernsby. Not Kate Smith.

'I'm looking for a man called Matthew Taylor. He lived in Brighton, on a boat in the marina. I never knew his permanent address. He has a spaniel called Bowie. He works for the fire service. He's white, quite a bit taller than me, with dark hair and dark eyes. Wears glasses. Oh, and he ruined my life.'

Chapter 44

Eve – Now

We're gathered in the office for the weekly team briefing, most of us clutching coffees and stifling yawns. It's first thing in the morning, and Gillian is pacing in front of the case boards. Things have really ramped up, with workload building and tempers flaring on a daily basis. The Lisette Dupont case is still on her radar, but it's fighting for her attention due to two stabbings in the city centre, a missing six-year-old and two reported rapes. It's been a week since DI Glenn Sloan's team shared what they knew, but it feels yet again like we've reached a dead end.

Zachary Samson's killer turned out to be nothing to do with Anya, just the result of a drug debt gone on too long. And with no new evidence to go on, we've well and truly hit a wall. Since that night at the pub, a worried frown has become permanently etched across Jason's stubbled face and shadows have formed beneath his already dark eyes. He's been less talkative, less caring. I'm wondering if I've done something wrong. But I'm trying my best to remain optimistic, spending long hours at the office discussing different avenues with him, Bella and Tiana, and taking my admin work home with me so I can spend more time on the puzzle of Lisette's murder. It's exhausting, but I know it's exactly what we need to be doing if we have any chance of catching this killer.

'This needs to be our key focus for the next two weeks.' Gillian jabs a finger at the word 'STABBINGS' which is underlined three times in thick black pen. 'We need to increase stop and searches. I want any cases going cold to be handed over. The papers and social media are all over us. Some scum-of-the-earth reporter has clocked on that there's a higher-than-average proportion of women in my team and the fuckwit's using it against us. This department's becoming a joke and I don't like it.'

I shrink back in my seat, hoping Gillian won't question us on the Lisette Dupont case, which is without a doubt going cold. I can't stand that feeling of getting close to solving a case and then running out of information and witnesses. All we know is that Anya is hiding in Scotland, probably somewhere along the Kyle line but even that we don't know for sure. Bella and I have spent hours poring over the CCTV, ANPR, road traffic camera footage, bank activity, and social media accounts, as well as consulting experts within the wider teams, but no one's able to get close to tracking her down. We've used up a substantial chunk of budget.

The Telephone Intelligence Unit have endured hundreds of calls from the public in response to the media campaign and newspaper articles, all of which have ended up leading absolutely nowhere. I've spent too many evenings going over every last detail entered into the HOLMES system by our indexers, convinced that hidden amongst the prank calls and false leads would be a shred of information that could kick the case back into gear, but so far . . . nothing. Just dead end after bloody dead end. Short of taking a road trip up to Scotland and searching every house in the Highlands, there's nothing more I can think of doing.

'Jason.' Gillian looks directly at him, breaking my train of thought. 'It might be time to hand over the Dupont case.'

My heart sinks. Jason frowns. 'Can we have a couple more weeks? We're getting closer. I want to finish this.' Jason punches his palm with his other hand for emphasis.

I look into Gillian's eyes, trying to silently communicate with her. *I'm not ready to let it go.*

She glances skyward, then back to us, her tone clipped. 'One week.'

***

I run a little ahead of Bella so we don't get in the way of pedestrians. After the day we'd had, we both agreed we needed to let off some steam, and going for a run appealed more than going for a drink. To me, anyway. Especially now the weather's taking a turn for the worse.

'We could be at the pub right now,' she calls from behind me.

'Pipe down,' I call back.

'I need a rest,' she whines.

I slow to a stop when I see a bench, dropping into it and letting my head fall between my knees. The September air is pleasantly cool against my sweaty skin. I stare at my neon green trainers as Bella drops onto the bench next to me. The tinny sound of heavy metal reverberates from the earphones dangling around her neck.

'We *will* do that marathon one day.' She gulps from her water bottle.

'Mm hmm.' I sit up and slide my phone out of my arm strap, and see a Facebook notification. With a flash of annoyance, I see a friend request from Tiana. 'Oh, come on, Banks.'

Bella glances sideways at me. 'What's she done now?'

'Requested me on Facebook.'

She doesn't say anything, instead choosing to stare out to sea with a frown on her face.

'What?' I say. 'Why are you scowling like that?'

Bella emits a sigh. 'Look, she's got some stuff going on.'

'Haven't we all,' I mumble.

'You're not the only one going through shit, Eve.'

'I know that,' I say, shocked at her tone. 'I didn't mean just me.' I don't want to tell her what I know about Gillian; it doesn't feel right to share.

'Sorry.' There's a subtle note of regret in her voice. 'It feels like sometimes you're so wrapped up in what happened to Frankie, you forget the rest of us have problems too. You're not the only one who goes home, weeps into yet another takeaway and listens to Dido on repeat.'

'I *know*,' I say again, resting a hand on her knee. 'What's going on with Tiana? And you? Clearly there's something.'

She waves a hand dismissively. 'I'm fine. Tiana will be fine. Amongst other stuff, she's feeling like she's not fitting in with the team. I've had to work pretty hard to convince her not to request a transfer.'

I feel a stab of guilt. 'I didn't realise she felt like that.'

'Well, she does.'

'I'm glad she can confide in you,' I say.

'You're not exactly warm to her,' says Bella, a hint of a smile playing upon her lips.

'I'll try harder,' I say, and I mean it. I pick up my phone again, and accept the friend request. Small steps. I glance back at Bella. 'Are you sure *you're* okay? What was going on with your phone ringing off the hook the other day?'

Bella's face flushes red, and she stands up to stretch out her legs. 'Spam calls.' She drops into a lunge. 'Shall we go?'

I think about pressing her further, but decide against it. She'll tell me in her own time, I'm sure. But that vile text from Tony . . . what was *that* all about?

Chapter 45

Anya – Then

The sun filters through a gap in the curtains and I squeeze my eyes shut against it, letting a quiet groan escape my lips.

'Morning, sleepyhead.' Lisette's voice is like melted caramel dripping from a spoon and I roll over to smile at her, to drink her in. We've been together for a month now, and I've only heard from Ruben twice since that night in the bar. The next day to apologise, and at 3 a.m. last Saturday morning, begging for one last handout. I told him not to contact me again, until he's sorted his life out. I'm done. And I haven't even heard from Matt, not once. I feel like I can finally relax.

'Good morning.' My voice is thick with sleep. 'How long have you been awake?' I ask, when I notice the laptop, open on her lap. She's still wearing the T-shirt she'd been wearing last night, and her dark coils of hair are pulled back from her face in a ponytail. One lock spirals free from its elastic, resting against her cheek and she is utterly beautiful.

'Not long. Just two hours.' She bites her lip as she taps away at her keyboard.

'What are you doing?' I hoist myself up onto my elbows and peer at her laptop screen.

'Some reports. Thought I would get them done before you emerge from your beauty sleep.'

I lean over and kiss her. 'I can't believe you've been sat there for two hours while I was dead to the world. I'm sorry.' I flop back onto the pillows.

'Don't be silly.' She closes the laptop lid. 'You only snored a little bit.'

I shove her with my elbow and she laughs. It's the most beautiful sound in the world.

'I'm getting a coffee.' I kick off the covers. 'Can I get you anything?'

'Iced tea, please,' she requests. It doesn't matter what time of year, or what time of day, Lisette's drink of choice will *always* be iced tea. Weeks ago, I'd tried to tempt her with a selection box of different coffees, but she wrinkled her nose at them.

I yawn as I make my way down the two flights of stairs to the kitchen. Lisette and Sylvie live in a beautiful three-storey Brighton townhouse, and it's so *them*. It's homely, and I love all the family clutter. Sylvie's paintings proudly displayed on most walls, alongside family photographs. Bulging bookcases and overfilled toy boxes. Jammy hand-prints and stray hair clips. I open up the kitchen blinds, letting the sunlight flood the room. It's a beautiful spring morning and I peer out into the back garden, watching an enthusiastic blackbird pecking at the bare patch of lawn underneath Sylvie's swing, which sways gently in the breeze.

She's at her dad's this weekend, but I'm finding that I miss her when she's not here.

Then I see it. Something tied to the seat of the swing. The blackbird makes a bid for freedom as I throw open the back door and storm over to the swing, knowing full well what it is before I get anywhere near it. Another bunch of dead poppies, this time tied with a child's hair bobble. Blue, with a yellow plastic star attached to it. Next to them, a decapitated toy alien. *Sylvie's*. Bile rises in my throat.

I don't understand. Ruben knows I've got nothing left to give him, that I refuse to help him any longer. Why is he threatening me like this? Threatening *Sylvie*? I drop them onto the ground and stamp on them, grinding them into the mud. I hurl the alien and its head into the bin on the way into the house. I can't do this anymore. I can't. Everything is so perfect, but this one thing threatens to ruin *everything*.

I pull my phone from my dressing-gown pocket and type a furious text to him.

Ruben, what do you want from me? I've told you, I'm not bailing you out anymore. And leave Sylvie out of this, please.

It buzzes with a text almost immediately.

Anya, what the fuck are you on about? I haven't texted you in days.

I jab at the screen in response.

The poppies, Ruben, and the alien. You know exactly what I'm talking about!

His reply comes through immediately.

Why do you keep going on about poppies? I genuinely have no idea what you're talking about. I think you need some serious help.

I bristle.

Don't you dare try and gaslight me.

He stops replying after that, and I cry into my hands. I was so sure it was him, but if it's not, then who? Who else knows what really happened to Poppy?

Chapter 46

I scrub the house until my hands are raw, making a special effort with the guest bedroom. Knowing this is going to be Peggy's granddaughter's first visit in years, I'm keen to make sure her visit's a pleasant one, so maybe she'll try and visit more often. I'd been out the day before to pick up some new lilac bedsheets and a bunch of sunshine yellow roses to liven it up, relieved to see the newspaper headlines had already moved on. All the clutter that was previously stored in the spare room has now been moved into the loft. We'd framed and hung two photographs that show off some of the beautiful sights of Plockton: fishing boats in the harbour, and rows of postcard-perfect coastal cottages. Peggy isn't hopeful, but I am.

I'm finishing up making a selection of sandwiches for lunch when the doorbell rings, and I hear Peggy greeting someone at the door. The sound of voices drifts down the hall and into the kitchen and my ears prick up. I bustle into the hallway, pasting on my best smile, as I watch Ingrid embrace Peggy tightly.

'Hi, Ingrid. So lovely to meet you.' Ingrid peels herself away from Peggy and shoots me a smile. I stretch out my hand to greet the plump-cheeked, younger version of Peggy who stands with her weight on one leg, suit jacket draped over her arm and a bunch of flowers balanced on top.

'Are you Nanna's cleaner?' She shakes my outstretched hand with her free one.

'Kate's my housekeeper, and a very good friend of mine.' Peggy smiles broadly at both of us, in the way a parent does when they really want you to make a friend.

'Oh, okay.' Ingrid frowns. 'And you live here?'

'Yes,' Peggy and I say in unison.

'Okay.' Her eyes dart between us both before resting on me for a few seconds. I shift uncomfortably. 'Well, it's great to meet you.' Her face splits into a smile.

'Come into the kitchen,' I say. 'I've made us lunch.' I gesture at the platter of sandwiches, carefully cut and garnished.

Ingrid's face falls. 'Oh . . . I don't eat gluten.'

'Oh, pet, I didn't know you can't eat gluten.' Peggy's voice carries a note of panic.

Ingrid sighs and places a hand on her stomach. 'I *can* but . . . I choose not to.'

Peggy frowns at her. 'Okay, love, whatever you want . . .' She looks helplessly at me, eyes wide.

'I'll pop to the shop and get something else.' I smile at them both, before grabbing my keys.

As I walk, I try to distract myself from the worries slinking around my mind. But the arrival of Ingrid has shaken me up, set me off-kilter. She *seems* nice enough, but I've got a bad vibe. I can't quite put my finger on it. I try to convince myself to give her the benefit of the doubt. Perhaps she'd had a terrible journey, or a bad week at work. Yes, that's got to be it.

I pop into the grocery shop to look for something gluten-free. My eyes scan the shelves, hoping for a big 'gluten-free' sign to jump out at me, but it's nothing like the big Tesco I used to take for granted in Brighton. In the end, I walk out of the shop with everything I need for a Greek salad, plus a loaf of special bread and some fresh fruit for afterwards. I'll have to catch the train out of town to a bigger supermarket if Ingrid decides to stay longer than a night.

When I arrive back home, I let myself in and close the door quietly behind me. I pause when I hear Peggy and Ingrid talking in hushed tones in the kitchen. Caught between not wanting to eavesdrop, but also wanting to know if they're saying anything about me, I hover in the hallway, chewing my lip.

'. . . so, she's *homeless*?'

'No, love. She lives *here*,' Peggy protests. I suppose I *was* homeless before I came to live here. I've never thought of it that way.

'Before she lived here then, she was homeless.' Ingrid's words sting. She has no idea.

'I don't know,' says Peggy. 'Why does it matter?'

'Of course, it matters, Nanna! You have a homeless person living in your house. She could be stealing from you, right under your nose and you'd have no idea. She could be a psychopath. A *murderer*.'

I feel a clutch of panic in my chest.

'You're being dramatic, lassie,' I hear Peggy say gently. 'She's a lovely girl.'

Oh no. I feel a sneeze building, and I pinch my nostrils together, desperately trying to fend it off. Instead of a sneeze, a weird, suppressed snort bursts out of me, and I silently curse myself. I hurry back to the front door, open it quietly, and slam it shut again, hoping they'll think I've just returned home. I bustle into the kitchen, all smiles, and put my shopping bag down on the table.

'I hope Greek salad's okay, Ingrid.'

Ingrid smiles widely at me. 'That sounds perfect.'

**

The rest of the day creeps by, and I find myself clock-watching, waiting for a reasonable time to slink off upstairs to bed. It's excruciating. I can't stop thinking about what I overheard. Is it jealousy? The fact I'm there for Peggy when she can't be, or won't be? Or has Ingrid recognised me from the newspaper? Surely not. After a couple of hours, I can bear it no longer, and I escape on a long walk, looping around the village twice and then ending up on the pebble beach with the wind in my hair. For the second time since I moved in with Peggy, I feel simmering fear creeping back into my blood.

Something tells me that Ingrid is bad news.

**

I open the door and a wave of relief washes over me when I see Hazel standing there. I grab her hand and pull her into the house. 'Thank God you're here.'

She shrugs off her jacket. 'Tense?'

'I'm convinced she absolutely hates me,' I whisper, my voice laced with misery. Things have got worse since yesterday.

Hazel pulls a face.

'That's a pretty good impression of her.' I laugh, but stop when I see Ingrid standing in the doorway.

'Of who?'

Hazel doesn't miss a beat. 'My mam,' she says.

Ingrid lets out a little chuckle before sweeping forward and gripping her hand. 'I'm Ingrid. Lovely to meet you.'

'And you.' Hazel smiles sweetly and holds Ingrid's hand with both of hers.

'Hello, love.' Peggy shuffles into the hallway, which is far too cramped to hold this many people, and gathers Hazel into a hug.

'You've got a lovely cottage.' Hazel untangles herself from Peggy's arms. 'Look at your photographs!'

I leave Peggy to talk Hazel through each of her family photographs whilst I crouch in front of the oven to check on the potatoes. They're pale yellow, sizzling in a shallow pool of glistening goose fat. My mouth waters in anticipation of the fluffy insides, the golden crunch. Always worth the wait.

'Why are you *really* here, Kate?'

I straighten up and turn to see Ingrid standing behind me, her expression unreadable. 'Excuse me?'

'Where did you come from?' She keeps her voice low, not wanting to be overheard. 'Why are you preying on Nanna?'

Anger simmers away in my stomach. 'I work for your grandmother, Ingrid. And we're friends. She wants me here.' I turn away from her, and fill a saucepan with water, ready for the broccoli and carrots.

'She doesn't see it, but I know you're taking advantage.'

I close my eyes in exasperation but stay facing the wall. 'What exactly *is* your problem with me, Ingrid?'

'She could've got someone from an agency. Someone vetted and checked. You could be anyone. You could prey on *anyone*, but you pick a defenceless old woman with MS.'

'I am not preying on Peggy.' I pick up a carrot and run a peeler down the side of it, trying to stop my hands from shaking. 'Can we just get on? Please? Peggy wanted us all here for a nice Sunday lunch. She's happy we're all here; you should be too.' I turn to Ingrid. 'It's not like she gets to see you much.' I can't help myself, and I twist the knife a little deeper. 'Is that what this is? Jealousy?'

Her face goes a shade redder as she storms out of the kitchen. I shake my head slowly. She's due to go home tomorrow, and I can't wait to see the back of her.

Chapter 47

It's late before I realise I'm the last one in the office. When did everyone leave? I seriously need to keep an eye on the clock. I yawn as I toss my phone and I.D. into my bag and sling my jacket over my forearm. I'm having an internal debate about what takeaway to order when Tiana bursts through the door I'm about to walk through.

'Tiana?' I've never seen her look so angry.

'Sorry, Eve.' She turns to leave, and I grab her gently by the arm.

'Tiana, what's wrong?'

'It's nothing.'

'Well it obviously isn't. Why are you here so late?'

She looks pointedly at me.

'I got carried away. Again. But there's no need for you to still be here.'

'Honestly. Don't worry about me. I'm going home.'

'Tiana. Talk to me.'

She turns around. 'Why? Why should I talk to you? You don't care. You're only pretending to care.'

'Hey,' I say indignantly. 'I do care. I'm sorry if I'm a bit . . . harsh on you sometimes. I don't mean to be. But I do care. Listen . . .' I hesitate. 'I'm not doing anything tonight. D'you want to come over? You don't have to talk about it, but if you could use the company, I'm getting a takeaway and you're more than welcome.'

Tiana eyes me suspiciously. 'Thanks, but . . . I'll be fine.'

'Sure. No problem.' I let my arms drop helplessly at my sides, the sting of rejection burning in my cheeks. No wonder she doesn't want to confide in me. I haven't exactly been nice to her. 'I'll see you tomorrow then?'

She nods and turns to walk away. I hurry in the opposite direction, down the stairs and into the darkness of the car park.

'Eve, wait!'

I whip around to see Tiana standing at the door I've just walked through.

'Is your offer still open?'

I smile. 'Sure.'

***

Within an hour we're planted on my sofa with plates full of Chinese takeaway on our laps.

'I find it hard to talk about personal stuff with work people, you know?' Tiana picks up a spring roll and nibbles at it without dipping it in the sauce first. I wrinkle my nose.

'I know what you mean.'

'No, you don't.' She puts down the dry spring roll. 'You, Jason and Bella – you're like . . . I don't know. Harry, Ron and Hermione. The Three Musketeers. No room for anyone else. You talk about *everything*.'

I laugh at the comparisons. 'Oh, believe me we don't. Not Jason, anyway. He's a closed book. And quite frankly, there's plenty in my life I'd rather he didn't know about, thank you very much.'

'Hmm.' She pops the rest of the spring roll in her mouth.

I frown. 'You don't dip.'

'What?'

'The spring roll. You don't dip it.'

'Oh. I don't like dipping stuff.'

'That's weird.'

'Is it?' She reaches for another.

'Kind of.'

'Not as weird as Bella's relationship with Jason.'

What does she know? What don't *I* know? She must be more observant than I give her credit for. I roll my eyes, not wanting to gossip. 'They're just mates.' Even though I'm not entirely sure that's true.

'Uh-huh.'

'Anyway, more importantly, what's going on with you? You don't have to tell me, but . . . you might feel better if you do.'

'It's Ben.' She self-consciously smooths her hair away from her face.

I look blankly at her.

'Ben. My fiancé.'

I should know that. 'Right. Of course. Ben. What about him?'

'He's backed out of the wedding. I think he's going to leave me.'

'Shit. Really? When is your wedding?'

'In two months.'

I really need to listen to her when she talks. 'Oh, Tiana. I'm sorry. Did he say why?'

'Just that he couldn't go through with it. I mean, I guess I should be grateful it's happening now and not on the day. But we've been together since school. I don't know anything else.' Her voice breaks.

'Tiana . . . that's shit. I'm so sorry.'

'It's fine. I found out a few days ago . . . and I had a bit of a wobble today, that's all. I'd just been on the phone to the venue to try and negotiate some money back. I'm sure you can guess how well that went. God.' She scrapes her fingers through her hair, then looks up at me. 'Do you have any alcohol in?'

'Ah, no. I don't drink. Sorry.'

She laughs. 'It's probably for the best.' She sinks back into the sofa and closes her eyes.

'You can crash here tonight,' I offer. 'You look pretty comfortable.'

'Thanks, Eve.' She opened her eyes and regards me warily. 'Sorry if I was a bit rude to you before. I'm not used to you being so . . .'

'Nice to you?' I offer.

'Yeah.' She laughs. 'That.'

'I'll work on it. Did you want to borrow anything? You can bung your clothes in the washing machine and I can get them dry by tomorrow.'

'That'd be great. Thanks.'

I heave myself off the sofa and head towards the bedroom, to dig out some pyjamas, or something that doesn't look old and grotty that I don't mind anyone else seeing. I'm sifting through piles of clothes, making a mental note to myself to buy new ones, when my phone buzzes in my pocket. It's the office number. I'd asked for any calls regarding the Lisette Dupont case to come straight through to me, day or night, on shift or off. Heart thumping, I wedge it between my ear and shoulder. 'Hello?'

'I've got a call for you from a Miss Ingrid Colton in response to the Lisette Dupont case. Shall I put her through?'

I frown. We've not had any calls through for this case in ages, and we're mere days away from Gillian handing it over as a cold case. My skin tingles in anticipation. 'Put her through please.'

I hear a woman's voice, laced with a strong Scottish accent, before I have the chance to speak.

'Detective Constable Eve Starling?'

'Speaking. How may I help?' I sit down on the bed and scrabble in my bedside table for a notebook and pen.

'Are you still looking for Anya Fernsby?'

A sudden rush of adrenaline floods my body. 'We are. What do you know?'

'I think I know where she is. Actually, I'm convinced

I know where she is.' A pause. 'She's living with my grandmother in Plockton. It's in Scotland.'

I sit up straighter, recognising Plockton as one of the stops on the Kyle line. 'Are you absolutely sure of this?'

'Aye. I found out a little while back that a homeless woman named Kate moved in with my grandmother, Peggy Colton, as a cleaner or something like that. I told Nanna she was being silly, and that she should've used an agency. I'd have paid. Honestly, I don't know what she was thinking. But she ignored my advice, so I went to see who this Kate person was. The minute I met her I knew I didn't like her. She seemed odd, and I didn't understand why she was living in my grandmother's house as a cleaner, or carer, or whatever she thinks she is. I'm not an idiot. I . . .' She paused, suddenly unsure of herself.

'What is it?'

'I looked in this woman's bag.' She has the decency to sound guilty. 'She's not who she says she is.'

I suspect what's coming, but I ask anyway: 'And what did you find, Ingrid?'

'Her debit card, her driving licence . . . it's all under the name Anya Fernsby. I googled her. I know *exactly* who she is.'

My pulse gallops. 'Does she know you've taken her I.D.?'

'Possibly. I took it an hour ago. She might not have realised yet. You've got to hurry.'

I stand up, thoughts ricocheting around my brain. 'And you have an address?'

'I do.'

***

I walk back into the living room after the phone call, feeling a smile spread slowly across my face as I lock eyes with Tiana. 'I believe we've found our woman.'

Chapter 48

Anya – Then

I'm out alone when I first have the feeling that I'm being watched. I'm in Tesco, trying to decide between what feels like a hundred different types of pasta, when I see a movement out of the corner of my eye. I glance behind me, but the aisle is completely empty. I can hear the rumble of a trolley as it rolls over the tiles a few aisles away, and the distant sound of a crying baby, but I've come at a quiet time of day. There aren't many people about. I decide on a bag of wholemeal fusilli and toss it into my basket before approaching the end of the aisle. I hover by the rice, listening out for footsteps close by, before stepping cautiously into the central aisle. My heart leaps but there's no one there. I sigh in relief and make my way to the back of the store where the coffee and breakfast cereals are kept.

I feel exposed with my back to the rest of the shop and I make a mental note to come back when it's busier. And then I hear it: two slow, deliberate footsteps that make my skin prickle. I whip around, expecting to see Ruben walking towards me, eyes flashing, ready to make a scene. But there's no one there. Are the noises in my head? I grab a box of Weetabix and hurry towards the safety of the checkout, hearing nothing but my own ragged breath and the blood pounding in my ears. The footsteps behind me start up again, this time faster, matching my own pace. What if it's not him? What if I've got a stalker? My mind explodes into a million possibilities, each ten times worse than the last.

I break into a run, the basket banging painfully against my leg, and the footsteps speed up. In a blind panic I change direction, attempting to dart down a different aisle to escape whoever is pursuing me, when I feel the blunt pain of running at full force into a solid object. I drop the basket, the contents skittering across the floor with a loud clatter, and I look up, dizzy with fear. I hadn't run into an object. I'd run into a heavyset man, who's currently reaching out two hands to steady me as I sway on the spot.

'Whoa, you all right?' He looks at me with kind eyes.

'I'm sorry,' I stutter, glancing around at the chaos. Six cracked eggs are oozing a gloopy, slimy mess into the tile grout and mixing with the milk that's rushing out of a split in the side of the carton. I feel a tap on my shoulder and a scream escapes my lips.

'Excuse me miss,' says a quiet voice from behind me. 'You dropped your purse.'

***

My face is still flushed with humiliation when I leave the supermarket with only half the items on my shopping list. I know the line between paranoia and reality is blurring, but it doesn't stop me quickening my pace on the way back to the car park. This happens each time I'm out alone. Those little movements just out of my line of vision. The footsteps behind me, matching my pace, close enough to make me feel uncomfortable but far away enough to make it hard to figure out exactly who it is.

Get a grip, I berate myself through gritted teeth as I frantically lock myself in the car, chest heaving in a ridiculous panic. It's probably nothing.

***

'Hey,' Lisette calls from the kitchen as I let myself in through the front door and cross the living room to meet her. I kiss her deeply, and wrap my free arm around her, breathing in her delicious scent.

'Are you okay?' She frowns, pulling back to look at me.

I nod. 'Just knackered.'

She brushes a strand of hair away from my face and tucks it behind my ear, her dark brown eyes full of concern. 'I am worried about you.'

'I'll be okay. I'm so happy to see you. How's Sylvie?'

Lisette smiles fondly, in that way she always does when she thinks of her daughter. 'She got back from Maman's an hour ago. She is in the garden, talking to her aliens.'

I laugh. Sylvie and her little plastic aliens that she loves so much. No other toy is as important.

As if on cue, Sylvie comes bounding in from the garden, her face lighting up when she sees me.

'Annie!' She wraps her arms around my waist and I squeeze her. She's probably the only person who can get away with calling me Annie.

'Hey, you.' I tap my finger lightly on her nose and she giggles. 'How are those aliens getting on?'

'Lulu and Mimi have just landed on Earth,' she says in that singsong way of hers, counting on her fingers. 'But Fifi decided to stay on Mars.'

'Ooh.' I stroke her cheek. 'I do hope Fifi comes to visit us soon.'

Sylvie laughs and then stops as if something has occurred to her. She turns to Lisette. 'Maman, have you seen Jojo?'

I freeze and Lisette frowns. 'Jojo?'

'The alien. I had four. Now I have three. Where's Jojo?'

Lisette looks at me and I shrug. 'I've not seen her, sweetheart. Maman and I will have a look, okay?'

Satisfied, Sylvie skips back into the garden, singing something incomprehensible.

I watch her closely from the kitchen window.

Chapter 49

Kate – Now

'Shall I pop the kettle on?' I call from the kitchen as I dry my hands on a tea towel. I feel so much calmer since Ingrid left. Peggy replies from the lounge that she could definitely do with another brew. I hum along to the radio as I potter around the kitchen, neatening up Peggy's odds and ends on the side, while I wait for the kettle to boil. Everything's looking so beautiful now autumn is settling in, and I'm bursting with ideas for the garden. I'll start by cutting back the climbing rose that is currently laying claim to the front of the house, so it no longer snags our clothes on the way in. I'm desperate to pull up all the weeds that punctuate the lawn and borders, and to see what space I've got to work with.

Images of blooming flowers dance in my head . . . I'll plant bulbs along the back fence – daffodils, tulips and lilies – they'll look beautiful once spring rolls around again. I smile, all thoughts of the newspaper article shoved to the back of my mind. I really can't believe I've managed to find such a wonderful place, with such brilliant people to settle with. Maybe things'll be okay, if I lie low.

As I place the tea cosy over the teapot, I hear the distinctive sound of footsteps crunching on the gravel outside, getting closer and closer. They stop. I see two shadows through the frosted glass. Then I hear the slow, deliberate sound of the knocker.

One, two, three.

Something in the way they walk, the darkness of their clothes, doesn't sit right with me. Call it intuition, call it paranoia, but something makes my throat dry up.

I take a deep breath and open the door.

Two young male police officers stand on the path outside, observing me cautiously, as if I'm a tiger ready to pounce. I can't be further from that. I feel like a mouse cornered by two wild cats. Nowhere to run. Nowhere to hide.

The taller one steps forward. 'Anya Fernsby?'

I manage a nod.

'I'm arresting you on suspicion of the murders of Lisette and Sylvie Dupont. You do not have to say anything. But it may harm your defence if you do not mention when questioned something which you later rely on in court. Anything you do say may be given in evidence.' I feel the cold, hard metal of the handcuffs knocking uncomfortably against my wrist bones. I don't fight. It's too late.

'Kate, what's happening?' I hear the tapping of Peggy's walking stick as she hobbles into the hall behind me.

'I'm being arrested,' I say quietly.

'Why?' I can see the betrayal in her expression and my face crumples in shame.

The other officer speaks. 'Anya is being arrested on suspicion of murder.'

'Murder? But her name's Kate. She's not Anya. You've got the wrong person,' pleads Peggy. 'She's Kate!'

'We'll update you in due course, madam,' he replies.

They lead me out of the cottage, through the garden and to a waiting police car. I avoid looking at the neighbours' curtains twitching as my head is firmly pushed down into the car.

I sit in silence as I'm driven to the nearest police station in Kyle of Lochalsh. Fifteen minutes later, I climb out of the car, shivering in the cold. My jacket's still at home. A home that's no longer mine, and a home I doubt I'll ever set foot in again. They steer me into the entrance of the police station, which opens out into a cramped waiting area. I'm then guided into a side room where I'm told to wait, as I'm to be processed shortly. The heavy metal door is closed and bolted, and I stand in silence, alone with my thoughts, four grey walls and little else. I suppose I've always known this day would come, but I'd never have been prepared for it.

Minutes pass, feeling like hours, and eventually, an officer unlocks the door and enters the cold, characterless room. 'Hello, Anya.' He closes the door behind him and gives me a curt nod.

'Hi.' My voice comes out in a hoarse whisper.

He passes me a bottle of hand sanitiser. 'Please wash your hands.'

I do as he asks, feeling the sting of alcohol on my skin, dry from constantly being submerged in cleaning products. He inspects both of my hands, and then, appearing satisfied, manoeuvres me towards a small machine with a glass plate at the front.

'I'm going to take your fingerprints first.' He takes my right hand, pressing each finger in turn on the glass plate, until the machine beeps. He repeats the process on my left hand. 'Thank you. I need to take some details from you before I book you into custody.' He motions to a table with two chairs either side of it, and I sit down opposite him. 'Please could you tell me your full name?'

I hesitate; it's been so long since I've spoken those words. 'Anya Fernsby.' I'm also asked to confirm my address, date and place of birth and my nationality. It all feels so formal, so cold. But I suppose I'm being treated like a criminal, because that's what he thinks I am. No, not what he *thinks* I am. It *is* what I am.

'Thank you.' He places the form into a plastic wallet and seals it. 'I'll take you through to the custody cell now. Is there anyone you'd like to call?'

My mind flies straight to Orla, but I can't let her find out I'm alive this way. So I shake my head. There's no one. Absolutely no one.

'Very well. Do you have a solicitor you'd like to get in touch with, or would you like a duty solicitor?'

'A duty solicitor please.' My voice is barely audible.

The officer nods once, before unlocking the door and leading me through the waiting area, down a cold corridor and into a holding cell – a small white and grey square with a bed and a metal toilet. My blood feels like ice as the door clunks shut behind me, and the reality of everything sinks in.

The only other person who knows the truth is the same person who's prepared to do everything in their power to conceal it.

Chapter 50

Eve – Now

Anya sits alone in the interview room after being brought back to Brighton a day after her arrest, staring with blank eyes at the plastic cup of water in front of her. She's quiet, one hand twisting a short lock of hair around her finger and pulling, over and over again, enough to lift the skin from her scalp. She looks so different to the pictures I've seen of her. The long, brown hair has been replaced with a deep red pixie cut. Her bohemian style had changed too; instead of the gypsy skirt and sandals she was so often photographed in, she's dressed in harsh black, her arms wrapped around her as if she's cold. When we enter the room, her eyes slide up to meet ours, and her hands drop into her lap. I notice her tattoo has been covered up with another one. She looks completely and utterly terrified.

'Hello, Anya.' I lower myself into the chair opposite her, and give her a smile. Her solicitor takes the seat next to her and Bella sinks into the one beside me. After our conversation about career progression, she's decided to work on her interview skills. I feel a stab of guilt for not bringing Tiana in on this interview, but it's too big a deal to let the office newbie loose in the interview room.

I feel a flutter of anxiety when I remember that Gillian, Jason and Tiana are watching from the next room, scrutinising every second of the interview. *This is it*. This is my moment.

I clear my throat and begin the spiel. I've said it so many times before, it's become second nature to me. 'This interview is being recorded and may be given in evidence if your case is brought to trial. My name is DC Eve Starling. The other detective present is DC Bella Cortez. Please state your full name and date of birth.'

Her voice is so quiet it's hardly decipherable as she mumbles her response.

'Thank you.' I keep my voice gentle, soothing. I need her to feel calm, believe that it's safe to talk. 'Also present is Rohan Dhillon, Anya's solicitor. Anya, do you agree that there are no other persons present?'

'Yes.' Her eyes are fixed on the table in front of her.

Bella leans forward and rests her elbows on the table and reads the caution. 'Do you understand?' she finishes.

Anya nods once and whispers, 'Yes.'

'And do you understand why you're being interviewed today?' Bella's usually confident voice is diminished somewhat, and I want to give her an encouraging smile but I can't.

Anya says nothing.

I fix her with an intense gaze. 'Miss Lisette Dupont and her daughter Sylvie died from smoke inhalation on—'

'Smoke inhalation?' Anya interrupts, her eyes widening.

'Yes,' I say, gently. 'They died from smoke inhalation, caused by a house fire that was set deliberately.'

'But . . . I . . . are you sure that's how they died?' Anya's eyes flit between me and Bella.

'Is there something you'd like to talk to us about, Anya?' I ask.

'No, I . . .' Her shoulders sag and her eyes shine with tears. She looks up and opens her mouth to speak, but then closes it again.

'Why does the cause of their death surprise you?' I give her some time to speak but she says nothing. I make a note of her odd reaction. How else does she think Lisette and Sylvie died? What does she know, or think she knows?

Bella glances at me and I give her a nod. She clears her throat. 'Can you please start by telling us about your relationship with Lisette?'

Anya trembles. 'She was my partner. We'd been together five months.'

'Did you get on well?' Bella asks.

'Really well.' Her voice cracks. 'I loved her *so* much.'

Bella nods. 'And you got on well with her daughter, Sylvie, too?'

Anya's eyes brim with tears. 'Yes. Yes, I loved her as if she were my own.'

'And how about Sylvie's father? Mark Maynard. What

was your relationship with him?' I think back to my theory that they'd been working together.

Anya wipes her eyes. 'Mark? I've never met him. Lisette thought it'd be best if we didn't meet. I was happy with that.'

'So, you never spoke to him when he picked Sylvie up?' I ask. 'Dropped her off?'

She shakes her head, confusion clouding her face. 'I . . . no. I couldn't even tell you what he looks like. Lisette always arranged things so that we wouldn't see each other.'

I watch her closely, searching her face for a hint that she's lying, but I don't see it.

'Can you tell us where you were between 11 p.m. on Sunday the 28th of June and 2 a.m. on Monday the 29th of June?' asks Bella. 'The time of the fire at 11 Buchanan Drive?'

She squeezes her eyes shut, as if she wants to pretend we're not there, that she's not in a police interview room discussing the murder of her girlfriend and stepdaughter, that everything in her world is safe.

'Anya?' Bella urges her.

She shakes her head and tries to speak but no words come out.

'Give her a minute, please.' Rohan's dark eyes slide from his client and then back to us.

Anya takes a few deep breaths, digs her hand into the tissue box that sits before her, and twists a tissue in her hands. 'I'd received this text from my ex.'

Chapter 51

Anya – Then

Can I see you?

I stare at the message from Matthew, rereading it over and over again. *Can I see you?* Why? What could we possibly have to say to each other after so long? I've not heard from him since I left.

What for? I eventually type back.

I just want to speak to you. I hate that we parted on such bad terms and I want to make amends. Apologise for the way I behaved, you know?

I stare at the screen. Why does he even care?

Why? I type back.

After a minute, the next message appears. *I feel guilty and I need closure. Don't you want it too?*

I'm not sure that I do, I respond.

Come on, An. I'm desperate here.

A pause.

I'm at Seaford Head.

Dizziness collides with me like a fist. Why is he at Seaford Head, of all places?

Matt, what are you saying?

Another pause. This time, too long. Then, eventually: *I can't bear it anymore. If I can't resolve things with you, I don't think I can take it anymore.*

I type fast. *Don't do anything stupid. Please. I'm literally begging you.*

I peer at the phone screen, trembling, waiting for a response. But there's nothing. Images of him stepping off the cliff edge blur with the flashbacks of Poppy that are never far from my mind. I have no choice but to drop everything and find him.

***

I pull into South Hill Barn Car Park, the closest place to park near the cliff's edge. My eyes sweep the car park, and there's just one car, black and glossy, parked in a shadowy corner. I don't recognise it. My eyes drift in the direction of the cliff top and I sweep my gaze from side to side, looking for him, hoping I'm not too late. I hurry across the grass, knowing that I owe Matthew nothing but at the same time, unable to bear the thought of him ending his life because of me.

As I stumble across the uneven terrain, my mind drifts to Lisette, how I wish I was in our front room, laughing over a bottle of wine, with absolutely nothing on my mind except for her. Lisette thinks I'm visiting Orla, but here I am, walking towards God knows what. Despite the gentle summer warmth, a chill settles within me. I hug my jacket close, my stomach churning at the thought of seeing Matthew again.

Then I see him. A figure, standing facing the glittering ocean, hair illuminated by the moonlight. There's no questioning it; I know that frame, that posture, inside and out. It's Matthew. Relief surges through me.

'Matt?'

He doesn't turn. Doesn't say a word.

'Matthew,' I say, my voice a little louder. I'm standing a few feet away, suddenly apprehensive.

'I knew you'd come.'

His voice, calm and quiet, breaks through the silence and I take a deep breath. 'Of course I came. I'm worried about you. Will you step back a bit? Please?'

'You're worried about me, are you?'

'Of course,' I say again.

He turns to face me and lets out a bitter laugh. 'You just don't want any more guilt on your shoulders.'

My stomach drops. 'What . . . what do you mean?'

His face is pale in the moonlight, with shadows under his dark eyes. 'I know you've been here before.'

'You brought me here, Matt,' I say, but part of me knew from the second I read that text message that he's here for another reason too. But *what* does he know? And how?

'Before that,' he continues. 'You've been here before that. To this exact spot, actually.'

I gaze around. He's right. It's the exact same spot.

I let out a yelp as something solid hits the back of my head. Before I can figure out what's going on, I'm being shoved face-first into the dewy grass and dragged across the ground, which suddenly gives way so all I can see is darkness. No, not darkness. *Water.* My head is over the edge of the cliff, my torso still on solid ground. My body goes into panic mode and I try to flip myself over like a fish on land, but the pressure of a hand in the middle of my back renders my attempt futile.

'Enough,' says Matthew.

'What's going on?' I stop thrashing about and try to focus on keeping my breathing calm, as I stare into the abyss of water below.

He doesn't answer. I can feel his hot breath panting on my neck.

'Matt. Answer me. *Please.*' Nothing. I've got to try and get him talking. 'I'm sorry about what happened, Matt. I really am. If I could go back and change things—'

'You'd do what, An?' He digs his fingers into my shoulders.

I'd never have gone near you, I say silently.

'I wouldn't have strung you along.' I think fast. I need to lie. 'I'd have been honest with you from the start. I messed up, Matt.'

'There's nothing I could've done to make you honest, Anya.'

'What? What does that mean?' I try to keep my voice level, but panic is rising and I'm quickly losing control.

280

He slams his hands on my back. 'I tried to get you to talk, to open up about her. About what really happened here that night. But you're fucking stubborn.'

My body feels like it's been flooded with ice water. It makes sense, why he asked so many questions, why he got me drunk and took me to Seaford Head to look out over the cliffs. I felt so ill that night. Did he drug me? I realise *he* must have left the dead poppies to scare me . . . but how does Matthew know about Poppy? And why does he *care*?

'Do you remember when I told you about the baby?'

'Yes,' I whisper, remembering what he said all those months ago . . . *I got a girl pregnant. We were . . . far too young. The baby died.*

The baby died because the mother died, a voice inside my head says to me. *And the mother died because of you.*

'You were Poppy's boyfriend. The older guy.' Terror bleeds into every part of me. 'She was . . . *pregnant*? She was only fifteen.'

The absence of his words confirms I'm right.

'It was an accident,' I insist. 'I tried to help her. I swear.'

'That's not what your cousin thinks.'

'My cousin? You spoke to Ruben?'

'I got him to talk, yes.'

Panic rises. 'It was an *accident*. What did you do to him to make him say otherwise?'

Matthew says nothing.

'Are you going to kill me?' I whisper.

After what seems like an age, he speaks. 'No. But I am going to make you pay.'

281

Another blow to the head renders me half conscious and I'm vaguely aware of being dragged away from the edge of the cliff. A strange blend of relief and fear ebbs through me until everything goes dark and silent.

***

What feels like seconds later, a vibrating sensation pulls me back to a state of awareness. My head is spinning and it takes me a few moments to realise I'm in the back of a car, my ankles and wrists restrained.

'Where are we? What are you going to do to me now?' I feel a tidal wave of panic rising in my chest.

Matthew's voice is dangerously quiet. 'I'm not going to do anything to you.'

I manage to heave myself into a sitting position and squint out of the window, realising with a flash of panic where we are. Opposite Lisette's house.

I swallow, my throat dry and sticky. 'How do you know where they live?'

Matthew gets out of the car, and for a split second I think he's going to let me out. But then I hear the locks go down and I watch him approach the house, carrying something. A clear plastic bottle. I twist myself into an unnatural position to allow my hands to scrabble for the handle, the lock, anything. Nothing works. The child lock is on. A scream rips through me as I watch Matthew unlock the front door with my keys and let himself into the house. I scream even louder, desperately hoping the sound will be enough to wake someone. But no curtains jerk open, no wide-eyed faces appear. Everyone's windows are tightly shut against the midnight chill. I feel like I'm waiting forever.

My attention flips back to the house as Matthew appears, closing the door behind him. What has he done? I don't understand. I stare at him as he walks back to the car and climbs back into the driver's seat.

'Matt, what's going on? Please tell me.' I inch forward in my seat, so my face is closer to him. 'Please.'

He continues to ignore me, his attention fixed on the house. I stare at it too, wondering what he's waiting for, and what's going to happen. I'm still wriggling my hands to try and loosen the cable tie, feeling my skin going red raw underneath the thin plastic.

And then I see it. A faint orange glow in the upstairs window. Lisette's room.

Fire.

'Matt!' I scream. 'What have you done?' I thrash my body wildly, panic surging through me and taking over what little control I have left. 'Let me out! Please, Matt, I need to get them out!'

'They're already dead, An. This is purely to cover my tracks. I paid them a little visit earlier. Just your friendly local fireman popping in to check the smoke alarms.'

A howl like a wounded animal lacerates through my throat as the words sink in. 'You wouldn't.' My voice is reduced to a whisper, my face soaked in tears. 'You wouldn't.'

The fight evaporates from my body instantly because I know, deep down, he would. All I want to do is tear my eyes away from the house, to cease this pain, but I can't stop watching. Desperately hoping it was a lie, and the door will burst open and Lisette will race into the street, Sylvie a living, breathing bundle in her arms. Every second that passes, more hope evaporates.

'You're sick,' I spit at him, fresh floods of tears spilling from my eyes. '*Sick*.'

Panic and fear rise in my chest at the thought of them both in that house. But he starts the engine and pulls away.

'No!' I scream, pressing myself against the window. 'Please, Matt. Please, I'll do anything. *Anything*. Don't leave them.' A hopeless sob forces its way out of me, and my entire body shudders with the strength of it. 'Why them, Matt?' I sob. 'What did they do to deserve this?'

He shrugs. 'They didn't. But you know what? I realised a few years ago that if you want to hurt someone, to *really* hurt them, then you hurt the ones they love. You killed my unborn baby, my girlfriend. The love of my life. Why would I not do the same to you?'

'It was an accident,' I sob helplessly. 'An *accident*. She fell.'

A few minutes later the car slows to a stop. The door opens behind me and Matthew's hand flies to my mouth before I have a chance to scream. He shoves me onto my front, and I feel the cold, hard metallic edge of a blade pressing against my wrist. My heart hammers in my chest but I feel only the release of the bindings. The pressure of his body on top of mine, his hot breath on my neck as he whispers into my ear.

'You're going down for this, Anya. I've planted evidence. I dropped your keys in the house. They'll trace the fingerprints on the white spirit bottle back to you. It's the one you used when you were helping me paint the boat. They'll think you splashed white spirit all over the washing basket outside Lisette's room and set fire to it. You're backed into a corner.'

'I didn't—' I try to speak but he shoves my face into the seat.

'I'm leaving.' He presses a hand into the back of my head. 'You will never see me again. You will never be able to find me again. You are completely alone, Anya. And now you know what it feels like.'

He drags me from the car and discards me onto the ground, then takes the car and disappears into the night.

I sit bolt upright, glancing around me. I'm down some sort of side road, with nothing but overflowing commercial waste bins and the distinctive, greasy aroma of a fish and chip shop. I scramble out into the street, and it doesn't take long to realise where I am. I can see the smoke rising over the rooftops, the sound of my harsh, ragged breathing blending into the background of my fear. I'm at Lisette's house in less than two minutes but I stop dead when I see how much the fire has taken over. *They're already dead, An.* Grief rips through me as I stand in the front garden, watching. There's nothing I can do.

I'm too late.

Sirens wail in the distance and panic rises within me. I turn around and reach for the gate, and lock eyes with a man across the road.

I've been seen.

I don't know what else to do.

I run.

Chapter 52

Eve – Now

I sit back in my seat, trying to absorb everything Anya has told us so far. It's like the floodgates have opened and she's telling us *everything* . . . or almost everything. There were a few times during her story where she paused, faltered, as if she was deliberating whether to leave elements of the story out. But is it the truth, or one huge, elaborate lie?

Even Anya looks taken aback at everything she's told us. Her eyes have lost focus and she's staring at the wall behind our heads. 'He told me he'd killed Lisette and Sylvie earlier that day, and set the fire to cover his tracks and make it look like it was me. But you said – you said they died from smoke inhalation. He *lied*. Oh my God. Oh my *God*.' She reaches a trembling hand for her cup and takes a sip, splashing most of it down her front.

'We're going to need to speak with Matthew Taylor quite urgently. Can you give us his contact details?'

'I don't remember his number because I got rid of my phone, but I can tell you where his boat was. He won't be there now, though.' She rattles off a location in the marina, her voice quivering. 'He worked at the fire station. But he said he was leaving Brighton. That I'd never see him again.'

'We'll do our best to find him,' I promise. 'Please excuse us for a moment.'

The door closes behind us, and Bella widens her eyes at me. 'Holy *shit*.'

Gillian, Jason and Tiana emerge from the next door along the corridor.

'That was quite a tale.' Gillian folds her arms across her chest. 'Thoughts?'

'It's so detailed,' I say. 'She knows exactly how the fire was set, down to the white spirit, the dropped keys, the washing basket. But it all seems so far-fetched.'

'She's had plenty of time to come up with a story.' Jason frowns. 'And it's all very convenient. Planted evidence? A missing ex?'

'It does sound a bit like a TV drama,' admits Tiana.

'The first thing we need to do is find out if this Matthew Taylor person really exists,' says Gillian. 'Eve, work with Anya to get an E-FIT pulled together. See if he matches any known suspects. Bella, speak to Poppy Fallon's parents, find out if they knew anything about this older boyfriend. Jason, can you get on the phone to the fire station to see if he ever worked there, and the marina to see if they have any records of him renting or parking a boat there?'

'Berthing,' Jason corrects her.

'What?' Gillian shoots him a look of utter annoyance.

'You don't park a boat, you berth it.' He takes in Gillian's irritated expression. 'I'll call them now.'

***

Bella and I enter the interview room for the second time, and sit down in front of a drained-looking Anya. We'd extended her custody period by twenty-four hours to try and find Matthew Taylor, but there was no trace of him anywhere. The E-FIT presented us with an artist's depiction of Matthew Taylor, a broad-shouldered, dark-haired man with deep brown eyes framed with thick-rimmed glasses. It didn't help in the slightest. Poppy's parents had no clue about any older boyfriend their daughter might've had. Jason got confirmation that no one under the name Matthew Taylor had ever worked at Preston Circus Fire Station, nor had he ever berthed a boat at Brighton Marina, and no firefighters had recently relocated.

The marina location Anya had given us had been used during that time period by a man called Robbie Griffiths who, when phoned, confirmed he'd never heard of Matthew Taylor or Anya Fernsby, and had never rented his boat out to anyone. Jason had even gone down to the marina to ask around, but no one had seen or heard of either of them. Given that the details Anya had managed to scrape together for him were minimal at best, I don't believe the bloke even exists, but of course, we did our due diligence.

'We can't find Matthew,' Bella informs her. 'There's no evidence to suggest he ever existed.'

Her eyes widen. 'What? What do you mean?'

'You have no number for him,' I begin. 'The staff at Preston Circus Fire Station have never heard of him. We can't trace him on social media. The marina location you gave us, well, someone else's boat was berthed there at the time. It wasn't Matthew Taylor, and they'd never rented out their boat to anyone. And the boat you described? Medium-sized, white with a navy-blue trim? That could describe roughly fifty different boats in the marina.'

'What does this mean?' Her eyes shine, threatening to spill over.

'Is Matthew a real person?' I ask, my voice brisk.

'Of course he is!'

'Have you got any further information about him?' I urge her. 'Names of family members? A phone number or email address?'

'I've told you everything I know. And I don't remember his number.' She drops her head into her hands. 'Can't you check CCTV at the marina?'

'It's only kept for thirty-one days,' Bella informs her.

'Okay, well what about other places we visited together? I have a list. Restaurants, cafés. You'll find him. I'll *prove* he's real.'

'Anya, months have passed. Cafés and restaurants . . . they don't hold CCTV for that long.'

'But they might,' she pleads.

I shake my head. 'Right now, we want to talk to you about your actions after the fire.'

'My actions?' She gazes back up at us.

I lean forward. 'We'd like you to tell us about your decision to run away to Plockton.'

Her eyes drop to the table. 'I . . . I knew how it looked. He said he planted evidence pointing to me. I'd touched that bottle of white spirit, after I helped him paint the boat. I knew my fingerprints were on it. And when I ran from the house, a neighbour saw me. I thought if I could get away for a few weeks, try and track him down and prove what he did, I could come back to talk to you.'

'But you stayed,' says Bella.

'I couldn't find him.'

'But why fake your death?' I try to make my voice sound as casual as if I was asking her how many sugars she takes in her tea.

Her shoulders droop. 'I . . . wanted to be someone else for a bit. And . . . I thought it would be better if everyone believed I was dead. That no one would come looking for me.'

'But we knew you didn't,' I inform her. 'We figured out how you made it look like you'd jumped.'

She closes her eyes. 'It all went so wrong.'

'And what about the money you withdrew in the months leading up to the fire?' asks Bella.

Anya freezes, a look of terror painted on her face. 'What?'

'You withdrew thousands of pounds at regular intervals over a period of nine months,' Bella supplies. 'Almost five thousand pounds. You emptied your bank account, and then you ran.'

'No. I promise that's not what happened. It's not what it looks like.'

I cock my head to one side, feigning an inquisitive interest. 'What *does* it look like?'

'You think I planned this. I didn't. That was money to help someone who needed it.'

'That's extremely generous, Anya.' I smile. 'You emptied your account completely, just to help someone? Who?'

She pauses, her eyes darting from Bella, to me, to Rohan, to her shoes. 'No . . . no comment.'

'Anya,' says Bella. 'Was it you who set fire to Lisette and Sylvie's house?'

Her eyes drop to the table and a tear splashes onto the smooth surface. 'No.'

'Did you have a fight? Did she say something to upset you? Is that why you wanted to kill her?' I urge her.

'No.'

Bella repeats my question as she leans forward. 'Did you set fire to Lisette and Sylvie's house?'

Anya breaks eye contact and shrinks back in her seat. 'No.'

I pull out my final weapon. I slide the sheet of paper out of my folder and place it on the table in front of me. 'It says here that you're a beneficiary in Lisette's will.'

Anya's eyebrows shoot up. 'What?'

I repeat myself.

'But I'm not,' says Anya, confusion clouding her face.

'You are.' I slide the sheet of paper across the table towards her.

'It must be a mistake. I'm not,' she repeats.

'It's a legal document,' Bella says simply.

'I had no idea.' Her eyes scan over the document. 'If this is true, she never told me.'

***

We have our MMO. Her prints are on the bottle of white spirit that fuelled the fire. She was a beneficiary of Lisette's will. And she was at the scene, by her own admission and that of a neighbour. She knows how the fire was set, down to the last detail. She faked her death and fled the country, after withdrawing her life savings. She conjured up an imaginary person to blame, who no one can prove exists. It all seems so clear cut.

I turn to face her. 'Anya Fernsby, you are charged that on Monday the 29th of June, at Brighton in the county of East Sussex, you did murder Lisette Dupont contrary to common law. You do not have to say anything, but it may harm your defence if you fail to mention now something which you may later rely on in court. Anything you do say may be given in evidence. Do you understand?'

Anya's whole body trembles. 'Yes.'

I move on to the second charge. 'Anya Fernsby, you are charged that on Monday the 29th of June, at Brighton in the county of East Sussex, you did murder Sylvie Dupont contrary to common law. You do not have to say anything, but it may harm your defence if you fail to mention now something which you may later rely on in court. Anything you do say may be given in evidence. Do you understand?'

'Yes.'

Chapter 53

Eve – Then

I try to link Frankie's arm as we stroll to the supermarket, but she shakes me off. She's angry with me. I try to make conversation with her, but she's stubborn. I suspect she's upset because she knows I'm going back to university soon. I give her some time.

When we arrive, I use what little scraps I've got left from my student loan to get enough food to fill the cupboards for at least a month. Tins of fruit and veg, boxes of cereal, long-life milk, bread, frozen chicken, orange juice. Anything cheap that lasts, or can be stored in the freezer. Plus the multi-pack of Dairy Milk bars I caught Frankie eyeing up. She can hide those under her bed. I admit that it's a peace offering, and I receive the tiniest of smiles in return.

We push our trolley with the wonky wheel over to the clothes section and she wanders around in a dreamlike state, delicately stroking all the fabric, delighting in the feel of the soft cottons and the glittering sequins that embellish the skirts and tops. Her eyes widen when I tell her she can choose some new clothes and shoes that fit her properly, but she quickly pretends she's not interested. Instead, I pick out a few things for her, while she sullenly watches me. Good thing I have my emergency credit card. I notice the supermarket is selling school uniform, so I pick out a couple of pairs of charcoal-grey trousers, white polo shirts, bottle-green cardigans and a pair of neat black shoes in the right size.

On the way back we stop at the little park where I used to escape. I don't feel ready to walk back into the house, and Frankie seems to walk slower and slower the closer we get to the house.

'Want to sit in the park for a bit?' I keep my voice tentative.

She slides her sharp little eyes to me, and then her shoulders soften. 'Yes.'

We cross the road to the park, flop onto the grass and lie side by side, staring up at the clouds without saying much at all.

After ten minutes or so, Frankie lets out a deep sigh. 'How long 'til you go back to uni?'

'A month.' I glance warily at her, but she doesn't react. Her tongue pokes out from the side of her mouth as she stares at the clouds. Her hair, so wild, so similar to mine, is tied in a loose ponytail, tendrils escaping around her face.

'Gilly says you can borrow her old laptop to Skype me. But maybe don't take it home, or Dad'll try and sell the sodding thing.'

'What's Skype?' She glances sideways at me.

'Like a phone call, but we can see each other. A video call.'

'Hmm.' She's quiet for a few minutes and then lets out another deep sigh. 'Why are Mum and Dad so rubbish?'

I close my eyes. 'Some people just . . . are. But we've got to make sure we don't turn out like them. That's really important.'

Frankie blinks at the sky and rests her hands on her stomach, her nails bitten down to the quick. 'Natasha's mum's lovely. She reads her stories and brushes her hair. They've never done that with me. Have they ever done that with you?'

I cast my mind back to the fading memories of Dad's bedtime stories. Cinema nights with my favourite films and bowls of hot, buttery popcorn. Mum tickling me until I finally agreed to go to bed. The feel of the soft brush through my hair every morning before tucking into Marmite on toast. Dad spinning me round in the kitchen to Bon Jovi, pretending to be a rock star. I used to think he looked a bit like Jon Bon Jovi, with his wild hair and handsome face. 'Someday I'll Be Saturday Night' was our favourite track; when it came on the radio we'd look at each other with serious facial expressions, pretend to pick up our air guitars and rock out while Mum rolled her eyes and pretended to find us exhausting, then eventually joined in. When things started going downhill, I remember reading the lyrics to that song and thinking how accurate they really were.

'No,' I lie. 'Never.' How could I tell her how great things were before she was born and everything crumbled? I turn onto my side, and prop myself up on one elbow, using my free hand to stroke Frankie's face. 'Anyway, you've got me.'

She jerks away from me and picks viciously at a patch of daisies on the grass. 'Not always. You keep going away.' There it is: the reason for her simmering anger.

The snake of guilt is back again, forming a tight coil in the bottom of my stomach that I'm convinced will take years to unfurl. But she's right. 'I won't go back. Not if you don't want me to.' And I mean it.

'You won't?'

I shake my head. 'I won't.'

Frankie bites her lip. 'But . . . does that mean you won't grow up and be a police lady, and arrest Mum and Dad for all the bad stuff they've done?'

I laugh. It's always been our secret plan. Every time Mum and Dad let us down, which was more and more often as time passed, I'd wink at Frankie and form my fingers into a little gun shape and point it at their heads when they weren't looking, and Frankie would stifle a giggle with her hand. In retrospect, it probably wasn't the best thing to be mimicking, but then again, we didn't have the best role models available to us growing up.

'Don't worry, chicken, I'll still be a police officer. I don't have to go to university to do that. I'll stay for you. Pinkie promise.'

'You don't have to stay.' She hesitates before linking her little finger with mine, and we lie back down on the grass.

'Love you,' Frankie whispers.

My heart skips. 'Love you more.'

But love isn't always enough.

Chapter 54

Anya – Then

I stop as close to the cliff's edge as I dare. I allow myself a few deep breaths before grabbing the phone from my pocket.

Hot tears prick at my eyes, threatening to trickle down my face, but I can't lose my nerve. Limbs trembling and palms clammy, I inhale the cool summer evening air as I take in the view. The grass illuminated by the sunrise, blades ruffling with every breath of wind. The sea glittering for miles, the horizon unbroken. The thundering noise of the waves crashing over the rocks below sounds closer than it actually is . . . almost three hundred feet to the bottom.

Such a long drop.

The sensation of the phone vibrating in my hand makes me start. Without looking at the glowing screen, I hurl it into the ocean with as much force as I can muster, watching it sail through the air before being swallowed up by the dark depths below. A spike of adrenaline burns through my body as I envisage myself stepping over, imagining the sensation of my body slicing through the cold air, plummeting into the darkness of nothing.

I take a step closer. Just a few metres away now. Any minute.

I'm standing in exactly the same place as the memories surge.

***

I weave through the crowds, small clouds forming in the air before my face as I run. Away from the bonfire, away from the parades and the fancy dress.

Away from Poppy.

I leave the sounds and smells of the bonfire display behind me, heading for the peace and quiet of the cliff's edge.

God, I need some air.

I'd invited Poppy over after school today. Aunt Andrea cooked us chilli con carne, except it wasn't really carne *as it was vegetarian. Poppy had wrinkled her nose when she'd told her that, and later she'd referred to Aunt Andrea as a* weird hippy. *I let her off the hook; I wanted to impress her. I laughed along, mocked her too. Even though I love how she looks a bit like Stevie Nicks. I smiled at the sight of her dancing around the kitchen to Fleetwood Mac's 'Gypsy', barefoot. Until I saw Poppy's face.*

When we got ready together, I watched from the safety of the mirror I was using to apply my make-up, as she'd stepped out of her school uniform. I was going to tell her tonight. I was going to tell her how I felt. How I was in love with her. Not how I wrote our initials inside little hearts on the inside cover of my diary though.

I couldn't tell her that. My cheeks flamed at the thought. She pulled on a leather jacket over a white T-shirt and blue jeans, a thick red scarf draped around her neck. Her hair snaked down her back like a mermaid's, and I thought she was utterly beautiful.

It took so long for me to find the words. I'd planned to do it before we left the house, but I backed out. Told myself I needed a little more time. We'd met up with Orla and Ruben, and after that, I couldn't focus on a thing anyone was saying to me. The thing is, I knew Poppy had a boyfriend. An older guy – she wouldn't give us his name. I'd started to believe she was making him up, because the way she looked at me sometimes . . . I knew there was something between us. Before we lost her, Mum always said, if you want to tell someone how you feel, then tell them. Even if they don't feel the same, they'll be glad you told them the truth. And at least you'd never be left wondering what if.

I pulled her to one side, as they were lighting the bonfire. We'd lost Ruben and Orla. Her face was upturned, the flames reflected in her shining eyes. She turned to me; flashed me a smile. I don't know what came over me, maybe it was the excitement of the evening, maybe the vodka we snuck into my room when we were getting ready . . . but I leaned into her and kissed her.

***

I shake my head. No. I don't want to go back to that dark place in my mind. Not now. I take another step. My head beats frantically now, screaming at me to step away, to step back to safety. I listen to it, and stagger backwards. What am I doing? This isn't what I came here to do.

I'm in the perfect spot. Part of me wishes I could leave a suicide note, telling the police everything. About Matthew, everything he did to me. My suspicions as to why. I know now that it wasn't Ruben who had been threatening me, leaving a trail of dead poppies for me to find.

I look down at my arms, realising the vibrant colours of the cardigan I'm wearing are far too bright for me to stay incognito. I wriggle out of it, ball it up and toss it to one side. At least they'll know I was definitely here. I wait. The sound of a dog barking in the distance makes me jump, and I turn on the spot, squinting in the weak light. I see a man walking his dog along the path, and then I cry out. It's not a fake cry to get someone's attention; it's real. Real, raw sobs that heave from my chest in great shuddering surges. I jump off the edge of the little knoll I'm stood on, and land in a heap, a couple of metres shy of the cliff's edge. When I hear the dog walker's frantic footsteps, I roll to the side.

And, crouched low to the ground, I run.

Chapter 55

Anya – Now

I've been charged with Lisette and Sylvie's murders, a fact that makes my heart rupture with an aching, devastating pain every time I think about it. Which is every second of every minute that passes. But what can I do? A witness saw me at the scene. I know how the fire was set, and I admitted as much. I faked my death and ran away. My prints are on the bottle. That damn bottle of white spirit I'd used to clean my hands after painting Matthew's boat. No one in their right mind would doubt the facts.

My court date is in a week, and Rohan has managed to work his màgic and convince the CPS to grant me bail, despite their attempts to argue that I'd run once, and might do it again. I'm wearing a tag, I've had to surrender my passport and I have to report to the police station daily. But I don't care about that. All I can think about are those words: *smoke inhalation*. They died from smoke inhalation. Which means both of them were breathing, and very much alive, when the fire began to burn. I could have saved them.

I could have saved them. Why didn't I listen to my instincts? Why didn't I *do* something?

The sun feels bright. Too bright for this time of year, surely. I squint and step onto a patch of sun on the pavement outside the police station, clinging on to Orla's arm for support. I'd been in police custody for four days, but it'd felt like four years. I haven't eaten in days, and I've ripped out so much of my hair on one side that it feels almost bald in places. I don't need to look in a mirror to see how bad I look; it's enough to witness my own sister's startled reaction when she sees me.

So many different things ran through my head during my time in custody. Who told the police where I was? Did someone recognise me? I don't know who to trust anymore. With a pang of sadness, I decide it must be Hazel. She's the only person up north who knew who I really was.

I climb awkwardly into the car, joints complaining from spending days on an uncomfortable mattress. Orla turns to look at me with a deep, hollow sadness in her eyes, so similar to my own. 'I can't believe this is happening to you.' She breaks the long, painful silence with her shaky voice. I can only hope that there's no element of doubt in her mind that I'm innocent.

***

I turn on my phone when we arrive at Orla's cottage in Blackbrook Wood, and there's a message from someone called *Facebook User*. But I know. I know it's him. A warning.

I don't want to read it, but at the same time, I can't stop myself.

Found you.

I run up the stairs, two at a time, as I feel the bile rise in my throat. I launch myself into the bathroom, but nothing comes up. There's nothing left inside me. Once the dizziness has passed, I approach the mirror for the first time. I don't recognise myself, even though I'm used to my new look. Instead of vibrant short red locks, my hair lies flat and dull. The dry, flaky skin on my face is greying, and the darkness around my eyes makes them look sunken. I look like someone who's done a long stint in prison, a homeless person or someone who's really, *really* ill.

I'm starving but the thought of eating makes me want to vomit again. I splash some cold water on my face and head into the spare room, curling into a ball on the bed. My mind drifts to the police interview, how I left out a crucial part of what really happened. How Matthew told me he'd spoken to Ruben. How he'd got hold of my phone during the break-in, the one he admitted he'd staged to rattle me, how my messages had still been coming through on that phone. The feeling of nausea, of sweat blooming across my body when I realised Matthew must've done something to Ruben to make him talk.

Guilt rips through me as I think about how I manipulated Ruben to keep quiet after what he saw, how he wrestled with the guilt of lying to the police about not being there on the cliff top that night. How that guilt probably drove him to drugs in the first place. I want to cry when I remember how innocent he used to be. Eventually, I sleep for the first time in days, but it's a broken sleep, punctuated with nightmares and peppered with terrifying images.

***

I don't move a muscle when Orla tiptoes across the bedroom floor and sits on the edge of the bed. I feel the weight of her hand resting on my calf, and that small gesture alone makes emotions stir up inside me like a whirlpool.

'Sis . . .' I can tell she doesn't know what to say any more than I do. How must it feel, to go through the pain of your sister taking her own life, then to find that she's in fact alive? How could it feel to know she was on the run from the law for a crime as heinous as murder?

She tries again. 'Whatever happened, please know that I . . . I'll always love you.'

I turn my head to face her and I see doubt in her eyes as she stares at the sister she thought she knew. 'You think I did it.' My voice doesn't sound like me. It's rasping, like I haven't drunk water in days. Then I remember I've barely swallowed anything since being arrested.

'No,' she stammers. 'You're a good person. You're my little sister. I *don't* think that.'

'You don't believe me,' I say. But then, I remind myself that it's my fault Lisette, Sylvie and Poppy are dead. 'I bet you wish I'd stayed dead, where I belonged.' The bitter words shoot out of my mouth like venom and I can't take them back.

Orla can't hide the hurt in her eyes. 'I would *never* wish that, even if you *had* done it.' Her voice escapes as a whisper, and she gazes down at the carpet beneath her feet. After a moment of silence, she stands up and walks to the door. She pauses and turns back to face me. 'I'll never stop being here for you, Anya. No matter how much you push me away.'

'All I need is a lift to court next Monday. Then I'll be out of your hair.' I roll over and press my face into the pillow, the pillowcase soaking up my tears. It sinks in that I don't just look like a completely different person now, but I feel like a different person. I *am* a different person. I think about what I'd be doing right now if I'd never met Matthew. I allow myself to indulge in a fantasy, where Lisette and Sylvie are still alive. I imagine picking out an engagement ring. White gold, with an emerald. I picture myself down on one knee, somewhere beautiful with icing-sugar sand, palm trees dancing in a tropical breeze. Then I think of Lisette, stunning in a wedding dress, elegant lace sleeves, a simple flower crown. Sylvie enveloped in a silky bridesmaid's dress, clutching a bouquet of posies. A sharp pain shoots through my head and I force myself to stop envisaging such impossible dreams.

My words and actions are causing so much suffering, it's almost too much to bear. I consider that prison could be a welcome relief, a distraction from this chaos I've become entangled in. It's a week until my hearing but there's no doubt in my mind that I'll be looking at a life sentence. And I know what inmates do to people like me in prison.

Child-killers. They'll tear me to shreds. It doesn't matter that I didn't mean for it to happen. As far as everyone else is concerned, I'm guilty as hell.

How has everything gone so wrong yet again?

***

I can't contain my sharp intake of breath when I see who's waiting for me in the living room the next morning. 'Hazel?' My jaw drops open.

She stares back at me for a moment, her eyes flickering over my pallid complexion, my lank hair. 'Kate – I mean, Anya . . . sorry. Bloody *hell*. Are you all right?' She stands up as if to hug me, then hesitates.

'It's okay.' I step forward. She pulls me close, and I close my eyes in confusion at the soothing feeling of another human's touch clashing with the sting of betrayal in my heart. I notice that Orla has made herself scarce in the garden. I lower myself into the armchair opposite, eyeing her with suspicion.

'Are you all right?' she repeats.

'Funnily enough, no.' My voice drips with sarcasm. 'But at least I'm allowed out, thanks to this lovely contraption.' I gesture towards my ankle tag.

'You're different. You look like a different person. I can barely recognise you. Are you eating?'

I fold my arms across my chest. 'Why are you even here? How did you find me?'

The hurt momentarily flashes across her face. She lifts her chin and eyes me defiantly. 'I had to take a train journey to

307

come and see you. A bloody long one. And I've got a deadline coming up; I should be editing like mad right now. I'm sorry I couldn't come sooner, but this has taken some planning. I found you on Facebook. You haven't been answering any of my messages. And then I found your sister. She gave me this address.'

Despite my anger, I feel a pang of guilt. I'd seen her messages. I shake my head as if to shake away the guilt. 'I'm sorry . . . but, Hazel, why are you here?' I ask again. 'Visiting me? You reported me to the police.'

Hazel sits up straight and looks at me right in the eyes. 'No I didn't. How could you say that? Maybe I shouldn't have bothered coming at all . . .' She tails off and gathers up her bag and coat.

My hand reaches out and grabs the air in front of her. 'Wait! I'm sorry. Please wait. You've come all this way. We can talk. Let's talk. *Please.*'

She pauses in the middle of putting on her jacket and sits down with a sigh.

'I'm sorry,' I repeat, 'but if you didn't report me to the police, then who did? You were the only person up there who knew who I really was.'

'You genuinely thought it was me?' She puts her face in her hands.

I fiddle with the belt on my dressing gown. 'Well . . . yeah. But I hoped I was wrong. Do you know who it was? No one will tell me.'

'It was Peg's granddaughter. It was Ingrid.' She looks up from her hands. 'Remember how you said she seemed suspicious of you? She saw your bank card and driving licence in your bag. Peg told me. The poor woman's so confused about it all. Doesn't know who or what to believe.'

I draw a sharp intake of breath. *Oh, Peggy.* 'I'm so, *so* sorry. It's just that within a few days of me telling you what I told you, I was arrested.'

She waves a hand dismissively; I appear to be forgiven. 'Never mind that. We've got a bigger problem.'

'We do?'

'Of course, we do,' she says incredulously. 'You're potentially going to prison and you've done nothing wrong. You were *framed*.'

'I've told them the truth but they won't believe me. I haven't got a scrap of proof.'

'Tell them again. Keep telling them your story, what really happened. They can protect you.'

I hug my dressing gown closer. 'Do you really think so?'

'Anya.' I notice how she hesitates when she says my name. 'If you're telling the truth, which I believe you are, then you *will* survive this.'

'I'm so scared. What if it all comes crashing down around me again?' Tears stream down my cheeks. I'm so exhausted, so fragile. All I want to do is curl up in Lisette's arms. I cry even harder, as I wish once more that I threw myself off those cliffs and ended it all when I should have, rather than hurting even more people, like Peggy and Hazel. I should never have got close to them.

'I'm going to speak to them.' There's an air of defiance in her voice as she stands up.

I gaze up at her. 'What will you say?'

'I'll think of something. You're *not* going to prison for something you didn't do; do you hear me?'

And all of a sudden I feel a flicker of hope in the bleakness.

Chapter 56

Eve – Now

The rain lashes against the office windows, made worse by the coastal winds that lacerate the building. I shiver. The weather is so up and down at this time of year but this is depressing.

'No running today?' asks Tiana from her desk, scooping yoghurt out of a pot with a spoon.

'Meant to be thundering later,' I say. 'Think I'd rather do circuits of my front room.'

'You think you've got problems?' says Jason. 'I got wet socks this morning. Woke up to a bloody pond in my kitchen from all the rain. Bastard window handle has broken. Had to hold it in place with an elastic band.'

I laugh. 'I guess that's worse. You're getting it fixed, right?'

'Got someone coming next week.' When he sees my face, he adds, 'Don't worry. I live in a nice neighbourhood. Not the ghetto, like you.'

I roll my eyes and return my gaze to the rain. I'm itching to run.

'Eve?'

I look back from the window. Bella is standing by my desk, damp hair sticking to her forehead, clutching half a croissant wrapped in a napkin.

'Hey, Bells.' I lean back and stretch my arms over my head. 'Sorry, I was miles away. Everything okay?'

'I was on my way back from Casey's. There's a lass downstairs who wants to speak with you. You free?' She takes a bite of croissant and a couple of flakes of greasy pastry land on my desk. She doesn't notice.

'Who is she?' I press my thumbs into my eye sockets and massage them.

'Hazel Morgan. D'you know of her?'

I shake my head. 'I don't think so.'

'She's Scottish. Could be to do with the Lisette Dupont case.'

'Now you've got my attention.' I down the dregs of my coffee and grab my notebook. I'm about to head down to reception to meet Hazel, when I spot Tiana at her desk. 'Want to join?'

She nods eagerly and follows me downstairs.

A young woman with impossibly long limbs and hair the colour of fire paces back and forth, and looks warily at me as we reach the bottom of the stairs.

'Hazel Morgan?'

She nods, her red polka-dot umbrella dripping onto the tiled floor.

'I'm DC Eve Starling. This is DC Tiana Banks. Would you like to come through?'

We lead her to a small room, before closing the door shut behind me and sitting down opposite.

'Our colleague said you wanted a chat,' I say. 'What's it about?'

She wrings her hands. 'Anya Fernsby.'

I nod to encourage her to continue, trying to stem my own eagerness.

'There's no way she did it. She didn't kill Lisette and Sylvie.'

'What makes you say that?' asks Tiana. I rest my elbows on my knees and watch her closely.

'Just . . . a few things.' She traces over some scratch marks on the low table in front of her as she speaks. 'She's a good person, you know.'

'Can you talk us through your thoughts?' Tiana flips open her notebook, pen poised and ready.

'She said that something bad had happened to her.'

'Did she say exactly what had happened?' asks Tiana.

'That her girlfriend and stepdaughter died in a fire. She says she was set up. I believe her.' The words tumble out of her mouth so quickly I have to work hard to keep up.

'Why are you so sure that she hasn't spun you one huge lie?' I ask.

'There's no way she'd have been capable of something like *that*. She's a good person,' she repeats.

'What makes you so convinced she's a good person?' Tiana challenges her.

'The way she looked after Peggy, doing way more than she was paid to do. The way she helped out her cousin,

313

Ruben. You know she almost bankrupted herself trying to help him out?'

That grabs my attention. Thinking back to the mystery cash withdrawals, I ask: 'Can you tell me more about that?'

'Well. He was going through a tough time. Got kicked out of his house, got mixed up in the wrong crowd. He needed to get back on the straight and narrow, and she helped him.'

'What was the money for?' I enquire.

'A deposit for a flat,' she replies.

I pause to think. Was it pure kindness? It's one thing to help out someone you love, but to give away all your money like that . . . and in chunks of cash, too. Was there a bigger reason behind it? I decide to ring Ruben once Hazel has gone, and do some digging. For now, I home in on Matthew Taylor. Knowing what she's going to say before she says it, I ask, 'Did she tell you who set her up?'

Hazel nods. 'She told me about this guy, this Matthew Taylor. She spent the whole time in Scotland trying to track him down online. I don't think she would've told me this stuff if it wasn't true. She was taking a massive risk. I could've turned her in.' Her face flushes red, and I know she's worried she's in trouble for keeping quiet.

'And why *didn't* you turn her in?' asks Tiana.

'I trust her.'

'You'd only known her a few months,' I point out. 'What makes you think she's innocent?'

'I know,' says Hazel. 'I'm a very good judge of character. And like I said, she *chose* to tell me this stuff. I didn't force her to tell me.'

I pause. 'She told us about Matthew Taylor. We can't find him. There's no evidence to suggest he even exists.'

Her face drops. 'Maybe he was using a fake name?'

I pause. 'Why are you only telling us this now?'

'I tried!' Hazel sits up straight in her chair. 'I called twice. You took my details and never called me back.'

Shit. She must have got lost in the sea of calls and emails we'd spent hours sifting through. What else might've been missed? I shake my head. 'I'm sorry. I promise we'll look into that.'

Hazel's eyes snap back up to me. 'Please don't give up on her. She can't be a murderer. She *can't* be.'

I snap my notebook shut. 'We'll certainly look into it.' I hand her a business card. 'Thanks for coming in to speak with us. Please get in touch if you think of anything else we should know.'

We watch her walk back to her car from the window, shielded by her polka-dot umbrella. I know there's more to this case than meets the eye, and if I'm honest, I can't say I'm one hundred per cent convinced Anya killed Lisette and Sylvie. The way she stuck to her story over and over again, never tripping up or contradicting herself like liars often do. I feel like I owe it to the Duponts to try one more time to find Matthew Taylor. But first, I want to speak to Ruben.

He answers the phone on my second attempt. 'Hello?'

'Am I speaking with Ruben Fernsby?'

A pause. 'Yes. Can I help you?'

'My name is Detective Constable Eve Starling. I'm ringing to speak about your cousin, Anya.' I keep my tone light.

'Oh.' Silence. Then: 'I hear she's been charged.' His voice sounds sombre.

'Yes. Are you okay?' I ask softly.

He sighs. 'Yes. Yes, I'm fine. How can I help?' His voice is brisk.

'I'd like to speak to you about the money Anya gave you.'

There's a long pause before he speaks again, voice full of something – regret? 'Sure. Yeah, okay. What would you like to know?'

'Can you tell me what it was for?'

'A deposit for a flat.'

'Why did you need to borrow the money? And why was it in cash?'

'I was going through a bad patch. If you must know . . . my mum kicked me out and I had nowhere to stay. No money. Nothing. And I prefer cash, okay? If I can see the money, it's more real. I'm less likely to spend it on . . . things I shouldn't.'

'You couldn't stay with Anya or Orla?'

'I didn't want to get under their feet.'

'But you felt fine about taking your cousin's life savings?'

'Look, she wanted to help me,' he protests. 'I'm very grateful and I always planned to pay her back. She's a kind person, you know.' His voice goes quiet. 'You have *no* idea.'

'And she wasn't paying you off in any way?' I ask. 'Covering something up?'

Ruben sighs. 'No. No she wasn't. I don't know what you're trying to get at, Detective, but Anya is a good person. She doesn't deserve any of this. *Any* of it.'

Trust no one.

316

I twist my fork into the chow mein I'd picked up an hour ago and take a bite. It's cold. I chew and swallow, too famished to be bothered to microwave it. I check my phone; still no reply to the text I'd sent Jason hours ago. No reply from Bella, either. So much for them being there for me.

I'm staring at the pile of notes, timelines, photographs and CCTV stills scattered across my coffee table, and running my hands through my dishevelled hair in frustration. I comb over what I know so far, plotting it into a new timeline in my notebook. Anya had been in a relationship with Lisette in the months leading up to her death. Lisette and Anya were blissfully happy, according to Lisette's sister Monique. There was no motive for the crime, which was always in the back of my mind. Well, apart from Anya being in Lisette's will, which she claims to know nothing about. But why would she have run away?

The evidence is stacking up against Anya though. It's not looking good for her. And yet . . . despite every single scrap of evidence that points towards her, my instincts scream at me to look elsewhere. We've got her prints on the bottle – circumstantial. Could've been planted. Her keys were inside the house and there was no sign of forced entry – she could have simply forgotten to take them with her. She was seen legging it from the scene of the crime . . . well. We all know Zachary Samson was probably drugged up to his eyeballs at the time. The faked death hadn't done Anya any favours, but then again, I've known people do worse things when they, or their loved ones, were threatened. And the money? I can't see how it's linked, or if there's anything more to it.

But I keep coming back to the same point – the thing I can't explain away, no matter what angle I look at it – she knows how the fire was set. *She knows*. How does she know if she didn't set the damn thing?

I think about what Hazel told me. How she told me exactly the same story that Anya did. That Matthew Taylor was the one who did this. The same Matthew Taylor we could never find. Anya had no texts, no photos – she'd thrown her phone in the sea so she couldn't be traced. The boat she supposedly lived on with him isn't there anymore. The staff at the fire station don't recognise the name or description. But *what if* she's telling the truth?

I flop back into the sofa, thinking it all over. If it wasn't for the force's insane targets, I'd have more time to investigate. More time to be thorough. More time to do things properly. At least by my standards.

But the date of Anya's sentencing hearing is looming. And if I can't figure out what's niggling at me, what feels so wrong with this conviction, we could be in danger of imprisoning the wrong person.

Chapter 57

Eve – Now

My trainers hit the pavement in a steady rhythm, as the cool September breeze licks my skin, flushing my cheeks. Autumn is just around the corner, and I'll soon be missing my early morning runs in the sunshine. It's my day off today, but I know there's no way I can lounge around and do nothing. Anya's hearing is in less than a week, and it's my last chance to crack this case.

I slow to a stop outside Preston Circus Fire Station, bending over and resting my hands on my knees as I catch my breath.

'Y'all right there?' A thickset man with an Irish accent and a shaving nick on his chin stands with one hand on the door handle.

I'm still trying to catch my breath as I reach for my warrant card. 'DC Eve Starling,' I say, flashing it at him. 'Wondered if someone could answer a couple of questions?' I shoot him a smile.

'Mick Webster.' He steps back to let me in. 'You chasing someone?'

'Just on a run. Day off,' I explain. 'But you know how it is.'

I follow him through to an office where a row of desks and chairs are occupied by a group of officers, two men and a woman.

'Guys, you got a minute?' says Mick. Three pairs of eyes fall on me.

'Sounds better than report-filing.' The female officer swivels in her chair to face me. 'How can we help?'

'I'm with Sussex Police,' I say. 'I'm looking for a man called Matthew Taylor who supposedly works here. Or has worked here in the past. I believe my colleague Jason Hooper has been in touch but I'm just triple-checking and covering my back.'

'Don't know either of those names.' The blond guy on the end desk shakes his head.

I frown. 'Either?'

'Yeah, I don't recall anyone coming in and asking,' says the woman. 'There are loads of us though; he could've spoken to someone else.'

'And none of you are aware of a Mathew Taylor working here, past or present?' I rattle off the approximate dates that Anya believes he was working there.

Mick peers at the E-FIT image of Matthew's face I'm holding up on my phone screen, and shakes his head. 'I've been here eight years, never met the guy. Sounds like someone's spinning you a yarn, Detective.'

'Sounds about right.' I smile tightly. 'Thanks for the help.'

***

When I leave the station, I ring Jason.

'Why are you ringing me on your day off?' he barks.

'I'm fine thanks, how the devil are you?' My voice drips with sarcasm.

'Wonderful,' he says. 'Tiana's been baking again. That girl will be the sweet, sugary death of us all.'

'Great,' I say impatience building. 'Can I ask you something?'

'Sure. Shoot.'

'You looked into Matthew Taylor working at Preston Circus Fire Station, right?'

'Sure,' he says. 'Spoke to a guy . . . Trevor something. Said there's absolutely no record of a Matthew Taylor working there. Why'd you ask?'

'No reason,' I say, not wanting him to think I'm using my day off to check he's been doing his job properly. There must be loads of staff who work at Preston Circus Fire Station. Why would they all know about this one conversation?

'Right, got to go. My friend's here,' I lie, fabricating a non-existent social life; one I wish I actually had. 'See you tomorrow.'

I turn on the spot and run back in the direction I came from. Towards the marina, to where Anya was one hundred per cent convinced that Matthew Taylor's boat was moored up.

***

The murky green water sparkles in a patch of sunlight that's broken through the clouds, and a couple of seagulls bob up and down on the gently lapping surface of the water. I weave through the crowds as people wander from restaurant to restaurant, trying to pick somewhere to eat an al fresco lunch, where they can make the most of the sun before it's firmly in September's chilly grasp. But I'm not interested in food. My trainers thump against the wooden panels of the boardwalk as I make my way to the far end of the marina, where Anya claimed Matthew Taylor's boat had once resided. I'd not believed a word she'd said then, but now . . . I owe it to Lisette and Sylvie to give this my all.

The noise of the marina dies off as I reach the quiet end, and I breathe deeply. It's easy to forget how insanely busy things are in the centre of Brighton, until you're somewhere peaceful. I reach the end of the boardwalk and stare at the empty space, wondering if I'm wasting my time. Criminals lie all the time. Why would Anya be any different to all the other lowlifes I deal with on a daily basis? It's that over-reliance on gut instinct that I've been pulled up on before. Sometimes it pays off, but I've been in trouble for acting before thinking before. Am I making a mistake by ignoring Gillian and Jason's instructions?

I'm about to leave, when a boat sails into the empty berth in front of me. The chances of it being the same boat are slim, I'm sure of it. But I need to know. As the boat slides gracefully into the space, I look at it, considering how it might fit the description Anya gave. But when I see the Indian man leap off the deck to moor up the boat, his brown hands expertly lassoing the rope to the mooring point, I know he's not the man Anya described. He glances up at me with smiling eyes and I give him a wave before trudging back in the direction I came.

I lean against a fence and watch the boats sailing lazily in and out of the marina. People come and go here, every day. I know the marina keeps records. I wonder about Robbie Griffiths, whether I could try and get in touch with him. What if there was a mix-up? I pull my phone from my pocket and dial the number listed online.

'Good afternoon, Brighton Marina Security and Information Centre, how may I help you?'

'Hello. I'm with Sussex Police. My name is DC Eve Starling. I'm hoping you can help with an ongoing investigation.'

The man on the other end of the line speaks with a brisk, efficient voice. 'Of course, Detective.'

'I'm looking for information about a boat berthed here.' I give him the location and dates, and wait for him to tap it into his computer.

'And what would you like to know?'

'I understand the boat is owned by a Robbie Griffiths, rented out to a Matthew Taylor—'

'I'm sorry, that's not the name I have here,' he interrupts.

I frown. 'Are you sure?'

'Absolutely. I have the name Derek Ackerman. And he doesn't hold a business boat licence, so if he was renting it out, he'd be in breach of our regulations.'

Interesting. I request the contact details for Derek

Ackerman, wondering how Jason ended up with the name Robbie Griffiths. Was there a mix-up?

***

I arrive at a tired-looking red-brick mid-terrace on the out-skirts of Brighton, with a front door that opens straight onto the street. When Derek opens the door, I'm greeted with a strong whiff of alcohol that reminds me so much of Dad on his bad days that I feel a gut-punch that nearly knocks me sideways.

'Derek Ackerman?'

'Who's asking?' It sounds confrontational but he's smiling with discoloured teeth.

I hold up my warrant card. 'DC Eve Starling. I'm inves-tigating a case and I think you might be able to help. May I come in?'

If he's shocked by the presence of a detective in running gear standing at his front door, he doesn't show it. He stands to one side and I enter the house, spying the tell-tale signs of empty vodka bottles bursting from the kitchen bin.

'Cuppa?' He gestures towards the kettle.

I smile back. 'No, thank you.'

He nods, and turns to the kettle anyway, tossing a teabag into a mug and opening the fridge to look for milk.

'Mr Ackerman, am I correct in thinking you have a boat berthed in Brighton Marina?'

The movement is slight, but I notice it immediately. He freezes for a split second, as if someone has chucked a bucket of ice over him, before reaching for the milk and closing the fridge door.

'I do. Are you sure you don't want a cuppa?'

'I'm sure. Can I ask if you rent out your boat at all?'

'No.' The reaction is fast, too fast, and I think even he knows it. He rubs a hand over his face before picking up a packet of digestives and offering it to me.

I shake my head. 'You won't be in any trouble if you have been renting it out,' I assure him.

He eyes me suspiciously but says nothing.

'You're not the one we're after,' I press him.

He drops into a chair and his shoulders slump. After what feels like an eternity of silence, he breaks it first. 'I don't have a licence,' he admits. 'I just . . . *really* needed the money.'

'I understand.' I give him my most sympathetic smile. 'I'm not here today to catch rogue boat owners trying to make some extra cash. I'm investigating a murder.'

The relief that had flooded his face drains as quickly as it appeared. 'Murder?' he stutters. 'In the marina?'

'No,' I say. 'But I'm looking for someone called Matthew Taylor who I've been told rented a boat in the marina, and I need to find him. The location we've been given is the one where your boat is berthed. I need to know if you rented your boat out to him, during these dates.' I tell him the dates, but I don't tell him that we aren't even sure if Matthew Taylor exists.

I'm so sure that I'm about to get the answer I'm looking for that the shock hits me like a slap in the face when he looks up from his mug of tea and shakes his head. 'No. No, I never rented to a man called Matthew Taylor. You're mistaken. I rented it out to a young family, but it was in the summer.'

Damn it, I think to myself as I walk back to my car. Why did I mention the phrase *investigating a murder*? I saw how he clammed up as soon as I said the 'm' word. But was his obvious anxiety just about getting caught renting without a licence, or is there more to this? And *how* had Jason missed this?

Chapter 58

Eve – Then

It's 11 p.m. on the night before I head back to university, and I've already left my friends at the bar. My mind had insisted on wandering back to my sister, and whether or not she was okay. Guilt had been rippling through me as I'd remembered how she'd asked if she could come with me, and I'd told her not to be silly, that she's only ten and can't possibly come to a bar. Then she'd asked me to stay, and I'd told her no but I wouldn't be long. The ripples of guilt had spiralled bigger and bigger until I'd decided I couldn't hang around any longer; I was feeling far too unsettled. My friends had given me sympathetic smiles as I'd made my excuses and left. They know a little of what's going on, but not everything. Just the highlights. A two-minute film trailer of my shitty home life.

I head to the nearest taxi rank, my heels precarious on the slippery, wet pavement, and count my steps to calm myself.

One.

Two.

Three.

Four.

I shiver as I wrap my bare arms around my body, cursing myself for leaving my jacket at home. It's Brighton; it's always bloody cold at night. I should've known better. But at least it's still early, and thankfully there are only a handful of people in the queue.

'All right, love? Cheer up, might never happen.'

I sidestep out of the way as a man staggers past me to the back of the queue, ignoring his drunken slurs. I soon climb into the inviting safety of a taxi, kick off my shoes and rub away the goose bumps that have erupted over my arms.

***

I don't notice what's going on straight away. I'm scrolling through a news article on my phone when the taxi turns into my street. When the driver slams on the brakes and swears, I'm thrown forcefully against my seatbelt, and my head jerks up to see what the commotion is all about. My eyes are met with a fiery blaze, illuminating the entire street. A strangled cry rips through my throat and I topple out of the taxi, leaving my shoes and bag behind and racing barefoot on the puddled pavement towards the house with my hand clapped over my mouth.

I stand rooted to the spot and watch in horror. Huge, angry flames flicker and lick hungrily at the windows. The bedroom windows, I realise with a paralysing sense of dread. I recoil, helpless on the pavement as a paralysing wave of terror drenches me. Then I notice that Frankie's bedroom window is open; did she get out in time? I stumble forward, hoping to see her limp but breathing form in the front garden, but all I can see are the origami creations that have fallen from her window, taken by a gust of wind and saved from the flames. I pick one up, an orange cat, and grip it with trembling fingers as if it's somehow connected to her, as if it can bring her to safety.

The stench of smoke overwhelms me. I heave as the contents of my stomach empty onto the grass in front of me with a sickening splatter. My body doubles over as dizziness takes hold like a parasite. I shake my head, not willing to give in to it.

Think.

Stay alert.

Call 999.

Where the fuck's my phone? I fumble madly in the pockets of my jeans, but it's not there. I stumble over to the gate, feeling like I'm wading through quicksand, my hands fumbling on the metal latch as the sounds I was hearing so clearly before morph into echoes.

Frankie. I've got to get to Frankie.

I'm through the gate, but my throat tightens as I lurch forward with my key, trying to jam it into the lock. *Why won't it fit?* My heart is racing as I slide it in on what feels like the hundredth attempt, and the door swings open. A wall of fire greets me and I stumble backwards. Darkness is closing in around me and my body is telling me to crumple to the ground.

Sirens wail.

Red light.

Yellow light.

Amber light.

I hear a scream, not knowing if the chilling sound is coming from the house or if it's escaping my own dry throat, but before I can figure out it, everything goes black.

I'm sure I feel someone catch me as I give in to the soothing safety of the darkness flickering at the edges of my vision.

***

I wake in a daze, in an unfamiliar room, lying on a bed I don't recognise, fully clothed and disorientated. I feel like someone has hurled a brick at my head as the memory of a house fire floods my mind, and I realise the disgusting stench filling my nostrils like a poison gas is the smoke that has settled on my clothes and hair. *Where am I?* I groan as I scramble out of the bed, stumbling with clumsy feet and shaking legs. I need to get back to the house to find out if Frankie's okay. But I stop dead when I realise where I am.

The white sheets. The blue curtain. The clinical smell.

The curtain is pulled back and a face appears, followed by another. It takes me a few confusing seconds to realise it's Charlie and Gillian, their faces creased in concern. I stumble towards them with a sob.

'Whoa, whoa, slow down, pet.' Charlie reaches out two big hands to steady me. 'You've had a shock.'

'Where's Frankie? Is she here? I need to get to her.' My voice sounds nothing like me. Stricken. I try to brush past them both without waiting for an answer, every possible scenario galloping through my head. I'm so selfish.

Why didn't I come home earlier? Why did I—

Gillian grabs my arm, firmly but kindly. 'Evie, wait. You're in shock. The nurses still need to check you over. And . . . we need to talk to you before you go out there.' The skin between her eyebrows crinkles and sadness fills her eyes.

I stop struggling, sensing something in her tone. Allowing her to steady my shaking body, I obediently sit back down on the bed, staring at the tiles underneath my bare feet.

Charlie's face looks strained as he lowers himself into the chair next to me. He runs a hand over his face, the dry skin on his palms catching on his salt-and-pepper stubble, and I notice that he's trying to wipe away tears.

'No,' I whisper, shaking my head in disbelief.

I know what you're going to tell me.

'Your mam and dad . . . they fell asleep on the sofa last night,' begins Gillian. 'Your dad's cigarette . . . it set the carpet on fire.'

Not yet. I'm not ready.

'They were drunk, weren't they?' I feel a cocktail of rage and guilt bubbling away in the pit of my stomach, and my nails dig painfully into my palms.

Charlie nods once, firmly. 'The fireman said there was booze all over the carpet . . . the place went up so quickly.'

No. Please no. Please don't let it be true.

'And . . . my sister . . . where is she?' I fight back tears, my voice catching in my throat.

Charlie says nothing and plants his face in his hands.

'I'm so sorry Evie,' says Gillian, her hand resting on my forearm. I watch as Charlie's broad shoulders shudder and he cries into his big hands. This man who is like a father to me and Frankie, who still has our drawings stuck on his fridge with a magnet, who'd eat the cupcakes Frankie baked, no matter how many sugary sprinkles she managed to coat them with.

If there's a god up there, please let this be a nightmare.

I sob with big, ugly tears as a nurse slips through the gap in the curtains. I barely notice as she gently eases me back into the bed and pulls the covers over me. I barely notice Charlie and Gillian eventually leaving. And I don't notice anything after that. I don't think I'll ever notice anything again.

All I can think about is Frankie.

What have I done?

Chapter 59

Eve – Now

'You did what?' Jason blinks at me.

I repeat myself, trying hard not to clench my jaw in frustration. 'I went back to the marina. They'd given you the wrong name. It wasn't Robbie Griffiths whose boat was berthed there, it was someone called Derek Ackerman, and—'

'Is this anything to do with that phone call yesterday?' Jason's expression is unreadable.

I feel my cheeks growing hot. 'I wanted to check some facts.'

A wash of beetroot red spreads over Jason's face. 'Double-checking the work I've done?'

'No, I—'

'Eve, why were you investigating on your day off?' Gillian wears a cool expression.

'We don't have much time,' I reply, my fists clenching and unclenching. *Do not lose your shit*, I instruct myself silently as I eye the wastepaper bin, wanting more than anything to boot it.

'Do you think you're some kind of lone ranger?' She folds her arms. 'Last time I checked, this was a team. I've told you time and time again, you rely too much on your instincts and not enough on the facts laid out in front of you. So if you want to be the Lone Ranger, or some kind of Mystic Meg, then you're in the wrong profession.'

The anger simmers away and instead I feel a stab of misery as Gillian fixes me with a stare, laden with bitter disappointment, as if she regrets hiring me. 'I'm sorry, ma'am. But maybe this means something.'

'That doesn't redeem you,' Gillian snaps, but drops her arms to her sides. 'Well, you might as well tell us.'

'Thank you, ma'am.'

'Don't thank me. And don't think you're off the hook.'

I nod. 'So I went to visit Derek Ackerman. It turns out, he's been renting his boat out to people despite not having his business boat licence. He claims he's been desperate. I got the impression he was funding his alcohol habit.'

'Go on.' Gillian presses her lips into a thin line.

'Well, he seemed really anxious that he'd been caught doing something he shouldn't. He said he'd rented his boat out to a young family in the summer, but denied renting it out to anyone called Matthew Taylor, or any lone men at all. But—'

'We'll need much more than a barely connected confession of an alcoholic to convince the CPS that Anya's hearing should be delayed.'

My heart plummets. 'But—'

'Thank you.' Gillian dismisses us and turns back to her computer.

I traipse out of the office behind Jason. The stiffness of his shoulders communicates how pissed off he is with me. He knows I went over his head, and rechecked the work he'd already done. All based on a gut feeling.

I drop into the seat at my desk and Bella and Tiana peer over their monitors at me, eyes laced with concern. I give them a small shake of the head and cast my gaze down. I'm convinced that what I've discovered could amount to something, but it's not enough. I think I know when it's time to give up.

***

'Come on, misog, I'm taking you to lunch.'

I wrinkle my nose at Bella and slouch further into my chair. 'I'm not hungry.'

'You might not be, but your stomach is.' She prods me in the side. 'I can hear it from my desk.'

'It's 4 p.m. It's too late. I've got shitloads to do.' I wave a hand at the reports on my desk.

'Never too late for lunch.' She pulls on the back of my chair and wheels me to the other side of the office. 'I'll wheel you all the way if you don't get up. And this thing doesn't have suspension.'

Everyone is staring now. 'Okay, okay. I'm coming. Get off my chair,' I grumble. 'And don't ever call me misog again.'

I'm still feeling stung and embarrassed about what happened earlier. Gillian's barely spoken to me; Jason won't even look at me. At least Tiana has given me a few sympathetic smiles, and delivered a couple of coffees to my desk, which I drank, even though they didn't taste good.

'You coming, Tiana?' I ask, and Bella raises an eyebrow at me. Does she look annoyed?

'Me?' She glances up from her desk. 'Um, sure. I just need to finish this. Go ahead without me; I'll join you in ten. Where you heading?'

'The Barley Mow,' says Bella, shortly. Why is *she* being snappy with Tiana now?

'Where's that?'

'Bellgate Street. Over near the church.'

Tiana's face looks blank.

'I'll send you my WhatsApp location.' I unlock my phone.

'See you in a bit.' Bella bundles me out of the door.

***

Once we're in the car, safe from the rain that falls from the sky in sheets, I realise why she was so desperate to get me out of the office, alone.

'I need to talk to you, Eve.' She leans her head against the steering wheel. 'I've fucked up.'

'What?' I reach out and grab her hand. 'What's happened?'

'It's Tony.'

My stomach jolts as I think back to the text I'd seen. *You slut.*

'Bells, talk to me.' I squeeze her hand, and she rolls her head to the side, looking at me from underneath her hair.

'I've . . .' She pauses. 'I've been having an affair.'

'Shit, Bells. With who?'

Her face flames, and I hear the name inside my head before she speaks it. 'Jason.'

So it wasn't just harmless flirting, after all. Was that why neither of them would text me back for hours the other night? Were they *together*?

'Seriously?'

She groans into the steering wheel. 'It was just a bit of fun. It was meant to be a one-night thing. I told Tony. He flipped out, *obviously*.'

'Was this around Jason's birthday?'

She frowns at me. 'Er, yes. How'd you know?'

'I saw a message flash up on your phone,' I say, feeling guilty. 'I didn't mean to look. I turned it over so no one else saw.'

'Ugh. Yeah, so that was *fun*. Anyway, I should've left Tony there and then. I guess I felt bad. I don't know. But things started up with Jason again, and Tony found out. He's found email addresses for half the force, including *Gillian*, and reliably informed them that I'm scum.'

'You're *not* scum,' I say. 'You're a bit of a prat, mind, but you're not scum. We all cock up from time to time.'

She shoots me a weak smile.

I glance through the windscreen, the car park blurred by rivulets of rainwater. 'This thing with Jason serious?'

She shrugs. 'Might be. I don't know. I like him. A *lot*. But he's my boss, Eve. That can't work.'

'Maybe it can.' I look back at her, wanting more than

anything to make her feel better. 'Look, Tony was bad for you. He didn't get your job, didn't understand what you needed. Expected too much of you. Yeah, you should've got rid years ago, and no, you probably shouldn't have ended it *quite* like this, but you might have a chance here. Someone who gets you.'

Chapter 60

Anya – Now

The day before my plea hearing, I can't focus on anything. It's an unfamiliar and unsettling feeling, knowing tonight will likely be the last time I ever sleep in a decent bed, eat dinner with my sister. Because I know there's no way any judge or jury will believe me. The evidence is convincing, thanks to the terrible decisions I've made. Orla keeps bursting into tears when she thinks I'm out of earshot. I can't console her; I can't even console myself. I feel nothing but numbness. I've failed her, and I don't deserve her efforts.

So, I lie on the bed, staring at the ceiling, trying to predict what life behind bars will feel like. It occurs to me that none of my other close friends have been in touch, which isn't surprising really. As far as they know, I'm a murderer. The circle of people who love me has shrunk to a number I can count on one hand. To occupy my mind, I reach into my bag and pull out my purse. There's a photo of Lisette and Sylvie in there that I haven't looked at for ages; it's agonising. Like a fist that squeezes my innards with an intense strength that takes my breath away. But I know I need to see their faces one last time, before I'm locked away for both their deaths.

As I slide the photo from its pocket, something else comes out with it. A receipt. I'm about to crumple it up when I glance at it. That's not my card number. I don't recognise it. Why's this in my purse? My eyes scan down the receipt; it's a purchase for two coffees, from the place Matthew and I went to occasionally. He was always meticulous about shredding his receipts, but I remember the one time when he forgot to take his receipt. I slipped it in my purse to give to him later that day, but I never did. My heart thuds as I realise what this means.

I roll off the bed and pad across the bedroom to retrieve my phone. It's only a quarter past five. If I'm careful, I can get to the police station, show them this receipt, and get back before my curfew. My heart thuds as I slip out the back door with Orla's car keys, knowing I don't have time to explain myself to her. Rain spits, and I shiver as I throw myself into the driver's seat and fire up the engine. I navigate out of the driveway and onto the winding road that leads away from the peace and quiet of Blackbrook Wood.

It's already getting dark as I pull up at the police station. I don't have long if I want to avoid setting off my tag. My chest burns as I race from the car and up the stone steps to the reception, breathless with anticipation.

'Can I speak to Detective Constable Eve Starling please? It's urgent.'

The man on the desk eyes me suspiciously, but picks up the phone. 'What's your name?'

'Anya Fernsby.'

His mouth sets in a grim line and he dials. 'DC Starling? Anya Fernsby here for you. Yes. Yep. Okay. I'll tell her to wait.'

'I've only got twenty minutes.' I point to my ankle tag.

'She's coming,' he says sharply. 'Wait over there.' He motions to a plastic chair but I pace, unable to remain still.

'Anya, what are you doing here?' Eve stands in the doorway, holding it open with her elbow.

I rush towards her. 'I need to speak to you. It's urgent. Please.'

She registers the desperation on my face and ushers me into a small room bearing two sofas and a coffee table.

'What is it?' She closes the door behind her. 'Your plea hearing's tomorrow. And your curfew kicks in at—'

'I know,' I interrupt. 'But look.' I hold the receipt in front of her face. Her eyes slide over it and she looks questioningly at me.

'It's his card details,' I say. 'It's Matthew. It proves he exists.'

She glances at me. 'It doesn't have all the details on it. Just some of them.'

'But . . . it proves he exists,' I insist again. 'You've got to listen to me.'

She stares hard at me, then sighs. 'Okay, I'll take a look at it.' She gestures at the receipt, which I hand over. 'I can't promise anything. But I'll talk to the powers that be.'

My shoulders sag. 'Thank you. I've got to go. But thank you.'

As I rush to the car park, all I can think is how this might prove the existence of Matthew Taylor.

This might save my life.

Chapter 61

Eve – Now

I watch Anya from the window as she scuttles across the car park, hood up against the never-ending rain. The receipt sits in my hand and I wonder if it's genuine. If Anya somehow faked it to buy herself some time, or if it really is the mysterious Matthew Taylor's bank account. If it's true, I might not have time to run it through Digital Forensics.

As I'm about to turn away from the window, Anya slows and looks over her shoulder as if she's heard a sound, or sensed me watching her. I shrink back so she doesn't notice me.

'*Damn,*' I whisper to myself, as Anya stops dead as she spots me staring. But then I realise her eyes aren't locked onto mine, they're looking to the left, in the direction of the door. A look I can only describe as pure horror floods her face. She pulls her hood down over her eyes and dives behind Tiana's sky-blue Fiat 500. What the hell has she just seen? I crane my neck to see if there's anyone coming out of the building, and I see Jason strolling down the path, clutching an umbrella, oblivious to Anya and her bizarre behaviour. He turns to the right, unlocks his car and climbs in, before driving out of the car park.

My eyes snap back to Anya, who is creeping out from behind the Fiat 500, watching Jason drive off down the street. Once he has rounded the corner, she races to her own car, throws herself into the driver's seat, and screeches out of the car park like she's being chased.

What the hell was all that about? Why would Anya be afraid of Jason? They don't know each other: he'd have said if he knew her. And suddenly, something clicks in my brain and I think back to the description Anya gave of Matthew Taylor. Tall. Dark hair. Dark eyes. Is this a doppelgänger situation, or . . . wait. *No.* No way. I think of the story about the boat, and the way Jason corrected Gillian on the right terminology for berthing a boat. Matthew's job as a fireman, and Jason's questionable investigation skills, both at the fire station and the marina. And as crazy as it sounds, Jason's David Bowie obsession. There were those songs he made me queue up on the jukebox, his phone's ring tone – 'Sound and Vision' – his dog's name. Dave. And Anya told us Matthew's dog's name was *Bowie* . . .

Imaginary puzzle pieces begin sliding into place inside my head before I can stop them, but it's madness . . . isn't it? Jason can't be Matthew Taylor.

I stare at the receipt in my hand again, imagining going into Gillian's office and telling her what I suspect, and I can picture the look of scorn on her face at the absolute insanity of the suggestion. It sounds crazy to me. But . . . what if it's true? I'd need proof. More than just my word that Anya was terrified when she saw Jason, as well as his dog's name. It occurs to me that Jason never once crossed paths with her during her time in custody. Oh *God*.

I rush upstairs and find Tiana, explaining to her what Anya had said, and hand her the receipt. 'Can you speak with the boss, see if she can speak to the CPS to delay Anya's trial?'

She stares at the receipt in her hand. 'Sure. You think it's genuine?'

I shrug, and pick up my rucksack. 'Hard to say. I'd rather not take the risk.'

'Where are you off to?'

'I've got to sort something out,' I say. 'I'll see you tomorrow morning.'

'See you tomorrow.' She's frowning at me. I must be giving off a vibe. I give her a cheery wave as I exit the room, dropping my hand as soon as I get into the corridor, power-walking to the car park, dodging puddles, wondering where Jason had gone. He didn't turn left like he normally does, which means he hasn't gone home. At least, he hasn't gone *straight* home.

Once I'm in my car, I punch Jason's address into the sat nav. If I need evidence, there's only one place I should look.

Chapter 62

Eve – Now

Minutes later, I pull up on Jason's street, across the road from his house. Detached, sandstone brick with a decent-sized, well-kept garden in a nice neighbourhood. I wonder what kind of place I'll be able to afford when I make DS. *If*, says a small voice in my head. *Pulling a stunt like this won't help.* The windows are dark; his car's not on the drive. I glance up and down the street, but I can't see it. I'm sure he's not home, but I climb out of the car, cross the road and press my finger to the doorbell anyway. I hear it ring out through the house, echoing in the empty rooms. I wait, but I hear no footsteps, no clearing of a throat.

I don't really know why I'm here. What was I expecting – to confront Jason and expect him to admit everything, going willingly to the station with me to give a statement? That's not going to happen. I need proof.

Casting my eyes around the shadowy street, wet pavements glistening in the moonlight, I see that no one's around. It's a Friday night, I expect everyone is out having fun after a long working week in the last of the mild weather as September draws to a close. As casually as I can, I walk around the side of the house and locate the back door. I remember being in this garden a few years ago when Jason hosted a barbecue for the team. I remember thinking what a great guy he was. And now I have no idea what he's capable of. If I'm even right. And if I'm wrong . . . I could be about to end my career in one of the worst ways possible.

I try the handle. It's locked, of course. My eyes slide to the kitchen window. It's low enough for me to reach it, large enough for me to fit through the gap. Could I smash the window? The house that backs onto Jason's garden is illuminated in the darkness. Every light is on. They're in, and they'll hear me if I smash the glass.

Then it hits me. What Jason said last week, after all that heavy rainfall . . . *You think you've got problems? I got wet socks this morning. Woke up to a bloody pond in my kitchen from all the rain. Bastard window handle has broken.*

The window handle was broken. Is it still? I approach the kitchen window and hook my fingernail underneath the UPVC frame. It doesn't budge. I reach over and try the other one, and to my disbelief, it opens straight away. What an idiot. He's had a *week* to get this fixed. I hoist myself up and through the window frame, landing with all the grace of a baby giraffe next to the bins. I freeze, convinced that he's lurking in the house and has heard me, but after a few moments, it's clear I'm alone. Darkness wraps itself around me, bleak and suffocating. And then I hear it. A tapping sound, followed by panting. *What the fuck is that?* I switch on the torch on my phone and shine it in front of me, my heart thudding when I see a pair of eyes reflected green in the darkness.

'Dave?'

The spaniel barks in response, but it's a friendly bark. He remembers me. Either that, or he's a rubbish guard dog.

'Hello, Dave. Had fun on the boat, did you?' I say, my voice soft as I bend down and entice him over. The last thing I need is Jason's dog biting my leg and giving the game away. But Dave trots over and licks my outstretched hand. I open up the fridge, find a pack of ham, and drop a couple of slices into his bowl. That'll keep him occupied while I root around for . . . well, I'm not sure exactly what I'm looking for. But I suspect I don't have long.

I shine my torch around the kitchen, but nothing looks suspicious. I fan out the paperwork that sits in a tray on the side, but it's all bills, bank statements and receipts. And a quick skim over them tells me there's nothing dodgy going on within the pages. I make my way through the living room. It's exactly the same as I remember it – minimalist style, minimal clutter, just like his desk and his car – only this time every looming shadow looks like someone about to attack me. But I'm fine. I've trained for this kind of thing.

The stairs creak as I edge my way upstairs. Dave, now finished with the ham, is following me, whining for more. I will him to be quiet. Once I reach the landing, I creep across the carpet and try the first door. Bathroom, no good. The next one along is the bedroom, and I make my way in, Dave hot on my heels.

The room is shrouded in darkness. I fumble around using my phone's light for a few minutes, but after bashing my knee on corner of the bed frame, I give up and switch on the bedside table lamp. Had I not been in a rush, I'd have found it terribly interesting, being inside Jason's bedroom. What strikes me as odd is the lack of personality. Perhaps he's too involved in his job to bother making his home cosy. Maybe it's simply a place to eat and sleep. As I rifle through various drawers, I think to myself how it's not dissimilar to my own flat. Maybe it's time for me to make my place more of a home; I've been there long enough.

I close the wardrobe I've just finished searching and turn to the bedside table. The only place I haven't looked yet. I slide it open, and my eyes land on a couple of iPhones nestled amongst the clutter. Jason doesn't have an iPhone; I know for a fact he has a Samsung. So who do these phones belong to? I pull them both out of the drawer and press the power buttons, but neither of them switches on. A little more rummaging amongst the odds and ends reveals a charger, so I plug one in, willing it to charge as fast as possible.

Then I see the photograph tucked into the drawer. It looks like a younger version of Jason, with a pretty teenage girl. A little sister, perhaps? He'd only ever mentioned a brother. My eyes land on a small reel of black velvet ribbon. I feel the soft fabric with my fingers, wondering why Jason would want or need something like this. It's sort of sinister. As the charging phone screen lights up, I tear my eyes away from the ribbon and wait impatiently as it loads. It feels like it takes forever, but eventually it turns on. It's password-protected

348

though, of course it is. What could it be? I stare at the screen. Jason's date of birth? Possibly too obvious but you never know. I try all variations – UK format, US format, the full date of birth or just the year, but none of them work. How many attempts do you get on an iPhone again?

I try some obvious ones – 0000, 1234 – knowing he's not that stupid, but I'm getting desperate. I get it wrong again and I'm locked out for one minute. It feels like the longest minute of my life. Once I'm able to attempt the password again, I know the next attempt will render the phone useless for a further five minutes. I don't have five minutes. *Think, Eve. Think.* What numbers mean something to Jason? What does he love? *David Bowie*, says a voice in my head. *Yes, but how does that help me crack this code?* I think about song titles. Isn't there that song by Frankie Valli and the Four Seasons – *December, 1963*? What if there's a David Bowie song like that? I don't know any; I can't say I'm a fan.

I turn to Google, which gives me two answers – *1917* and *1984*. Shit. Which one might it be? How does he have *two* songs with four digits in the name? *1917. 1984. 1917. 1984. Make a decision, Eve.* I go with *1984* and I hold my breath as I tap the last digit . . . and I'm in. My fingers fly over the screen, navigating straight to the messages. And the first name I see is Anya's.

My heart thuds as I read the last words Anya sent to Jason, the night of the fire: *Don't do anything stupid. Please. I'm literally begging you.*

I was right. Jason and Matthew . . . they're the same person. I drop the phone onto the bed as if it's red-hot, and fumble in my back pocket for my own phone. As I scroll to Gillian's number, I'm vaguely aware that Dave is no longer sniffing around my ankles.

'Pick up, pick up, pick up,' I whisper to the dial tone.

'Eve?' I've never felt more relieved to hear Gillian's abrupt voice at the other end of the line.

'Gilly,' I say, forgetting her rank, forgetting my manners, wanting only to share this terrifying news with her. 'I've found something. It's about Matthew. I've found him. He's Ja—'

The phone is snatched from me. A hand clutches my throat.

Chapter 63

Eve – Now

I jerk my head around and lock eyes with Jason, who emanates pure fury.

'What are you doing in my house, Eve?' His voice is cold, disturbingly quiet.

'What were you doing with Anya Fernsby?' I retort, twisting out of his grip.

He ignores my question. 'Did you think you could just break in without me knowing? I saw your car down the street.'

Before I have time to react, something hard comes crashing down into the back of my head in an explosion of pain. I burst through the bedroom door, onto the landing, and quickly roll out of the way as a boot is aimed at my head.

I clamber to my feet, staggering on the spot and grasping my head. As my vision clears, Jason shimmers into focus in front of me, one arm raised above his head, his face settled into an expression of cool unreadability.

I lunge for him. He gasps as my fingernails find his

throat, and he swings his baton at me. I twist out of the way and aim a sharp elbow at his face, hitting him squarely in the eye.

I duck as his fist swings for my head again and retaliate by aiming a knee directly between his legs. When he doubles over in agony, I spot my chance and dart towards the staircase, my sweaty hands slipping on the banister. I run faster than I've ever run before, taking the stairs three at a time before landing, cat-like, at the bottom.

A blinding, white-hot pain shoots through me as something hard connects with the back of my head before I can reach the front door, and I crumple forward. I'm dragged by my ankles to the other end of the hall and my wrists are cuffed to a radiator pipe.

Jason stands in front of me, his facial expression transformed from rage to worry. 'Eve. Why did you have to put me in this position?'

'What position?' I look up at him, various parts of my body throbbing.

Jason fades in and out of focus. 'You're my friend. You know I care about you . . . but you broke into my house and tried to expose me. You know too much. But I can't—'

'Can't what?' I spit. 'Silence me? *Kill* me?'

He closes his eyes. 'Things got out of hand.' His voice is quiet and I have to strain to listen. 'I did it for *her.*'

'Who?' I strain at the cuffs. '*Who*, Jason? Anya? Lisette? Sylvie? Who are you talking about?'

'Shut up.' He presses his hand to his forehead. 'Let me *think.*'

I'm silent as I watch him work through whatever he's trying to figure out.

'You know too much,' he repeats, his hands falling to his sides. 'You'll talk.'

I think fast. 'Jason . . . you know I won't talk. You say you care about me? Well, I care about you too. I don't want to see you locked up. Let me go, and let's make a plan, okay? I've got your back, like you've got mine. Like we always said.'

He looks at me, considering what I said. A dark look crosses his face, and I feel a pang of fear. The tense silence is broken by the sound of his phone ringing. He glances at it, before heading for the kitchen. He comes back, phone still ringing in one hand, a knife glinting in the other. He holds it to my throat. 'You say a word, you know how this ends, okay?' But his voice shakes; I don't truly believe he wants to do this to me.

I nod, trying to avoid contact with the blade. He picks up the call. 'Boss?'

Oh God, it's Gillian. If I can just get her attention. I inhale, ready to make a sound, clear my throat, cough, but the knife presses harder against my skin as he feels me tense, and I freeze. Can I take the risk? I'm no good to anyone if I'm dead.

'I'm all right. Yeah. No, haven't seen her. Did she? I think she went over to Seaford Head again. Oh right? Yeah sure. Thanks for letting me know, boss. Speak soon.'

He shuts off the call and stares down at me. 'Gillian wants to try and delay Anya's hearing. Said Anya visited the station today. Told them she'd found some evidence that Matthew

Taylor exists.' His voice is distant and monotonous, like he's drifted off somewhere. I can't work out if it's him, or me feeling flaky. I say nothing.

'I've got to go.'

'Where?' I splutter.

He pauses. 'I'm going to check on Anya. See if she's . . . okay. I— I'll deal with you later.' He stares at me for a few more seconds, something unreadable in his expression, then leaves. The sound of the door slamming shut rings in my ears, and I'm still feeling dizzy from the impact of Jason hitting my head.

Think, I instruct myself. *How the hell am I going to get out of this mess?*

It dawns on me that Jason isn't on his way to check up on Anya, he's on his way to kill her. He knows she's finally cracked him, and he wants revenge . . . and then he'll be back for me. I might not know the Jason who was stood before me a few minutes ago, but I know if he's determined to do something, then he's going to do it.

The cuffs clang against the metal pipe as I yank them, hoping he hasn't locked them properly. Who am I kidding? He's a cop. Yet I tug and pull anyway. If I pull hard enough, could I wrench the radiator from the wall? Drag it outside with me, scream for help? I cry out with pain as I pull so hard the metal cuts into my wrists. I try twisting around and using brute force to untwist the nuts and bolts that hold the radiator together, but my hands, now slick with blood, slip on the smooth metal and struggle to gain any purchase. I shout with every ounce of breath I have left in my lungs, but no one comes.

After a few minutes of quiet, Dave emerges from his

hiding place behind the sofa and lies down in front of me, his head resting on my knee. I relish the warmth, a scrap of comfort in this horror show.

I don't know how much time passes as I sit in the darkness, drifting in and out of awareness, panic ebbing and flowing. Not just for me, but for Anya and her sister. Are they dead already? Is he on his way back to finish me off? I try working out all the ways I could reason with him, trick him into trusting me. Long enough for me to get hold of Gillian.

I think I hear footsteps on the street outside. I freeze. I couldn't breathe even if I wanted to. I wait for the inevitable key in the lock, the creak of the door as it opens. The feeling of Jason's eyes on me. The knife against my neck, pressing into the artery, warm blood flooding my skin as the life drains away. I strain my eyes in the darkness, trying to make out the shape through the frosted glass panel in the door, but the consciousness I've been trying to grasp hold of slips away. I need a couple of minutes' sleep . . . just so I can focus on what to do next.

Chapter 64

Anya – Now

The temptation to floor the accelerator is strong, but I resist. I'm completely rattled by seeing Matthew outside the police station. I know I should've gone back in and told them, *He's right there under your noses, don't you see?* But how can I trust the police now, when it looks like he's one of them? He said he was going to disappear. So why is he back?

He never left, says a voice in my head. *He's been watching you.*

The realisation hits me so hard I almost feel the wind being knocked out of me. *The poppies.* Matthew knew Poppy, that much is clear. But how did he even know to target me in the first place? When Poppy's death was in the papers, I was never named. After a handful of interviews, they'd been satisfied that I tried to talk her down, and I've never been questioned again.

A fresh flush of anxiety consumes me, and I press harder on the accelerator. What if he saw me speaking to DC Starling? What if he overheard our whole conversation? What if he's gone to Orla's house to kill me, thinking I'm where I should be, and my sister pays the price? What if another person dies because of me? What if, what if, what if . . . I'm fifteen minutes from Orla's home, driving down a quiet road. Rain splatters the windscreen and my wipers swoop from left to right, frantic and fast. I push even harder on the accelerator and the car picks up speed. I take a corner a little too wide, and an oncoming car honks angrily. My pulse accelerates too, and my hands grip the steering wheel so tightly my knuckles turn white. I need to get there and make sure she's safe.

Worry spikes when I see flashing lights in my rear-view mirror. Desperately hoping it's a police officer responding to an incident, I slow and pull to one side, expecting them to pass by in a blur of white, red and blue, but they too pull to one side and slow to a stop behind me. I turn off the engine and wind down my window to speak to the tall, stringy-looking man I can see approaching in my wing mirror.

'Can you come with me please?' he asks in a bored voice.

My legs might as well have been made from two sticks of jelly for all the use they are. I'm guided into the back of the police car and the door is shut and locked. My hands are slippery with sweat, with rainwater.

The police officer twists in his seat to glance at me. 'Do you know how fast you were going back there?'

'I might have been a couple of miles over. I'm sorry.'

'You were doing sixty-three in a fifty.' He glances at my car and taps something into his phone. 'What's your name?'

'Anya Fernsby.'

He glances down at the device in his hand, tapping at the screen, before looking back up at me. 'This isn't your car.'

'It's my sister's. Orla Fernsby. I'm insured on it. And I'm sorry. About the speeding. I was just—'

'You're currently on bail.' He raises an eyebrow at me.

'I—'

'Your curfew ends in ten minutes. Where are you heading?'

I give him the address, my voice shaking uncontrollably. 'I'm so sorry. I'm going to my sister's.' I think about telling him about my worries, but I stop. I don't trust the police, not after what I've just discovered about Matthew. 'I'm running late. I want to get back before my curfew ends.'

He takes a deep breath, puffing the air out through his cheeks. 'Three points on your licence is probably the least of your concerns right now. We'll be in touch.'

The doors unlock and he releases me from my temporary prison. I scuttle back to my car, wet hair sticking to my face, knowing I'm about to break my curfew and there's nothing I can do about it. I can't risk getting caught speeding again. I hope and pray I'll get to Orla's in time. Before someone else gets hurt.

***

Twenty minutes past my curfew, I arrive at Orla's. The sun has set, and I'm surrounded by unsettling darkness. As soon as I open the car door, a gust of cold air and horizontal raindrops hit me in the face. I expect to see flashing blue and red lights but there must be some kind of time buffer on the ankle tag.

'Orla?' I call out once I'm inside.

'Anya?' my sister shouts back to me.

I shut the door behind me and rush into the kitchen. 'Are you okay?'

Orla is holding a tea towel, a worried expression on her face. 'I'm fine. Where the *hell* did you go?'

I drop into a dining chair. 'I'm sorry. I had to go to the station to tell them something about Matthew. And then I got caught speeding—'

'For God's sake, An.' She flings the tea towel onto the worktop in a burst of anger. 'You don't need anything else going against you right now!'

'I know, I just—'

'Don't.' She glares at me. 'Do you know how worried I've been? Haven't you put me through enough? You're literally *all I have left*.'

I feel a stab of guilt. 'I'm sorry. For everything.'

She's silent, leaning against the worktop, resting her head against the cupboard above. 'Dinner will be ready in about half an hour. And I'm sorry I burnt the garlic.' She turns back to the bolognese that's simmering away on the hob.

'It's okay.' Sensing she needs some space, I leave the room, heading up to the spare bedroom to lie down. This isn't how I wanted my last night with Orla to go.

***

359

Somehow I manage to drift off into a light sleep, but then I'm jerked awake by a sound. I can't figure out what the noise was. Was it even real, or was I dreaming? I rub at my eyes, and heave myself off the bed before padding downstairs. As I reach the bottom, I'm met with an uncomfortably cold breeze; the front door is wide open.

'Orla?' I peer out into the front garden, but it's pitch-black; I can see nothing. I've been on at her to get some security lights fitted but she hasn't sorted it yet.

I close the door shut behind me and head towards the kitchen, the smell of burnt cooking drifting through the air. I'm met with silence. But when I set foot on the cold kitchen floor tiles, I let out a strangled cry at the sight of my sister gagged and tied to a chair. Her face is pale and she looks unconscious. 'Orla!' I scream, rushing to her, ripping off the gag and leaving her skin raw, fingers fumbling with the knots but they're so tight, *too* tight. I can't loosen them—

I feel a hand at my throat and I'm thrown to the ground with rough force. My vision is blinded with black spots but I can see him; I can see his face. It's—

'Matthew?' My voice chokes as I say his name. His facial expression is cold, unreadable, as he brings his foot up into the air and presses it down onto my face so I can't speak.

'You couldn't leave things alone, could you?'

My eyes widen at the sight of him and I try to speak through the rubber sole of his boot grinding into my face, but my jaw is being crushed.

'You can add your sister to the list of people who are paying the price for what you did.'

I swing my leg out to try and knock him off balance and he budges, but only slightly. In retaliation, he brings his foot up and slams it back down into my face. I cry out in pain. My cheekbone feels like it's been shattered into a thousand pieces.

'Why?' I manage to beg, tasting blood, feeling blinding pain. I need to buy myself some time, hoping Orla would regain consciousness. 'Why now? Why wait so long?'

The pressure on my face lessens slightly as he considers my question, as if weighing up whether or not to talk.

'Come on.' My voice is muffled through the dirt-encrusted rubber sole of his boot. 'You're going to kill me anyway. I just want to know. Why did you wait so many years to track me down?'

'I was a mess,' he snaps, leaning down towards me. I can feel his breath on my face. 'All right? Is that what you want to hear? I was a fucking *mess*. I thought Poppy killed herself. I thought she was so distressed about the pregnancy that *I* caused, that she threw herself onto the rocks to end it all. I blamed myself,' he shouts, a spray of spittle landing on my forehead. 'So I moved to Brighton and joined the police force. I thought in some way it would help me make up for the pain I caused. And it did, for a bit. But then, another detective was transferred to our team. A detective who I know worked on the original case. Janet Kane.'

I feel a prickling in my scalp. *Janet Kane*. I remember being interviewed by her. She was terrifying.

'I couldn't bring myself to speak to her about it; I was finally moving on. But one day, I swear I saw Poppy walking down the street. She looked so much like her, even the way she walked. And I couldn't get her out of my head. So I got chatting to Janet, and she let slip that there had been another person up on the cliffs with Poppy. A school friend. *You*.'

I can almost feel the cold wind against my skin as if I'm back there. But that information was never released to the papers. Janet Kane had seemed satisfied with my version of events.

Matthew continues. 'I started to think. What if someone else was to blame? What if she was pushed? What if *you* pushed her? I remember her telling me about you, how clingy, how *obsessed* you were. So I tracked you down.'

My chest tightens at the thought of him following me. I remember how I felt when we first met, how I thought I'd recognised him from somewhere, how he'd played along. I must've seen him when he was stalking me.

'And now I know, thanks to my little chat with your cousin.' He removes his boot from my face and presses it hard into my chest, forcing the oxygen out of my lungs before I have the chance to think about what Ruben has said, and why he would speak to Matthew. 'You couldn't take the rejection from Poppy, that she wasn't like you. You were *humiliated*. You killed her.' His face looks manic. I've never seen his eyes this wide, this white. 'You killed Poppy, and our unborn child. I thought it would be enough to inflict the same thing on you. Kill your girlfriend, your stepdaughter. But seeing you again . . . it's not enough. I want you to *burn*.'

Chapter 65

Eve – Now

The tunnel is murky, and eyes peer from the shadows, following me with every step. It goes on forever; no sign of it ever coming to an end. On and on I traipse, completely and utterly alone.

'Evie!' A reedy little voice from beside me makes me start, my eyes straining to adjust to the gloom.

'Frankie?' I crouch to scoop up my younger sister from the grimy ground. She's so much smaller than I remember. No bigger than a toddler. 'What are you doing here? How are you here? You're . . . you're d—' No. I still can't bring myself to say it. Frankie doesn't speak but continues to stare at me with big, round eyes. I look resolutely ahead and carry on walking, desperate to reach the end of the tunnel, and get us both to the safety of the light. The heat in the tunnel is stifling, but I can see a welcoming glow in the distance. I trek on, carrying the warm bundle of my sister in my arms, struggling over the terrain that's becoming more rutted and rough the further I walk. The pinprick of light grows, a bright circle in the distance that beckons me, enticing me into its warmth and safety.

I look down again, and the ground is covered with broken glass.

'Turn back, Evie.' Frankie's terrified face peers up at me, drained of colour. 'Get away from the glass.'

I feel so sick. 'What? I'm getting us out of here. I'm taking us somewhere safe.'

Frankie shakes her head frantically. 'No, you're not. You're taking us closer to the fire.'

Fire? My head jerks up and I realise with a wave of fear that the distant circle of light is all of a sudden very close indeed. It dawns on me that it's not light at all; it's a blazing ball of fire, and it's getting bigger by the second. Before my eyes, it morphs into a burning house. Our house. I pivot on the spot, trying to run away, but now the fire is surrounding us. We're completely trapped.

A cry tears from Frankie's throat. She leaps from my arms and turns to face me, her sweet little face twisted with ugly rage. 'It's your fault!' She repeats the cruel words over and over again, pointing a finger at me. I shrink back in shame. 'It's your fault, Evie! You killed me.' She pummels at me with tiny fists.

My eyes dart around, searching for an escape, but the circle of flames surrounds us, drawing ever closer.

The last thing I see is my mother, running out of the flames, sooty and sweating, and pushing us both to safety.

***

I wonder what that bright thing is, I think. Everything's blurry and fuzzy. Did I die? I really hope I'm not dead. But this isn't like anything I've ever experienced before, so I conclude that I must in fact be dead. Frustration bubbles away inside me. Little sounds echo in the distance, but they're not close enough for me to worry about right now. All I want to know is what that strange light is, more than anything else in the world. I try to lift a hand to reach out and grab it, but I feel it flop helplessly at my side.

'Jason . . .' I mumble, wondering if he'd died too. 'That you?'

Jason.

Why does that name suddenly make me feel so wildly angry? An unexplained surge of fury pulses through me as a memory seeps in from the edges of my awareness, but as I grasp it, it ebbs away into nothing. A mix of confusion and aggravation swirls around inside me. I blink and try to force my eyes to focus, wishing this new world would become a little clearer to me. The force of straining my eyes makes my head sore. God, this hurts like hell. I feel as if I've been beaten repeatedly around the head and kicked in the face. Isn't death supposed to be painless? Maybe I'm still dying.

Jason. Did he do this to me? No. Not Jason. I feel a confusing combination of contempt and fondness for him but can't remember why. Did we fall out? We're so close . . . we have each other's backs. Why am I angry with him?

With a jolt, I realise I'm lying on the ground, something hard and metallic digging into my wrists. Coldness seeps into my skin. I'm definitely not dead, but I'm yet to rule out the dying part.

'Eve.' A woman's voice calls out, stern yet laced with concern. 'Can you hear me?'

I squint to work out who the familiar voice belongs to.

I blink as I see an eye staring at me through a letterbox, accompanied by torchlight. 'Gilly?' I croak.

'Shit,' she says, her eyes adjusting to the darkness. 'Can you let me in?'

'No. I'm cuffed to the radiator.' The words catch in my throat. 'He fucking *attacked* me.'

Gillian says nothing, and for a terrifying few seconds, I think she's on his side, and he's sent her to finish me off. If Jason's a bent cop, how do I know if Gillian is who she says she is?

An ear-splitting bang breaks my frenzied, paranoid train of thought and the glass pane shatters into thousands of pieces. The sound threatens to unearth a memory but I shove it down. I can't deal with it right now. Gillian's hand reaches through the gaping hole in the door, fiddles with the lock, and opens it wide. She rushes in and drops to her knees in front of me. I've never seen her look so distressed.

'How'd you find me?' My voice shakes.

'I heard a scuffle when your call got cut off. Knew you were in trouble. It was easy to find you, you left your bloody WhatsApp live location on when you invited Tiana to lunch. Thank your lucky fucking stars. What the *hell* happened in here?' She fumbles for a key and unlocks my cuffs. 'Where's Jason?'

'He left,' I say. 'He cuffed me and left.'

'Jason did this to you? Are you *sure*?'

I nod as I free my hands from the cuffs, and a rush of memories comes flooding back in an order that makes no sense. I try to piece it all together as I stretch my arms out, flex my fingers, trying to get some semblance of feeling back into them. 'After Anya left the station today, I watched her go. She was heading back to her car, and she stopped suddenly. She looked *terrified*. She hid from someone. It was Jason. And I thought . . . why would she be so scared of him? She's at a police station. She would've known there'd be officers around. And he wasn't even in uniform.' It takes a monumental effort to form full sentences. 'Then I thought, she knows him. It was *recognition* on her face.'

A series of images unfold in my head with the clarity of crystal: Anya's face when she saw Jason in the car park. The messages on his phone. Jason's face twisted in rage as he smashed me over the head, the furious fight, the smashing glass, the fire at my house, my sister's tiny casket being lowered into the ground. As the two memories blur into one, tears threaten to cascade from my eyes. 'Then it hit me. The man she described sounded exactly like Jason.' As I say the words out loud, more and more of the pieces begin to slot into place. 'Jason knows about boats – remember when he corrected you on the terminology? And then there's the dog. Bowie. Jason's dog is called Dave. *David Bowie*,' I say in response to Gillian's puzzled expression. 'I wanted to find you, to tell you, but . . . I wanted solid evidence, not a hunch. You said I rely on gut instinct too much. So I just . . . went.'

I see a flash of guilt on Gillian's face as she reaches for my blood-soaked hand. 'I didn't mean for you to bloody—'

I cut her off. 'It doesn't matter now. I found a phone, and it had messages from Anya on it. We need to find him,

Gilly. He knows she's finally found him. He's going to want revenge.' My eyes widen as the reality of what I said sinks in.

Gillian falls into a shocked silence. Her face wears a deathly pallor, her mouth hanging open. 'Jason,' she says finally, blinking at me. 'He's got Orla Fernsby's address. I've got to stop him, he's going to— The absolute fucking swine.' She pulls her radio out of her pocket and drops my hand. 'Eve, I need to go. I'll call you an ambulance—'

'No,' I protest. 'There's absolutely no way I'm leaving you to stop him alone.'

'But—'

'Come on.' I stagger out of the house towards her car, the searing pain in my head subsiding, replaced with pure determination. Rain hammers down, soaking my hair and plastering it to my forehead.

Gillian slides into the driver's seat, pressing a finger to her radio, requesting the Armed Response Unit and rattling off the address.

A reply crackles over the speakers as I punch the address into the sat nav. A cold, hard realisation hits me as the map loads. 'Her house is in the middle of nowhere.'

Chapter 66

Eve – Now

A deluge of rain falls from the sky and gravel crunches under the tyres as we pull up outside the cottage, the windscreen wipers racing from side to side almost as fast as my heart is thumping. A glossy black car is parked to the left of the house. Jason's car. I'm vaguely aware of Gillian calling in the fire service as I topple out of the car before it rolls to a halt. The pounding in my head returns as I stare in horror at the cottage, cloaked in darkness, and my nostrils are assaulted by a terribly familiar stench before I lay eyes on the thick clouds of black smoke spiralling from the house. The memories aren't holding back, and I'm unable to shake them off as they fly at me with sharpened claws.

Flames.

Smoke.

Hospital.

Casket.

I hear footsteps behind me, and Gillian appears by my

side. 'They're on their way, but from the other side of town. It's going to take at least twenty, twenty-five minutes. Traffic-depending. *Shit*. We don't have much time. Any sign of Jason?'

I nod, eyes transfixed on the house. 'His car's still here.'

No wonder Orla didn't pick up when I rang her from the car. 'Ma'am . . . we—' I scoop wet hair from my face and swallow hard, my throat dry and sticky. 'We've got to go in there.'

She turns to face me, eyes wide. 'Not you. I'll go.'

A movement behind her head catches my eye. A figure, sprinting from the cottage and into the woods. 'Stop!' I yell hoarsely. He doesn't look back, but I'm certain of one thing.

It's him.

Gillian whips around and sees what I've seen. She looks at me, her face deeply apologetic, before springing into action and tailing him without looking back.

I know what I need to do.

With one deep breath, I move swiftly towards the cottage, feet pounding hard on the grass with every step, determination flooding my body and numbing all feeling.

I can't let Anya down. I refuse.

I skirt the perimeter of the house, finding a downstairs window that's far enough away from the fire. I pull the baton I'd grabbed from Gillian's car and hammer it into the glass. It breaks easily, and I haul myself through the small frame, feeling shards of glass snagging on my clothes. I land with a thud on the tiled floor of a tiny utility room, my shoulder complaining, my head still throbbing from the earlier impact. The washing machine is spinning as if everything's normal . . . I climb to my feet and hesitate at the closed door, testing it with the back of my hand. No heat. Yet.

I push it open and step into a kitchen. A smoky haze curls into every corner of the room, and the stench of chemicals stings my eyes. I grab a tea towel, run it under the tap and tie it around my face to cover my mouth and nose, before heading into the dining room. The crackling sound of flames is louder now. I'm close. The door's shut, but I know it'll lead to the entrance hall where the fire will be climbing the walls. Snaking into each corner, devouring everything in its path.

I step into the hall, where the sound is unbearable, and memories dance within the flickering flames, taunting me. A huge, towering inferno spreads across the carpet and licks hungrily at the walls. I'm rooted to the spot. The stench of smoke and burning carpet overwhelm me. I cover my mouth as I heave. *The heat. Oh God, the heat.*

'Is anyone there?' I shout, and I hear a hoarse yell from upstairs in response. 'Stay where you are,' I instruct, my voice muffled through my makeshift mask. Then I run through the fire. Flames lick at me as I reach the bottom of the stairs, scaling the steps two at a time.

I stumble onto the landing, prepared to fling open each door to find Anya and Orla, but it's immediately obvious where they are. Two dining chairs are wedged underneath the handles of two doors. One door is being battered repeatedly; the other is worryingly still. Disturbingly quiet.

'Anya? Orla?' I shout out as I pick up both chairs and fling them over the banister into the fire below.

'Help!' One of the doors bursts open and an ashen-faced Anya spills out of it, a bruise blooming on one side of her face, blood trickling from a split lip. I whip the tea towel away from my mouth and she stares manically at me before flinging herself towards the other door, behind which Orla lies unconscious on the floor. Anya drops to her knees beside her sister, shaking her roughly.

'Wake up,' she screams in her face. 'Wake up. Please.'

I can see from the rise and fall of Orla's chest that she's still alive, but we don't have much time.

'She's unconscious. I can't wake her.' Anya's voice is high and panicky.

'Let's get her out of here.' I haul Orla into a standing position, her head lolling to one side. 'We've got to find an escape route. *Now.*'

Anya glances towards the window. I squint out into the darkness, but realise with a crushing sense of dismay there's no way we'll be able to drop Orla out of that window without killing her. Not at five metres onto cold, hard concrete. She won't stand a chance.

'It's too far. We've got to find another way.'

We cough and splutter as the smoke thickens. I frantically motion for her to get down. We both crouch, and I lower Orla as we do so.

'The conservatory,' I say, remembering passing it on my

way to the utility room. 'On the other side of the house. If we can get over there, we should be able to lower her onto the roof and climb out that way.'

Anya stares at me, understanding in her eyes.

'We'll have to crawl across the landing,' I say. 'The smoke's too thick now.'

The flames are still going strong, working their way up the stairs, step by step. I shuffle backwards as I drag Orla by her ankles. Anya pushes her shoulders forward as she shimmies across the landing. It's a slow and awkward movement, the thick carpet making it extremely difficult to drag Orla between us. The fire reaches the top step and creeps onto the landing.

'We need to move quicker,' I shriek. My entire body is covered in a layer of sweat, and the bitter scent of burning is filling my lungs and making me wheeze. An intense heat hits me as I draw level with the flames, inches away from my face. I freeze, every limb unable to move.

Flames.

Smoke.

Hospital.

Casket.

No. I shake my head violently from side to side. I will not succumb to the memories that have spent the last ten years flickering at the edge of my vision. I refuse to allow someone to die because I'm too terrified to act. With a strangled cry, I force myself to stand, heaving the dead weight of Orla's unconscious body onto my back with a strength I didn't know I had, and dash to the end of the landing. I stagger through the door and throw open the window, gasping as the fresh night air fills my lungs. My vision blurs, the view partially blocked by little black dots, a sea of tadpoles swimming wherever I try to force my focus. But I see it: the conservatory roof.

Anya has followed me into the room, closing the door on the wall of flames that have now engulfed the landing. Her face is washed out and shiny, eyes red and chest heaving as she leans against the closed door.

'Climb out so I can lower her down to you,' I instruct. 'Careful on the glass.'

She scrabbles through the open window and steps tentatively onto the metal framework of the roof, cautiously avoiding the panes of glass. I heave Orla feet first through the window, and Anya grabs hold of her ankles, and I shift her so I can clamber through the window whilst still keeping hold. Below is a glass box of fire. An intense heat radiates through the panes, making the metal structure dangerously hot to touch as we slide Orla across the roof. Anya lowers herself to the ground and reaches up her arms to help pull her sister to safety. She gasps in relief when she's safely cradled in her arms, but I know she's not out of the woods yet.

I prepare myself to scrabble down from the roof when a sudden scream from the woods resounds through the air. *Was that Gillian?* My body jolts with a start, and I step to one side to steady myself. The sound of the glass shattering beneath me is the last thing I hear.

Chapter 67

Eve – Then

The glass bottle in my hand shatters into a million tiny fragments as I bring it down onto the kitchen lino, a decade of anguish and despair funnelled into that single act of defiance. Of rebellion.

But it isn't enough. How can it *ever* be?

Dad's face is twisted in rage as he rounds on me. 'What the fuck are you doing?'

'You sold Frankie's mobile, Dad!' I grab another bottle and hurl it at the floor in front of his bare feet. 'I bought that for her so she could call me when I'm not here. So she's not completely alone!' Vodka splashes up the cupboards and against his feet, and he staggers back to avoid the jagged shards of glass littering the floor.

He lunges for me as I raise another bottle into the air, and I duck out of the way. He stumbles drunkenly into the fridge, making it teeter, sending the bottles on top of it crashing to the ground around him. 'It's just a fucking phone!'

'It was her only way of contacting me since you stopped paying for the fucking internet!'

Down goes the bottle in my hand. The sound is ear-splitting, but I don't care anymore. I storm into the living room and feel under the sofa cushions. More bottles.

One.

Two.

Three.

Shatter.

I reach a hand under the sofa and pull out another bottle. I turn on the spot and launch it at the wall next to Dad. Vodka streams down the wall. The house stinks of it.

'Have you lost your fucking mind, Evie?' His face has transformed from angry to terrified.

Yeah, maybe I have lost my mind. I can't think straight but in that moment, I don't care. It's not just this; it's everything. *Every fucking thing.*

I work my way around the room, plucking half-drunk bottles of vodka from their hiding places and bringing them out into the light. Letting him know I realise the extent of his problem.

He's marooned in the middle of the living room, sur-rounded by a sea of broken glass, feet bleeding, panting in fear, eyes darting around for an escape route. No, not an escape route, I realise, as I notice his eyes sliding to the battered old biscuit tin shoved unceremoniously under the TV unit. The one full of family photos. Happy snaps, taken before everything went to shit. I make a grab for it, tearing off the lid, and I find the last bottle. Resting on top of a photograph of my seven-year-old face. I screech out in fury and send that one flying into the wall as well.

Glass, everywhere.

Vodka, everywhere.

That'll teach them.

Chapter 68

Eve – Now

The broken bottles. The vodka. The reason the fire in my family home took hold so fiercely. The reason I cannot bring myself to drink a drop of alcohol. I will never, *ever* stop blaming myself for Frankie's death.

I shake away the memory as shards from the conservatory roof rain down on me, landing in my hair and on my shoulders. Anya's pale face stares helplessly at me through the glass. Seconds. That's all I've got. I feel the heat from the flames licking at my trousers and blistering my skin, and the pain from the broken glass that tore a jagged zig-zag into my leg when I fell. The fire is so close now. I swallow down the sick feeling of terror, reach back and then drive my elbow into the pane, but it doesn't budge.

My eyes search the blazing room and fall upon a small wooden side table. I grab it with both hands and swing it with enough force to shatter the glass. It's ear-splitting. I kick away the large shards that stick out of the framework, before leaping out of the conservatory onto the ground, rolling back and forth until the flames on my body are extinguished. I lie on my back on the cool, damp grass, my breath forming little clouds in front of my face as I pant. But now there's no escaping from the memories that parade before my eyes. I squeeze them shut, forcing the tears to stay inside my eyes, but the memories are inside my head and they're more prominent than they've ever been.

I sit up with a start, remembering the sound of the scream, the reason I fell. The fact that my boss, my friend, is in serious trouble. I climb to my feet, body screaming in pain, and turn back to Anya, cradling the limp form of her sister. 'Stay here. Help's coming,' I gasp. 'Send them to the woods.'

'Where are you going?' Anya screeches towards my retreating back.

'After him. Stay here,' I shout over my shoulder as I sprint towards the foreboding darkness of the woods, in the direction I'd seen the dark figure running earlier.

Towards Jason.

Chapter 69

I tear my eyes away from the detective and stare back into Orla's sickeningly pale face, sooty smudges all over her cheeks, nose and forehead. She's breathing. Wheezing. We're bundled together under a tree, which is keeping most of the rain off us. The sound of the fire ripping through her cottage is at odds with the soothing sound of the rain hitting the canopy of leaves above, pattering onto the grass surrounding us. The air smells smoky yet cool.

'Please, no,' I repeat over and over as I grip on to her with desperate hands. 'Don't you dare leave me.' A cry rips through my throat as I fear the worst. I scream into the darkness of the murky sky, 'Don't take my sister, please. She's all I have left.'

The weight of her body shifts ever so slightly in my lap and she coughs, before taking in a gulp of cool, night air. 'Such a drama queen,' she murmurs, wincing in pain.

I bury my face into her chest. 'You're alive. Thank *God* you're alive.'

She coughs violently, rolling off my lap and onto her front. She heaves and throws up on the grass, then takes more gasps of fresh, cool air.

'The ambulance is on its way.' I rub her back gently as she takes deep breath after deep breath. I'm desperate to ask her what happened, how Matthew ended up in her house but I can take a guess. If a friendly police officer shows up at your door with I.D., you typically don't question it – especially when your sister is on bail. I feel another stab of guilt that my actions have brought pain and destruction to another person I love. But this time, it's mixed in with a heavy dose of revenge. I want to find him. I want to *kill* him. I'm going down for a double murder I didn't commit; what difference will it make if I kill someone for real?

I look at Orla, trying to stem the combination of fury and fear in my voice. 'How are you feeling?'

She drops back into a sitting position, evaluating herself. 'I . . . I think I'm okay. I think you got me out just in time.'

'It wasn't just me. He locked us in while we were unconscious. It was DC Starling who got us out.'

Orla's eyes widen. 'Where is she?'

My eyes are dragged to the woods, remembering her words . . . *after him*. She's gone after Matthew. The anger inside me isn't simmering anymore, it's a red-hot melting pot of pure rage. Something snaps inside me.

Chapter 70

Eve – Now

The wind and rain lessen once I'm under the cover of the trees. A fusion of scents weaves its way up my nose: damp, spongy moss growing on wet tree trunks, earthy mushrooms and decaying leaves. Twigs snap loudly underfoot as I run, avoiding deep puddles of muddy rainwater, torch swinging from side to side as I search for a sign of life.

Or death.

Cold wetness seeps into my trainer as one foot lands in a puddle; a stinging breeze finds its way through the trees. I listen hard, but the sound of the blood rushing in my ears is deafening. I stop when I see a pool of torchlight up ahead, and a body lying in the centre of it.

Gillian.

I push dripping strands of hair out of my face. The smell of sopping mud is strong as I slow my pace and creep forward, remaining hidden in the shadows of the trees. The light up ahead grows brighter. Voices echo in the darkness, mixed in with the rustling, scuttling sounds of the woods around me. I grasp on to any words I can hear floating towards me on the breeze.

'. . . too late for them. They'll be long gone now.'

'You don't . . . have to . . . do this.' Gillian's voice is thick with pain, gasping for breath between words. 'Let me . . . save them.'

Fear grips me as I try to edge closer, but the leaves rustling beneath my trainers threaten to give me away. An owl hoots. I pause. I don't know whether it's a surge of adrenaline, or pure, unadulterated fury, but there's nothing for it. I sprint towards the light that shimmers in the pitch-black, pointing my own torch directly into Jason's shocked face. He squints in confusion, eyes dazzled by the bright light.

'How the hell did you—?'

Thwack.

I swing the heavy torch into the side of his head, and he roars in anger, reaching to grab me. I shine it in his eyes again and aim a sharp kick at his knee. The two torchlights perform a dizzying dance as we aim blindly for one another, sometimes hitting, sometimes missing. I feel a hard blow to my chest, and I wheeze.

'You interfering little bitch,' says Jason.

The spinning lights make me dizzy, but I'm not letting him get away with it. Not again. We continue to grapple, and I howl as I feel the hard metal casing of the torch connect with my cheekbone. My own slips from my hands and rolls out of my reach, into the damp of the undergrowth.

Darkness shrouds us as he drops his torch, both hands on my shoulders as he drives me up against a thick tree trunk.

He holds me there with the weight of his body and grips my head roughly with both hands. I'm sure there's a slight hesitation before he smashes my skull into the tree with a sickening crunch. Images shimmer in my mind.

Gillian's limp body on the ground.

Anya's helpless face from behind the flames.

The photo of Lisette and Sylvie, smiling out of the pasta-decorated photo frame.

Then I see a movement in the shadows. A face. Someone's standing behind Jason.

My eyes widen and I hold my breath.

Chapter 71

Eve – Now

My eyes struggle to focus on the image of Anya standing before me, holding a tree branch, pale face staring at Jason lying limp on the ground in front of her, as if she can't believe what she's just done. *I* can't believe what she's done. She's saved my life.

I take a tentative step forward, my hand reaching for her shoulder, and she snaps back to reality, steadying me on the uneven ground. I squeeze my eyes shut. I'm in agony but I think I'll be okay. Unless I'm dreaming, which I could well be. I stumble over to the other figure lying unconscious in the dark.

'Gillian?' I try to shine the light into her eyes, but my vision is blurred and I struggle to see clearly.

A groan.

I feel a wetness in her side, and bring my hand away. It's warm and sodden; he must've stabbed her. The dark patch underneath her tells me she's lost a worrying amount of blood. I press my hands to her skin to stem the flow, trying desperately not to let panic consume me.

'Here. Use this.' Anya peels off her hoodie over her head and tosses it towards me.

I press it over the wound, hoping it's enough to stem the flow until the paramedics arrive. 'Thank you.' I stare at her, still at a loss as to how she's here, right now, saving my life.

Gillian stirs and I turn my attention back to her.

'Eve . . .'

'It's okay, I've got you. Help is coming. And Jason's unconscious.'

I turn my face to Anya. 'Your sister . . . is she okay?'

'She's alive.' Her face is grey in the torchlight, mouth set in a grim line.

'Okay,' I say, turning back to Gillian and watching her closely. 'Okay. We'll be all right.' The pain in my head is almost unbearable. 'We'll be all right.' I repeat the words, hoping they are true, until the sound of heavy footsteps thudding our way interrupts the quiet rustling of the woods; a team of paramedics appear alongside dancing torchlight up ahead.

We'll be all right.

The nightmare's over.

***

You see a lot as a detective. Memories that drag you from your sleep each night, just as you're on the edge of drifting off. Stuff that makes you squirm, even years after witnessing it. Things that make you want to dig out your own eyes. But the strangest thing I think I'll ever experience is sitting in a dark and windowless interview room opposite Jason

Hooper, who I never would have dreamed would be slouching in a plastic chair on *that* side of the table.

Gillian eases into the seat beside me. I can tell from her movements that she's still in pain from the stab wound, but she won't clutch her side, nor will she wince. She won't show Jason how much he hurt her. The doctor wanted her to stay in hospital another night and take some time off work, but Gillian, being Gillian, flat-out refused. I don't blame her for wanting to be present at this interview.

I stare at Jason. 'Talk to us about Poppy Fallon.'

I notice a subtle change in his demeanour. A slight widening of the eyes, a squaring of the shoulders. He hadn't been expecting this question. 'We were friends. Why are you asking me about her?'

'Poppy died when she was fifteen, and you were . . .' I make a show of peering at the sheet of paper in front of me. 'Twenty-three. Now, I'm not sure about you, but I don't know many fifteen-year-old girls who would be friends with a man eight years older, and keep him a secret from her friends and family, unless there was something more to the relationship.'

'She didn't keep me a secret.'

'Neither her parents nor Anya knew anything definite about you. Anya did, however, inform us that Poppy mentioned dating an older man in the weeks leading up to her death. Is there anything you'd like to tell us about that?'

Jason laughs bitterly. 'You think I killed her.'

I flash him a smile. 'No, I don't. But I know that Anya was present on the night Poppy died. It was ruled an accident, but what I'm struggling with is how you ended up dating

Anya years later. Brighton's a big place. That's a pretty big coincidence isn't it?'

Jason lifts his chin. 'I didn't date Anya. You're barking.'

'Jason Hooper didn't date Anya Fernsby. But Matthew Taylor did. However . . . Jason and Matthew appear to be one and the same person, according to Anya.'

He leans his face closer to mine. 'That's bullshit, and you know it. She's a lying little—'

'If it's bullshit, why did you knock out Orla Fernsby and set fire to her home?' Gillian challenges him.

'I didn't knock her out.' His voice is sharp as he turns his face to her. 'And I didn't set that fire.'

'You ran into the woods,' she accuses him.

'I was visiting on your instruction to check up on the Fernsby sisters.' He shrugs at Gillian. 'The fire had already started. I ran because I thought I'd be blamed.'

'And you stabbed me because?' asks Gillian.

'Self-defence.'

She laughs. 'You're a brilliant detective, Jason Hooper. But you're a shit liar.'

His face reddens.

'Here's what I think happened.' I lean forward in my seat. 'You were in love with Poppy Fallon at the time of her death. You still are.' I think of the photograph in his bedside table drawer that I now know to be Poppy. 'You read the newspaper article that mentioned a teenage girl was present on the night of the incident, but you couldn't find out who it was. If you did any digging, you'd risk outing yourself as a paedophile. So you waited. You joined the police force, worked your way up. And last year, when she was working in our division, you met DI Janet Kane who worked on the case when she was a DC. You got hold of Anya's name, and you tracked her down. How am I doing so far?'

Jason glares at me, fury radiating from him.

I continue. 'You fabricated a new persona as Matthew Taylor, a fireman. You preyed on a desperate alcoholic, convincing him to rent you his boat without registering any records so you could operate under the radar. How did you do that, Jason? Offer to renovate it for him? Anya told us you both painted it. That's quite a job, and conveniently meant Anya had to handle the bottle of white spirit, leaving her prints all over it.' I pause, giving him a chance to speak, but he remains silent. 'You wormed your way into Anya's life, making her trust you, hoping she would fall in love with you and tell you the truth about what happened with Poppy. She told us you got her drunk, asked her relentless questions. But it didn't work, did it? She left you for Lisette. So you retaliated by killing Lisette and her daughter. Why did you wait so long though? That's the only bit I can't put my finger on.'

He says nothing, but the look on his face is thunderous.

'We're charging you, Jason,' says Gillian. 'Eve found the phone at your flat, the one you used to pretend to be Matthew, and Anya has identified you as Matthew Taylor. You tried to kill both of us. You know what happens if you cooperate. And if you refuse.'

Jason closes his eyes for a few seconds, and opens them again, his expression changed. 'When I looked at Anya's phone, I saw messages from her cousin, Ruben Fernsby,' he

389

says reluctantly. 'He kept hinting at something that had happened in the past, and asking Anya for money. She handed it over so willingly, I knew there'd be a reason. It took me a while to track him down and question him myself. Once I got the answers I needed, I wanted to make her pay.'

'And what did he tell you?' I ask, remembering the large amounts of cash Anya withdrew from her account in the months leading up to her disappearance, to help her cousin out. I think back to the conversation with Ruben and kick myself for not pushing him harder.

'Anya and Poppy were at Seaford Head. Anya shoved Poppy over the cliff edge. She. Killed. Her.' He jabs his index finger into the table to emphasise each of his last three words.

'And Ruben would corroborate this?' I ask.

'I'm convinced of it.'

'And you didn't coerce him into speaking?'

'No,' he snaps, but his uncomfortable expression says otherwise. 'Look, Anya had already told me something had happened. She never told me the full story. She freaked out when I took her to Seaford Head. Ruben just gave me the missing piece of the puzzle.'

'Under duress.'

'No.' His voice is firm.

'So he told you off his own back?' I say. 'I don't believe you.'

Jason raises his palms to the ceiling and drops them into his lap. 'I don't know what to say to you, Eve. I didn't coerce him.'

'You'd better think of something,' snaps Gillian, leaning forward, hands pressed against the table. 'Because we're going to speak to Ruben, and right now we don't believe a word that comes out of your lying mouth.' She can't hide the betrayal she's feeling.

'Jason, I don't believe that Ruben would willingly talk to you when he wouldn't tell *me* any of this,' I tell him. 'There must be a reason. Otherwise, it doesn't make any sense. You must see that?'

After a moment of consideration, Jason sighs and speaks again. 'He wasn't going to throw his cousin under the bus without a bit of persuading.'

I shake my head. Speechless. I think about how Jason has been throwing his weight around, bullying Ruben into talking, screwing up Anya's life, mindlessly killing Lisette and Sylvie, just to complete his own personal mission, to exact his revenge. How he tried to bury his crime, making it look like it was the work of the arsonist who'd been setting fires locally. Then another thought strikes me. *Zachary*. His murder was so convenient, so timely. What's the death of another druggie to Jason? I wonder . . .

'Jason, can you tell us anything about the death of Zachary Samson?'

Gillian tenses beside me, but says nothing. Jason glares at me.

'Look,' I say, once I realise he isn't going to talk. 'I get it. I know what it's like to lose someone you care about. You know I understand, right? How you'd do pretty much *anything* for someone you love?'

He stares up at the ceiling.

'Remember the time I told you that in my darkest moments

I wished my parents were still alive so I could punish them? Because if it wasn't for them, Frankie would still be alive? I get it, Jason. I really do.'

Jason drops his gaze back to me, eyes glassy. I feel like I'm getting through to him. 'You killed Zachary too, didn't you?' I press him.

After a brief pause, he says, 'Yes.'

I say nothing, waiting for him to confess what I already suspect to be true.

'I needed to cover my tracks.' His voice is quiet and steady. 'I went round to see him, on my own. After you and Bella spoke to him. As soon as he saw me, he recognised me. He spotted an opportunity, threatened to blackmail me. I was having none of it. We had a scrap, and he hit his head on the TV unit. Died instantly. I set it up to look like a drug deal gone wrong.'

It's my turn to fix Jason with my hardest stare. 'Three people.' I shake my head. 'You're a *police officer*.'

Jason ignores me, directing his attention to Gillian. 'You need to speak to Ruben. You need to know why I was driven to do what I did. Why I had no choice.'

Gillian makes no promises. 'You killed Lisette and Sylvie Dupont, and Zachary Samson. You attempted to murder Anya and Orla Fernsby. You attempted to murder us *both*. Regardless of the reason behind your actions, you're being charged with three cases of murder, four cases of attempted murder and two cases of arson.'

Jason closes his eyes, beaten. I know how I should be feeling . . . triumphant. Exuberant. But what I really feel is betrayal.

Chapter 72

Anya – Now

I'm a free woman.

It didn't take long for the case against me to be dropped. After I'd knocked Matthew unconscious, he'd been taken to hospital with DC Eve Starling and the woman who'd been stabbed. Eve still looked awful a week later, when she'd visited me to update me on my case. Bruises and cuts blossomed across every inch of visible skin and she'd walked with a limp and winced whenever she'd moved. I owe her *everything*. She'd confirmed that his real name is Jason Hooper, and that he's a detective sergeant in her team. She'd also told me how he'd tracked me down and set up a fake identity to try and get to the truth of what happened to Poppy. His strange behaviour, his intense questioning, it all finally made sense.

And now . . . I still can't get my head around the fact that he's locked up in police custody, and no longer hunting me. He'll have to undergo a trial of course, but I've been told there's enough solid evidence against him to charge him. And he's going to be locked up for a very long time indeed.

***

The first thing I do after visiting Orla in hospital is go to see Ruben. I don't know how I'll feel when I see him . . . him speaking to Matthew set in place a chain of events that ended with the deaths of Lisette and Sylvie. But I know he was vulnerable and coerced. I also know he denied ever saying anything when the police spoke to him last week. Ultimately, Matthew was to blame.

When he answers the door, I'm relieved to see his face free of bruises and some meat on his bones. He glances warily at me from the gap between the door and the wall, before opening it and stepping back.

'I'm sorry I blamed you for everything,' I say, once I'm inside. 'I know you weren't behind the poppies. I'm sorry I accused you.'

'I'm the one who should be apologising,' he says. 'I let that policeman bully me into saying what he wanted to hear.' He shakes his head as if trying to forget something, 'I don't even know what I really saw; I don't want to know.'

'It was an accident,' I remind him sharply.

'I know, I know. But then there was all that money I took from you—'

I wave him off. So much has happened, I don't even care about the money anymore. And Matthew is evil and manipulative. I can't blame Ruben for that. Especially when I manipulated him myself.

'No, listen,' he insists. 'I've sorted myself out. For real this time.'

I raise an eyebrow but let him continue.

'After you . . . left. I confided in Orla. I told her everything. She was angry. God, that woman has a fiery temper when it comes to protecting you. But after a while, she helped me. Gave me a job at Melody Laine. I've saved up a quarter of the money I borrowed from you. And I'll keep saving until I've paid you back in full.'

'I don't *care* about the money, I care that you're better now.' I reach out and grab his hand. 'You were in the worst possible place when all this happened. I've got a lot of perspective now.' Losing the love of your life will do that to you.

He reaches out and pulls me into a hug. We stay like that for a long time.

***

As I walk down the path from his flat later that afternoon, my phone pings. I glance at the screen; it's a notification from HSBC. I log in, and see a bank transfer from Ruben: £1,250, as promised. I glance back at the flat and smile.

And now, I'm heading back to Plockton. I hadn't lived there long, but I'd become accustomed to the slow pace, the serene beauty of the place. It took me a while to pluck up the courage to phone Peggy, apologies and explanations streaming out of me like a river, and I've been forgiven for the chaos I've caused. At least by Peggy . . . Ingrid might take a bit of work. Whatever happens, I know I can't stay here; all Brighton holds for me are smouldering memories. I hope Orla and Ruben understand.

But first, I have one more thing to do.

Chapter 73

Eve – Two months later

Our glasses clink together and something cold splashes down my arm.

'So proud of you, Eve,' says Gillian quietly, once our cheers have died down into a gentle hum of conversation.

'Thanks, ma'am.' I grip my Coke, feeling awkward. With Jason's arrest leaving a gaping space in the team for a detective sergeant, Gillian has promoted me in his place. I have mixed emotions about it.

'How are you feeling about . . .' I wave a hand pathetically, trying to encompass everything that has happened in the past five months without words. Jason was convicted today. When the news that one of our own had been the arsonist behind three brutal deaths and the stabbing of a DCI, the distress had reverberated through the whole force.

She takes a swig of red wine and shrugs. 'I've been better.'

I nod. I know how she feels.

'But I'll *be* better.' She squeezes my shoulder. 'And so will you. We need to keep an eye on her, though.' She cocks her head towards Bella, who's laughing with Tiana about something, but there's a distant expression in her eyes that I understand. I think the whole Jason thing hit Bella the hardest. Things between those two were more serious than I'd realised.

'Ladies,' says Gillian. 'I've been mocked for my female-heavy team but we've proved ourselves time and time again. You're all bloody *brilliant*. Please don't ever leave me.'

We cheer again. Bella locks eyes with me and I smile in encouragement. She smiles back and this time it reaches her eyes. And when I glance around the table at my colleagues, my work family, I know I'll be fine. Gillian, Bella, Tiana . . . we'll all be fine without Jason.

***

The sun shines weakly on me as I make my way to the cemetery, clutching three small bunches of roses with trembling hands. I use my elbow to open the creaking gate to the churchyard and let it close with a soft thud behind me. My sharp eyes sweep the area before entering – a habit I can't break even when off duty. It's quiet, save for a lone seagull screeching as it passes above. I'm very much alone. I walk along the flagstone path that hugs the perimeter of the church, shivering as I pass through the shadow cast by the old building. I can't remember the last time I was here, I realise with a pang of guilt. But I finally feel ready to put my own demons to rest.

I remember exactly where Mum, Dad and Frankie are

buried. In a quiet corner of the churchyard, nestled amongst well-tended headstones adorned with floral garlands and elaborate ornaments, I find them; bare and unkempt, sticking out like sore thumbs amongst the strange and eerie beauty of the other graves. I drop to my knees before each headstone in turn, wiping down the surfaces with a cloth and tugging at the weeds crawling up the sides. Nature taking over, in the way it so often does without human intervention.

With muddy hands, I carefully arrange the flowers on each grave. It's a soothing, methodical process that calms me, and distracts me from the purpose of the visit. Am I truly ready to forgive and forget? The case against Anya Fernsby had unleashed a barrage of raw and painful memories, and every step of the process had felt like a sharp blow to my heart . . . inspecting the burned-down house on Buchanan Drive, mourning Sylvie as if she were my own sister, and learning about the way fire destroys homes and lives, as if I didn't already know that from my own experience.

But finding out that my colleague and friend was the one responsible for the savage attack was the hardest pill to swallow. I know I'll find it hard to trust anyone in the same way again, but I've got a duty to my colleagues, and to my county, to be able to move on from this and demonstrate the leadership and integrity that Jason Hooper had ultimately failed at. This is my life, bringing justice to a world that often feels cruel, evil and unforgiving. It's my job to expose the dark parts, otherwise how can the light win?

I remember the promise I made to Frankie, all those years

ago. 'I won't let you down,' I whisper, placing my hand gently on the headstone of *Frankie Starling, aged ten, taken from us too soon*. 'I promise.' And to my parents' headstones: 'I forgive you. Both of you.'

Epilogue

I'm back again. One last time before I leave England for good. But this time, I'm not here to fake my death . . . this time, I'm here to say goodbye . . . and to say sorry.

To Poppy.

***

I pulled her to one side, just as they were lighting the bonfire. We'd lost Ruben and Orla. Her face was upturned, the flames reflected in her shining eyes. She turned to me; flashed me a smile. I don't know what came over me, maybe it was the excitement of the evening, maybe it was the vodka we snuck into my room when we were getting ready . . . but I leaned into her and kissed her.

For a second or two, she melted into the kiss. But it was as if lightning had struck and she backed away, her face a million times worse than it had been when she watched Aunt Andrea dancing barefoot in the kitchen. 'What the fuck are you doing?' She'd frantically scanned the crowd to make sure no one had seen what had happened.

'Nothing,' I'd stammered. 'Sorry. I'm drunk.'

'You dirty lesbian.'

Tears ran down my face like rivers, and I broke away from the crowd.

'Don't you dare tell anyone about this.' She grabbed my arm, but I'd broken free and I ran towards the cliffs.

And here I am. All I wanted was some fresh air, to clear my head. To work out what had happened. How I'd misread the situation so badly.

A crackling sound echoes through the night sky, and I see a shower of golden sparks exploding in the distance. The fireworks have started.

And then suddenly, she's standing in front of me. 'I knew you'd be here.'

I shrug, annoyed that she finds me so predictable.

'You forced yourself on me,' she accuses, and it stings.

My mouth opens and closes stupidly. I don't know what to say. 'No,' I manage. 'I thought—'

'You thought wrong. I have a boyfriend, you know.' She folds her arms over her chest.

I laugh bitterly. 'Yeah, we all know about your paedo boyfriend, Poppy.'

'What the fuck?'

'You're fifteen!' I shout. 'He's in his twenties. It's wrong.'

'Do you know what's wrong?' she says, her words dangerously quiet.

I say nothing.

'People like you.' The words are shooting out of her like venom. 'I can't believe you tried to kiss me. I'm not gay. I don't like you in that way. I can't believe you forced yourself on me.'

'I didn't,' I protest, confusion clouding my mind. 'You kissed me back, Poppy.'

'Stop it.' She shoves my shoulder. 'Just stop spreading lies. I thought you were my friend, but you wanted to get me into bed.'

Now I'm crying again. Am I a horrible person? I thought I was in love. How could I have been in love with this spiteful, angry girl shoving me and hitting me? 'Stop it,' I say, suddenly finding my voice. 'Just stop it!'

But she doesn't listen. I back away from her, before I realise we're close to the edge of the cliff. Way too close.

But she carries on. I can't even make out what she's saying but I catch the words your dirty hippy aunt probably invites you to her sex parties before the red mist descends and I fight back. I shove her with both hands, and she screams.

Everything happens so fast.

Poppy's foot slips.

She screams out.

And then she tumbles over the edge.

I drop to my knees, fingers clawing at the edge of the cliff, and then I see her, fingertips gripping the edge. They told us at school that it's almost three hundred feet to the bottom. I reach my hands out into the darkness, and feel her hand clinging on to mine.

I have every intention of heaving her to safety. I imagine us falling into a heap on the grass, scared but safe, laughing nervously about what a close call it had been. Apologising to each other for the fight. Agreeing to be friends again.

But I remember her vile words, and I pause.

She must have seen something in my eyes because she pleads.

'Anya. Please.' Her harsh voice is now weak. Terrified. And something in me snaps.

'No,' I say firmly.

I let go.

***

I stare at the spot where it happened, replaying the moment over in my mind fully. Right after I'd let go, I'd realised Ruben was standing there, mouth gaping open in horror at what he'd witnessed. He'd followed me up there because he'd seen me running through the crowds, face tear-streaked and scared. And he'd seen that. As far as he knew, it was an accident, but I couldn't take any risks. It had taken quite a bit of persuasion, manipulation even, to get him to promise to pretend he'd never set foot up there. To protect him, I'd said. But really, it was to protect me.

I let out a deep breath. That heavy stone of guilt I've been carrying – I know I'll carry the weight of it forever. Even more so, now I know about Poppy's pregnancy. Not for the first time, I consider turning myself in. Facing up to what I did all those years ago, paying the price for my crime. But what good would it do? Who would benefit from this, apart from easing my own guilt? It's not like I'm a danger to society. It's not like I'd ever harm anyone ever again. I'm not Matthew. I'll do better, make up for it somehow. I know I will.

'Goodbye, Poppy.' I press a hand lightly to the grass, and hold it there for a moment, before turning around and leaving Seaford for good.

Acknowledgements

The Deadly Spark may have my name on the cover, but there's an unbelievable number of people who helped make it happen, and it wouldn't be the book it is without them.

I want to start with my biggest thanks of all, which goes to my wife Laura. Without her, this book would still be an incomplete draft languishing on my computer. I must confess I spent more hours drafting this book than I probably should have during the first few months of our marriage, but Laura remains my rock, my inspiration and my biggest cheerleader despite this. Laura, I love you so much. Thank you for everything.

Another huge thanks goes to my always brilliant agent Maddalena Cavaciuti, who believed in me and my book, worked tirelessly with me on my manuscript and provided endless support, enthusiasm and inspiration. Maddalena, I appreciate you more than you'll ever know! Your faith in my story kept me typing through many a long night.

A massive thank you to my editors, Finn Cotton, Rebecca Jamieson and Cat Camacho, for your invaluable input, and for sharpening *The Deadly Spark* into a much, much better story (believe me, it's been quite the transformation!). I still can't quite believe it's a real book now. Thank you for taking a chance on an unknown author and her debut novel. Huge thanks to my publicist, Sarah Lundy, for everything you've done to try and get me and my book on everyone's radar! And last but not least, everyone at HQ who has been working behind the scenes to make this happen.

To my parents, Liz and Colin, for always encouraging my writing, even if tales of cats with superpowers weren't exactly bestseller material... thank goodness I switched genres. And Dad, thank you for all the bedtime stories; you're the reason I love books so much. And to my fab in-laws, John and Julie, for stepping in as babysitters so I could hit my deadlines – I honestly don't think I'd have done it without you. A special shout out goes to John for all the advice on fires and arson – it never hurts to have a retired firefighter in the family!

To the wonderful friends and generous authors who have supported me, encouraged me and cheered me on – there are far too many of you to name but know that you're all absolutely brilliant. I appreciate everyone who read draft after draft, providing feedback, suggestions and for being so excited for me. That support really kept me going! And I can't finish without some special shout outs to the Circle of Trust (quite frankly the best thing to come out of lockdown), the Penguin WriteNow class of 2020 and the Avon Copy Queens. What would we even do without WhatsApp and gifs to get us through the day?!

I can't write my acknowledgements without mentioning

my Year 10 English teacher Katie for planting the seed. Katie, if you hadn't suggested I try to become an author back when I was 14, who knows where I'd be now?

And finally, to you, the reader. By buying my book or borrowing it from a library, you've helped make this author's dream come true. Hate to be cheesy, but it's true. If you love this novel, please leave a review wherever you like to leave reviews, and let people know what you think. I'm always happy to connect with readers online – you'll find me on Facebook, Threads, Instagram and X, as well as roxiekey.com. Let's chat!

ONE PLACE. MANY STORIES

Bold, innovative and
empowering publishing.

FOLLOW US ON:

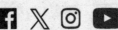

@HQStories